THE ADVENTURE OF

FAXMAN

AND THE

CUT TOE GANG

E.D. SHIFFMAN

CONTENTS

The Adventure of Faxman and the Cut Toe Gang

© 2022 By E D Shiffman

Paperback ISBN: 978-1-66784-312-4

eBook ISBN: 978-1-66784-313-1

CHAPTER ONE

Impound Lot Auction

City of Ukiah

May 25, 1998

Auction begins at 10:00 a.m., inspection period 8:00–9:30 a.m.

All sales are final.

CHESTER SULLIVAN QUICKLY SCANNED THE LIST OF VEHICLES at the Mendocino County impound lot, looking for something that would pique his interest. Six months had passed since he'd gotten embroiled in the securities fraud scheme that had brought down Capital Triangle Properties and assorted brokerage firms. He had benefited financially from a fund started by the Securities and Exchange Commission to award whistle blowers and clamp down on white-collar crime such as the Terra Auri IPO. But the reward had come at a cost.

Months of interrogations to clear his name and depositions to help convict Morris Poulsen, John Marking, and the rest of the participants in that fraud had seemed like a huge effort in comparison to the $250,000 award he received from the fund. Still, it was the most money he had ever garnered in his entire life. It would have taken him a lifetime to save such a sum at his former parking lot attendant job. Chester was emotionally fried and was looking for a project to work on while he took a few months off from the working world in order to plot his next career move.

Incredibly, the press and law enforcement remained clueless about the amazing ability his friend Arnie had acquired to fax himself anywhere in the world. The chance exposure to the supermoon while covered in fax toner and the resulting ability to fax himself anywhere on the globe was a power of enormous potential. Without Arnie's special ability, the securities fraud perpetrated in the Terra Auri IPO would have gone undiscovered. Poulsen and Marking would have secured a fortune, and unwitting people would have seen their investments in the security slowly erode over time as the inferior share class they had purchased dropped in value.

"Let's see," Chester mused as he scanned down the list of impound vehicles. He was looking for a future project while he decompressed from the recent events and developed a plan for his upcoming career change. His fascination with cars had followed him all of his life. His first love had been a baby-blue, wood-trimmed 1951 Buick Roadmaster station wagon his father had faithfully restored and maintained under a tarp in the Sullivan car collection barn on the family estate. Thereafter, Chester had been the proud owner of a variety of cars during his high school and college years. There had first been a '69 Volkswagen Beetle with a blown engine that he had fixed and converted to a Baja Buggy. That had been followed by a series of pickup trucks, all Chevrolets, and one AMC Pacer, inspired by the 1992 cult movie *Wayne's World*.

Chester viewed the advertisement from the *San Francisco Chronicle* for the impound auction. "1995 Chevy Astrovan . . . too domestic. 1989 Ford 250 four-wheel-drive, three-quarter-ton truck with utility bed . . . too utilitarian. 1990 Dodge Caravan . . . too plebian."

Then at the bottom of the list he spied a potential find. "Hmm," he uttered as he read the vehicle description. "1971 VW Westfalia

Campmobile. Now there's one with potential." He conjured up a multitude of ways this van could be restored. Surf van to relive his youth on the beaches of Santa Bonita. Perhaps a full-on, frame-off restoration for resale and profit. Maybe just a retro van he could fix up and repaint with some bright metallic colors to tool around the city in or take to the mountains on the weekend. An early spring trip to the Saline Valley in Death Valley would be at his fingertips with a van like this one, he thought. He imagined himself exploring the desert, Erika with her fire-red hair streaming out the window, pointing out all the photo ops and potential hiking excursions as they sped along and breathed in the clean desert air. The Racetrack, Scotty's Castle, maybe the discovery of a long-lost gold mine . . . this was the world that could open to them with the purchase of such a van.

He noted the date and time for the pre-inspection at the impound yard. It would not be as simple as just making the drive to Ukiah and attending the live auction. Erika had convinced Chester to safeguard his reward proceeds by opening a joint account with her so that she could help him conserve his funds and perhaps save for a down payment on a house for the two of them. She was confident their relationship would continue and grow into something permanent. "It's your money, Chess," she had cooed when he brought the large check to her. "If you handle it well and only spend the interest, perhaps you can leverage this money into something bigger by way of an investment. Your dad will be so proud of you." He had readily agreed. After all, it was his naïveté and lack of experience in the first place that had caused the danger to his girlfriend's life during the Terra Auri affair. He was indebted to her and was grateful to still have her.

Maybe this van purchase won't be so hard after all, he thought. Getting a good buy on a classic vehicle and restoring it for a profit was something he could do. If he had failed in the fast-paced arena of IPOs in his recent career as a budding stockbroker, he certainly would not fail in a straightforward car restoration. He knew cars in and out, backwards and forwards. There was no way he could fail. All he had to do was convince Erika that a profit could be made from this wise investment.

His time at Argus Securities had not been a total waste. While his financial acumen had not grown appreciably during his short tenure at the firm, he had been able to design a basic framework for how to present a product to a potential client and begin a discussion that might eventually lead to a sale. That was all he really needed to do with Erika. A sales job on Erika so that she would support his new van restoration project and agree to let a few dollars from his nest egg be released for the venture.

He immediately launched into sales pitch assessment mode. What would be the grabber for her, he wondered? He methodically began to hone in on the primary sales motivation that would get her to support this purchase. "After I fix it up, we can take it to the beach on weekends or go on vacations to national parks." He rejected this option as too frivolous. He knew she wanted a home, somewhere to put down some roots. Anything that moved away from the picture of a house with a white picket fence was not going to be supported.

He thought back to his sales calls for the Terra Auri deal. In all cases the major initial selling theme was the chance to get in on the ground floor of this new investment with the goal of making a ton of money. Each prospective client had a subtheme to which he had appealed once he had ferreted out the client's needs and motivation. Some simply wanted more income in order to improve their lifestyle. Others were trying to provide for a wife or grandchildren once the client was no longer in the picture. Erika was no dummy, though. He would have one chance to broach the subject and he had to make it good. She was not going to be swayed by the chance to have fun driving around in a newly restored classic van. No, Erika was a person of numbers, facts, and reason. This would have to be a financial undertaking where he could combine his mechanical skills and some modest financial investment to show how a profit could be made and how his savings account would grow once he had fixed up the van and sold it.

The sound of footsteps coming up the sidewalk outside of his house broke his train of thought. They echoed louder as they approached the door, stopping so the visitor could knock on the door. Chester answered the door to find Arnie standing before him with a cardboard tray of fresh coffee and croissants.

"Hey, Chess," Arnie greeted him. "Did you forget we were supposed to have breakfast at Peet's today?"

"Damn," replied Chester. He had the familiar sinking feeling that, once again, he had left his friend high and dry while he daydreamed.

Arnie was not at all put out, however. After five minutes of waiting, he had gone ahead and ordered the usual fare for the duo. He had not been completely surprised that Chester had failed to show up. Chester could easily be diverted, and Arnie had long ago become accustomed to adjusting for him instead of becoming angry or simply terminating their friendship.

"No big deal," he said as he entered Chester's house. The financial reward of the Terra Auri affair had been equally bestowed upon Arnie. The one substantive change in each of their lifestyles had been the termination of their longtime roommate arrangement. With each of them now in possession of a modest bankroll in the form of the SEC reward money, they had mutually decided that now was the time for them to each get their own living space and progress into adulthood. Arnie had been the natural choice to remain in the old apartment the two had shared for some time. Erika and Chester had decided to take their relationship to the next level and had rented a house nearby.

Of course, the $250,000 reward was not enough to enable them to live the life of Reilly. In the back of each of their minds was the need to continue in a new job search, or in Arnie's case, the need to keep his office machine repair business alive and viable. He had deposited his award into his savings account after spending a small percentage on a new paint job for his van and an upgrade of all of his computer, diagnostic, and phone equipment. Arnie was not the emotional spender Chester was, but he could make a practical case for upgrading some of the components of his business and personal life.

"What's up?" he said to Chester as he placed the coffee and croissants on the coffee table. "Looking in the want ads for your next career move?"

"Nah," replied Chester. "I think I can be more productive working for myself than trying to get another job in the corporate world." He folded the newspaper in half and tossed the classified section over to Arnie. "What do you think about this deal?"

Arnie caught the paper in midair and plopped down on the black leather couch across from Chester. His appearance was decidedly different from his former pre-Faxman self. The black-rimmed glasses had been traded in for a new un-bespectacled look thanks to the latest Lasik surgery. He was no longer an office machine repair nerd, at least on the outside. He had also changed his hairstyle from the former shaggy, unkempt look to a neatly styled coiffure to augment his recent fame and notoriety from the Terra Auri affair.

Unfolding the paper, he skimmed it and observed the local news and various advertisements in the business section. His friend's new investment opportunity did not immediately jump off the page. "Where?" he asked as he flipped the page over and continued to skim the sections for a likely business opportunity for his friend.

"Keep looking," replied Chester. He wanted validation for his latest idea but enjoyed the cat and mouse aspect of seeing if Arnie could figure out what he was up to. Arnie continued to skim the paper and finally noted the impound lot sale in Ukiah. "What? Are you looking for another set of wheels?" he said. "You already have a sweet ride with that Mazda 6 you bought with your reward dough."

Erika had been instrumental in talking Chester down from his dream of owning a new limited-edition Corvette with a price tag of $129,000. Instead, she had searched the Internet for a modestly priced sports car and had found a *Consumer Reports* recommendation for this

Japanese alternative. At one-fourth the cost and with a simple, less expensive maintenance schedule, she had convinced Chester of the benefits of conserving his cash while at the same time satisfying his boyish needs for speed and cornering ability. "Besides, honey, this one is a four seater. That leaves room for the kids, if and when they come along." This last comment had been a joke. They had never seriously discussed marriage, and Erika knew the male psyche well. Just the mere mention of the bonds of matrimony could cause a man to take off like a scared rabbit, retreating far into an emotional shell.

"The Mazda is my daily driver," replied Chester. "It's good for around town and long trips. But I like the VW van on the sales list. It could be cherried out in a frame off restoration. I could make some good money on it. Besides, we could have a good time using it for weekend trips to the beach or camping in the mountains."

Arnie lifted his gaze from the newspaper to look at his friend's face. The realm of possibilities for this enterprise was very appealing. After all, Arnie was already a fan of that particular make and model, using one for his mobile office machine repair business. It was a simple thing for him to clear out his tools and parts inventory anytime he wanted to take off for a short road trip, sleeping and eating in his van as he searched out some new techie convention or beta tested one of his new inventions in the field. It would be him and Chester up against Erika on this idea.

The duo sat quietly in their seats as they imagined what the van might look like fully restored. In Chester's mind, it was a powder-blue beach van with bamboo mats on the floors and surf stickers on the windows. An old-time surf rack with the green metal frames and black rubber straps held two longboards with laminated wood fins on the roof. A garish Hawaiian hula doll, complete with grass hula skirt, bobbed and wiggled on the dashboard.

Arnie's mental picture of the impound vehicle was decidedly different. Satin primer black with all the side windows tinted dark charcoal. It was a resto-rocket with chrome wheels and a cherry bomb muffler and chrome tailpipe protruding out of the rear engine compartment. The fire-engine-red muffler protruded out at a garish angle, midway up on the left-rear-quarter panel, evidencing the nature of the hopped-up four-banger engine.

He imagined modifying it to double the standard power of the rear-mounted, air-cooled pancake engine. A lowered suspension completed the exterior look. Inside was every electronic navigation and audio gadget known to man. The instrument panel was lit with digital red readouts against a black background, all programmable to the color scheme choice of the driver.

"Oh, you gotta get this van," Arnie said. "It's a cruiser." The two smiled at each other and high fived. It would be a team effort to get Erika to buy into the investment.

CHAPTER TWO

THE SUN HAD BARELY RISEN OVER THE MEDITERRANEAN town of Casablanca when a tall, gaunt figure emerged from the central post office with a bundle of mail under his arm. He wore his hair in the style typical of the early 1970s hippie. Dark brown and fully flecked with gray, it evidenced a man of some years. He wore it gathered in a ponytail that hung down his back. An untrimmed beard and mustache covered his face. He had no need to wear a turban, common on the streets of the Middle Eastern town. His swarthy countenance was largely hidden, enabling him to mix in with the crowds, anonymous to the casual observer.

Shopkeepers in the bazaar were opening their stores and street merchants began to stock their stalls and booths with all manner of merchandise as the sun rose higher in this former metropolis of the Ottoman Empire. The tall figure passed by this hubbub of activity and proceeded along the street until he arrived at the café where he habitually took his first meal of the day.

Selecting the same table and chair he had used virtually every morning for the last five years, Jack Morrison sat down in a chair facing the street and lit a cigarette and unrolled the newspaper he had brought with him.

He was dressed in white cotton peasant pants and shirt, and this and his huaraches and hippie hair gave him away as a product of that free-spirited time. His sleeves were partially rolled up, revealing forearms that each carried multicolored tattoos. On his left forearm was an image of Jesus wearing a crown of thorns. His other arm bore the traditional anchor symbol of the US Navy.

As he unrolled the paper, the mail from his post office box slid out before him onto the table, spilling against the flowerpot centerpiece that was filled with bright red geraniums. One letter from the thick stack fell to the sidewalk. With a look of irritation, Jack Morrison stuck his cigarette into the corner of his mouth, squinted one eye to avoid the smoke, and reached down to retrieve the letter. He stopped for a moment as he observed the address of the sender. "CTG" had been scrawled in the upper left-hand corner of the letter by the sender along with an address in Tiburon, California. He paused only for an instant but then casually deposited the letter back into his pile of mail and gathered the clutch back into an organized stack to be looked at later after he had scanned the morning paper.

Jack was a man of habit and control, a man who took measured steps throughout the day and evaluated every move and action before the fact as if someone were watching him. Indeed, as a former Navy Seal with black ops experience, he was used to surveilling others. The waiter delivered his meal with little conversation, only a cursory "Will there be anything else, sir?" as he topped off the coffee. Jack Morrison was well-known to the waiter. Jack was a man of few words and not one to make casual conversation. Just the meal order, delivery of the bill, and a quick refill of his coffee was all that he desired. The size of the tip was usually inverse to the amount of time spent in conversation. This customer just wanted to be left alone. A waiter's dream from a time and energy standpoint.

Jack finished his meal, paid the bill, and rose to leave as he had done for hundreds of breakfasts. Each time, with mail tucked under his arm, he would meander through the shops back to his apartment to throw out the mail that had no further use to him and perhaps lay aside a magazine or letter for further reading. This time was different though. He had only picked through his mail, opening none of the letters and only briefly scanning the newspapers and magazines. Giving the semblance of a man of leisure, unconcerned about any matters of the day, he had held the batch of mail a little tighter than usual as he strode back to his apartment. The errant letter with the "CTG" notation on the return address was on the top of the bundle. As he walked, he glanced down every few minutes to be sure the letter was firmly in his grasp.

He paused briefly as he entered the vestibule to his second-story flat and glanced quickly down the street along his back trail to see if he had been followed. Seeing no one, he continued up the stairs and down the darkened exterior hallway to his room. The hallway was of a Moorish design. White tiles festooned with turquoise inlay adorned the floors and walls. The exterior wall of the hallway was finished with whitewashed stone panels, each with large decorative openings to let in the outside air for cooling purposes, a style typical of that hot Mediterranean region.

He unlocked his door and quickly entered his apartment, tossing the stack of mail onto the dining room table, keeping only the top letter in his grasp. A ceiling fan turned slowly above him as he settled into a leather recliner and ripped open the letter. It was not long, only one handwritten page. His brow furrowed as he read the contents of the communiqué. His eyes moved quickly from left to right down the page then rapidly began again at the top. He read slower this time, letting his mind wrap around the full meaning of the text, giving his imagination time to fill in the blanks and the intent of the person who had sent the letter.

He let his trembling hand holding the letter fall to his lap and sat motionless in the chair, gazing first at the floor and then across the room to the wall, seeing nothing. His mind worked rapidly as he began to sort out what must happen next. The letter was a call to action, a lit fuse, the first step in a yet unwritten sequence of future events that he was powerless to change. Like the seed that stays buried in the desert until the correct amount of time, heat, and scarification has occurred, he was a sprout, about to emerge from his dormancy after a long five-year hiatus.

He reran the movie of past events through his mind. Northern California five years previous, a late-night meeting to exchange prohibited substances for payment, a plane crash in the Everglades, a deal gone bad, a fortune not collected but waiting with a hidden code to be unlocked at a later time. Fear, anger, and resolve moved across his countenance as events of the past flooded back to him.

As if returning from a trance, he focused his gaze on the letter in his lap. He folded it and returned it to its envelope. He retrieved his Vietnam War–era Zippo lighter from his pocket, leaned over the metal trash can next to his chair, and touched fire to paper. He deposited the flaming communiqué into the trash can, gazing at it for a minute, then, banging the can against the floor, he verified that all was now ash. No one would be able to reconstruct the details of the letter. Patting his pants pocket to be sure he had his cell phone, he left the apartment and went downstairs to catch the intercity bus. After traveling for several minutes, he exited at a neighborhood park and deposited himself on an empty park bench. Across from him a group of children were playing soccer. He was far enough from the clatter of their play to not be overheard and removed from the crowd enough so that he could observe his surroundings and be aware of unwanted visitors.

Just as he reached into his pants pocket to retrieve his cell phone, a loud whack hit the back of the bench on which he was sitting, startling him. He stood up quickly, looking around behind him to see what had caused the sound. A soccer ball was bouncing lazily away. A young dark-eyed boy was giggling as he trotted after the ball, his friends shouting and laughing in the background. Jack could understand their jokes and ridicule, which was targeted at the young boy, who had apparently made an errant kick that had sent the ball in Jack's direction. Jack was not amused. Standing tall and silent, he returned the boys' gaze with a long stony "don't screw with me" stare sufficient to keep the group's soccer game well away from him. The boy returned to his group with ball in hand, chattering and laughing to his friends with a comment targeted toward the tall, bearded American who had been interrupted by their play.

Returning to his phone call, Jack placed a foot on the seat of the bench and pulled out his wallet, retrieving a small piece of paper from one of the credit card slots and unfolding it. The paper was old; the folds were deeply creased and yellowed. It had been stored in the wallet for such a long time that he had to lay it out on the bench seat and smooth it out with both hands in order to read what was written on the paper. A phone number was written on the paper in pencil. Time, sweat, and storage in his wallet had worked on the writing to smudge and partially erase it, but it was still legible. The note bore an Australian area code and phone number. He alternately gazed over the top of his reading glasses at the number and the keypad of his cell phone, dialing the number with slow firm strokes of his middle finger. The half stub of his index finger rested alongside his dialing finger. It was largely a useless appendage, smooth and deeply purple on the end. It was the only finger on his right hand that was without a silver ring. His North Vietnam captor had taken the digit during a weeklong interrogation after Jack was captured while involved in an operation in Laos. He was reminded of his wartime experiences each time he used his middle finger and also of how he had drowned his captor inside his partially submerged bamboo cage one evening after luring him inside.

Jack was not a man to be trifled with.

CHAPTER THREE

ERIKA MCCONIKA SAT AT THE COFFEE TABLE IN THE HOME she and Chester had recently rented with her eyes closed and her hands held out before her, waiting for the big surprise Chester was about to place in them. Unlike the life of leisure Chester had chosen after receiving his reward money, Erika had chosen to continue to work at Capital Triangle Properties, albeit no longer as a financial analyst. The fortunes of the company had taken a 180-degree turn after the Terra Auri debacle and her role in uncovering the fraud had not sat well with many of the company staff. The company was now in receivership. The courts trusted her since she had played a role in unveiling the fraud. Now, she was involved in winding down the affairs of the company and safeguarding as much of the company's assets as possible so that the pool of Capital Triangles investors and creditors could be paid at least a portion of their funds.

Morris Poulsen could not, of course, take any direct action against her. As one of the triad of characters who had masterminded the real estate scheme, he had quickly announced a sabbatical from his role as CEO of the firm to "refresh and reenergize to fight the spurious allegations and charges that have been made against myself and others." He had been released on a five-million-dollar bond. In his press conference, held just outside the county jail, he had resolved to fight to the end to restore his name and reputation and the jobs for all his staff who were egregiously affected by the incipient charges laid at his feet by the Securities and Exchange Commission. In actuality, he had undertaken steps to be sure his wealth was properly safeguarded and hidden. If it appeared he would be convicted on the charges brought against him by the SEC, he had made plans to go on the lam and live off of the substantial assets he had been able to hide in various offshore banks in a country without extradition agreements with the US.

As she sat at the coffee table, Erika mused on how large the diamond might be on the engagement ring Chester must be about to present to her. His tone during the phone call earlier that day had been nervous and excited. "I have a big surprise for you and I want this night to be special for us," he had said. A dinner reservation at the trendy Chanticleer had been made for the couple and all she was required to do was slip into a dress, grab a handbag, and wait to be picked up at seven that evening. She had arrived home earlier than usual from work to prepare for the event. He had indicated that he has something to show her and she had been waiting and hinting for a long time about this surprise. What else could it be but an engagement ring, the male gesture of commitment and surrender, the equivalent of admitting "I cannot go on any further without permanently having you in my life"?

Some little girls dream of the day they are walked down the aisle on the arm of their daddy with family and friends all in attendance to see the most beautiful woman in the world join with the man of her dreams. They daydream of this event, discuss it in detail with other like-minded little girls, and pretty much have the entire event, from the guest list to the menu and table decorations picked out long before the actual offer of marriage is proffered. It is the final opportunity to laugh, cry, fight, and make up with friends before those solemn words "I now pronounce you husband and wife" ring down like the bang of a judge's gavel at the end of a trial. Erika had definitely been one of those little girls.

She had selected a black sleeveless cocktail dress with a small matching diamond-studded purse for the evening. As she waited for Chester to arrive, she alternately crossed and uncrossed her legs while occasionally holding her hands out before her to check her freshly done nails. She was quite the package, if she did say so herself. There would be no cold feet for Chester on this outing. She was simply irresistible.

At that moment, she heard footsteps approaching her front door and she rose to greet her boyfriend. Chester stood on the front steps, awkward as usual, neatly dressed in a country club casual ensemble of camel slacks, powder-blue long-sleeve shirt, and an argyle sweater vest. In his hands, he held a small envelope. Handing it to her, he gave her a peck on the cheek and took her hand, guiding her to the sofa. "This is what I want to you to take a look at," he said as the two sat down thigh to thigh. "This is really important to me, and I know I agreed to let you sign off on any business ideas I wanted to get started, so take a look at this and let me hear what you think."

It was now obvious to Erika that this was not going to be a ring and a marriage proposal. She was disappointed, but this was not the first time she had lathered herself up into thinking that today was going to be the day. Her relationship with Chester had the typical ups and downs of any semi-serious union. She had acquired the ability to talk herself down from past experiences where instead of being offered the engagement ring, she had ended up with tickets to a sporting event or some exotic activity such as kite surfing or bungee jumping. With a quick sigh, she opened the flap of the letter and removed the contents. Several papers had been stapled together into what appeared to be a business plan. The top page boldly stated in large print "Business Plan for a Classic Car Acquisition and Restoration Project." The rest of the page was devoted to before and after photographs of a Volkswagen van. At the bottom of the page was a notation in eight-point type with the usual disclaimers and waivers typically found on a financial prospectus for a private equity offering. She smiled internally as she noted the fine print and turned the page to see the details of Chester's proposal. Some of the skills he had acquired during the Terra Auri debacle had migrated over to his personal life after all.

The proposal looked very much like the ill-fated Terra Auri IPO that had enabled Chester to assume his current life of leisure and present his van resto project to Erika. She suspected that he had taken one of the IPO draft word documents from his old job and had cut and pasted portions of the format to use as a structure in the presentation. What Chester lacked in ingenuity and creative ability was not lost in his ability to copy and duplicate the work of others to suit his own purpose.

On the second page was a photo of an early 1970s VW van labeled "Before." The photo portrayed a van resting in a field of cut hay. Off to the side of the field was an old oak tree shielding the vehicle from the elements. One of the rear tires was flat and the van listed to one side. Grass was growing in the roof channels above the windows, evidencing it had not moved in some time. Behind the smoky gray windows, one could see the remnants of original, now well-worn upholstery.

Page three was boldly labeled "After" and showed a newly restored van painted bright green with black accents. The wheels were chromed, the rear tires slightly wider than the fronts, looking a little like the slicks used on drag strip funny cars. A pair of surfboards adorned the retro-style roof racks, held firmly in place by black rubber straps. The rest of the presentation was a discussion of how the van would be acquired, the intended improvements, and the way Chester would sell the vehicle and recoup his costs and return on investment. An appendix section had a detailed breakdown on each improvement Chester would be making to the van, a time and labor estimate together with parts costs, as well as a time line. He had used the format and template from the Terra Auri affair, albeit in a much-abbreviated form, to show the investment profitability. His last line included an internal rate of return calculation of 35 percent over a one-year investment period.

Erika could not help but smile at his ingenious attempt to convince her that this was a business proposition when in fact, she knew he would probably never fully restore the van as proposed. The likely outcome of the endeavor would be for him to put on a quick coat of paint, hose out the interior, and install new seat covers and start to use the van in a couple of months. The two of them would be spending a lot of time at the beach and this would be their mode of transportation. She could think of all the financial reasons Chester should not buy the van, but she did not have the heart to rain on his parade. Did it matter that best case he would recover his investment and perhaps a few extra dollars? If it gave him some focus and feeling of self-worth while he waited for his next career move, what could it hurt?

"So, what do you think, honey?" he asked as she closed the cover on the presentation and looked up at him. He braced for her logical business-headed response. He had an answer ready for every objection she might raise.

"I think you should go for it," she replied, reaching out to him and rubbing his thigh. "This is right up your alley and you should just go for it. Maybe I can get a ride in it after it's done, before you sell it and rake in all that cash."

Chester sat silently beside her for a moment, waiting for the next shoe to drop. He had expected a resounding rejection of his plan for spending a small part of his reward money, or perhaps a series of follow-up questions on costs, specifications for the improvements, and the like. But Erika's nonplussed acceptance of his proposal, lock, stock, and barrel, caught him by surprise. He defensively searched for the pitfalls that awaited him in her quick acceptance, but could not deduce anything other than her whole-hearted support for his van purchase and restoration plan.

"That's great, honey!" he gushed. "I will just park it inside the carport so I can work on it out of the rain and keep the mess from bugging the rest of the neighborhood." He was relieved and excited to get started. The sale was only two weeks away. He had plenty of time to get prepared and make travel and hotel plans so that he would be ready for the day of the sale.

"So, what's the next step, sweetie?" Erika asked. "Do you take a wad of cash up there? Will they accept personal checks or a cashier's check?"

"I don't have a clue yet" he replied, reclining against the back cushion of the couch. "I will have to research the value at the library or on the World Wide Web and see what these vans are going for. If it is running it will bring more than if the engine is trashed. I also need to attend the presale inspection so I can see how much body rot there is and what the interior looks like. This thing could go from as little as a couple of thousand dollars if the body is pretty straight but the running gear is shot, to as much as seven or eight thousand dollars if is running. If I get a range of values from the Internet and parts and repair costs upfront, I can spend the night before the sale working up my bid and hit the ground running at the sale."

"Don't forget to figure out a way to bring the van back with you," added Erika. "Also, are you going to have enough room in the carport to work on it? We don't want any beef with the neighbors."

He paused for a moment, realizing he had detailed out the logistics of attending the auction and had a good idea of the series of events that would be involved in the restoration process. But he had given no thought to the actual logistics of bringing his prize home. "I guess I haven't thought about it that far," he replied. He had some work to do, but the nuts and bolts of those pedestrian activities could be resolved with a little time and effort.

CHAPTER FOUR

THE LAW OFFICE OF JOHN RIGGS WAS LOCATED ON THE SEC-
ond floor of a low-slung, two-story commercial condominium complex
several blocks from the downtown central business district of Santa Bonita.
The nondescript building was in an area known for what the legal community termed grade-B lawyers. A legal caste system of sorts existed in Santa
Bonita, aligned along the quality of the law school the local bar member
had attended rather than socioeconomic status. Lawyers who had attended
well-regarded law program such as Harvard, McGeorge, or UCLA were
eligible to enter the A class. They held positions in the small cadre of top-
flight legal firms that conducted most of the corporate and estate planning
work for the high-profile businesses and wealthy families in the area. Their
offices were all situated within a two-block radius of the superior court and
law library. Attorneys and judges would commonly mingle or at least have
lunch or coffee in close proximity, affording them an informal chance to
emphasize a current or upcoming case to the judiciary. B-grade attorneys,
having attended less prestigious law schools or assorted attorney mills,
were located in the lower-cost section of the business community that was
a long walking distance from the court and the public records. The rents
were lower, but so were their fees. Divorce cases and personal injury claims

made up a high percentage of their work. Occasionally a business transaction or a probate came their way to provide some relief from their regular fare of divorcing clients seeking help on how to divide savings accounts and pickle forks or dressing a client up in an oversize neck brace to convince a jury about a large financial award in an auto accident case.

The first thing Riggs saw when he entered his office was a large yellow sticky note on his computer screen. A scrawled message, obviously from his janitorial service, stated, "man call many times, you call him first thing, very portant!" The time on the message was noted as 2:00 a.m. He did not recognize the number but it appeared to be an international call. Riggs plucked the message from his computer screen and frowned as he read the message again. Who would be calling him at this hour from an unrecognizable phone number? During his checkered law career, he had had the occasional late night or weekend call from a distressed client. The reasons ran from the annoying to the ridiculous. He recalled the time a female client who was seeking a divorce had frantically called to inform him that her soon to be ex had piled all their possessions on the family room floor and was set to light them all on fire if she did not agree to his version of a fair property settlement. Another time he had been contacted on a Saturday afternoon to bail out a client who had been arrested while cruising the red-light district of a nearby town. He chuckled as he recalled how the client had pleaded innocent of attempting to partake of a local prostitute's services. He had convinced the judge that he had merely been asking for directions to a local bakery so that he could pick up a surprise for his wife's birthday. That client, a retired police commissioner, had gotten off with only a warning to be more careful the next time he went shopping for hot buns in a bakery.

Riggs had had his share of unusual cases over the years. Since the upper elite of Santa Bonita's legal community shied away from cases that didn't pay that well or might damage the law firm's reputation, Riggs had handled many of the seedier assignments. They had included drug dealers and domestic disputes, as well as a litany of trip and fall situations. He knew all the private detective agencies in town and had used most of them during his career.

He could think of no one in his stable of active clients who might be calling long distance with such an urgent purpose. He eased into his overstuffed black chair and booted up his computer. Now was a time of caution, he thought to himself. There was no end to the number of ex-husbands who harbored lingering plans for his harm—or even, he imagined, demise—to even the score in divorce property settlement matters where he had prevailed. Using caution customary to his trade, Riggs navigated to an Internet search engine and entered a search for the origin of the international call. The results to his question was instantaneous. Casablanca, Morocco. He frowned as he gazed at the results. The image of the famous movie starring Bogart and Bergman came to mind; the black-and-white scene of the leading lady at the airport bidding farewell to Bogy was his mental association with the city. He knew no one living or vacationing in that region. He had neither friends nor clients who might be calling him from that locale. At the bottom of the message were the initials JM. He searched his mind. "JM," he mused. Perhaps an old client or a long-lost acquaintance or lover? His mind worked through all the possibilities, seeking a clue to the sender of the early morning message. He came up short, no answer or even a hint of where to look in his records.

At that moment, his paralegal, Manita Parsons, burst in the front door. "Good morning, John," she called from the reception area as she rushed into the office and deposited her purse and assorted packages onto her desk. "Sorry I'm late, but the bus was held up by some accident on the freeway. I had to get off a couple of blocks early with all these packages I am returning to Nordstrom today. What a hassle." Manita was a short, plump woman of Korean descent. Her parents had come to this country a decade after the Korean conflict, and she had been able to complete a college education while helping her parents run a successful restaurant. A mix of old Asian values and modern American culture, she spoke fluent Korean and was not afraid to roll up her sleeves and attack any project that Riggs threw her way. But she was also a fashion whore and food snob of sorts. All the latest Apple products found their way into her possession within moments of their release to the retail market. She also knew where the best dim sun eatery was located.

"Manita, let me give you a quick item to research for me before you get started on reviewing that deposition for the Ripaldi divorce," he called from his office. Manita appeared at his door and plopped down into the brown leather chair in front of his desk. "Here," he gestured as he handed the yellow sticky note to her. "I need you to try and find out who might have sent this message before I call them back. Can you look through all our old files and my contact list and see if you can get a match for these initials?"

"Sure thing," she replied, snatching the note from his hand.

"I don't want to get bogged down by some nutcase or an old client who is having trouble getting over a divorce or trip and fall award," he added. In his line of work, it was not uncommon for old cases to resurface in the form of a weeping woman who had squandered the entirety of her divorce winnings, or a client who had run through his workers' compensation funds and was looking for a way to prolong his hiatus from work by extending those payments. None of these conversations ever turned out well. People were never happy to be informed that they had had their one bite at the apple. He was careful about taking on cases where his fee was paid at the end of the case as a percentage of the award. No sense in spending time on a case that would burn up large amounts of his time with little chance for success.

Manita strode across the office into the small kitchen that also served as the file storage area for the business. She poured a cup of hot black coffee, added a nondairy creamer substitute and sugar, and sat down in front of the file room workstation. As she logged into the network and waited for the machine to boot up, she read the handwritten message and pondered the initials. "JM," she muttered to herself. She could not help but smile as she thought of the juvenile joke with the punch line "Jack Mehoff." She began using the search function in her word processing program, trying female first names, starting with the letter *J*. June, Jackie, and Jill all proved fruitless when combined with the last name starting with the letter *M*. "Maybe it's a guy, "she muttered to herself as she shifted her search. Impatient, with a full day's worth of work in the form of deposition summations for a litany of personal injury cases that were currently active ahead of her, she began searching for various male names starting with the letter *J* that would coincide with a last name beginning with *M*. She was unable to find any files, current or closed, that might be a clue to the late-night message taken by the cleaning staff.

On a whim, she reversed the order of the names and instantly came up with a single name of a former client: "Jackson." There was no first initial or name, just a single name for a file that appeared to be over five years old, closed long ago. She reviewed the summary information accompanying the file name. There was little information. It was not clear what the case had been about or even what the result of the action had been. Under the summary description of the case, she noted a cross-reference to an unnamed case that had been given a pseudonym of "CTG." With the heavy workflow ahead of her, she quickly e-mailed Riggs the results of her file archive search. "No such initials in any old cases, did find a reference to an old file for someone named Jackson, no first name, pretty old case," she wrote. With the reference to the CTG matter she ended her communiqué by asking if he wanted her to look any further.

In a matter of seconds, Riggs was standing in her doorway, his face drained of color. "Let me see that file record," he demanded. Manita turned her computer monitor at an angle to permit him to view the list of files. He leaned over and peered down the list of closed cases until his eyes landed on the notation "CTG." His hands trembled as he placed his index finger below the record, reading the brief case description summarizing the matter.

CHAPTER FIVE

THE NEON SIGN ABOVE THE BLUE AGAVE RESTAURANT CAST A
pale blue light on the entrance to the eatery. The locals' favorite diner and
watering hole was filled with the usual Friday night crowd of upper-mid-
dle-class professionals recently arrived from jobs in San Francisco. A few
tourists traveling through to wine country for the weekend peppered the
crowd. Chester and Arnie stood out as a couple of smaller city bumpkins
sitting at their table next to the bathroom in the rear of the restaurant.

"Ready to order?" hailed the waitress. She leaned suggestively over
their table, wiping water that had spilled from the ample pitcher she had
just placed on the table before them. Grease, spilled condiments, and other
assorted smudges were vigorously swabbed into a dull uniform sheen on
the table surface to give the bacteria-laden coating a sanitary appearance.
"You boys in town for the Dipsea Race this weekend?" she queried as she
prepared to take their orders.

"Nothing as exciting as that," replied Chester. "Just having a look at
some cars being sold off by the county tomorrow over at the impound yard."

"Is it time for that thing again?" she replied. "I got a real deal on an
'83 Corolla last year. A real ugly duckling, but it gets me to work."

Before Arnie could stop him, Chester enthusiastically recounted their goal of snagging the VW van along with the restoration plans they had for the vehicle.

"Sounds like a great project," she commented as she wrote down their order for a couple of chili burgers with fries.

"Why did you do that?" hissed Arnie under his breath. "You need to put on your poker face and not let anyone know how much you want that car. If there is anyone else interested in the van, or if the auction company has placed a shill in the crowd to bid things up, you could end up paying way more than you have to and you might not get it at all if the crowd starts to build interest in it. Lay low, man, lay low. No more talk about why we are here or what we are doing. "

"Okay," apologized Chester. "We're a folk group from Salt Lake City, just like at the end of *Wedding Crashers*, right?"

"Something like that," replied Arnie.

Chester's enthusiastic report on the upcoming van purchase had not gone unnoticed. At the end of the bar, within earshot of the duo, John Riggs sat atop one of the newly upholstered bright red barstools. It was mere coincidence that he has ended up in the same bar as Chester and Arnie on the eve of the pending car auction. The note left by the cleaning crew the day before had set off a rapid chain sequence including a phone call to a long-ago client, tracking down info on the pending impound lot sale, and a hurried trip to Mendocino County so that he could be on scene to attend the auction on behalf of his client. Wearing a ball cap festooned with a Porsche logo, his coat collar pulled up around his neck, he sat quietly, trying to blend into the boisterous Friday night crowd around him. He was on a mission. Visibility was his enemy and he was taking no chances at leaving any impressions that anyone would be able to recall. He wanted no one to be able to tie him to the area. His head had turned slightly in the direction of Chester and Arnie's conversation with the waitress at the mention of the VW van and the impound auction. The slight quarter-turn of his head, the momentary cessation of his chewing—these were small, unnoticed expressions of his surprise and concern. His mission to the area was now more complicated and troubled than he first thought.

Arnie and Chester finished their meal, topping it off with a hot fudge sundae and a piece of apple pie. Their exit from the restaurant was followed by Riggs's nonchalant glance. The short, nerdy-looking guy was the brains of the outfit, he observed. The tall, good-looking one who had his heart set on buying the van was another harmless boob, apparently dead set on spending a lot of money fixing up an underpowered box on wheels that had a limited cult following. He seemed equally harmless. However, John Riggs felt the need to report what he had overheard to the client who had sent him to Tiburon to attend the impound auction sale. Downing his beer, he signaled to the waitress for his bill and placed a twenty on the counter before twirling around on the stool and exiting the building. He stayed in the shadows as he followed Chester and Arnie up the street to their hotel. His client would want to know all about them as a matter of precaution. The hotel clerk could be plied with a fifty-dollar bill to supply cursory information as to the origin of his apparent auction competitors.

"How was your meal, sir?" the hotel clerk greeted Riggs as he walked past the reception counter to the elevator for his wing of rooms in the Bayside Inn.

"Fine, just fine," Riggs replied as he quickly entered the elevator and the door closed behind him. This older two-story hotel had been a last-minute choice, the only hotel with a vacancy the weekend of the popular Dipsea Race, which would be held in Mill Valley, across the bay. This trail race, the second oldest in the county, always put pressure on hotel and motel operators. Riggs had been lucky to find a room with such short notice.

He entered his room and closed the door behind him, locking the dead bolt, hanging the safety chain into the slot on the door, and giving the door a shake. Eighty years of wear and tear on the mechanism was evident. The door rattled and gave just a little, but both locking mechanisms seemed to be in working order. Countless coats of paint, new carpets, and slabs of inexpensive marble in the bathroom did not entirely hide the age of the historic hotel. In the corner of the room by the sofa, a squat light with a yellowed lampshade cast a dull light. Riggs sat down on the couch, lit a cigarette, and placed the telephone on his lap. He stared at the rotary phone for a moment, as if trying to recall how to operate the antiquated apparatus. Thinking better of it, he took out his cell phone and dialed. He was greeting on the other end by a message machine. The recording had been made by someone with a heavy Australian accent. "Good day, mate, I'm not in at the moment. I'm out surfing but give me a ring later or leave your number after the beep."

Riggs's message was short and to the point. "I am at the location. Nothing unusual so far. At least one bidder looking at the subject. Call when you can." He put out his cigarette in a glass of water and set it on the end table, next to a sign that read "Thank you for not smoking in this room."

The phone rang at 3:00 a.m., startling Riggs awake from a deep sleep. He had been dreaming about one of his former divorce clients' husbands, who was chasing him with a gun. The soon-to-be ex-husband had found out Riggs had been dating his soon-to-be ex-wife while representing her during the divorce proceedings. Barely able to move and with the irate ex-husband in hot pursuit, the early morning phone call had rescued him from an almost certain death.

"Hello, mate," the voice on the other end greeted Riggs. Riggs recognized the voice instantly.

"For God's sake, it's three a.m.!" he exclaimed.

"Well it's five p.m. down here, mate, and I just got out of the water after a three-hour session at my favorite break. So, give me the skinny. How are things shaping up over there?"

Riggs struggled with the time zone difference between the west coast and the east coast of Australia, where the caller resided. It had been some time since the two had spoken. Over the course of the past five years, there had been only a few conversations each year to confirm that each was alive and well, certain payments were being made, and most importantly, a vital but yet unplanned act was still waiting to be accomplished. Five years was a long time, but the process had been a worthwhile and necessary endeavor.

"Have you checked to be sure the van is still in the lot?" asked the Australian.

"Not yet," replied Riggs. "It is listed on the schedule of property going to auction tomorrow. I am counting on it being there. The bidding should not take long. How good can it look, sitting there after all these years? No one is going to make a huge bid for it, and after all, it has not run since they towed it from the motel."

"Righto," came the reply. "Take no chances, though. Get there early and station yourself in front of the crowd so they can see you bidding. We have waited this long. Don't take any chances on losing the bid."

"I've got it covered," replied Riggs. "There were a couple of guys talking about the van in the bar last night. Just a couple of car guys who are looking for a restoration project. I will just outbid them and have the van shipped back to my home. We can store it in the garage out of sight until you get what you want out of it."

"Ah yes, the house. How is your mansion by the sea these days? After all of this time, you are the only one who has enjoyed any of the fruits of labor from our joint venture. It's my turn now." The house he referred to was the former residence of one Lester Sherman, known to some as Lester the Molester. An attorney by trade, he had had a reputation as a womanizer and legal counsel to drug traffickers and other local ne'er-do-wells. He had come to an untimely demise after being knifed by the son of a woman he had married. All manner of scandal had broken out over the killing when the public found out about the seventy-plus-year-old's relationship with a thirty-two-year-old local party girl/socialite. A struggle had broken out in the parking lot of his beachside abode centered on who would be staying in the house. The son, coming to the aid of his mother, had produced a knife and abruptly ended the argument by stabbing Lester in the neck.

During the administration of the Sherman estate, Riggs, flush with cash from a recent transaction, had been able to move up several social classes by buying the tainted, scandal-associated house at a discount.

"John," the voice on the other end of the phone continued, "you were well compensated five years ago. I have been waiting down here all of that time for my payday. If your ire and energy has waned with the passage of time, you need to reinvigorate yourself and get muscled up for this trans-action. If the van slips through your fingers, I will not be pleased. Do you have a game plan for the auction tomorrow and have you made arrange-ments to get the van to a safe location?"

Riggs paused for a moment before giving his reply. "I will buy the van tomorrow. I looked at one of those publications that prices old cars and trucks and I think five thousand is more than enough to cover this purchase. I have an old friend a few miles from Tiburon who will let me park the van at his place for a few days until we are able to deal with it."

"Okay," replied the voice on the other side of the call. "Ring me tomorrow after the sale is over and we can discuss what has to happen next."

Riggs hung up the phone and crawled back into bed. It was 3:30 a.m. but he was now wide awake. A movie was running through his head of a series of events many years ago. A rainy night in the Florida everglades, a plane going down in the storm. DEA agents questioning him at his office about a missing client. The Jojoba Ranch in eastern Santa Bonita County. Later, a missing person report to the court and the petition for authority to conduct business as conservator of the estate. And finally, five years later, the court matter to declare the missing person dead and collect the insur-ance proceeds. It all came back to him like a bad dream. He had hoped that he would never have to revisit this series of events again, but here they were, as he knew they would be, staring him squarely in the face. He would simply have to deal with the task at hand and then be done with the affair.

He tossed and turned in bed the rest of the night as he waited for the sun to come up. He would get an early breakfast and get over to the impound lot with enough time to inspect the van and more importantly, see who else in addition to the pair of characters he had overheard in the bar the night before might be bidding on the vehicle.

The next morning, Arnie and Chester were just getting ready to leave their hotel room for the complimentary breakfast downstairs when Erika called.

"Hi sweetie," she greeted Chester. "How are things shaping up for today's auction? Have you seen the van yet?"

"We're headed over there in a little bit," Chester replied. "Gonna get some chow and then give it a good looking over so we know what we are getting into. We don't want to overpay, you know."

"Well, just be careful you don't buy a mess of problems you will have to throw a bunch of money at," she replied. They ended the conversation with a promise from Chester to let her know how things turned out after the impound sale was over.

The drive to the Mendocino County impound lot just outside of town was uneventful. As they approached the yard, the traffic began to build up, and they could see a small crowd of people waiting outside the chain-link fence that surrounded the lot. Parking was difficult to find due to the influx of bidders for the annual sale. Finding an open parking spot on the side of the road, Arnie parallel parked in the dirt just off the pavement, being careful to position the car so as not to become stuck in the mud from the overnight rainstorm that had passed through the area. The pair then joined the group of presale bidders who were all waiting to kick the tires on the cars that would be sold that morning. Inside the yard were a couple of Mendocino County sheriff patrol cars. The officers standing outside the vehicles were drinking coffee. A sad-faced baseball-capped yardman came out of the small metal-sided office promptly at 8:00, walked down the wooden steps, and began talking to the two deputies.

The crowd standing expectantly outside the impound lot gate were an odd mixture of working folk, college students, and a few flashily dressed professional auction bidder types. These last few were talking loudly among themselves and obviously knew one another. Their business was to purchase late-model cars that found their way to these types of auction sales, fix them up and make them drivable, and turn them over for a profit. They were spending their time verbally jousted with one another about past bidding wars, disasters they had purchased, and the ones that they had made killings on.

Grim-faced working people stood quietly, murmuring among themselves and peering through the chain-link fencing to get an early peek at the cars. Along with the college students who made up the balance of the crowd, they were intent on finding something that was still running and needed very little work to make it their daily driver. Fuel economy, mechanical soundness, and a good set of tires took precedence over the color, popularity, or style of the car.

"All right, folks," one of the deputies barked as he approached the closed gate. "Burt here is the yardman for the lot and he will be opening the gate in just a minute." He spoke with the tone and mannerisms of authority typical to the law enforcement profession. Theirs was a job of order and control. Be it a public disturbance, crowd control, or a simple DUI traffic check point, they were trained to take the upper hand and direct the event at hand. "You will have ninety minutes to look the cars over and inspect them. Some of them run and some do not. Burt can get them started for you so that you can determine their condition. Don't try to drive any of them. They are being sold as is, where is. The auctioneer will go over the terms of sale just before the bidding begins."

As Burt unlocked the padlock securing the heavily chained gate, the crowd began to surge forward. The concertina-wire-festooned gate squeaked loudly on its rusty hinges as he swung it open, revealing the vehicles within. To Chester and Arnie, it was as if the gates to the emerald city had just been thrown open before them. Treasures abounded in the forms of a few 1950s-era sedans, several late-model vehicles, and a large assortment of ten to twenty-year-old cars, trucks, and boats. They were all arranged in neat rows, parked side by side, with just enough room to open the doors, hoods, and trunks in order for the public to inspect the interiors. Painted in white paint on the windshield of each was a number that identified the car by lot number so that there was no confusion when it came time for the bidding.

Each of the prospective bidders began inspecting the inventory for the cars they were interested in. There was no particular planning for the placement of the vehicles. Each had been placed in its location as it had come in. Some had been abandoned on the side of the road at various locations in Mendocino County. Some had been confiscated during the investigation of crimes in the county or had been towed for being parked illegally, their owners never having raised the cash to pay the tow and impound fee. There they sat, each with an untold story on how they came to be in the impound lot. The stories would no longer matter. The winning bidder would begin a new chapter for the vehicle with a winning bid. They would postpone for a time the vehicles' ultimate destiny of being recycled through a car crusher before being reborn as a completely new Honda, Chevy, or Toyota.

"Come on," growled Arnie as Chester looked over a 1952 Pontiac Chieftain. It was painted a solid flat black with yellow and red flames on the front fenders. Red rims and a poor attempt to re-chrome the front and rear bumpers evidenced the car as someone's attempt at a hot-rod restoration. "You never see these around anymore," said Chester excitedly. "Look, it's all here. Straight eight, three on the tree, all the glass is in good shape and no rust. We could hammer out these little dings easy. I say we do a complete frame-off restoration, give it some better rims, keep the drivetrain all original, and turn it for some sweet profit."

"No problem, just call Erika and let her know your budget has qua-drupled and you are getting this old beater instead of the van. I am sure she will be pleased. I will bet you parts abound for old stuff like this, right?"

Chester's face fell as he considered his friends' comments and logic. Arnie was right, of course. Erika would be pissed if he spent more than his budgeted amount. Unlike the prospective VW purchase where aftermarket parts were readily available, it would be expensive replacing parts on the old Chieftain. It was a great-looking car but a potential quagmire of costs, delays, and frustration. "I know, you're right, man. Let's get over to the van so we can check it out and be sure we know what I am getting into."

The 1971 Volkswagen van was at the far end of row 39, partially hid-den behind an old Weber's Bread bakery van. The pair spotted it as they checked the information sheet, which had the vehicle descriptions and locations for the inventory being sold that day. They appeared to be non-chalant, not particularly interested in any one car. They had rehearsed their plan and bidding strategy that morning while having coffee in the hotel lounge. They would stroll up and down the rows of cars, pretending to be interested in several vehicles and showing only casual interest in the VW van. People in their vicinity would hear them discuss the van but also hear them talking it down as only a secondary choice. Chester's earlier inter-est in the old Pontiac, while genuine, would throw other prospective van purchasers off the track. The pair had agreed to not place any bids in the early going and just sit back and wait to see what type of interest developed in the van. They did not want to turn their hand early and drive the price up unnecessarily.

A retired couple was giving the van a going over when Chester and Arnie strolled up to look at it. Decked in green two-tone paint typical of that era, with the original narrow rims and tires, the hippie van had had a relatively good life. The rear window was festooned with a happy face sticker implanted on a sunflower decal and a second sticker with the cap-ital letters "HR." A peeling sticker of Che Guevara was slowly making its exit from the rear bumper. The retired couple remarked about how similar the van was to the one they had owned thirty years previous when they had met after college. "Look, honey," the husband had remarked, "it has the same aftermarket 8-track tape deck we had in ours. The color scheme is exactly like ours was, right down to the upholstery." Chester and Arnie went through the motions of being casually interested in the van. They each noted to themselves the items that would need work. Their plan was to compare notes off to the side, out of earshot, and decide what the top bid should be. The pair began spending a lot of time going over the Weber's Bread van, pretending to be interested in it and speaking freely about what they could do with it to turn it into a camping vehicle. The bread van's proximity to the VW gave them additional time to assess the van and the level of interest from other people walking up and down the rows of cars and trucks.

CHAPTER SIX

TERRY KORMAN HAD RISEN EARLY THAT SATURDAY MORNING
as was his usual practice as the caretaker of the Wasiola Canyon Ranch in
eastern Santa Bonita County. He had made a pot of coffee but had skipped
his usual breakfast of ham and eggs. With a travel mug full of coffee, he had
loaded his ranch dog, Mego, into the cab of his pickup truck and begun the
ten-mile drive into town for breakfast and to place a phone call from the
phone booth located in the rear of the diner. Tall, blond, and tan, he looked
every much the part of a southern California surf dude except that his attire
was decidedly Western. A surfer of sorts, Terry had been a big wave rider in
Hawaii during the late sixties and early seventies. He had followed the surf
crowd to Sunset Beach and Waimea Bay, trying to be the next Greg Noll
or Buzzy Trent. Three decades later found him doubling as a real estate
agent in Santa Bonita County along with his caretaker job at the ranch. He
wore the pant legs on his Levi's just a little too short, and the sleeves of his
cowboy shirt were rolled up to his elbows, with shirt tails hanging out of
his pants. The old-guard stockmen of the Cuyama Valley could spot him a
mile away as a dude, but to visitors to the area, he appeared very much to
be a bona-fide cowboy.

The drive out of the canyon to the main highway involved an old, paved road, rutted by years of poor maintenance. In the 1950s the use of the road by heavy oil-field trucks and equipment from a short-lived oil boom had hastened its demise. It was a narrow two-lane affair that wound back and forth along the canyon floor until it connected to the main highway, which ran east and west through the valley. Terry was the sole occupant of the road as he traveled into town. The sun was already well up in the sky and he could see a dust devil boiling in the distance as he turned onto the main highway. It was going to be another scorcher, 101 degrees by midafternoon and only light winds to provide any relief to the valley occupants. Mego paced back and forth along a bale of oat hay in the back of the truck, tail wagging in a lopsided circular motion, nose to the wind, sniffing the local breezes. As Terry drove along the highway into town, he started thinking about the events that had brought him to this remote area. The promise to a friend, the exchange of cash, and dire consequences of not following through on his part of a five-year-old agreement had kept him in this game of part-time ranch manager for far too long. He passed the headquarters for the Rummell Ranch Oil Field. Decrepit buildings and an abandoned gas plant evidenced the oil boom that had brought a measure of prosperity to this valley fifty years ago. A few rusted pump jacks were lazily at work, extracting their meager mix of heavy crude oil and saltwater from the oil-bearing sands below. The easy oil had been found years ago. Now, the process that remained, of flushing the strata with water, injected it into old wells, and pushing forgotten globules of oil toward an extraction well, was a long and tedious one.

As he drew up in front of the Buckhorn Saloon and parked his car, a roadrunner stalked across the highway, holding a rattlesnake in its mouth. The herd of doe-eyed crossbred Brahma cattle in the pasture across from the eatery tossed their heads and snorted as they shied away from the bird and its breakfast prize. Giving Mego a pat, Terry hurried into the diner to take the table next to the phone booth before it could be occupied by someone else. He passed the dimly lit bar to his left as he entered the diner. Both the bar and diner opened each morning at six. The diner closed at eight. The bar remained open until the last customer left. It was the only watering hole for sixty miles in any direction. The locals commiserated about the dealings of the day over assorted mixed drinks. Long-haul truckers used the diner and bar as a rest stop to refresh themselves and restock their coffee thermoses as they continued to the coast. There were no scales along the highway. Many of the drivers were behind on their logbooks and past the required mandatory rest periods. Coffee was part of the program to help them deliver their loads and prepare for a return trip with fresh cargo.

Herb Rummell was sitting in one of the rear booths with his wife. Herb gave Terry a disapproving glance over the top of his reading glasses. He was the son of one of the founders of the famous Rummell Brothers Cattle Company that had owned virtually all of the Cuyama Valley at one point in time. The Rummell family story was a history lesson in the boom and bust nature of early California real estate fortunes. His family had come to the state in the mid-1800s from the East Coast after Frémont took the region from Mexico. Early auctions had enabled the family to acquire land in what was later to become the San Fernando Valley. Several generations of Rummells had been ranchers in that arid region. With the acquisition of water rights from the Owens Valley at the beginning of the twentieth century, irrigation had sprung up and the family had become positioned to take advantage of rising land values to expand their cattle holdings. Ill-timed loans from banks, just as the effects of the 1929 stock market crash had begun to ripple through the economy, had resulted in the family defaulting and being in danger of losing all of their San Fernando land holdings to their banker. Their bank, not being eager to take over more land holdings in foreclosures and recognizing the political power of the Rummell family, had offered a land trade of the valuable San Fernando ranch in exchange for the large Cuyama Valley ranch the bank had already foreclosed on. The Rummell family knew owning this droughty Santa Bonita County ranch was a better alternative than to losing their San Fernando ranch in a foreclosure sale and ending up with nothing. Cattle fortunes rose and fell across time. Better to take the deal and hope for better cattle prices than to close down the family ranching enterprise and try to start new careers.

They had made the trade and maintained their family ranching reputation on the Cuyama ranch. Rainfall was a quarter of that on their former ranch, and resulting cattle numbers and income was much reduced. But the family had been able to survive on much reduced financial circumstances.

A surprise oil discovery on their ranch in the 1950s was so large that the Caliente Oil Company, which had made the discovery and locked up the entire ranch under an oil lease, had later built the town of Cuyama as housing for its oil field workers. The later bust of the oil field had resulted in the oil company pulling out and selling the homes to its residents. Schools, parks, pools, and infrastructure were turned over to the county when the oil company left the valley. The town had slowly decayed with the lack of oil money to maintain those improvements.

Herb Rummell contained the full summation of his family history in his soul. He had been a child during the ranching and oil field heydays and had been witness to their demise as his parents aged and he became an adult. Educated at Berkeley (the Rummell children attended the finest finishing schools and colleges), he had grown up working on the ranch as a child, but in an atmosphere where cattle ranching was not the primary source of income for the family. Substantial oil royalties had enabled his father and uncles to run their cattle operation with less of an emphasis on cost controls. They had converted the herd to purebred Herefords and ran the ranch, which was better suited for seasonal steer grazing, as a year-round cow and calf operation. Hay was grown on part of the ranch to provide supplemental feeding for the livestock during the summer and early fall season after all the grazing resources had been used.

At the same time, oil royalties had fallen off dramatically with the exhaustion of oil production just about the time of the passing of the first Rummell brother. Herb's father had put his fortune into a trust with a large bank, and the bank had rigidly began doling out income from the small remaining oil royalties. The bank trustee was unable to continue running the cattle business. The ranch has been divided among the family trusts and instead of income from the cattle business, Herb had been forced to accept the smaller cattle lease income. He smarted under the reduced living resources provided to him by the trustee and resented the newcomers to the valley who had bought up small ranches carved out from the family's holdings. To him they were usurpers, fake country folk who knew nothing about his former way of life. Herb had continued to live on the ranch after the death of his parents as a caretaker for the trustee. He had never held a nine-to-five job. But he could remember his days as a child on the ranch when the real work of fixing fences, maintaining water systems, and the gathering and branding of cattle had taken place. These people new to the valley had no connection to its past, and Herb placed Terry into this class of people. To him Terry was just another townie with a cowboy hat and a pickup truck.

As for Terry, he was not happy to see Herb sitting so close to the phone booth. Herb was a busybody and kept his eye on all the happenings in the valley. With Herb and his wife sitting right there, there were two people who would closely observe his phone call and speculate on whom he might be getting a call from.

He ordered a cup of coffee from the waitress. She was young and attractive, especially in contrast to most of the daytime shift of middle-aged women who were all now home with their families. His waitress was unattached and available. She had been cool and nonchalant to him as she took his order. But he had noted her deeply plunging neckline and a nicely turned calf as she sauntered away from him with his order. Their eyes locked briefly as she placed his order and rung the cook's bell. She was available, ready to hook up with anyone who offered a way up and out from the monotony of that one-horse town. Terry mulled over the possibilities of such an encounter and how he might enter into further conversation with her. She would return with his coffee. He could start up some small talk over ordering his meal, or perhaps wait until she asked if he wanted anything else when she gave him the bill.

His thoughts were interrupted abruptly by the ringing of the telephone. Herb looked up from his meal curiously as Terry sprang up from his seat to take the call. He saw Herb observing him as he entered the phone booth and knew he was suspicious.

The waitress heard the muffled ring coming from inside the phone booth too. She paused and looked at the phone booth in amazement. It was rare that anyone used the apparatus anymore with the advent of the cell phone. And it was even more curious that someone would be calling that number.

"I wonder who that could be," she said, regaining her composure and heading quickly to the phone to answer it.

"I got it," Terry interjected, jumping out of his seat and almost knocking her out of the way to intercept the call. "I think it's for me," he continued. "Phone is out at the ranch, so the boss is calling in here this morning to see how things are going." A little put out at having been hustled aside so abruptly, she picked up the coffeepot and returned to the front of the diner. Looking back over her shoulder, she saw Terry close the door firmly behind himself and pick up the receiver. He turned his back to her as he began talking.

"Hello," Terry said into the phone.

"Korman, is that you?" The voice on the other end of the line was faint and scratchy, like sandpaper.

"Yes, this is Terry," he replied.

The voice was not familiar to him. The accent was decidedly Australian, and the call was hard to understand. "What did your buddy Riggs tell you about this phone call? Do you know what you're supposed to do and what this is all about?" the voice asked.

"Uh, who am I speaking to?" Terry questioned. "All I know is I received instructions to be here today for this call, and I was not to use my landline or cell phone."

"Affirmative," came the reply on the other end of the line. "There may be some people who want to look around the ranch in the next few weeks. Can't say who they might be or how many of them there will be. They might just be people looking for arrowheads. Might be law enforcement with an interest in some of the past goings on at the ranch. In any case, kick them out of there and don't give anyone permission to enter the place."

The scratchy voiced person was short and to the point. Terry had been instructed to take this call by his longtime surfing buddy John Riggs. Riggs had told him to be sure to be on time for the call, which was going to come from a different time zone. He was to follow the instructions of the person on the other end of the call and confirm to Riggs that the conversation has taken place. Up to this point, Terry's part-time job as the ranch foreman—which had also come courtesy of John Riggs—had been a lark, a diversion from the monotony of being a real estate broker in Santa Bonita County. He was just one of hundreds of brokers, each with an army of sales agents, who clambered for listings and jockeyed for position to be the first in line to present offers for their clients. He had chosen to specialize in rural ranch properties since they were few and far between and harder to market and sell. Over the years he had built up a clientele of customers and had become known as the go-to guy for rural land and ranches. It had been fortuitous that Riggs had given him this part-time foreman assignment. It paid enough to defray his broker's office overhead and provided an excuse to get away for a few days a month and play rancher at the Wasiola Canyon Ranch.

On his way back to the ranch after the call, he noticed that he was clenching his teeth. His hands gripped the wheel tightly. He took a deep breath and tried to relax. He had begun to recall bits and pieces of stories that had been relayed to him about strange goings on at the ranch over the years. Some time ago a big splash of a story had hit the papers about how the Cuyama Valley had become a haven for drug runners. The remote location and lack of law enforcement provided the perfect setting for late-night deliveries of drugs via airplanes. Eventually a DEA task force had partnered with local law enforcement to bring a stop to the practice. Terry had found it odd at first when he had visited the ranch for the first time and had met the neighbor, Herb Rummell. Herb had sped up to him in a cloud of dust in his green 1965 Chevrolet pickup truck to find out who he was and what his business was in the canyon. They had introduced themselves and Herb had warmed up to Terry once he found out the particulars of his job on the jojoba ranch. Terry had remarked about the long dirt road on Herb's ranch that seemed to lead to nowhere. It appeared to be about a quarter of a mile long and ended abruptly as it began. It was no more than twenty feet wide, straight and level, with no connection to any of the other roads in the area. The Rummell ranch was across the road from the entrance to the Wasiola Canyon Ranch. "Your boss can fill you in," Herb had replied, suddenly acquiring a chip on the shoulder. "The guy who planted all of those darned jojoba trees asked me if he could land his plane in my field when he came to visit his place. I told him okay. Thought it would be one of those puddle hoppers that can set down anywhere but no. He has Jake Stubblefield bring out his D8 and skin off a full-fledged landing strip. Turns out he owned a twin-engine jobber that used to be a commercial passenger plane. He had ripped out most of the seats so he could haul in ranch supplies, or so he said. I gave him a piece of my mind for taking out all that grass, but he threw a few hundred dollar bills at me and I just looked the other way. Looked the other way too when the DEA agents staked out the place during one of those sting operations they were running in the valley a few years ago. They had SUVs and ATVs and men on horseback all hidden among the trees in these canyons just waiting for someone to land on the strip. Nothing ever happened though. I think they finally caught some of the drug runners on the Chimineas ranch down the road."

As Terry recalled the conversation, he thought of another incident that had occurred on the Rummell ranch. A burned-out shell of a late-model Mercedes-Benz had been discovered a couple of miles off the main highway that ran east to west through the valley. It had been discovered by an oil field worker who was on his daily rounds to check on the pumps in the Rummell Ranch Oil Field. It had been parked on the side of the dirt road next to a well and set afire. The car was destroyed. It had been eventually traced back to John Riggs, who had been using it after a mutual friend, Rick French, the then-owner of the Wasiola Canyon Ranch, had disappeared. The police had investigated the arson and remarked that someone had been sending a message by burning the car and leaving it on the ranch. Most likely a message for someone in the local drug trade, they had thought, perhaps something to do with a turf war conflict or maybe an unpaid drug debt. The fact that Rick French had gone missing several months previous to this event was of interest to the police who were following up on a missing person report on French. Nothing further had come out of the matter. Terry had eventually been hired by Riggs to take care of the ranch after French's disappearance. Riggs had been appointed conservator of the French estate several months after French's disappearance. The parents and siblings of the French family had not opposed the appointment.

The Cuyama Valley had always been the equivalent of the Wild West in Santa Bonita County. Indeed, the local sheriff substation uniform of the day was the usual khaki brown shirt and olive-green pants. Instead of the standard issue patrolman's cap, the valley deputies wore cowboy hats. The preferred sidearm was a forty-five-caliber single action revolver as opposed to the nine-millimeter Glock of their city brethren. The investigation of the burned-out car had consisted of a quick physical inspection and a few pictures for their case file. No prints, fabric samples or other physical evidence had been gathered. They did not put a lot of time into the investigation. The car had been removed from the ranch that afternoon to eventually be recycled at an auto dismantler in Los Angeles.

Terry had always held an odd feeling in the back of his mind so far as his ranch foreman job was concerned. Several years ago Riggs had called him up for lunch to discuss an upcoming surf trip to Baja, which had become an annual event for them and a few other middle-aged buddies. It was their habit to take longboards and stay at the new hotel that had been built overlooking the popular K38 point break and relive the days when they were carefree teenagers from southern California spending the summer surfing and chasing the local girls in Mexican surf towns.

This time the conversation had been different, though. They had met at the Chase Restaurant in Santa Bonita. Riggs had chosen a table in the back, away from the lunch crowd. After they had ordered their meals, Riggs had become very somber and serious. "I have some bad news about our old surfing friend Rick," he had reported in a lowered voice. "I don't have all the information yet but I got a call from his girlfriend, Monica Durley. He has been missing for several days and she is afraid something bad has happened to him. They also found a plane registered to him that had gone down in Florida. It was loaded with cocaine but the pilot was nowhere to be found. She is at her wit's end. I did all his legal work for him so I will be petitioning the court to become conservator of the estate until such time as he is located or until they find out what happened to him."

Terry had not been surprised about the plane and its contents being traced to French. He had known French for a few years. The two of them had ended up in Santa Bonita after spending time in Hawaii on the north shore. French, a tall handsome athletic type with long blond hair, held himself out as one who was spiritually connected to a higher plane of thought. To the world and the women he chased at the Chanticleer and other local watering holes, he was a jojoba farmer in the Cuyama Valley who led a semimonastic life of meditation, spiritualism, and the production of jojoba oil. His life's work was the pursuit of spiritual growth and harmony for the planet. Terry knew the whole image was contrived. French was in the drug trade. His intelligence, need for an adrenaline rush, and abhorrence of physical work or a normal nine-to-five job had naturally led him into this lucrative occupation. He had the smarts and nerves of steel to become successful in the business and had been able to build up a sizeable portfolio of properties in the Cuyama Valley for which he had paid cash from the earnings of his trade. The properties had served two purposes. Primarily, they had given him the outlet to pursue his jojoba farm facade, which served as a cover for his success and cash flow. Secondarily, the tree hugger aspect of his jojoba bean enterprise sold well with the local female crowd in Santa Bonita. Between his aura of spirituality and his organic jojoba business, he had the perfect conversational entrée to harvest a crop of the romantic sort from the unattached women of that town.

A cloud of dust was boiling up behind Terry's truck as he sped along the dirt road that led up to the ranch headquarters. The double bump sound of his truck passing over the cattle guard brought his attention back to the present. The springs on the truck's vinyl seat creaked twice as he lifted and settled back down. He glanced back to be sure Mego had not been launched out of the bed of the truck. She stood there in the front corner of the bed, legs splayed and stiff, head down, recovering from the rough ride over the cattle guard.

He could not resolve in his mind how the occurrences of the past might be related to this current situation. He began to have the sinking feeling that his cushy role as the part-time ranch foreman was no longer going to be simply a lark. Someone was expecting him to fulfill an important role. A role that was neither safe nor secure. He brought the truck to a stop in front of the low-set house that served as the ranch headquarters and his living accommodations. Built long before the oil boom years of the 1950s, the board-and-batten structure was a squat affair. Whitewashed with faded green trim around the windows, it was spartan in its design, with just the basics in the way of improvements. The original water system had consisted of a buried cistern that would catch rainwater from the roof during the winter and then be used sparingly throughout the year. Years ago, someone had upgraded the water supply to a modern well which the Soil Conservation Service had paid for through a government grant program for livestock water. A line had been run to the house and the old cistern system had been abandoned, its roof now beginning to cave in from neglect.

Terry pulled the truck to a stop in front of the house and parked it under one of the ancient cottonwood trees that supplied shade to the home. Witnesses to the comings and goings of the assorted past and present owners of the ranch, the monstrous trees stood as sentinels, mute observers of the transition of the land from the original Chumash Indian occupants, to seasonal sheep grazers, followed by fenced-in cattle operations. The scraped and plowed jojoba fields, which eked a marginal existence from the droughty sandy soils of the region were the latest iteration in the ever-changing character of the Cuyama Valley.

Terry trudged up the well-worn steps to the porch and went inside, plopping down into the old leather chair in the living room. The screen door closed behind him, its coiled spring smashing it against the doorframe. The sound of the door hitting the house repeated itself, increasing in cadence as it echoed off to nothing in the warm morning air. He heard Mego circling on the porch, her wolf ancestor brain smashing down unseen grasses prior to plopping down in a lump at the top of the porch stairway. The air was still and warm, not a hint of a breeze. That would change soon as thermals began to form from the heat of the day, gathering moisture from the land and fauna to form huge puffy white clouds that would later threaten the region with rain and flooded streams, spilling over their banks. Terry sat in silence in his chair, pondering what other changes might also be in store for him.

CHAPTER SEVEN

AT FIVE MINUTES TO TEN, THE CROWD OF BIDDERS BEGAN TO drift in from the lot and assemble in front of the gate. The deputy sheriffs stood off to the side, lending their crowd-control talents to the affair. Auctioneer Myron Veneer emerged from the office and stood on the steps to the impound lot office. He was a middle-aged, balding Southerner with a decided drawl. His was not the thick southern speech of the Deep South, nor was it the almost undecipherable Cajun speech of Louisiana. It was the slow gentlemanly way of speaking typical of the old Civil War border states. He spoke slowly enough to enable the listener to translate his drawl. The listener could fill in the misunderstood words by listening to the entire sentence, then filling in the blanks. An ill-fitting brassy brown toupee adorned his head. Patches of gray hair peeked out from his neckline where the hairpiece did not fully cover his untrimmed natural hair. His pants were dark brown polyester. A bright orange shirt was accompanied by a black Western-style sports coat trimmed with heavy white stitching that matched his white loafers. A silver Navajo style ring with a large turquoise stone adorned the pinky finger of his right hand, which he used to gather the crowd of auction bidders around him as he began to address the crowd.

"Good morning, folks. We are going to start the auction in a few minutes, so let me give you the ground rules. We will begin with lot one and take them in order from first to last. I will move to the location of each vehicle and call out the lot number and give a brief description of the car so there is no mistake on what you are bidding on. You have each been assigned a bid number. Each time you want to raise your bid just hold up your number. The first one I see becomes the active bid to beat, and I will call out your number and the amount. As we get close to the end, you can call out the amount you are raising the bid to. I will give you all final notice that the gavel is going to come down on the final bid, but don't wait too long if you are going to make one last bid. When the gavel comes down the bidding is over and the sale becomes final. Immediate payment will be made to Monica Early, my assistant. She will escort you to the sales office to complete the paperwork. Burt, who is the watchman for the yard, will hand you the keys and paperwork so that you can register your new vehicle. Monica, give a wave to the crowd so they can all see you."

A tall comely blond waived her hand from the back of the crowd. Bright red lipstick accented her pale complexion and a black ribbon and bow held her locks back from her face in a tight pony tail. A black-and-white checkered blouse, short sleeved, open at the neck, completed by white short shorts, very much portrayed a fifties-era ensemble. Monica, a recent retiree from a Midwestern roller derby circuit, knew how to play to the crowd and control the flow of winning bidders through the process of cash payments for the car title documents.

"Are there any questions before we begin the bidding?" Myron asked. The meat of his job was about to begin. The group of bidders had been charmed by his southern drawl and forthright manner. Most of them had never attended an auction sale before. They would be unfamiliar with the process and hesitant at first to step forward and raise their paddles. But with time, his singsong cadence, abrupt halts to the bidding, followed by humorous chastising of the crowd when the bids were too low, would suck them all into the process. Many of them would end up paying more than they had intended for the cars on the lot. Each sale would become a celebration of sorts as the crowd would congratulate the winning bidder and gain hope and courage when it was time to bid on the vehicle they were interested in buying.

"All right, folks we are going to start with lot one, a 1973 Ford Pinto station wagon." The crowd assembled in front of the metallic blue wagon with pseudo-wood-trimmed doors. It had American Mag wheels with whitewall tires, giving it a sporty, surf car look. A few people in the crowd still remembered that the Pinto was one of the most dangerous vehicles the Ford automotive giant had ever produced. Known for exploding in rear-end collisions because they collapsed the gas tank, few of them were left on the road. Ford Pintos had been making a steady march to the auto dismantlers' yards for years once it was learned of the safety flaw in the vehicles design. The result had been to drive up the demand and price for the few remaining cars still on the road. They had become a cult vehicle, much like the AMC Pacer of *Wayne's World* fame. People snapped them up and restored or modified them just for the chance of having a one-of-a-kind ride.

"We are going to start the bidding at five hundred dollars," Myron began. The car was not in running shape and the blue leather interior was cracked and frayed. The metallic blue body with the fake woody trim was flawless though. The interest in the car was high. "I've got five, will ya give me six," Myron began to yammer in the age-old auctioneers' cadence. "I've got six, who will do seven," he continued. Bid cards flashed and the bids crossed over into quadruple digits. The final two bidders consisted of a young teenaged surfer, father in tow, and a Hispanic car club guy wearing blue jeans and a white T-shirt. The emblem on the back of his black leather jacket read "Brown Sensations," calling out the name of the southern California car club to which he belonged. The young surfer was intent on buying the car to use as a surf vehicle. The latter was going to strip the entire body down and turn it into a resto-rod, barely recognizable as a former grocery getter of the seventies. The bidding seesawed back and forth, the car guy raising his bid with barely a nod, while the young high school student enthusiastically raised his bid paddle and shook it vigorously each time the bid came back to him. Eventually the surf car was his, the older bidder finally giving up in disgust and turning his back on the crowd. The crowd of bidders hooped and hollered congratulations to the young man and he and his father strode off to the office with Monica Early to pay for the car and collect the paperwork to transfer the title. Her job was to deliver the paperwork from Myron and the buyers to Burt and talk up the car as they walked across the lot to forestall any buyer's remorse that might crop up before cash traded hands and title papers were provided to the new owner.

Up and down the rows went the auctioneer, followed closely by the crowd. A few bidders had gone directly to the cars they were intending to bid on and waited patiently by their prospective purchases for the crowd to assemble and bid. Arnie and Chester had followed the crowd for a while but eventually followed suit and went over to the VW van. They made another final inspection of the van, trying to pick out repair items they had missed and to again go over the costs to bring the van back to running condition. As the crowd approached the van for the next round of bidding, Arnie reminded Chester of their strategy. "Keep a lid on it, Chess," he hissed under his breath. "Let's see where the bidding goes and try not to bid this thing up too high. I will give you a nod when it is time to make our strike." Chester nodded and the two positioned themselves in the middle of the crowd of bidders.

"Okay, folks, lot number 27 is a 1971 VW Westfalia Campmobile. It runs but has been sitting here about five years." He glanced over at the office where Burt the yardman was issuing bills of sale to the successful bidders. "What the heck. Burt, the yard watchman, must have been living in this thing. That's why it has been here so long!" The crowd chuckled at the joke. "All right folks, we are starting the bidding at one thousand dollars. Here we go. Who will give me a thousand for this fine example of a seventies beach van?" The couple who had been interested in the van quickly raised their paddle. Before Myron could confirm their bid, John Riggs pushed his way to the front of the crowd and announced, "I bid two thousand dollars." He looked around the crowd haughtily, confident that his high bid would seal out any other bidders who had been considering the van. He wanted to get in and out. To get this thing over with quickly so that he could finish his business and return home. The couple who had been looking at the van lowered their gaze and exited the crowd of bidders. No one else made a higher bid. "Well," Myron chortled, "this guy is serious about the van, I guess. Is anyone going to come up on the price or am I just about to make this the fastest sale of the day?" He looked over the crowd, seeing no one willing to raise the bid. Chester was stunned and grabbed Arnie by the shoulder. "What do we do, man, I only brought thirty-five hundred bucks with me and if this guy is serious, we are shit out of luck."

"Only one way to find out if this guy is for real or if he is going to fold," replied Arnie. Chester raised his paddle and shouted "Thirty-five hundred bucks!" The blood drained from Arnie's face and his jaw dropped as he realized his friend had just responded with an all or nothing bid. Myron swung his gaze in the direction of the two and licked his lips. His interest in obtaining the highest price possible was strictly financial. At a fee of 10 percent of the winning bid for his services in running the sale, each increase in price meant more bucks in his pocket. He also knew his cars. Two grand was plenty for this old van. This new bid was simply outrageous.

The crowd of bidders and onlookers grew quiet. They all stared in the direction of Chester as he lowered his paddle slowly. It was as if someone had said the wrong thing, exposed the unexposable, crossed the forbidden line, shit on the sidewalk. They began to murmur among themselves about the last bid, glancing back and forth between Arnie and the two recent bidders. The couple was done. They shrugged their shoulders. The husband signaled with a slicing motion of his finger across his throat that they were out. All eyes turned to John Riggs. He was just standing there, arms folded on his chest, staring intently at Arnie and Chester. He appeared unfazed to the crowd. Internally, his heart rate had begun to rise. He had to have this car, regardless of the price. To fail meant things which he did not care to consider. He stared at the duo coldly as if trying to intimidate a witness at a trial before asking the one final question that would sway a jury. He wondered how much money they had. Could they go higher? He raised his card. "Five," he stated coldly. Myron began his chanting again, "Gave me five, I've got five, who will give me six," trying to keep the excitement and momentum moving forward. It was not unusual for this kind of thing to happen. On occasion, bidding would get out of hand, resulting in a new price level for the particular vehicle. This price would be noticed in the car community and either would remain as the new standard, or would fade as an aberrant, emotion-fueled sale that would quickly be discounted by the car collector community.

Arnie and Chester stood silently, hands in their pockets. Chester shook his head in response to the auctioneer's wrangle, signaling that they were done. "Going once, going twice, sold!" boomed Myron as he brought his gavel down on the front bumper of the van. "Take your lot number and your payment up to the office with Monica, please, and Burt will take care of you." The crowd moved off to the next auction item, leaving Arnie and Chester standing in front of the van. "I'm sorry man," Arnie said to his friend. "Who would have thunk it. Five grand for this hunk of junk? It's only worth half that at best."

Chester was deeply disappointed. He took one last walk around the van, pointing out the modifications he had planned for the vehicle. He resolved to pick up his search for an alternate vehicle to work on. The pair decided to take one last tour through the cars still unsold in the auction to see if an alternative might present itself.

Riggs strode up the stairs to the impound lot office trailer to conclude his purchase, Monica following close behind. The sound of his classic black wing-tip shoes on the rough sawn wood gave off a tapping sound as he climbed the stairs.

"You got the deal of the century" she said to him as they entered the office. "You just don't find these kind of vans in this kind of condition these days. What do you have in mind, a full restoration and selling it at the next Mecum auction?"

Riggs gave her the brushoff with an evasive answer about having had a van like this one when he was a teenager. He had spent enough time with divorcee clients to not be roped in by her fully filled tight blouse and skimpy shorts, which rode up enticingly on her long lanky frame.

Burt knew a successful bidder was soon to enter his office. The normal sound coming from those stairs was the loud clumping of the steel-toed work boots of a tow truck operator, or the urgent steps of someone trying to retrieve their impounded daily driver from the yard. These footsteps could only be coming from one of the buyers.

"Hi," Riggs greeted the yardman. "I am paying for lot twenty-seven this morning." Burt fumbled through the stack of tickets Monica had just deposited in his inbox, locating the slip for the van on the top of the stack. "Ah yes, the hippie van," Burt commented. "Hate to see that old one go. It's been here so long it's like one of the family."

"That will be five thousand dollars," stated Monica as she opened her cash box to receive payment. "Cash, cashier's check, or a certified money order will do."

Riggs was already filling out a check. "Personal check okay?" he asked, not waiting for a response. He signed the check and quickly removed it from the check book, placing it in front of the pair. The yardman stared at the check for a moment and then slid it back across the table to Riggs.

"Cash, cashier's check, or certified money order," he repeated.

"There won't be any problem with this check," replied Riggs. "You can see it is written on the account of my law firm. I do business with bail bondsmen and the court and they all accept my checks."

Burt looked up from the stack of paperwork on his desk and again repeated the payment methods acceptable for the sale. "These are the rules printed in the auction brochure. They are also on the county website. I can't change them, even if you are an attorney. It could mean my job."

"This is preposterous," replied Riggs, his voice beginning to rise in tone and tenor. "I've never had anyone unwilling to take a check. I am an officer of the court. Is there anyone I can call? Do you have a boss I can speak with?"

Monica closed the lid on the cash box and calmly explained that the administrative staff for the impound lot were off for the weekend and while the deputies at the sale could speak with him, they were equally powerless to approve his personal check. "If you can't provide the payment in full, they will go to the next bidder in line and let them take the van. Sorry, but there's nothing I can do about it."

"We will see about this," stormed Riggs as he picked up his check and walked out of the office.

Standing on the deck outside, he looked around for the auctioneer. Myron was now positioned in front of lot 30, a 1985 Toyota Camry, talking up the vehicle's dependability and gas mileage. "Don't let the 240,000 miles on the odometer fool you, folks. This one's got a lot of miles left in her yet. Who will give me five, five, what will ya give me?" he chanted as the bidding began again. No one in the crowd raised their paddle and no amount of prodding, pleading, or cajoling from Myron could induce the bidders to step forward. "All right, this one is for the crusher," concluded Myron. Riggs strode up to him as the crowd moved over to the next car up for auction and grabbed Myron's elbow. "Can I speak with you a moment, sir?" he asked, speaking low with an even tone.

"Sure, buddy, what's your pleasure?" Myron replied. "Got a low bid to take this Camry off my hands? Make a great grocery getter for your wife or a sweet ride for one of your kids to get to school."

"I'm not married and my ex gets enough dough out of me. The only car she will drive starts with a B and ends with a W. I need to speak with you about the van I just bought. Your assistant will not take my business check for the purchase and I need to see how we can finish up this sale."

"Cash, cashier's check, or certified money order," replied Myron. "Payment in any of these forms will be acceptable. The rules of the sale are clearly stared in the auction materials and on the county website."

"Will you hold the car until I can get to the bank Monday and get a cashier's check for you?"

"Sorry," Myron replied. "If it was my car I would have no problem with it, but this is a county sale and they have strict rules. If you can't make the payment in the required form, the car goes to the next bidder in line. Deputy," he called out to the officer who was standing behind the crowd. "Can you go find those two boys who made the last bid on the VW van and get them over here? I think I saw them down by the row of pickup trucks over by the back fence. Tell them they get the van if they can make immediate payment." He looked back through his sheets of paper. "Thirty-five hundred bucks is what their bid was. Tell them to cross my palm with thirty-five hundred bucks and the van is theirs."

Riggs's face began to flush as he realized he was dealing with the rigid bidding rules of the county auction. In some other situation, back in Santa Bonita County where he was known, perhaps, the outcome would have been different. Some cash via a palmed hand, the calling in of a favor, the implied promise of a future payback, were all options usually open to him in these kinds of dealings. But he was out of his territory, and no one knew him here. Without saying a word, he turned on his heel and walked out of the storage lot, back to his car. As he closed the car door behind him, he sat in the seat for a moment, thinking about his next move. He would have to tell his client that he had not gotten the car and admit that sloppy planning had led to his failure. That he had been dragged into the assignment on short notice with little time to plan for the event would bear little weight with his client. It had been a simple assignment. Buy the car and put it in a safe place. He had blown it. The client would not be happy.

Chester was leaning over, peering into the engine compartment of a 1962 Chevrolet pickup truck, verifying that the original 235-cubic-inch, Blue Streak straight-six engine was still with the vehicle. "Yep, it's got the straight six in it, still the original blue paint. This could be one sweet ride."

"Excuse me, gentlemen," the deputy sheriff interrupted. "Are you the two fellows who put in the losing bid on the VW van, lot twenty-seven?"

Upon verifying Arnie and Chester had been the bidders, he informed them of the situation. "The guy who had the high bid could not come up with the purchase price. Seems he did not read the auction rules and came with just a checkbook. If you two still have the thirty-five hundred bucks in cash or a cashier's check, head up to Burt's office and the car's yours—that is, if you still want it."

Arnie and Chester stared at each other for just a moment. Smiles grew on their faces as they realized that the van had not been sold out from under them after all. They had snagged the van! "You bet, thanks, officer!" replied Arnie as the pair closed the hood on the truck and trotted off to the office to pay for the van and receive the title to the vehicle.

Arnie and Chester took the stairs up to the office two at a time then hurriedly opened the door and greeted Burt, who was handling paperwork with another purchaser. "I will be with you in just a moment," he stated, barely looking up from the papers in front of him. He was a methodical person. His was a job of repetition and procedure. First, identify the buyer by the signed card from Myron, which had all the information on the lot number, vehicle, and purchase price. Then retrieve the court documents empowering the county to transfer the title over to the buyer. There was never a pink slip to give to the buyer. Only on rare occasions was a current vehicle registration available. These were cars that had been left on the side of the road by people who could not afford to fix or tow them. Most of the time, the registration had lapsed. If the license plate had current stickers, it was likely they had been appropriated from another person's car and glued on to the license plate.

Burt completed the sale transaction and turned his attention to Arnie and Chester. "Auction slip and personal identification please," he said, extending his hand to receive the requested paperwork from them. Chester dug deep into the front pocket of his pants and retrieved a rolled-up wad of bills, wrapped in a rubber band.

"Here you go. Thirty-five one-hundred-dollar bills, for the lot 27 van. Fresh off the press."

Burt was not amused. "Remove the rubber band and smooth out the bills so Monica can count them and verify that they are all good," he replied. "Now, auction slip and personal identification please." Arnie did as instructed, laying the smoothed-out stack of bills in front of Monica like an offering placed on an altar. Monica began methodically counting the bills, periodically creating individual stacks containing ten bills. When she had three full stacks and a fourth partial stack, she began to examine each bill, looking for the telltale evidence that each was authentic. Fine cotton threads, heavy ink, properly spaced serial numbers, all indicators of authentic bills were noted. "All right, gentlemen, payment in full has been received." Burt signed a receipt ticket for the cash with a slow, deliberate hand. Arthritis in his hands and wrists from years of manual labor restricted his signature to a series of up and down, barely recognizable scrawled lines. He followed this up with the loud bang of an official county stamp that noted "Paid in Full" in bold red ink.

"Here is the transfer paperwork. We don't have a pink slip or current registration form. This one has been on the lot for almost five years. Some kind of problem with an estate or something. Just give this paperwork to the Department of Motor Vehicles when you are ready to register it."

Arnie looked quickly at the papers that Burt had stuffed into an envelope and handed to them. The bill of sale, an affidavit of transfer, and a preprinted form from the county referencing court proceedings that authorized the car to be sold by the county. It all seemed in order. They would have preferred the traditional pink slip endorsed over to them on the back, but with papers in hand and a key to the ignition and doors, they were ready to load up the van and make the long drive back home.

"Before you go, gentlemen, do we have your current address and phone number in case we need to contact you?"

Arnie verified that the information on their bid registration form was correct and complete.

"Why would you need to contact us?" he asked as they rose to leave the office.

"Once in a great while someone turns up after the fact and wants to see if they can buy the car back. Sometimes they left personal property in the car and are willing to pay a finder's fee if you come across it. It is a pain in the ass for us so we just send them on to the buyer to work out whatever needs to be handled. Good luck with the car, gentlemen. See you at next year's auction, we hope."

The pair thanked Burt for his time and retrieved their truck and trailer. Chester carefully checked that the ball hitch was still safely connected to the truck and that the safety chains and electrical cord for the trailer lights were still well attached and functioning.

"Come on, let's get rolling," complained Arnie, tired of the pretrip truck inspection routine Chester was going through. They had done the inspection the day before they left Santa Bonita, and it seemed redundant.

"Slow down, little guy" Chester replied. Repetition and routine were part of his makeup. He had previous commercial truck driving experience from his post-college days before his coat and tie job at Capital Triangle Properties. Driver safety had been ingrained into him and he had extrapolated this mind-set and procedure into his personal driving habits. Equipment failure leading to a breakdown or accident while on the road was something he could control and guard against.

Arnie knew the drill. He trotted around to the front of the truck and began giving Chester the thumbs up sign at Chester turned on and off the headlights, turn signals and emergency flashers. They went through the same process for the rear lights on the trailer. Finding everything in order, they pulled the truck and trailer around and positioned it in front of the van. "Help me with these ramps," Chester asked and he began pulling on the two loading ramps that were housed underneath the rear of the trailer. He unhooked the rusty chain that kept the ramps from sliding out from underneath the trailer and they tugged on the first ramp, fighting years of rust, debris, and bent metal to extract it.

When the second ramp was in place Chester grabbed the hook at the end of the large winch cable on the front of the trailer and rolled it out to hook on the front of the van. "Jeez," he said, exasperated, "there is nothing to hook this thing to." The uni-body construction of the boxy van had few points strong enough to hook on to. They decided to simply hook the chain to the front bumper and gingerly haul it up onto the trailer. The electric winch ground away as the van began to move for the first time in many years, leaving a collection of weeds and trash behind it as the front wheels touched the ends of the two ramps and began to slowly lurch aboard. When it was finally securely sitting atop the trailer, they began passing smaller chains across to one another and used chain binders to lock the van firmly in place to the trailer. Chester made one more walk around the truck and trailer, kicking all the tires and pulling on the chains to be sure his precious cargo was not going to become loose during the trip home. "All right, let's roll!" he shouted to Arnie.

As he climbed into the truck he saw John Riggs approaching him, waving his hands to slow him down and saying something to him. "Are you guys interested in making a quick profit on this van? I really want the van and can give you an extra thousand bucks if you are willing to part with it." The hard work had been done to get the van loaded and Chester had already started the thought process of how he was going to strip the van down to the frame and rebuild it from the ground up with all new gaskets and door trim so that it would be like new, just like when it came off the factory floor. He was mentally invested in the project now. No amount of money was going to divert him from this project. "Sorry, man. These old vans are not that common and I have been looking for one in this kind of shape for a long time."

Riggs shrugged his shoulders and reached into his wallet for a business card.

"Well, if you change your mind, here is my phone number. Just don't wait too long. I need the van in original condition with no work started on it. Give me your contact info just in case my client wants to talk to you directly about the van after you get done restoring it."

"No problem," answered Chester, quickly writing his name, address, and phone number on the back of Riggs's business card and handing it back to him. What could it hurt to have a potential buyer in his pocket when it came time to realize his profits from the project? They bid their goodbyes and drove off and headed for the main street through town.

In the impound yard office, Burt looked up from his paperwork and saw them driving off, VW van in tow. He had watched Riggs try to buy the van from them. "Can you wait outside for just a moment," he asked the next buyer who was about to enter his office. With the door closed behind him, he pulled out his cell phone and sifted through his wallet for a faded yellow folded piece of paper. Carefully unfolding it he dialed a smudged phone number and waited for a response on the other end of the line.

When someone picked up, Burt spoke tersely.

"The van is sold and headed out of town. Your guy did not get it. The dumb shit did not bring any cash or certified checks with him. I had to let it go to the next highest bidder, a couple of young guys from Southern Cal." He read off Chester's name and address from the paperwork in front of him. "Okay, I am all done in this deal now. I have held up my part of the bargain. You can send me the other half of the C-note and our business will be done."

Hanging up the phone, he opened the top desk drawer and retrieved a small manila envelope. In it was a half of a crisp one-hundred-dollar bill. An unsigned handwritten note accompanied the bill .The instructions had been clear if he wanted the other half of the bill. If anyone other than a certain John Riggs purchased the van, Burt was to provide information on the person who took possession of the van immediately by calling the phone number at the bottom of the note.

He had not been sure what this was all about but had called the number on the outside chance that the communiqué was legit. It had been a short conversation. The speaker on the other end of the line had been curt, to the point, a hint of menace in his speech. "Do you have a cell phone? When the van is sold, call this number again and let me know who bought it. If it's not John Riggs, I will need an address. Use your cell, not the office phone. That is all you have to do. Call as soon as it is sold." Then the speaker had abruptly hung up, the conversation ending as quickly as it had started. Burt kept the letter and phone number. He could use an extra hundred bucks, and the task seemed easy enough. Just a phone call and a minute or two of his time.

CHAPTER EIGHT

ERIKA MCCONIKA TOWELED HERSELF OFF AFTER HER LATE-AF-ternoon workout at the gym. The light-green towel held her fiery red hair in a turban while she wrapped another color-coordinated green towel around her body. She heard the rustling sound of a truck pulling into the gravel driveway in front of her home. Peeking out the frosted window in the shower, she saw Chester and Arnie parking the truck. Behind the truck, the trailer was loaded with a green, two-tone Volkswagen van. Chester had called her from the truck on the trip home to excitedly inform her of the successful purchase. He had relayed the details of the day, including how they had almost lost out on the van and the last-minute change of events that had catapulted them into the winning bid position. "Can you believe that guy? Showing up to an auction and not having cash to seal the deal?" She had agreed with him that the situation had been fortuitous. It signaled that this restoration project was starting off on the right track.

Their new home was a modest, one-story ranch-style abode. The home was situated at the end of a cul-de-sac. The neighborhood was decidedly blue class. In the side yards of many of the homes were parked an assortment of boats, camping trailers, and the occasional derelict car.

The van restoration project would blend in well with those of the rest of the neighbors. The home was clean and recently remodeled, faux wood flooring throughout, composite granite counters in the kitchen and baths. Complete with new drapes and appliances from Home Depot, the previous owners, who had sunk their savings into the home, had become overextended. They had lost the home through foreclosure when the real estate market had slowed and retrenched. The successful buyer had quickly put it on the market as a rental. Their loss had become Chester and Erika's gain.

Erika hurriedly dressed and went outside. It was a great-looking van, she thought, as she looked it over, sitting atop the trailer the guys had borrowed from a neighbor to retrieve their prize. It had the original faded paint. There were a few scratches, but the van looked none the worse for wear, given the length of time it had been sitting in the impound lot. She greeted Chester with a hug and a long, slow kiss.

Arnie began rattling the chains as he removed the chain binders on the passenger side of the trailer. "Come on, Chess, let's dump this thing off so I can get out of here." The couple separated and Chester removed the chains from the van and trailer, throwing them in a heap in front of the trailer. Crawling up onto the trailer and into the van, Chester released the parking brake and took the transmission out of gear. Arnie released the locking mechanism on the winch, removed the hook from the bumper of the van, and began pushing on the front of the van. The trailer began to tilt and the van slowly rolled off the trailer. Arnie ran around to the driver-side door and jumped behind the steering wheel and pushed down on the brake pedal to stop the van. The pedal went all the way to the floor. Thinking quickly, Arnie pulled on the emergency brake. The van slowed to a stop as the ratcheting sound of the emergency brake handle signaled that the device was working.

"That could have turned out differently," exclaimed Arnie as he opened the door and got out of the van. "Brakes are shot. The pedal went all the way to the floor. Master cylinder is shot or maybe all the brake fluid has leaked out."

"Doesn't matter," Chester replied. "I am going to strip the brakes down to the backing plates and rebuild them from the ground up. Once I get this thing running, I don't want to risk having a wreck from forty-year-old brakes that have been sitting for years."

"Are you going to just leave it here in front of the house?" Erika complained. Chester was putting wood blocks in front of the wheels.

"Just for a few days, honey," he replied. "I will clear out some of the stuff from the side of the house and then we can push it over there so I can put it up on blocks and start working on it."

"Push it?" she repeated. "Do you think the two of us can move this heavy old thing ourselves?"

"Don't worry, baby, I have a way to do it that is so easy, you will be amazed. All those years working at the gas station taught me a few things. You'll see."

CHAPTER NINE

THE LATE AFTERNOON SUN BLAZED OPAQUELY THROUGH the rain clouds, casting an orange-tinged light upon the beachgoers frolicking in the waves at the Australian community of Surfers Paradise. A conglomerate of local surfers, body boarders, and tourists were catching the last sunlit hours of the day before the pending rainstorm arrived to sweep them from the beach, driving them to the warm safety of their homes and hotel rooms. It had been a rainy fall, a quick end to a summer of warm days for the local Queensland residents and the throngs of seasonal tourists who flocked to the area each year.

On the patio of the Paradise Café, a tall middle-aged man sat on the balcony overlooking the point break where three-foot ankle slappers were still providing fun waves for the small gang of surfers who were busily getting in their last few waves before dark. He watched the interaction of the group with casual interest as the timeless jockeying of the surfers to gain priority and the best position on the waves took place. The younger groms, darkly tanned, some with sun-bleached hair, paddled aggressively around the larger pack of surfers, talking back and forth among themselves, attempting to signal to the rest of the pack that they were locals and entitled to any wave they chose. Tourists sitting on rented surfboards gave them a wide berth. The older locals ignored the young groms. They were the alpha males of the pack. It was understood that when they turned to paddle for a wave, no one was supposed to snake them or get in their way. The groms would not hesitate to take a wave from one of the tourists, but they knew their place in the wave priority food chain and left the old guard alone.

"Good day, Mr. French," greeted the waiter as he busily cleaned off the dirty dishes and glasses from the balcony table. "What can I get you today?"

"How about a Fosters and a bucket of ice," the customer replied. Rick French was the epitome of the US expat surfer who had migrated to Surfers Paradise to retire and ride the waves. An entire community of former businessmen, doctors, and other professions had chosen to drop out of the working world and retire early in this southern hemisphere locale and enjoy the relaxed beach-going lifestyle. Tall, tanned, with long wavy blond hair reminiscent of the free and easy lifestyle of the seventies, French maintained a guru-like spirituality that spoke of his centered, calm approach to life. He did not become rattled by the small inconveniences of daily life or impressed by the fits and emotional responses of people around him. Indeed, upon arriving in Surfers Paradise five years ago, he had become accepted by the local surfing community as one of their own in a short amount of time. It had not hurt that he had contacts already living in the community; they had helped to escalate the rate of his acceptance by the locals. The young single women who frequented the cafés and bars found his aura of controlled spirituality irresistible.

His waiter returned with his beverage and took his order for fish and chips. He took a long pull on the ice-filled mug of beer and gazed out onto the beach below, deep in thought. After a moment, he pulled out his cell phone and placed it on the table in front of him. Reaching to retrieve his wallet from his back pants pocket, he opened the billfold and pulled at a threadless seam that held the wallet together. Lifting the seam up, he exposed the underside of the leather and viewed a phone number written in india ink. The number had smudged slightly with years and perspiration but was still legible. Placing his wallet back into his pocket, he took another drink of beer and resignedly dialed the number. After a long delay and some clicking sounds, he heard the familiar raspy voice on the other end of the call.

"Jackson, go."

"It's French."

"I know. Is the deal done? When do I get my money?"

"I don't have the van but I know where it is and who bought it. I will get you what you need from the van in a few days once I check it out and see the best way to access it."

"You were supposed to have this under control. It's been a long time. We have bird dogged the van for five years and I'm running out of patience."

French sat there for a moment not responding. Five years was a long time to have waited for the moment of opportunity he knew would some-day happen. The van, which now was in the hands of the two young resto-ration aficionados in Santa Bonita, had once been his. He could still picture the vehicle and remember his camping and surf trips to Baja. When it had been confiscated and sent to the Mendocino County impound yard, he had not been in a position to retrieve the van or make any plans on how to pay the county storage and towing fees. Indeed, that was not a time for him to show his face anywhere or give even the slightest suggestion that he still walked the earth.

It had been a rainy winter night five years ago, in a modest motel in Tiburon. An exchange of money had taken place and he had given the sig-nal for his twin engine Cessna 340A to leave the airstrip from the drug-car-tel-controlled airstrip in the interior of Columbia. Its destination was an undisclosed location in Mexico. In the makeshift Colombian hanger was a contract pilot. The pilot was a former Vietnam-era warrant officer who had experience in both helicopter and fixed wing aviation. He had done the Colombia to Mexico trip numerous times before with the plane loaded with cocaine fresh from the Colombian drug cartels. Jack Morrison, known as Jackson to his friends, had a contact at the hangar to verify the quality and quantity of the hashish. On his phone call approving the purchase, French would instruct his pilot of the location in Mexico where he would land.

French had been running this three-stage drug smuggling tactic for years. The Drug Enforcement Agency was aggressively pursuing the drug cartels' typical routes to import their products into North America via Florida. No attention was given to transportation leaving from Florida though. Private passenger planes, sailboats, and even personal vehicles transported to these locations were all suspect. Aviation was the preferred mode because of the rapid delivery and the ability of pilots to avoid radar via circuitous, low-level flights. Having surfed the lonely central California coast for years, Rick French had devised a scheme of transporting his product from sources that had already been successful in getting it into Florida. He would first fly it to Mexico. From there he used panga boats from locations in Mexico to transport his inventory to various beaches between Point Conception and San Simeon on the California coast. There was never anyone out along the coast during the late night / early morning hours. All one had to do was locate a cove with an accessible sandy beach at low tide, drive a loaded flat-bottom boat up onto the sand, and quickly off-load the bales of product into waiting vans for delivery to his remote Cuyama ranch. For a fee, he would inventory the illicit drugs far from the eyes of law enforcement until such time as the buyer was able to make full payment for the product. He had been able to modernize the illegal drug value chain by providing a less risky delivery system combined with an inventory storage and credit program for his sold inventory.

He had gotten the idea from what he observed happening among the alfalfa growers in the Cuyama Valley. The locale was dotted by large pole barns in which farmers would store their baled alfalfa hay after harvest. It had been a common practice to sell the entire barn of hay to a dairyman or feedlot and permit the buyer to keep the hay in the barn for a year. There it would be protected from the weather, and the buyer could remove it as needed instead of having to use higher value land in other parts of the state for storage. For the buyers of his hashish or marijuana bales, he was also a type of banker. He required a cash payment up front to cover the cost of his product, but he extended credit and his storage services to his buyers. This lowered their upfront cash outlays and also reduced the risk of having their entire inventory seized in a drug raid. If one of their mules was arrested, their loss was limited to that smaller delivery, not the entire load purchased from French. French did not have to be a traditional extender of credit. He covered his costs and some of his profit upfront. In the event the buyer did not perform on the rest of the purchase, he had the inventory in his possession and could resell the balance of the inventory to collect his profits.

But something had gone wrong this last time. An exchange of money had taken place at night on a ranch in the Cuyama Valley. French had verified receipt of the payment via his cell phone with his contact on the ranch from a turnout on one of the windy dirt roads that traversed the heavily forested mountains surrounding Tiburon. The money, an even five million dollars of it, was neatly packed in crisp one-hundred-dollar bills inside of a new leather briefcase. French had instructed his contact to hide the cash before the sun came up the next morning.

After the handoff of the briefcase, French had called his pilot, who was sitting in the plane on the remote runway and had given him instructions to fly the plane to the drop-off point in the Sonoran Desert of central Mexico.

French had returned to his motel room for the trip to Santa Bonita in the morning. All of those plans had rapidly changed with the 2:00 a.m. phone call he had received from his pilot. With the noise of the airplane buzzing in the background, he could barely make out the voice of his pilot telling him he was being pursued by another airplane, presumably law enforcement, and they were trying to force him to land. Wind and rain were making it difficult for the pilot to maintain control, and at the same time, the DEA agents were equally challenged to keep their quarry in sight, much less escort it to a proper landing site where they could make an arrest and take control of the contraband.

French had given the okay for his pilot to ditch the plane in the jungle and make use of his parachute to do his best to avoid capture. Bad weather and poor visibility had enabled the pilot to safely eject from the plane and parachute to the ground. He had avoided detection, and by morning, he was safely encamped at the home of a local campesino. He was never found by law enforcement. The plane had eventually run out of gas and crashed in the Florida Everglades. It was found several days later, more or less intact, along with its illicit cargo.

French had concluded that the local DEA would be waiting for him at his motel. After a quick call to Jack Morrison to alert him of the danger, he had invoked the doomsday plan that he had prepared for just such a situation. With the aid of a fake passport and a new identity, in twenty-four hours Rick French no longer walked the earth.

"It's been five years, I've waited long enough," he heard Jack repeat on the other end of the line. French was oblivious to the casual beach scene around him. He briefly acknowledged his waiter refilling his drink order in front of him. The memories of the past were like a bad dream to him. His greatest fear had always been serving a long prison sentence for drug trafficking. That had not happened. His second greatest fear had been physical harm or death from dealing with the drug lords of Bogota and the various intermediaries involved in the purchase, transport, and eventual sale of the product. He had long ago rationalized away the social impacts of the drug trade, passing it off as part of the natural selection process for the human race. The strong survived. The weak succumbed.

In the past, he had been involved in several sketchy situations where he thought his life was in danger. The torture and assassinations that made front-page news from time to time were all too familiar to him. After avoiding arrest, avoiding pain and death was his next greatest concern. He did not want to end up gunned down in the alley of some backwater Colombian town or have some of his appendages mailed to his family in Southern California.

Jack Morrison was a concern. Ever since the plane had crashed and Jack's product had not been delivered, he had been in the back of French's mind, lurking in his subconscious. He owed him a debt from this botched hashish transaction in Colombia. He had a way to get cash to Jack from a hidden location on the ranch, but the DEA involvement had forced him to leave Tiburon quickly and flee the country, leaving behind all his possessions. When the drug task force broke down the door to his motel room, they found only his clothes. His Volkswagen van was later discovered abandoned on the side of the road in the mountains above Tiburon. There had been no trace of French.

The phone call with Jack was brief and to the point. Jack had been short changed on the drug transaction with the loss of the plane and its cargo. Five million dollars was a lot of money to lose. He suspected French might have turned informant and set him up in a sting operation with the DEA, but French's rapid disappearance thereafter followed by a phone call to Jack with a proposition had calmed his suspicions. He had been receiving steady payments since then. Money to postpone the resolution to the financial problem he had suffered by nondelivery of the hashish. If French had intended to screw him on the deal, he would never have heard from him again. The two had been in a standoff. Jack, the ex-navy seal, now international drug dealer and enforcer, was willing to hold off before resorting to resolving his problem with French with the use of a gun. French was able to make periodic payments of cash with the goal of getting access to replacement cash that for the time was hidden away in a safe place, not currently accessible but available upon the occurrence of future events. And the stop gap, a life insurance policy he had purchased before his disappearance, which would guarantee that he could keep Jack at bay and continue his new life in the southern hemisphere.

"I have a line on the cash," French said. "It is hidden in various locations near my ranch. As far as I can tell, no one has touched it. My old ranch foreman hid it for me in Cuyama and left me a map of the locations. I have had a guy keeping an eye on the ranch for me to be sure no one has tried to look for the cash. He knows nothing about the map. The map of the locations for the stuff is hidden in my old van. The van was finally sold from the impound yard in Mendocino. I have good intel on where the van is headed and who bought it. I should be able to access it in a few days once I make my travel plans. Plus, the life insurance policy has been paid into my estate as well. I will pay you your money once I get the map back and access my cash."

"I'm leaving nothing to chance," replied Jack. "I'll meet you in California and we can get the map together. Then we can be done with each other."

"Slow down, Jackson. Getting to the map before the kids who bought the van know anything about what is going on should not be hard. But I don't think this is more than a one-man job. I don't want you lurking around with a nine millimeter or an uzi where this could all go down bad. Let me case the situation first and then I will tell you what it will take and if it is more than just a grab and go deal."

Jack ended the conversation abruptly after indicating he was willing to wait a day or so for French to size up of the situation.

CHAPTER TEN

BURT WAVED GOODBYE TO THE TOW TRUCK DRIVER AS HE closed the gate to the impound yard. It had been a week since the annual car sale and half of the inventory had been sold and removed from the lot. The rest of the cars were now deemed junk and a regional salvage company would begin to remove them. They would be hauled to a crusher, flattened into car pancakes, and sold by the pound. Much like the proverbial decaying trees of the local redwood forests, the junker cars would again spring to life. After being sent to a smelter and melted down, they would be recycled back into new cars in the form of Fords, Chevys, or Hondas.

He ran the heavily rusted chain through the gate and placed the large padlock through the ends of the chain, locking the gate firmly before returning to his apartment, which was located behind the salvage yard office. Part of his compensation as the yardman included these living quarters. They were neither spacious nor particularly attractive. The apartment shared a common wall with the office on the property and both structures were modular buildings that had been hauled onto the property by a mobile home moving company. They had been placed off the ground on metal stands commonly used in mobile home parks and were spartan in their design and decor. Over the years Burt had assembled a collage of yard art obtained from the cars being stored on the property and from local yard sales. Several plastic pink flamingos had found their way into his yard as had a few discarded toilets and bathtubs. He had added color to the yard by planting geraniums and fuchsias into the old plumbing paraphernalia. Here and there were displayed chrome bumpers from 1950s automobiles. His favorite was a row of smiling teeth from the front grill of a 1951 Buick Roadmaster. The crankshaft from the straight-eight engine block served as the base for a birdbath made from the blade of an old farming disk.

His dog, Bingo, greeted him at his porch and the two of them climbed the stairs to begin dinner and settle down for the evening. The door to his apartment was slightly ajar. "Must have forgotten to close it after lunch," he muttered to himself as he reached for the doorknob. In the corner of the room leading into his bedroom, he saw the dark form of a man emerge from the doorway. "Who the hell are you?" he yelled. "How did you get in here?"

The following morning in Santa Bonita, Chester was up early and busy tearing into his van project. He had determined that the engine did not run but it did turn over when he tried to start it. He had hooked the battery charger up and let it charge all night and his first order of business was to get the van off the street and locate it around on the side of his house so that his neighbors would not complain about having the restoration project trashing the look of the neighborhood. Many of his neighbors had similar projects or toys, but cars being worked on, camping trailers, and off-road vehicles loaded on trailers were usually hidden in backyards or on the side of homes behind closed gates, out of view of the neighbors.

Erika hurried out the front door, holding two cups of coffee, and met Chester at the front of the van. Her hair was up on top of her head, held in place by an elastic scrunchy. Chester noticed she was not really dressed to help him work on the car. She was wearing a short pair of shorts and a tank top that showed off part of her well-toned midriff. Flip-flops were not the best choice for helping him push the van around to the side of the house. He had not planned for her to do any actual restoration work with him, but he did need her to help him move the van so he could begin working on it.

"So what do you want me to do?" asked Erika, handing him one of the cups of coffee. She was always nervous about helping on car repair projects. She had no mechanical knowledge and did not really like getting her hands dirty. She also did not fully trust Chester's skills and work habits. Most of the car projects he worked on turned out eventually, but he took short cuts and risks along the way that at times made her nervous. He had always looked out for her safety when he asked her to help out at a critical moment in the project, but loud banging, pulling on things hooked to chains, or setting blocks under cars while they were being jacked up made her cringe.

"All I need you to do is help me get this thing around to the side of the house," he replied.

"How do you intend to do that?"

"We will just take it out of gear and push it. It is a pretty light vehicle and the street is slightly down hill. Once it gets rolling, you will jump into the driver's seat and steer it up by the side of the house. I will keep pushing and you will stop it by pulling on the hand brake when I tell you to. We should get enough downhill action to just roll it up there." He positioned Erika by the driver's side of the van and opened the front door. "Just put one hand on the wheel and one here on the doorframe. I will be pushing from the back. When I yell 'go,' take the hand brake off and start pushing. When we get in front of the driveway, jump into the seat and close the door. Just steer it around to the side of the house. I will keep pushing."

It was a seemingly simple plan but the execution came off poorly. As Chester began pushing, Erika forgot to take off the hand brake. "Is the brake off?" he yelled as the two of them pushed. "Oops, do I take it off now?" she replied.

"Yup!" he yelled from behind the van as he began pushing again. The van began rolling down the street and Erika aimed the front of the vehicle toward the target area. As the van turned by the side of the house and headed uphill its speed slowed and Chester pushed mightily. Erika jumped into the driver's seat and slammed the door shut. When the forward speed slowed more, Chester yelled for Erika to set the hand brake. The van came to rest ten feet from its intended destination.

"Now what?" asked Erika as Chester met her at the front of the van. "We can't leave it blocking the garage."

"Watch this," he replied, opening the door and motioning her to get out. "I charged up the battery last night just for this occasion. This is not a recommended way to move a car but in a pinch it will work." He sat down in the driver's seat and put the shift lever into first gear. "Stand back," he warned as he turned the ignition. The van lurched forward as the starter began to grind. He turned off the key after a few seconds and let the starter rest. A moment later he again lurched the van forward using the starter with the transmission engaged.

"Voilà," he trilled as the van arrived at the parking place he had cleared along the side of the house. Erika breathed a sigh of relief. No one had been hurt and Chester was in a good mood. She knew that his restoration project would have its successes and setbacks. Starting off with this small victory was a good way to begin. The couple returned to the kitchen for a coffee warmup before tackling the project any further.

The tow truck driver in Mendocino County who had towed a car from a morning head-on crash had been the unfortunate party to find Burt's body sprawled inside the entrance way to his apartment. An entry wound to the front of Burt's head resembled a third eye, small and neat, a contrast to the exit path of the bullet, which had removed most of the rear of his skull. Bingo was equally dead, both having been shot by a nine millimeter semiautomatic weapon, popular with the amateur home defense crowd of gun rights activists. The pistol was both affordable and easy to operate. For several hundred dollars, a pistol in good condition could be acquired after the mandatory ten-day waiting period in California. Five empty shells were strewn around the room. Three of them had been used on Burt as he had tried to flee from his assailant. Bingo had taken the other two as she had tried to defend her master.

The sheriff's detective had reconstructed the crime scene from the evidence at hand. The victim did not know his assailant. Entry to the apartment had occurred through a broken window in the rear of the unit where the apartment was obscured from the view of the county road. The drawer to Burt's desk was still open but it did not appear to have been rifled through. Clutched in Burt's hand was half of a torn hundred-dollar bill. The other half was nowhere to be found in the apartment. This torn bill was puzzling to the investigator. Why was it in Burt's hand? Who would want to kill the old curmudgeon? The impound yard was a likely spot for a thief to consider robbing. Most people paid their fines in cash. But the security cameras and security lights were a deterrent for most would-be thieves. Equally puzzling was the record book where Burt tracked the receipts of funds for fines associated with impounded cars and the sales of cars from the periodic auctions and sales to recycling companies. The pages from the most recent transactions including the recent auction sales were missing. They had been ripped out.

The investigation was limited to taking the obligatory crime scene photos and pulling prints from around the area of entry. Tire track marks were not going to be much help with the daily traffic flow from towing companies and the public seeking to pay their fines and retrieve their cars from the lot. The security camera was pointed toward the fenced lot and away from the rear apartment area. Burt's murder would likely become a cold case without some further help from an informant.

CHAPTER ELEVEN

CHESTER WAS IN HIS ELEMENT. MECHANICS COVERALLS would be the uniform of the day for the next few months while he tore into the Volkswagen and turned the flower power hippie van into a radical surf mobile. He had placed jack stands under each corner of the van to make the under carriage safely accessible. His plan of attack was to check the mechanical systems first to see what needed to be done from a safety stand-point. Before that though, he would quickly troubleshoot the nonrunning engine and determine the extent of the problem.

He removed the old oil bath air cleaner from the carburetor and hooked up a remote starter tool to the battery so he could start the engine from its rear-mounted location without having to bother Erika with turn-ing the key from the driver's seat. Spraying a healthy dose of starter fluid down the carburetor, he pushed the button on the remote starter and let the engine cycle several times. The engine turned over rapidly, giving of a repetitive whine as it attempted to start. After several unsuccessful attempts Chester stopped and put down the remote starter. "Crap," he muttered to himself. He removed the fuel line from the carburetor and again turned the engine over. A healthy flow of fuel spurted from the fuel line. "Gotta check for spark," he thought as he reattached the fuel line and popped off the two metal clips holding down the cap to the distributor. He was going to check the condition of the points but was instead surprised to see that the rotor was worn and corroded, incapable of carrying a spark to permit the engine to run. "Criminy!" he exclaimed in excitement. After a quick trip to the parts store, the engine had coughed to life in a cloud of blue smoke from the exhaust pipe once Chester had installed the missing rotor and turned the engine over. It ran roughly on the mixture of recently added fuel and the gummy mix of old fuel that had been aging in the tank. As the engine warmed up and Chester revved up the fuel linkage, the engine progressed from loping along on three cylinders to a full-throated roar of all four cylinders fully firing.

Chester had been tempted to drive the van around the block, but as he was about to take if off of the stands, a black BMW pulled up in front of his house and a man got out of the car and approached him.

"Starting on your project already," the man said as he walked up to Chester. Chester recognized him from the auction sale in Mendocino County—he was the guy who'd tried to outbid them. He was now casually dressed in a Hawaiian shirt and khaki Dockers shorts typical of the baby boomer generation.

"John Riggs. You remember me, I trust. I was in the neighborhood and thought I would drive by just to see if you were having second thoughts about maybe making some quick money on the van. These projects always take more work than you think they will, and foreign car parts can be pretty pricey."

Chester was surprised to see Riggs, remembering him and his attempt to buy the van from him after the sale. "This guy just won't take no for an answer," he thought as he rose to meet the approaching Riggs.

"No thanks," replied Chester. "I am just getting into it and things are turning out better than I thought. She runs after all and once I compression test the old girl all I have to do is rebuild the brakes and run down all the electrical and she will be a daily driver."

"Look, buddy," replied Riggs, "I know you are amped up to take this restoration on and see it through to the end, but I have a client who is a real nut for this model. These are hard to find in this condition. My client has authorized me to offer you six thousand dollars cash for the van as is. You can double your money."

"Nope," Chester replied. "Come back in a couple of months when this thing is all done and then we can talk".

Riggs could see no amount of money or further inducements were going to sway Chester into selling him the van. "I might just do that," he replied. Erika walked out of the house with a fresh cup of coffee in hand at that moment. Riggs made a quick retreat to his car. The rear end of the BMW hugged the ground as Riggs gave it full throttle and sped away.

"Who was that"? Erika asked, handing the coffee cup to Chester.

"Oh, just some guy from the sale that is sour grapes over us getting the car."

"Is he the one who didn't bring enough cash?"

"That's the guy," he replied. "You would think we had bought an Aston Martin or Ferrari, the way he's kept trying to buy this old thing."

Rick French was not amused when he received the phone call from Riggs that evening telling him Riggs had been unable to convince Chester to sell the car to him. French had ended a sunset surf session early and had missed a gathering of the local surfing group over drinks to take this phone call. Now he mulled the problem over in his mind. What could be done to get access to the van? The new owner was obviously not swayed by money. He would pay any reasonable amount to get the van, but raising his price again would only cause suspicion. He discussed his options with Riggs. "We really don't have to buy the van to get what I need, John. All I need is a map."

"Map? What kind of a map?" replied Riggs.

"It's a map of where my cash is stashed in the Cuyama Valley. I need it so I can get Morrison off my back and get on with my life. Remember my old foreman, Emory Calloway? For the last few years when I was active in the business, I had him hide packages of cash and gold for me throughout the ranch as a hedge against the possibility of my arrest or in the event I needed to leave the country on short notice."

"But I thought the life insurance policy you bought was supposed to take care of all of that," replied Riggs. "I have been making payments for you to your family as instructed and approved by the court. The money has been laundered and sent down to you every few months. How much more is there left on the ranch?"

"You have been paying Jack money from time to time with the understanding that I will someday get access to the ranch and be able to retrieve the rest of the money I owe him, or pay him from the life insurance funds you are holding in my estate," replied Rich. "These payments have been small enough to avoid being detected and reported within the bank reporting system. I have been able to survive down here and conduct a little business to make ends meet but it has been hard for my family to get the insurance money to me without getting caught. My folks are old now and my siblings are about ready to retire. I need to settle this thing once and for all so everyone can get on with their lives."

"So how do you plan to accomplish this?" asked Riggs.

"I need to get that map. Time to turn up the pressure. Make owning the van unpleasant for them. This guy has a girlfriend, right? Perhaps it is time to snatch her and make a trade of her for the van."

"I am not going to be part of that!" exclaimed Riggs. "Kidnapping was never part of the deal. If you can't get the van through proper means, I am out."

"You're out when I say you're out," replied French. "You are up to your elbows in this thing with the phony estate, getting me declared dead and, siphoning money to my family. Things will not go well for you if I suddenly surface after all these years of being dead. Insurance fraud is a serious matter."

Riggs was silent on the other end of the line. He could quickly determine how bad things could get if he pissed off his client and former friend by trying to back out now and disentangle himself from the situation at hand. "There is an easier way to go about this," he replied finally. "You're right, you don't need the van. All you need is what is inside of it. I have a client who has some experience in breaking into cars and removing electronics and such. He runs an auto repair shop and I got him off recently on a smog facility licensing problem. He still owes me my fee. Let me talk to him about getting into the van and getting your map for you."

French mulled the proposal over for a moment and agreed. This was wise counsel. Avoid escalating the matter unnecessarily at this point and see if they could get in and out quickly with a minimum of attention from law enforcement. Better to have the local police deal with a smash and grab in a car instead of a kidnapping and hostage situation. "All right, get it set up and let me know when you are ready to go so I can plan on making the trip up. To be safe, tell your ranch manager I am going to call him again, same as last time, the number in the old phone booth at the Buckhorn. I want him to pay attention to anyone snooping around in the old oil fields until I can get back and access my money."

Riggs heard the sharp click of the phone on the other end signaling the end to the conversation. He thumbed through his rolodex and located the address and number of his client who would be awarded the task of breaking into the van and retrieving the item.

The muffler shop on Chapala Street was an old whitewashed wood-frame building with a Quonset hut style roofline. Originally built for use as a distribution location for a regional bakery, it had suffered as the economic fortunes of that part of the city had changed over time. Elias Espinoza now ran a muffler shop from the location. Its high ceilings allowed Elias to operate multiple lifts so he could ply his trade of exhaust system repairs and smog certifications. He was an aficionado of classic motorcycles, specifically 1950s choppers. Parked outside the muffler office was his 1956 Harley-Davidson panhead that served as his daily driver.

He was not thrilled to see John Riggs pull up in front of his establishment. He owed Riggs money for recent legal services, money he did not currently have. "How's it going, homie?" Riggs said as he extended his hand in a white man's version of a homeboy handshake.

"What's up?" answered Elias guardedly. "I told you I would pay my bill next month. Business has been slow."

"I have a little job I need you to do for me," replied Riggs. "Take care of it, and we can call it even Steven."

What kind of a deal? Elias knew that it was going to be something off the record. Something that might be illegal or perhaps blurred the lines between societal norms and the need to get something done. He motioned for Riggs to follow him into his office and closed the door behind them.

"I need you to retrieve something for me from a car one of my clients used to own," said Riggs. "He had it impounded and did not pay the storage fees in time. It got sold to a guy in town and I need to get inside and get some personal property."

Elias stood motionless for a moment, mulling over the request. "Did you ask the guy if you could get your client's property out of it?"

"It is not that simple. My client cannot disclose what the item is or give any information to the new owner about what he is looking for. I have already raised too much attention with the owner by asking him a couple of times to flip the van to me at a big profit. If I show up again and try to get him to just get the property that is hidden in the van, he'll only become more suspicious. I can't risk him keeping the item and figuring out why it's important."

"So what are we talking about here?" Elias asked. "Is it just breaking a window and getting something off of a seat, or would I have to tear things apart to find it?"

"It's a rolled-up document that is hidden in a Volkswagen van. In the pop-up roof part of the van, there is a false bottom in which the document is located. All you'd have to do is get inside the van, extend the roof up, pull out the false bottom, and then grab the document. Deliver it to me and we can consider your bill paid in full."

Elias mulled this information over. It sounded like an easy job. No electronics to deal with or cutting electrical leads to remove a stereo system. This older model car would have no original security alarms or other theft deterrents, and the new owners would have no reason to add one while they were still fixing the car up.

"Okay, where is the van and when do you want the job done by?"

Riggs was pleased by this answer. He was not one to forgive a financial debt easily. The implied threat from Rick French though had brought him up short. Riggs was a bluffer and an actor in the world of legal actions and court processes. He had no problem intimidating witnesses on the stand as a finder of truth and an officer of the court. All of his clients, even those least able to pay, eventually paid his fees. No one wanted to spend any more time than necessary involved in the court process. But when it came down to real physical threats against his person and the need for courage, he was woefully deficient. Elias would be his fixer. His services would get French off of his back with the retrieval of the map.

"The van is parked on the side of a house over on the west side of town near the beach. It is up on blocks but probably not even locked. Some guy is starting a restoration project and I need you to get in there ASAP before he monkeys with the interior and finds it." He relayed the information on the address and description of the vehicle to Elias with the expectation of the job getting done that evening.

CHAPTER TWELVE

HE WAS HAVING TROUBLE OPENING THE DOOR. NORMALLY Elias was able to use his lock-picking tools to work the lock release on the driver's side door. But the van had been parked close to the house by its new owner. Assorted tools and equipment sat between the passenger's side of the van and the house. It looked as if the owner had purchased a portable lift but it was not yet assembled and sat on wood pallets alongside the van. Elias had tried to pick the lock on the passenger's side front door with no success. The interior linkage that would have permitted him to slide his tool down between the window and the rubber door molding and lift the lock to open the door appeared to be missing.

He could not risk being discovered by trying to move some of the equipment on the left side of the van. He had positioned himself across the street and down the block by a few doors earlier in the evening to survey the house and wait for the occupants to go to bed. The house had gone completely dark around eleven but shortly thereafter the lights had gone on again. He had observed a male opening the rear yard door and a small dog exiting the house. The small dog had sniffed around the backyard as if on a scent trail. Stopping finally, he had lifted his leg over an area of interest and had proceeded to mark his territory.

Elias had waited a full hour after the house went dark again to be sure that the occupants had fallen asleep. The practical entry point into the van was the side sliding door. Famous for being difficult to close, he was having an equal amount of trouble trying to pick the lock on the sliding passenger side door. After years of non-use, it too was frozen solid. He considered ending the evening and coming back with a can of liquid wrench or WD40. But time was of the essence. He did not want to return to a partially dismantled van up on blocks or hoisted on a lift. Ground entry now was the only option. Pulling a large crescent wrench from his tool bag, he held his breath and smashed the wrench down sharply on the side door window. It took several blows to fully break through the tempered glass, and he could see a light in the bedroom come on as he reached inside and opened the door using the inside handle. He would have only seconds before someone emerged from the house to confront him. Quickly sliding the side door open, he jumped inside and began prying the interior roof lining off from the ceiling of the van. He had it partially pried open when the resounding boom of a firearm filled the air with a report. Elias did not hesitate. Dropping his tools, he jumped from inside the van and sprinted down the street to his car.

Chester turned on the light to the side yard of his house and viewed a dark form running down the street and jumping into a classic Chevrolet. The black-primered car pulled out from the curb and did a 180-degree circle in the middle of the street, rear wheels burning rubber as the driver sped away. The acrid smell of burning rubber and smoke filled the air. Chester ran down the street, trying to read the license plate of the car. He was unable to get a clear view.

As he walked back to his home, he lowered the shotgun he was carrying next to his side so that he could hide it from his neighbors. He had purchased his Remington 870 model shotgun through a registered gun dealer. But standing out there in the dark at one o'clock in the morning, he did not want to be approached by law enforcement and have to explain the discharge of a firearm within city limits.

Erika was waiting for him by the side door when he returned. Lights were on in several of the other homes on the street. Neighbors peeked out upon the scene from the safety of their homes. Theirs was a middle-income neighborhood that was not subject to home invasions or robberies. "What happened?" asked Erika as Chester walked up.

"I don't know," replied Chester. "All I saw was a guy in dark clothing running down the street. He jumped into a Chevy, pulled a brody in the middle of the street, and took off. I tried to get the plate but his lights were off and I was too far away."

"That's incredible," she replied. "What was he after? Was he trying to break into the house?"

"I don't know," replied Chester. "As soon as I heard breaking glass, I jumped up and ran out the door. It all happened so fast, I am not sure which window he was breaking into." The couple walked back to the side of the house and began looking at the doors and windows to see where the sound of breaking class had come from. All the glass along the side of the house was undamaged. They stood there puzzled, unable to decode the sequences of events.

A patrol car turned onto their street and slowly drove down the block. An officer trained his spotlight on each house and side yard as he patrolled. Chester walked out to the curb and motioned to the officer. Deputy Tim Treadwell pulled his patrol car up to the driveway and turned on his light bar. Emergency lights began flashing, bouncing off the homes on both sides of the street. More homes became lit with the arrival of officer Treadwell.

"We have a report of a possible robbery in progress. Are you the caller?' asked the patrolman.

"No, we did not call it in, but this is the house the guy was trying to break into," answered Chester. "We've looked for the broken window but can't find anything broken on this side of the house"

"I am 1023 at 5420 Hillcrest Circle," the officer spoke into his portable radio. "Interviewing the reporting party. Stand by for a further report." He turned toward Chester. "Can you tell me what happened here this evening?" He removed a small spiral notebook from his breast pocket and began writing down Chester's statement describing the sequence of events.

"I know I heard breaking glass. That is what woke us up," Chester started, as he relayed the happenings of the night. "There is no damage to the house. Maybe the guy just threw a bottle."

"What's all this glass by this van?" asked Treadwell. He pointed his flashlight along the poorly lit side of the van, exposing a damaged side door window on Chester's restoration project.

"What the hell?" exclaimed Chester as he walked over to the van. "What was this guy trying to do? There is nothing here to take."

"Was there anything else of value in the van?" asked the patrolman. "Your wife's purse? CDs? Any packages?"

"Girlfriend," chimed in Erika. "We're not married."

"No, nothing of value," interrupted Chester. "I just picked this up at an auction in Mendocino County and literally just brought it back yesterday. There were some old clothes and junk inside and a trashed wetsuit. But we removed all that and took it to the dump yesterday."

Treadwell took their statement, noting the time on his report, and closed his book. "These things happen sometimes. A random break in, the guy might have been given some incorrect information from an informant. Maybe he got the wrong house or car. In any event, I will make my report and we will patrol the area for the next few evenings to see if anyone tries to come back again." He keyed his portable radio. "Dispatch, 2932 is 1024."

He took his leave and turned off his emergency flashers. Erika and Chester watched as he drove away.

"That is so strange," muttered Chester as the couple walked back to the house and went inside. The lights began to go off in the nearby homes with the exiting of the patrol car and the silence of the evening fell over the neighborhood. Chester and Erika could not get back to sleep. The activity of the night right outside their home was too alarming, too concerning to permit them to simply fall back asleep.

"Why would anyone be interested in getting into that old van?" asked Chester. "There is nothing of any value in there, only the old crap left by the last guy who had the van."

"Maybe it was some homeless guy strung out on drugs or looking for a place to crash" replied Erika. "It could have been a simple smash and grab deal that you interrupted before the guy could get away with anything."

"Maybe he used to own the van and wanted to get something out of it," replied Chester. "There is that guy who wants me to sell him the van. He has some bullshit story about a client that is looking for this specific model to restore. How bizarre is that for this guy to go after me at the sale and then again yesterday, all over this innocuous old VW." The couple continued their musings on the reasons behind the happenings of the night and eventually drifted off to sleep.

Erika rose early the next day. She was in the middle of new job search and as was her practice, she was taking diligent steps to locate her next position in the accounting field. She had become a commodity of sorts with her recent assignment as a receiver for the now defunct Capital Triangle Company. Her forensic accounting skills and executive duties winding down that entity would provide her entry into higher-paying positions. As she sat drinking her first cup of coffee, she heard Chester rustling around in the bathroom. "Gonna join me for coffee?" she hollered down the hall at him.

"Yup, be out in a second!"

She walked over to the cupboard to get a clean coffee cup. The selection of non-matching cups sat before her, stacked on top of one another. They were the result of the couple's impulse buys while on vacations and weekend getaways. The cups bore the names of various towns, states, and foreign locations where they had traveled. Some were specific to a venue or event. Erika usually tried to select an appropriate cup to match the mood or activity Chester was going to be involved with for the day. She selected a cup that had ATHS emblazoned across the front. In the center of the cup was the picture of a 1955 International West Coaster logging truck loaded with a huge single tree. "Five at the butt" was emblazoned at the bottom of the picture. The five-foot-wide base of the old-growth cedar log dwarfed the man standing beside it. "What better selection than this," she thought as she remembered their trip to the American Truck Historical Museum the summer before. Chester had reveled in the museum and had sat in many of the restored big rigs as he had pretended to go through the gears. Five and fours, four and fours, ten speeds, eighteen speeds, there he had sat pretending to up and down shift as he went along imaginary grades, all the time pulling a load just shy of the maximum weight limit. He had mimicked the sound of a jake brake and the final use of air brakes as he brought each truck to a stop.

As Erika filled his cup, she saw Arnie pull up to their house. "Arnie's here!" she called down the hall.

"Good," replied Chester as he walked into the kitchen, dressed in clean mechanics overalls. "He is going to help me take out the master cylinder and get the brake drums off so I can get this thing to stop."

"Stopping is a good thing," she quipped.

Arnie gave a quick knock on the side door and opened the door slightly to see if they were up yet. "What's going on with all that glass by the van? Did you get started on the interior without me and break a window by accident?"

"We had a break in last night," answered Erika solemnly.

"The cops came and everything," added Chester. "I got out there in time to shoot off a couple of rounds from my twenty gauge. The guy ran off before the cops could get here."

"That's wild," replied Arnie. "Maybe that guy we met at the auction is really serious about getting your van."

"Well, that Riggs guy showed up again and tried to get me to sell him the van again," answered Chester.

"Probably not," interjected Erika. "Just some guy looking for valuables. He was parked down the street and probably was casing all the cars looking for one that was not locked or had something worth stealing. With the van up on blocks, it's not like anyone was going to hot wire it and drive off with it."

Chester and Arnie finished their coffee and went outside to the van to begin their brake repair work. The broken side door window proclaimed the happenings of the previous evening and Arnie was drawn to inspect the damage.

"I see you could not resist doing a little interior demo work," observed Arnie.

"What do you mean?"

"Here, where you were pulling off the ceiling trim in the pop up roof."

Chester walked over and noticed the partial dismantling of the interior roof. The rubber trim was lying on the floorboard and half of the ceiling fabric was limply hanging down. He whistled. "Oh, this wasn't me."

"Maybe whoever did this got scared off by your shotgun blasts. Looks like he was well into pulling the ceiling material off," observed Arnie.

"Why would anyone be interested in this part of the van?" asked Chester. "It's not like you can't find replacement interiors for these things. I found a full upholstery kit available in the J. C. Whitney catalog just the other day."

"This guy was not looking for stereos or car parts," replied Arnie. "If he had wanted the van, he would have used a tow truck to hook on to it and drive off. Repo companies do it all the time. The owners get behind on their payments, the bank gives them a call, and with the proper paperwork, they show up and tow the car. Most times the people don't even know it is going down until they see their car being hauled off by the repo man."

"So what could the guy have wanted from inside this old junker?"

Arnie stepped inside of the van and sat on the bench seat that accompanied the space where the center table was located. "Let's see," he mused as he contemplated the ceiling area of the van. He reached his hand up into the void and felt around. The underside of the metal roof was rusty and had pieces of gray insulation glued to it. Years of wear had resulted in the insulation becoming detached from the roof. Pieces of it floated down, causing Arnie to cough as it drifted through the air. Arnie pulled on the hanging piece of ceiling fabric to give better access to the void in the ceiling. A long, rolled-up piece of paper fell out from the ceiling fabric and landed on the table in the middle of the camper. Chester and Arnie grabbed the roll of paper and began to remove the rubber bands that were located at each end of the roll. The rubber bands were so old that they had lost their flexibility. They now were the consistency of glue and had to be pried and peeled from the roll of paper. They had been there for some time.

"Maybe it's a treasure map," said Chester.

They rolled the paper out slowly so as not to rip or damage it.

"It is a map" replied Arnie and they held down the corners of the paper. The map was yellowed and printed on heavy gauge paper. On the bottom margin were details pertaining to the California Department of Oil and Gas. There were numerous dots located on the map and each dot had a name and number associated with it. Some of the dots were solid black, others were partially black. Many of the markings were small circles. A legend at the side of the page noted the difference between these locations.

Some denoted producing oil wells, while the others signified wells that were no longer active or ones that had been dry holes.

"Cuyama Valley Oil Field," read Arnie. "This looks like a map of an oil field in eastern Santa Bonita County. Look here—Cuyama River, highway 166; the town of Cuyama."

"So why would a map like this be hidden in the van?" asked Chester. "Is it really a treasure map of some kind? It must be valuable to have been hidden up there in the roof. Whoever put it there obviously did not want anyone to find it."

"This is a map that anyone can get from the DOG."

"DOG?"

"Department of Oil and Gas," replied Arnie. "One of my old clients was a petroleum engineer. He used to download PDF files of these maps for his business. I know because he was always having trouble with his printer trying to handle these large sheets."

They rolled the map back up and went back inside the house to show Erika the discovery.

"Check this out," announced Chester as they sat down with Erika at the coffee table and rolled out the map.

"What is it?" she asked.

"Arnie found it in the ceiling of the van. It shows an oil field in Cuyama and all the wells out there, but Arnie says it's not of any value. We could get the same map just by going to a regional office of the DOG.

"Do you think this is what the guy was looking for last night?" she said.

"It must have been, but why?"

"Well, let's get to the task at hand," interjected Arnie. "Enough of the high jinks. I gotta do some work at the office this afternoon, so let's get started on pulling the master cylinder and the brake drums so you can get this thing road worthy."

The pair returned outside to the van and left Erika at the table with the map set before her. She carefully studied it, verifying that no special notes or markings existed. Her analytical and detail-oriented thought process noted the printed notes, statements, and legend pertaining to the oil wells on the map. She observed the clustering of wells noted as producing and that dry holes were located on the fringes of the identified oil field. Her family in Texas had been involved in the oil business by way of an old lease on the family farm that dated back to the beginning of the twentieth century. That was the times of booms and busts in the oil game. Wildcatters had leased the family farm for the right to explore for oil. A discovery by the Texas Company had resulted in a series of gusher oil wells. The discovery of the field has been so successful that the company had later become the conglomerate known as Texaco. Royalties still flowed from the field in reduced, but steady, monthly amounts.

Erika continued to stare at the map. "What's this?" she exclaimed to herself. She quickly ran upstairs and returned with a magnifying glass. Bending closely over the map, she continued to study the locations of the wells that were producing and those that had been put on inactive status.

"I got it!" she shouted. She sprang up from the table and called out to Chester and Arnie from the window. "I think I know what this guy was looking for and why he was after this map!"

"Look closely at the markings on some of these oil wells," she continued after Chester and Arnie had come inside. "What do you see on well number 325?" she continued. Arnie took the magnifying glass and began to look at the map.

"And look at 419 and 301 too. What do you see?'

"Nothing, just wells and numbers," he replied.

"What is the marking on the well?" she asked.

"It's x-ed out like some of the other ones on the map."

"Look closer, check out the legend. What kind of wells are they?" she continued.

"Hmm, looks like these are abandoned wells, but the lines are in a crossed pattern, not x."

"Exactly," she replied. "There is no such marking on the legend, and if you look closely, you will find that these were made by hand. They were added to the map some time after it was printed.

"Yes, I can see that," replied Arnie. "The ink is not the same color and the lines are fuzzier than the others on the map."

"So someone marked up some of the wells on the map for some reason," interrupted Chester. "But why?"

"Anyone's guess," replied Erika. "You are going to have to ask the guy who hid the map. Maybe he was involved in the oil business and was working on some confidential transaction with the oil company."

"Good luck trying to find the guy," replied Arnie. "Didn't the lot guy say that the van had been there for five or six years? If this map was valuable, don't you think the owner would have showed up and paid the impound fee or bought it at the auction?"

"Who knows?" replied Erika. "Maybe he is dead. Maybe he didn't have the dough to get his van back. I bet the guy who keeps trying to buy the van from you has some connection to this map."

"Yeah, maybe that attorney's client used to own the van and hid the map there."

"Maybe the map is of no value and you guys need to get back to work," replied Erika.

All they had were questions and no answers. The brake job task was at hand and further speculation on the purpose of the map or what information it might contain would have to wait until another time.

"Here, I will roll it up and put it in an old storage tube case I have. That way it will be safe and some rainy day you can think about what the secret of the map might be," said Erika.

They reluctantly agreed and returned to the van and began pulling the stubborn brake drums off.

CHAPTER THIRTEEN

TERRORIST ACTIVITIES IN BELGIUM HAD SLOWED AIR TRAVEL to a trickle at the Brussels airport. Jack Morrison sat apart from the crowd of travelers who were gossiping among themselves about the eventual departure time for the flight to Havana. He had no interest in conversing with his fellow travelers or speculating about when they would be permitted to leave for their destination.

Despite efforts to restrict entry, it had always been possible to enter the United States if preparations were made in advance through under-the-radar channels. Jack had been an expat for the last five years, unwilling to come back to the States. The DEA knew of his drug distribution activities and he had ascertained that it was healthier for him to remain out of the country than to risk capture by attempting to reenter the United States. His business activities were of course harder to conduct from his location in North Africa, but he had adjusted his methods and had forged new contacts in the trade to permit him to continue a low level of activity and keep his hand in the business.

It was a risk, trying to get back into the country with so many eyes watching the major ports of entry, but he had decided that time was of the essence and he could no longer wait and trust that everything Rick French had been telling him was about to occur. French had been living the life of a retired businessman, living the dream of residing in Surfers Paradise in Australia. Jack had no such luck. He had been living a frugal life in the hot desert climate of Casablanca. He was constantly on the watch for people who might want to do him harm, be it former business contacts, families and friends of people he had killed, or the local Muslim fringe groups who were always looking for the opportunity to kidnap and ransom wealthy foreigners.

Direct entry into the US would be problematic for Jack. Equally as risky was attempting to travel via Mexico or Canada. He needed to get to a country in close proximity to the States but not with the closely monitored international flights. Many countries had maintained relations with Cuba since the Castro revolution and the resulting embargo on trade between Cuba and the United States. Travel to Cuba for US citizens had always been possible if one was willing to risk traveling from another country and hope that US customs did not look too closely at their passport on their return. Educational or humanitarian purposes had been exceptions to the Cuban travel ban for US citizens, and medical and related imports were still permitted between the two countries. Jack had none of these as believable travel excuses. He now reasoned that he needed to get back quickly to verify that what French said was going on was really the truth. He did not have the time to book travel from Africa by sea on a freighter, and direct flights into the U.S. were carefully monitored. With the ability to fly to Cuba, he had surmised that now was the best time for him to reenter the States by way of Havana. He would mingle with the other travelers, keep a low profile, and hope no one questioned the dates on his passport, which showed he had traveled extensively outside the United States. Upon reaching Cuba, he would devise a way to board a freighter bound for one of the Gulf States.

"What happened to your finger?" asked the little boy who had bounced up to him. He had been chasing a Nerf soccer ball that his family had been kicking around the waiting area.

"Someone bit it off when I was a small boy about your size. That's what you get for sticking your nose into someone else's business."

The little boy had run off laughing, returning to his group and relaying the missing finger story to his family. They all stopped what they were doing and stared at him. They were no longer laughing. The father was looking over at Jack with concern on his face. The group picked up their carry-on items and moved away to the other side of the waiting area.

With the attention now off of Jack, he picked up his backpack and walked down the row to where the airport food court was located. He felt very much like he was back in the United States. Many of the fast food franchises were located there together with other restaurants offering local dishes. He decided on a premade chicken Caesar salad from a deli that carried premade meals from the Wolfgang Puck eatery in the airport food court.

As he picked at his salad, he heard the announcement that his flight was ready to board. He was in the last boarding group. He hurried to finish his meal, holding the edge of the plate up to his mouth to shovel in the last few pieces of chicken and lettuce. As he dumped his trash in the receptacle and walked over to his gate, he could hear the gate attendant calling off the groups who would be boarding first. "Platinum card members, military service members, families traveling with small children, and anyone needing assistance," called out the boarding agent. This was followed by lower levels of priority, all tied to precious metals signifying the reduced level of service provided to the successive boarding groups. "Gold and silver members," she called out next. "Let me know when they get down to lead," someone in the crowd mumbled. "Folks traveling with a one-eyed dog," another joked.

Jack's last-minute arrangement for his flight had left him without a seat assignment. When Jack finally boarded, he found that most of the seats were taken. He looked for a row with an empty seat and spotted a couple who were occupying a window and row seat. The undesirable middle seat was empty. As he approached them he could see them staring straight ahead as if he might overlook them and continue on toward the rear of the plane. They of course acted surprised when he stopped and asked if the seat was taken. Their passive plan to get some extra room for the flight evaporated. The husband, noting Jack's formidable appearance, acquiesced and moved to the center seat, giving Jack the aisle.

As the plane lifted off, Jack mulled over the recent conversation he had had with Rick French. He had placed the call from the park bench in Casablanca, fully aware that he could be under surveillance at any time. The passing of time had lessened the risk, but he still had been cautious, making an effort to keep the conversation vague.

"It is going to take a few days for me to get to the location, but everything is on track," French had stated. "I am having a delay in getting the material I need. I only need to locate the source document and get out to the location and retrieve the packages. Should not be more than a week or ten days."

"Why all the smoke and mirrors?" Jack had replied. "This day has been coming for five years. I don't want to hear about any delays or problems. You said this deal was nailed down and as soon as you could buy your old van back, I would get my money. I'm flying out and will be on the ground in two days."

The call had been quickly ended. French had been warned. Now was the time for him to deliver on his promise. There were more people involved in the transaction than just Jack. Rick's ability to escape the country and reside undetected for years with funding provided to him had required the assistance of family, friends in law enforcement, and one superior court judge. Several of them were expecting payments for services rendered. He also needed to be sure his family would not be drawn into this mess just as he was about to be in a position to settle it once and for all.

The next morning, John Riggs had received a call from French and had learned that Jack was going to be on the ground in a matter of days.

"I don't like the smell of this," Riggs had replied. "You told me this would be a clean deal and all I would have to do was wire some money for you. Now this guy is showing his face. Did you fuck up? He wouldn't be showing his face again unless he thought he had to. What is going on?"

"Your screw up with buying the van has thrown a wrench into the whole thing. Now he is suspicious that I am not giving him the straight story. For all he knows I spent all the money, or it does not even exist. He is coming down here and we both need to fix this pronto," French had replied. "Did your guy get my map yet?" he asked.

"Not yet. He was over there but the guy came out of the house with a gun and chased him off. The police showed up. He is not going back."

"So how do you intend to get it now that the cops have been involved and the guy is on night watch over his van?" asked French.

"We can get the map. All we need to do is get a private dick to provide surveillance and listen in on what goes on in the house. They have probably found it by now or certainly will when they start to pull the van apart to work on it. I will get a man on the job and report back to you on what he finds out. It may take some time depending on when they find it and whether they just throw it out in the trash or actually look into it," replied Riggs.

"Rolled-up map hidden in the roof of a van," stated French. "You can bet your ass they are going to try to see why it was there. Get your guy on it today!"

John hung up the phone and called Manita into his office. "Who do we like for investigation services these days?" he asked her. "We have an immediate need that I have to get resolved for an old client."

"I like what the Casebeer Detective Agency did for us last year on that alimony case you won," Manita replied. The agency had ads on the local television station touting their security services and investigation capabilities. Craig had been a local celebrity of sorts, having invested in a semipro women's soccer team along with a local investor named Billy

Blevy. Blevy had been a successful real estate investor in Santa Bonita and for a time had ridden the wave of real estate development in the town. But a later failed bank investment and soured real estate developments had been his undoing, and the pair had lost control of their sports team. Craig had worked hard to rebuild his reputation and the image of his security firm. Blevy was now long gone, and Craig had successfully restored his reputation in the community.

"Remember the divorce you did last year where the ex was trying to hide her business income from your client so she could double dip and get alimony too?" she continued.

"Yeah," he replied. "Wasn't that the one with the dumpster diver who waited outside her home each trash pickup day and would go through her trash with a fine-toothed comb?"

"That's the one. Didn't he find those motel receipts where she was dating her divorce attorney along with her business records?"

"Yup. I am the only attorney in Santa Bonita County to ever have alimony payments expunged for a marriage that lasted as long as that one," he replied. They recalled how the judge had thrown up his hands upon learning of the subterfuge and improper conduct by an officer of the court. Riggs's client had been relieved of future alimony payments due to the ingenious efforts of the private detective. "Let's get Casebeer over here for a meeting today. I want to get him started on this case," directed Riggs.

"Okay, what is the file name on this one?"

"Don't need to start a new case file. Let's just open an old file under CTG," replied Riggs.

Later that day, a meeting took place at the offices of Craig Casebeer. The Casebeer Detective Agency was an old-line business that had been founded by Craig's father. His father had started the business after retiring from the Santa Bonita police force after thirty years of service. He had been well respected in the law enforcement community and when Craig had taken over the business, much of the goodwill and connections to law enforcement had remained. Outside the detective offices, several white sedans with the decals of the business were parked. The on-duty staff had the clean-cut law enforcement appearance about them. Clean shaven with trimmed mustaches and sideburns that were high and tight, they gave the appearance of a paramilitary unit in their neatly pressed uniforms. They provided protection services for the elite of Santa Bonita County and could be seen patrolling those neighborhoods or standing guard at the wrought-iron gates that led into the estates of the wealthy.

"So what can we do for you today, John?" asked Craig as John and Manita sat down in front of Craig's large cherrywood desk. It was an antique from the federalist period. Crotchwood panels dominated the facing and the square-edged legs sat upon knurled eagle-clawed feet, giving the appearance of strength and security. The heirloom had been passed down to him from his family, which traced their roots back to Massachusetts pilgrims.

"We need help getting information from some people in town as to the location of a certain item."

"Another property dispute?" asked Craig. "Let me guess, the husband has run off with the wife's jewelry and you are trying to find out if it still exists so you can put in on a property division schedule, right?"

"No, nothing as exciting as that," replied Riggs. "It involves property that used to belong to my client, which he left in a car he used to own. The new owner is going to find it someday and my client wants it back."

"So what are we doing for you? Asking the owner to return the stuff? Why doesn't your client just pick up the phone and give them a call?"

"It's not as simple as that," replied John. "My client's vehicle was sold from an impound lot before my client could retrieve it. The item is a map that on the surface has no value to anyone except for him. It contains markings or symbols that, if interpreted, would permit the holder of the map to potentially locate items, valuable items, which my client secreted away years ago as a kind of insurance policy. He did not deal with banks in his line of business. There are reasons he cannot contact the owners of the van currently, which are related to his sudden disappearance five years ago. If I again contacted the van owner and ask for the item, assuming they have found it by now, it would only draw further attention to my client and myself as his attorney in fact for the past several years."

"And what are the valuable items marked on the map?"

"My client owns property in the county and he had used the map for his development plans for his property. He would like to get it back rather than start all over."

"I see," replied Craig. He knew John's reputation for dealing with some edgier clients. He was probably not getting the full story. But a job was a job and he had the staff to cover any assignment brought to him, from simple security services to surveillance.

"Do you want us to contact this person and ask for the return of the map? Will you offer a reward for finding it?"

"I don't know if the guy has actually found the map yet," replied John. "I had a guy go over there last night to see if he could just enter the van and remove the map from its hiding place but he got busted before he could complete the job."

Craig mulled this response over for a moment. "Hidden? Guy got busted? Sounds like this is no ordinary map and you have got yourself into a mess."

"The map is of no value to anyone but my client. I don't need you to contact this guy and try to get it back. I need someone to watch what is going on at the house and listen in on their conversations so I can see if they have found the map and what is happening with it."

"That is something in our wheelhouse," replied Craig. "Sounds like you need us to get started ASAP. How about we start twenty-four-hour surveillance of the home and use listening equipment to monitor conversations. We probably cannot plant devices in their phones after the break-in activity last night. Let's see what we can come up with in the next few days."

"That will be fine," replied John.

"The file name for this assignment will be CTG," added Manita.

CHAPTER FOURTEEN

THE HIGHWAY TO THE REGIONAL OFFICE FOR THE Department of Oil and Gas in Bakersfield was a narrow two-lane affair that handled commercial truck traffic from the coast to the central valley of California. As Erika drove her fire-engine-red Mazda Miata, she noted with heightened interest the details of the Cuyama Valley. She had traveled several times before through this remote region of eastern Santa Bonita County, but the features of the region had gone largely unnoticed during those travels. As she passed the Rock Front Ranch and turned sharply east, she began noticing the sprawling, sparse ranches of the valley. Every few miles an old ranch house and farmstead could be found, the improvements noticeable in the distance by large cottonwood trees that sheltered the buildings from the blazing summertime sun. The eastern side of the county was a sharp contrast to the western beach scene. Here there were few people. The ones who resided here were a throwback to the ranching and oil boom days of the early part of the twentieth century. She passed through the former Humble Oil company town of New Cuyama. A sign proclaimed the grand reopening of the Buckhorn Saloon and she noticed a few oil field workers congregated in front of the establishment. On a previous trip through the valley, she and Chester had stopped off for a meal at the Buckhorn but had been disappointed to learn that it had closed for the winter season. Their quest for the famous buffalo burger had had to wait until another time.

She took a renewed interest in the occasional oil wells that could be seen from the highway. They were congregated in groups next to batteries of rusty storage tanks and she noticed that most of the pumping machinery was motionless. Here and there she observed a single pump jack working its slow, vertical up-and-down motion as it operated to draw oil from deep below the surface. These wells were not like the freshly painted ones pictured on the front page of the annual report from industry giants such as Exxon or Shell. These pumps were rusted hulks, mechanically operational but one step away from the scrap heap where they would be sold by the pound once they were no longer needed for their current task. She pulled over to the side of the road next to a well that was a stone's throw from the highway and turned off her engine. The sound of an engine droned out to her. She watched it make its pumping motions. The engine's speed increased slightly each time the slick silver pump rod pulled in an upward direction and slowed down slightly as the rod then reemerged back into the oil well casing. A horizontal walking beam sat in the center of the well head pump mechanism. Directly over the well at the end of the bar was an irregularly shaped piece of steel that resembled the head of a grasshopper. The large counterweight on the rear of the pump bar thrust in a downward motion each time the pump rod lifted upward, drawing oil from the oil-bearing sands below. Warm summer breezes painted Erika's face as she watched the oil well labor as it extracted the gooey black liquid from a Pleistocene stratum deep within the earth. The moving metal parts creaked and groaned a rhythmic mechanical melody, repeating the monotone pattern as the pump cycled. Erika could find no clue for the importance of the van's map and the derelict oil field.

She started up her car and pulled back onto the highway. She was greeted by an eighteen wheeler careening toward her in the opposite lane. She saw the driver's eyes widen as he wrestled the wheel to put his rig back within the confines of his narrow lane. Summer was carrot harvesting season in the Cuyama Valley and Erika was greeted by successive trucks hauling empty double trailers as they returned from the central valley packing sheds to pick up their loads of orange cargo. She hugged her side of the highway each time she met one of them coming at her from the opposite direction.

She arrived at the Truxton Avenue address of the Department of Oil and Gas shortly before noon. Gathering her purse and the rolled-up map, she sprinted to the building to see if she could meet with counter staff to discuss the map and its notations. She was coldly greeted at the counter by administrative staff. They had been busily discussing lunch plans and did not appreciate being interrupted so close to the noon hour. They had made a call to someone in the back and Erika was soon being helped by Steve Engleson. Steve was the junior petroleum engineer on staff and was eager to help the red-haired woman who waited for him at the counter. "What can I help you with today?" he asked as he handed her his business card.

"I found this map in a car we bought and I was wondering if you can explain it to me, what some of the notations mean?"

"Sure, let's see what you have here," he replied. She handed him the cardboard case and he removed the map from the cylinder, spreading it out on the counter before them. "Yup, I see, this is an old map of the Cuyama oil field in Santa Bonita County. I have done some work over there on some well abandonments and gas plant environmental clean ups."

"I just drove past there today on the way over here," she replied. "Seems like a pretty dead area to me. Why would someone be hanging on to a map like this?"

"You're right, that area is undergoing secondary production and wells keep being taken off line as production drops."

"Secondary production?" she asked.

"When oil was first discovered out there in the 1950s, there was so much pressure in the field that once the structure containing the oil was drilled into, the oil gushed out of the hole, just like you see in the movies and old pictures of that era. They would call the well a gusher. Over time the wells would cease to flow and then they would install pump jacks like you see out there today."

"I saw some of those on the drive over today. Most of them were not working, but a few were still going."

"Yes," he replied. "Those fields are now under secondary production. When the easy oil has been found and production drops off, the majors like ARCO or Conoco sell their leases to smaller operators that start a water flood."

"Water flood?"

"Under the best of situations only about 30 percent of the oil can be removed by conventional pumping," he explained. "Secondary efforts usually involve injecting water into the production zone to remove more oil from the sands and to push that oil and water mixture to a collection well where it is pumped out. The wells you saw still running are in secondary recovery efforts and the big steel tanks you saw beside them collect the mixture. Oil rises to the top and is removed and trucked to a refinery. The water at the bottom of the tank is reinjected back down other wells that are used to recreate pressure in the field and recover more of the oil."

"Okay, I have this old map of this field and it looks like it is on its way out, right?"

"Not necessarily. There are new treatments being discovered all the time using gases or chemical injections to wash more oil from the sands. Fracking, for example, is being used a lot in some areas."

"Can you explain some of the markings that have been made to some of the wells on this map? I see the legend at the bottom of the map but it looks like some of the wells have been marked with crosses instead of x's. Are those wells also abandoned or no longer being pumped?"

Steve peered over the map and used a magnifying glass to look closer at the detail. "These were marked by hand by someone and do not denote any official status of the department. According to the legend, before these wells were hand marked, they were shut in but not abandoned. Sorry," he continued as he noticed the blank look on Erika's face. "When a well cannot be operated at a profit due to declining production or mechanical failure, the oil company will typically refer to it as shut in. This lets them keep the well hole open and save the costs of abandonment. Sometimes they will bring them on line again or use them for water injection wells. But most of the time they are trying to postpone the costs to officially abandon the well and plug the hole under standards issued by the DOG. They kick the can down the road as long as they can until we lean on them to abide by the regulations."

"So these marks made on shut-in wells could mean anything?"

"Pretty much," Steve replied. "Could be a landman was looking at the field and identifying wells he wanted to collect data on or had identified as candidates for resumed production. Sorry I can't be of more help. This is just not a very active area and no one is looking into new investments out there currently. I would not be surprised to see the rest of the operators out there walk away from their leases with oil as low as it is today."

Erika thanked him for his time and gathered up her map for the return trip home. She stopped off at the Buckhorn for a late lunch on her way back to the coast, ordering their famous buffalo burger and a salad. She looked at the oil field map again while she waited for her order. She stared at the part of the map where the wells had been marked by hand. The wells in that area were closely placed in neat rows and columns. As she stared at the grid pattern she suddenly noticed something that had previously been overlooked. Taking a pencil from her purse she began connecting the wells that had been hand marked. She made several attempts, erasing her light pencil marks until at last her efforts resulted in clearly formed characters. She stared at the results. Much like the connect-the-dots puzzles she had played with as a child, her adult effort had resulted in a series of large capital letters: CTG.

She arrived home in the late afternoon. Chester and Arnie were working on the van. She could hear some pounding coming from the rear of the vehicle and she walked over to see how their project was going. "Does it stop yet?" she asked. She could tell that her timing was wrong. A red-faced and sweating Chester looked up at her from his crouching position at the rear of the van. She recognized that look. Things were not going well. She could see Arnie's legs sticking out from underneath the van.

"Give it another whack!" yelled Arnie, his voice a bit muffled.

"Hold on a second," Chester replied to Erika. He began pounding on the side of the brake drum while Arnie pried at the slot between the drum and the backing plate. The drum began to cock to the side as a small pile of rust dribbled out from behind the drum. Seeing some movement, Arnie extracted himself from under the van and rolled himself into view on a small dolly. Grabbing the brake drum in both hands he pulled from side to side and nearly fell over backward as the drum finally came free.

"See, I knew it was hanging up on the brake shoes," he exclaimed, pointing to the deeply ridged shoes and scored drums. "We could have been here all day if we had not backed those shoes off all the way. The rest of them are going to be just as hard to get off," he continued.

"So, what did you find out about our map?" asked Chester. "Is there a buried fortune out there in no-man's-land? Can I stop working on the van and just pay someone to finish the resto now that we are about to find the pot of gold?"

"It was pretty much a wasted trip," she replied. "The guy I talked to did not have any idea why the map had been marked up. In fact, he pretty much told me that the wells out there are about done and will all be closed down in the next few years."

"If that map had any value to someone, don't you think the guy who owned this van would have got it out of hock or arranged to remove the map before the van got sold? They let you get your personal property out of your car when they tow it, you know," said Arnie.

"I don't know. Defunct old oil field near a dying town? No prospects on the horizon for any new oil discoveries out there? But why did someone try to break in and get your map. Let me do some more digging before we just toss it in the trash," she answered.

Erika left them to finish fixing the brakes on the van and sat down in the kitchen over a fresh cup of tea to digest the matter. What would be the next step? A sudden impulse came over her and she picked up the phone and called information.

"City and state, please," came the greeting from the 411 call.

"Tiburon, California," she replied.

"State the name of the person or business you are calling," continued the voice recording.

"County of Marin, administration," she replied. She was quickly connected to the central number for the county and after some searching, she was connected to the county impound yard through the sheriff's department. She was greeted by the voice of a middle-aged woman.

"Impound, Beryl speaking."

"I am calling to get some information on a van we bought at your sale last month. We found some personal property in the vehicle and want to return it to the owner. "

"I'm new here," replied Beryl. "If you bought it last month, I did not handle that sale."

"Is the guy who handled the sale available? I think his name was Bob or Burt, something like that."

"Burt's dead. Someone shot him just a few days after that sale and all I am doing is babysitting the place until they find someone to take things over."

"Dead? Shot? Did they catch the killer?" Erika asked.

"The investigation is ongoing. I cannot discuss any details of the case."

"I understand. We bought a Volkswagen van at the sale and found some papers in there that we think should be sent back to the owner of the van. If I give you the license and sale lot number, can you get his address so we can mail these back to him?"

"All those records were shipped up to the detectives as part of the investigation. I don't know where anything else is in this office. I am a patrol officer and don't have any idea of how they keep their records for the impound lot."

Erika thought a moment. "Can you at least run the plate of this van for me to get the name and address of the last registered owner? I hate to just throw this stuff in the trash."

"Hold on for a moment. A lot of times these records fall off our system once we impound a car and it sits for a while on our lot." Beryl went out to her squad car and entered the license plate number Erika had provided to her. The name and address quickly came up on her system. She noted some additional comments to that record and quickly jotted the information down in her notebook.

"Richard French, 1261 Las Almas, Santa Bonita, California, 93105, is the last known address," relayed Beryl. "But you probably are not going to have any luck contacting this guy. I see file notes that indicate he was listed as missing and a probate was later opened. That is probably why no one came to retrieve the vehicle. You can try mailing the stuff to that address. Maybe they will forward it on to the guy. Worst case, you get it back and then you can pitch it."

Erika thanked the officer for her time and finished sipping her tea. She looked at the address she had been given and thought about the area of town where the street was located. Her late grandmother had lived on the street for many years up until she lost her house in one of the wildland fires that periodically ravaged the city. On an impulse, she grabbed the map and jumped into her car.

"Where are you headed?" asked Chester as she started up her Miata. "I got a name and address from the impound lot and am off to see if this guy still lives there or if anyone there knows where he is," she replied.

"But what if it is a treasure map of some sort or has clues to a big oil discovery?"

"Think about it, Chess. Someone broke into your van to get this. We don't know what it means but it is important to someone who is willing to break and enter just to get it. The guy at the sales yard is dead and this guy French went missing. I think the sooner we get rid of this map the better for all of us. We are playing with fire here and I don't want any part of it."

"Dead. The old guy at the impound yard? What happened to him? Did he die from a heart attack or stroke or something like that?"

"The sheriff's office only said the yardman was shot and the case is under investigation and they cannot discuss it," she replied.

Chester and Arnie stared at each other in silence.

"Nothing seems to get clearer with this van and the people who have been connected to it," said Erika. "The sooner we find out what this map is all about, the better I will feel about you owning this van."

She sped off, map safely stowed beside her in the passenger's seat. She began to drive up onto the mesa behind the city through neighborhoods that were familiar to her. Turning onto Las Almas, she drove up to what had been the adobe home her grandmother used to own and stopped for a moment to see what the new owners had done to the place. It looked undisturbed from the time her grandmother had owned it. Bright-red bougainvillea draped across the low-set adobe brick walls that surrounded a courtyard. Here and there blue-gray agaves stood as silent sentinels around the steel casement windows. Sour grass was sprouting bright yellow flowers in the rose beds in the garden. She recalled how she and her siblings had picked them as children and chewed on the stems to extract their sour juices.

She pulled back onto the road and began looking for the twelve hundred block. "1251, 1257," she muttered to herself as she slowed in anticipation of coming onto the address of the former French home. "1263," she muttered, stopping the car. She backed up slowly and stopped. She saw the number on the house before her: 1259. "What the heck?" she exclaimed to herself and she pulled over to the curb. 1261 did not seem to exist. Then she noticed what appeared to be the large side yard to the home she had parked across from. She exited her car and walked across the street, looking at the home and then walking back up the lane toward the home listed as 1263. She noticed a water meter cover in the curb adjacent to what appeared to be a vacant lot. Removing the cover, she peered inside. A black widow had built a web within the bowels of the concrete water meter box. Its white silky web was spread over the water meter, hiding it from view. She grabbed a stick and began moving the web to get a better view of the apparatus. A large black widow spider scurried out from the web and tried to hide farther down in the hole. She flicked it aside, noting the large red underbelly. Shivering with an involuntary reaction to seeing the spider, she noted that the meter was in the off position with a large water district lock installed in the brass clasp.

"Excuse me, can I help you?"

Erika looked up to see a small thin woman approaching her from the downhill home next to the empty lot. "Is there something I can help you with?" the woman asked again.

"I was looking for a house at 1261 on this street but it looks like it does not exist."

"What's your business? Are you a real estate broker?" asked the woman.

"No, I am looking for a Mr. French or his family to return some property to them."

"French. Are you with the insurance company again? I thought you guys were all done with your investigation!"

"No, I am not with an insurance company," replied Erika. She relayed how Chester had purchased French's former van and how they simply wanted to return some papers and personal property to him they had found in the van.

"Oh," the woman replied, extending her hand to Erika. "I am Wendy Pulte. Rick disappeared many years ago and was declared dead by the courts. Sorry I was so abrupt, but for many years we were questioned by the police and a life insurance company about his disappearance. There were shady people always coming over to his house at all hours of the night when he lived here. It burned down after he disappeared and we all started to feel uneasy about who he was and why people were so interested in his old house."

"Burned to the ground? Shady people?" Erika asked.

"Rick was a free spirit jojoba farmer who seemed to have a lot of time on his hands. He spent a lot of time traveling or at the beach, surfing. He was gone a lot. Never struck me much like a real farmer. He was more the leather safari hat and sandals kind of a guy. Not the meat and potatoes farmer type you see in Levis or overalls."

"Disappeared?" asked Erika as she tried to appear nonchalant.

"Yes, it was kind of sad for Margaret. One day he is here and then next you never hear from him again."

"Margaret?"

"I'm sorry. Margaret Hurley was his longtime girlfriend. Girlfriend of course when he was not down at Chanticlair, cruising that scene for someone to pick up."

Wendy rattled on in her chatty Kathy style about Rick and his Jesus-like appearance, his ability to charm young unattached women with his organic jojoba farming and mysterious world-traveler aura.

"Anyway, poor Margaret was displaced when the house mysteriously burned to the ground just a few months after Rick went missing. That is why you can't find the address you are looking for. The house used to sit where this large empty area is," she further elaborated, pointing to the land between Wendy's home and the next home on that side of the street. "I used to complain to the lawyer for the estate about cleaning up the lot but after a while they removed all the burned wood. I kind of like it now. No neighbor next door, more privacy, you know."

"Lawyer?" questioned Erika.

"Some fellow named Riggs. He has an office in town near the courthouse. Said the heirs still want to hold on to the lot to maybe build a vacation home someday. I guess they all got real rich from the life insurance money that was paid to the estate."

"Estate? Don't you have to be dead to have an estate?"

"Yes, of course. I think this guy Riggs, he was running things for Rick while he was missing, got the court to declare him dead about a year ago. That is why I thought you were from the insurance company. Those guys were hounding me for years about Rick and his lifestyle. Typical insurance company, they did not want to pay the five-million-dollar policy to the family. Anyway, that is the story as I know it. You can probably look up the attorney and give him the stuff you found. He still represents that family, I think."

Erika thanked Wendy for the information and returned to her car. "Riggs," she muttered to herself. Why did that name sound familiar? Suddenly she recalled seeing the name on a business card Arnie had shown her that they had brought back from the impound lot. She had thought it was just a coincidence that the other bidder interested in the car was also from Santa Bonita. Now she thought differently. Disappearing owner, burned-down house, family getting rich from a life insurance policy. It sounded like something you might find on *20/20* or another late night forensic crime television show.

She drove back home and began to get dinner ready for Chester and Arnie. "How's it going, boys?" she greeted the pair as she walked in the door. They were sitting in front of the television watching the early local news. The mountains on the cans of Coors Light beer were a dark blue, indicating they had just finished working on the van.

"Got all the drums pulled and removed the master cylinder. Drums are scored but can be turned. The master cylinder is toast, full of rust and such. We'll just order a rebuilt one when we take the drums in to be turned. I think we can ream out the wheel cylinders and just rebuild them ourselves," reported Chester.

This was all Greek to Erika. The details of automobile mechanics and how they worked was lost on her. They either made a varoom sound when they were running and got her to where they were going or a clunking sound they were broken. She had tried in the past to help Chester determine what was wrong with her car when it had broken down or was making a different noise than usual, but she was rarely able to be helpful. The usual "my car is broken" phone call would go like this:

"Chess, my car won't start and I'm stuck at work."

"What does it do when you turn the key?"

"It just makes a noise but doesn't start."

"What kind of a noise?"

"What do you mean, what kind of noise? It doesn't start."

"Well, is the starter working?"

"I don't know. It makes a *wa wa wa* noise when I turn the key."

"Does it sound like the engine is trying to run at all?"

"I don't know. Now all it does is just make a clicking noise."

Chester was usually able to determine the cause of the trouble and arrive on scene with the appropriate part or tool to get her car running again

"Sounds like we will be driving that van to the beach soon," she said now. "I found out some interesting things today about the guy who used to own the van."

"What was he, some international spy?" asked Chester.

"Yeah, did he work for the CIA and used the hippie van as a disguise to throw off all the other secret agents?" joked Arnie.

"Nothing as interesting as that," replied Erika. "Seems like this guy was part of the hip social scene here a few years ago and just up and disappeared one day. He was some kind of jojoba farmer who just went missing and was finally declared dead."

"Did he get lost in the backcountry or something?" asked Chester.

"Don't know. The lady I talked to who lives next to the house he used to live in gave me the history on the guy from what she remembered, but his disappearance remains a mystery."

"You should have talked to the folks who own his house now. They probably know where the guy lives now. What was his name?"

"Rick French, and there is no one to talk to at the house. It burned down years ago after he disappeared and was never rebuilt."

"This sounds like a murder mystery you see on TV," said Arnie.

"It gets stranger than that," answered Erika. She retrieved the manila file that contained the papers related to the van purchase and pulled out the business card that Riggs had given Chester at the impound lot at the day of the sale. "See the name on this business card? The card from the guy who has a client who wants your van so badly? This is the guy that handled the estate for Rick French."

"What a coincidence," murmured Chester.

"That's more than a coincidence," said Arnie. "What are the odds that a guy from Santa Bonita goes missing and his van gets sold to us in an auction in Marin. And then the guy who first got the bid tries to buy it from us. Then he looks us up the next week and tries to buy it again. And then Erika finds out he is the lawyer for the guy who used to own the van and that guy disappeared and his old house burned down? That is more than just a coincidence. There is something going on here that we have no idea about."

"Don't forget the impound lot guy ending up dead. I think you should just call this guy Riggs and offer to sell him the van and get away from this thing as soon as you can," urged Erika.

"No way," replied Chester. "We've spent too much time on this project and besides, what does all the mystery surrounding the guy who used to own it have to do with us? He is dead. I own the van. I have legal title. This guy French is going to have to pull a Lazarus and rise from the tomb before I even think about getting rid of it before I am done with my restoration. This is an investment, remember Erika?"

"Don't forget the map too," added Arnie. "It must be valuable to someone or else no one would have broken into the van and tried to steal it the other night. I think we need to do some more digging and flush this out before we even think about selling the van early. We could be sitting on a pot of gold that could make us rich."

"Yeah, we can double our money on the van after it is done. But we could become millionaires if we find out why this old oil field map is so valuable. We could be the next oil barons of Santa Bonita County," added Chester.

"All right, I will do some more digging and see what I can find out," replied Erika. She had the sinking feeling that she was about to become involved again in another edgy situation like the recently concluded Terra Auri affair.

CHAPTER FIFTEEN

TRAVELING TO MIAMI VIA HAVANA HAD BEEN RELATIVELY easy for Jack Morrison. He had blended in with a number of travelers from North Africa who were traveling to European destinations. He had first flown to Frankfurt. The customs agents had processed him to his next flight to London quickly, noting his travel plans to Cuba. He had used a fake passport issued in Morocco. To the authorities, he was just another tourist visiting Cuba. He had landed at Heathrow International Airport and had taken the tube to his hotel in south central London and had walked the several blocks to his hotel. Jack was not unfamiliar with the city. As a teenager, his family had taken a trip there to explore family roots related to his father's side of the family. His grandmother had immigrated to the states from London in 1910. She had recounted tales of the family history and being related to the landed gentry and members of the royal family. His father, an amateur genealogist, had indeed found that they were distantly related to a Captain Mosse whose plaque hung in tribute in the basement level of Saint Paul's cathedral. "Limey bastards," his father had exclaimed upon finding the plaque of the distant relative hidden behind a cafeteria table in the lower level food court for the cathedral. The plaque had cited the heroic actions of the captain and his death during a battle involving

Lord Nelson's fleet and Danish warships. The ill-fated Mosse had placed his vessel between the grounded ship of Nelson's and the Danish fleet to shield Nelson from certain destruction. The Danes had been thwarted but during battle the unfortunate Masse had taken a bullet to the chest and had died instantaneously. "The bastards should show more respect," his father had muttered as the family had read the notations on the plaque.

Jack checked into a three-star hotel with a rear view of the South Kensington Station. Dinner had been spent at a local pub located two blocks from his hotel. He had ordered his favorite meal of fish and chips. He had been taken aback by the presentation of his dinner. The fries had been stellar but the entire body of a deep-fried fish that had been set before him was quite different than the chunked pieces of fried cod he was used to eating. He had to make an effort to get past the visual of an entire headless fish sitting on his plate, complete with fins and a tail that curved upward as if it had suffered a tragic death in the frying pan. The flavor had been what he was used to though and he had worked his way through the carcass, leaving the fried tail fin on the plate at the end of the meal.

He was a little worried about his flight from Havana to Miami. Air France would fly him to Havana the following day and he expected security screening to be routine but troublesome. His passport would most likely be scrutinized more closely if he chose to travel on to Miami. There was too much at stake financially for him to rely on Rick French's reports of the progress being made on getting him his long overdue money from a drug deal gone wrong.

He spent the next day sightseeing in London before leaving on the early evening flight to Havana. The Tower of London, Kensington Palace, and Big Ben were all easily accessible via a one-day pass to the integrated public transportation system between the tube and various bus lines. His father had traced the Morrison family line back to the late 1700s but had regrettably never connected the dots to the royal bloodlines of the landed gentry. He had assumed his mother's story of having come from long ago wealthy English lords was a fantasy. Nonetheless, he had tried to imagine his family's life in London during the nineteenth century and how they had been able to survive as cobblers, printer's assistants, and later, pawnbrokers.

The officer at the security checkpoint had scrutinized Jack carefully as he looked at his ticket and passport. "Traveling a little light, aren't you?" the guard had commented as Jack presented himself and his one item of carry-on luggage. The functional lightweight backpack with a Rick Steve's logo emblazoned boldly on the back flap of the item proclaimed Jack to be an aficionado of the travel light drumbeat.

He had presented himself to the agent dressed in khaki pants and a short-sleeved cream-colored shirt, untucked in the current casual style in Morocco. A panama hat and open-toed leather sandals completed the ensemble, which he used to underscore his tourist-focused trip to the island. Everything appeared to be in order to the security officer. Jack was a foreigner from North Africa. His dark complexion and silver rings and bracelet were typical of jewelry worn by people from that region. He was traveling under the name of Trinidad Ferhat. He had not risked having an additional passport prepared for entry into the US. There would be cargo ships traveling between the two countries. He would devise a plan to gain passage in any manner he was able once he was ready to enter that country.

He had a current driver's license, which the California DMV had faithfully sent to his address of record every five years. No tickets meant an automatic reissue of his license. That was the easiest piece of documentation for him to maintain. He had no plans to leave the US again once he had retrieved his long overdue fortune. He could live off the grid in the States with that pile of cash. Except for the usual nuisances of driver's license renewals, and perhaps the IRS questioning a tax return, he would be able to resume his stateside life and resurrect his old contacts in the drug trade. The players might have changed over the years and the distribution methods were different, but the insatiable demand for illicit drugs had not ebbed in the slightest. Middle-class families still paid more attention to careers and lifestyles than they did to their children's after-school activities. Drug use was still prevalent in low-income neighborhoods where the use of drugs helped mask the grinding poverty and lack of opportunity.

He passed on through the security screening and took a seat in the gate waiting area. It would be a full flight. People milled around anxiously looking at the flight monitors, which showed the status of arrivals and departures. Jack noticed his plane was on time and settled into a seat in the rear of the boarding area. There he could keep his eye on the crowd and look over the newspaper he had picked up at the newsstand on the way to his gate.

CHAPTER SIXTEEN

"THE BEST PLACE TO LOOK UP PROBATE RECORDS IS AT THE superior court records office for the county where the decedent resided," stated Andie Moloney. The in-house legal counsel for Capital Triangle Properties was a tall, thin, thirty-something who had been brought up in the school of hard knocks in her native country of Ireland. Seeking greater opportunity than that offered by her family in the form of a job on the family sheep farm or a career living in town working as a barmaid, she had emigrated to the US after high school. She possessed none of the sense of entitlement exhibited by citizens of her age in America. She had quickly found a job working in a trust department for a local bank where she diligently applied her farm work ethic. She had quickly charmed her workmates with her heavy Irish accent and was equally loved by trust beneficiaries and the trust attorneys and other estate professionals she came into contact with. She had made full use of the junior college opportunities to improve her lot and an online undergraduate degree had qualified her to enter law school. She had worked her way through law school with a part-time job as a real estate assistant and after passing the bar, had specialized in real estate transactions for a local law firm. The opportunity to go out on her own had come through the firm of Mulroney, MacGregor, and

Hanratty, where she had toiled after becoming an attorney. M, M, and H had represented a class of investors in the Capital Triangle real estate debacle and when the court had placed the firm into receivership, she had been recommended by the firm to become in-house counsel. Her real estate experience would be beneficial in recovering investors' money and having one of their former associates in the position would be beneficial to their client's financial recovery.

"All you need to do is look up the name of your person on the probate index. It will give you the date the will was filed with the court and the case number. All the records are on microfiche," Andie said.

"Microfiche," repeated Erika. "What are they over there? In the dark ages?"

"Yup," Andie replied. "The county puts money into things the public can easily see, like police protection and public bike paths. You're not going to see cutting-edge technology in the court records system just for the occasional project like yours. What are you working on anyway?" she asked.

"It's this dumb van project Chester and his friend are working on. They found an interesting map hidden in the roof of the van and they want me to find out what happened to the former owner."

"Former owner?" asked Andie. "Don't they know who they bought it from?"

Erika relayed the sequence of events starting with the auction sale up to her visit to the last-known residence of Rick French. "Interesting," Andie replied. "Let me know what you find out over at the records office."

Erika left work early in the midafternoon and parked in the public parking garage across from the Santa Bonita County Courthouse. It was a large three-story affair with white-painted stucco and Spanish tile roof to fit in with the Spanish-themed architectural requirements of the downtown tourist area. As she proceeded to the second parking level, she approached the circular exit ramp into which exiting cars were fed on their way to pay for parking fees. A skateboarder came rocketing down the exit ramp, nearly losing control and spinning into her lane. She slammed on her brakes, barely avoiding the teenage rider as he continued barreling down the concrete tube. She was familiar with the drill. More than once Chester had tobogganed down the exit ramp after a late night movie, tires screeching all the way down as he held the steering wheel tightly and slammed on his brakes at the end just before reentering the flow of traffic. She usually objected to his antics but secretly, she enjoyed the wild ride down the ramp. It was a quick thrill ride and reminded her of the Space Mountain ride at Disneyland.

She found it necessary to park on the top floor of the garage. Shoppers and tourists had filled up all the prime spaces on the lower levels. She walked past a homeless man who was going through a garbage can. She was accustomed to the urine smell of the parking garage that served as bathroom quarters for the transient homeless population of Santa Bonita.

The County Courthouse was of a similar architectural style. Large and imposing, the L-shaped building was bordered by a large sunken garden. A large fountain with sandstone statues marked the main entrance to the building. She took the stairs with black ironwork railings to the second floor where the Hall of Records was located and approached the counter. There she was greeted by a young woman who was in charge of the counter.

"I want to look at an old probate file," she stated.

"Do you have the name and case number?" the clerk asked.

"His name was Richard S. French," Erika replied. "I don't have a case number but I think he died about five years ago."

"I can look for it that way," the clerk replied. "Let me check the list of probates by year and see if I can locate the file."

She returned from her computer with a piece of notepaper that had the case number and decedent's name on it. She handed the note and a form to Erika. "Just fill out this records request and I will pull the file for you. I will also need to see some identification."

Completing the form and showing the clerk her driver's license, Erika took a box of microfiche to one of the large readers and began going through the records. There was a lot of information and much of it had to do with notices of hearings, petitions, and requests for payments from the estate. The first document was the most interesting to her. The petition to admit the will and approve the appointment of executor had been filed by John Riggs. "That's the guy who tried to buy the van," she muttered under her breath. More interesting to her was the recital in the petition that mentioned an earlier case dealing with the appointment of a conservator for the decedent five years previous to that date. The file showed that Rick French had gone missing and Riggs had been appointed to manage his assets. She wrote down the conservatorship case number in her notebook for future reference and continued looking through the microfiche records. As she came across various filings that looked interesting, she printed them off from the microfiche reader. She had just enough time to go through all of the records before closing time. Quickly gathering up her belongings, she paid for the printed pages at the counter and returned to her car.

As she took the stairs to the top level of the parking garage, she noticed a police cruiser exiting the building. As the car approached her she saw that it was a private security company vehicle with logos, and exterior lights that looked very much like an official police car. "Wannabe policeman," she thought as the car drove past her and exited the parking lot. The driver in the car stared straight ahead, not noticing her. He wore sunglasses and dark nondescript clothing. Erika retrieved her car, paid the parking fee, and drove home. She would have to review her paperwork in more detail at home. From what she had gleaned so far, her interest in the estate of Richard S. French had been piqued. She failed to notice that she was tailed by the security service vehicle as she drove back to her house and that the car had parked down the street from her.

The van was still up on blocks and Chester and Arnie were sitting inside at the kitchen table having a beer. "So what did you find out down at the courthouse?" asked Arnie.

"Well, this guy French did own the van and he died and had a probate. Riggs handled the estate and all the court work. Funny thing though. This French guy went missing five years before they opened the estate and Riggs was appointed conservator of French's assets and has handled a bunch of transactions during the time since he went missing. I will have to look at this conservatorship file also to see if there are any clues in it."

"Let's see," replied Chester. "A guy goes missing. His lawyer goes to court to handle his affairs, has him declared dead five years later, and then we buy the van from an impound lot that the missing, now dead guy, used to own. Later, Burt the old guy who ran the lot dies. Then the lawyer for the guy tries a couple of times to get us to sell him the van and we find an oil field map in it with some markings."

"Don't forget the break-in," added Arnie. "We would never have found the map if that guy had not smashed the window and started to pull off the ceiling fabric."

"This is all as clear as mud," replied Erika. "I will ask Andie at work what I should do next, but I don't think we are any closer to finding out what this map is all about. The more we look into this the more questions we have."

"It's kind of like a murder mystery or treasure map deal," added Chester.

"Let's not get ahead of ourselves," replied Erika. "There is a lot of hair on this thing and none of us wants to get involved in something that might be dangerous. Let me see what I can find out from Andie about what I have found so far and we will see where the trail leads us."

CHAPTER SEVENTEEN

"HERE IS YOUR STATUS REPORT ON THE CTG MATTER," SAID Manita. She had printed off the morning's e-mails, placed copies in the CTG case file, and handed the report to John Riggs.

"What does it say?" replied Riggs, not looking up from the papers on his desk.

"Observed female subject exiting the superior court records office at sixteen hundred hours. Followed subject to her residence. Listening devices indicate subject and two male companions are aware of the details of the missing persons case of a Richard S. French and following probate matter. Subject plans to look at more files. Parties are trying to find out the facts pertaining to what information is contained on a map they discovered in the van. Standing by for further instructions."

` "Tell him to continue surveillance and monitor conversations in the residence for another day," directed Riggs.

"Will do," replied Manita. She returned to her desk and sent an e-mail to the Casebeer Detective Agency instructing them to continue on with their surveillance.

Rick French was just getting out of his truck and retrieving his surfboard after a midafternoon surf session when he received a call from John Riggs. Noting the number, he quickly stowed his board in the rope hanger in his garage and answered the call.

"I have bad news and good news," Riggs relayed on the other end of the phone.

"Okay, it's not all bad, so that is a good thing. Tell me what you know so far."

"It seems these guys that bought your old van have made a connection between the van and you. They know about your disappearance and the court case declaring you missing and later dead," Riggs relayed. "They still know nothing about what the map has on it or why it is useful to anyone, but they are still curious. One of the guys' girlfriend is going to look at the missing person's report they did on you and the conservatorship file. I don't think anyone is going to be able to connect any of the dots. I have a private investigator monitoring them and will report to you if anything of interest happens."

"You are probably right," replied French. "They will hit a wall pretty quickly and probably just drop it. The insurance company could not find out anything on us. These kids won't either. But I am going to have to get that map from them at some point."

"Okay, but you are going to need to tell me why this particular map is so important," replied Riggs.

"My insurance policy that I had you take out on me before the last shipment I did from Florida was supposed to take care of my living expenses in the event I found it necessary to leave the country quickly. When the deal went bad and I had to disappear, I was able to keep Jack off of my back by having you send him periodic payments until such time as I could access my stashes of cash. I had my ranch foreman Emory Calloway hide cash for me from time to time at various well sites on the Rummell ranch next door to my place. He noted the location of each well where he hid cash for me and I kept the map hidden in the roof of my van for safe-keeping. When my van got impounded with the map in it, I had to wait all of these years for the missing person case and estate to close so that the county could finally sell the van. It was just dumb luck and your failure to bring cash to that sale that these guys were able to buy the van out from under you."

"Can't you just ask this guy Emory Calloway where he stashed the cash?" asked Riggs.

"Maybe. I have not talked to him since I made my departure from the States and he does not know anything about our arrangement or that I am still alive. He might even be dead by now but you can ask around in Cuyama and see if he still lives there. He marked down the locations where he hid stuff on the map and I will need it back to retrieve my stuff".

"Will he talk to me about this hidden cash?" asked Riggs.

"I don't know" replied French. "He and I were the only two people who knew about hiding the cash in the old oil wells. I told him I just did not trust banks. He was a cranky old guy who grew up during the Depression and had similar feelings about banks and such. If you approach him with the idea that you are in charge of getting cash back to my family that I hid from the government, he might talk to you," answered French. "Get Terry Korman to meet with him and look over an oil field map of the Cuyama oil field. It is worth a shot. Tell Korman to pick up an oil field map just in case Emory kept a list of the well numbers he used to hide the stuff. If we can't get my map, maybe we can use a list of the wells to find them on a map of the area."

"Okay, I will report back what I find in a couple of days," replied Riggs. "Get me Terry Korman on the phone," he then barked to Manita, after ending the call with French.

Manita scrolled down through her contact list on her computer and found the listing for Terry. "Which listing, business or ranch office?" she replied.

"Ranch office," answered Riggs.

When the phone rang at the ranch office, Terry was out in the backyard practicing his roping skills on a pair of plastic roping horns he had attached to a bale of hay. He had been instructed to stay at the ranch until further notice and finding things to pass the time had not been easy. The shade from the hot summer sun was provided by the large cottonwood trees next to the house. The leaves shimmered in the afternoon breeze that welled up each afternoon in the valley. He had found an old nylon rope in the barn along with the roping dummy and had hauled it out into the open lawn area behind the house to help pass the time while he waited for instructions from Riggs. It was hot, ninety degrees in the shade. The thin single wall construction of the old board and batten ranch house did little to keep out the heat of the day and the shaded area around the house was the only oasis for miles from the blazing summer sun.

Setting down his rope, Terry was greeted on the other end of the line by John Riggs.

"I need you to look around for an old map of the area that Rick might have kept in the ranch house. It might be a Department of Oil and Gas map of the Cuyama Valley oil field," Riggs said.

"What kind of map is this? Are you interested in oil wells on this ranch? You know, there are a couple of old sites where they looked for oil but never found any."

"No," replied Riggs. "I am interested in the entire Cuyama Valley, not just the wells on the ranch."

"Okay, what is going on? Are we going to start doing some oil lease acquisitions for the estate?" asked Terry.

"I am not at liberty to discuss that at this time. Just get me the map. If there isn't one at the ranch, you can get it from the Department of Oil and Gas. And let me know when you have it. See if you can find out if Emory Calloway is still around also so we can meet with him."

"Emory, sure, I think I saw him last week in the bar at the Buckhorn. Let me get ahold of him and we can set up a meeting for later this week."

"Friday will be fine, noon at the Buckhorn," replied Riggs.

Terry located his pocket notebook where he stored the names and contact information on clients and retrieved the page for Emory Calloway. Emory had been the foreman of the ranch for many years before retiring and passing the duties on to Terry. Well into his eighties, Emory had grown up on the Carrizo Plains area of eastern San Luis Obispo County. He had been raised as a cowboy on his father's spread. When his family had lost the property during the Depression, he had found work on the ranch French had eventually purchased. Working his way up from breaking horses and later working cattle, Emory had eventually become the cattle boss for the ranch. In an industry where job advancement was based on an ability to learn the cattle business on the ground and in the saddle, Emory had been able to progress to becoming manager of the ranch by his natural ability with livestock, and the ability to work long hours in less than ideal conditions. He had decided to retire after French had purchased the ranch. It had become apparent that French had no interest in the cattle business and had in fact, taken some of the prime grazing ground out of grazing and planted it with jojoba plants. The rest of the ranch had been leased out to other local cattlemen and Emory had no interest in ending his career simply babysitting the ranch and overseeing the new jojoba investment. When French had gone missing, he had given notice. Riggs had asked Terry to watch over the ranch for their mutual surfing buddy, French, until such time as he resurfaced. Emory had provided Terry with a general tour of the ranch and the water systems to enable Terry to continue to oversee the ranch.

Terry picked up the phone a little nervously and dialed Emory's number. He was never comfortable talking to Emory. Emory knew he was a "dude" and knew very little about the ranch or the practical aspect of dealing with ranch problems when they came up.

"There is more to handling a ranch than just driving around in a pickup with a dog in the back and a gun in the rack," Emory had chided Terry when he had turned over the duties to him. During his term as manager, Terry had had to call Emory several times for advice on who to call to fix a broken waterline, or how to get the spring boxes cleaned and working again to supply water for the house and barns. It had taken him some time to determine the difference between the large irrigation wells that drew water for the jojoba farming operation and the simple gravity-fed water system that accessed spring water from the hills in the rear of the ranch.

"Tell your boss to quit pumping the ground water so much," Emory had chided Terry the last time he had called when the water to the house had stopped working. "That country was never meant to have irrigated farming," Emory had scolded. "You are running into a wreck out there with all those jojoba fields."

Terry heard the phone ringing and then the sound of Emory's voice.

"Emory, this is Terry Korman at the ranch."

"What is it now, Terry. Are you out of water again? Did you get the truck stuck again in the China pasture"?

"No, nothing like that," replied Terry. "John Riggs wants to meet with you about some oil wells in the valley and go over an oil field map."

Emory did not respond.

"Emory, can you meet us Friday over lunch to go over this map with John?" Terry asked.

Emory remained silent for a moment. He knew what the significance of this map was. He had spent many nights on horseback years ago making long night rides across the ranch and onto the neighboring Rummell ranch where most of the oil wells in the field were located. There he hid small waterproof packages that Rick French had given to him from time to time. He had been instructed to wait for nights when the moon had waned. Under the cover of complete darkness, he had been instructed to locate old abandoned oil wells that had been capped in a manner that would permit him to make easy entry. These wells had not been easy to locate. Many of them still had all of the pumping and downhole equipment located in the well. Others had been surreptitiously abandoned by removal of the oil well equipment and then covered illegally with dirt to hide the location. When and if the Department of Oil and Gas ever got around to following up on the proper abandonment of those wells would be a problem for future owners of the ranch.

Emory had been able to locate wells through discussions with crews in fields that were being idled and taken offline pending future potential use. The likelihood of these old wells ever coming back online was remote. French had determined that the clean, dry, oil well bore holes would be good locations for him to hide his packages. No one would ever think of looking in them for the contraband that French needed to hide. It was safer than trying to store his cash in a safe deposit box or risk trusting his wealth to someone who might be tempted to dip into his financial stash of cash. Emory had ridden out a total of thirty times over the course of several years to make these deposits. He never asked what the packages contained. He suspected that they contained precious metals such as gold and silver or cash by the size, shape, and weight of each package. It was none of his business. Emory was equally suspicious of the government and the system and had no reservations complying with his employer's requests. If French's attorney was involved with questions on the map, it must have something to do with the estate. Besides, French was long gone and recently declared dead. Those packages had value to someone.

"Yeah, I guess so," replied Emory. "I don't get out much anymore and you are going to have to pick me up. Those bastards at the DMV took my license away and I don't want to get caught driving around town in the daytime."

"Okay, we will stop by around noon to pick you up," replied Terry.

On Friday, Terry and Riggs pulled up to a green single-wide trailer on a side street in Old Cuyama. The small community was five miles from the former company town of New Cuyama where the only gas station, restaurant and bar in the valley were located. If the town of New Cuyama had seen its better days, Old Cuyama was even more well-worn. Several old industrial buildings that used to serve as carrot packing sheds and oil field service businesses stood dark and empty. Their windows were boarded up and sand had piled up against the warped and sagging doors.

A few old homes and duplexes still were being used as farmworker quarters, but the lack of maintenance and tumbleweeds in the yards bespoke of the transient nature of the occupants and the viability of the town. Old Cuyama was in transition to becoming a ghost town.

Emory's trailer sat on the site of a former farmworker residence. When Emory had retired from the ranch, he had taken his savings and purchased the old single-wide trailer from a local landowner who had purchased land to develop a vacation property for his family. A house had burned down on the old town lot and he paid a small monthly rent to the lot owner for the right to have his trailer there. There was little concern that the lot owner would ever give him notice to move. Prospects for a revival of the town were remote.

"Riggs, is that you?" called out Emory as he rose from the porch and walked down the bowed trailer steps into the front yard. "You look none the worse for wear."

"Yes, still kicking, I suppose" replied Riggs. He noticed that Emory had aged since the last time he had seen him. Emory still wore the same old cowboy uniform. Sweat-stained hat, cowboy shirt with fake pearl buttons snapped at the neck. A well-worn Santa Bonita Fiesta Rodeo belt buckle attached to a stained leather belt held up a pair of Levis. None of the fancy boot-cut wranglers for Emory. Levis had been what he had grown up with and Levis would be what they buried him in. His legs were even more bowed than Riggs had remembered. Time, thinning bones, and gravity had taken their toll on the once vibrant old cowboy.

The two shook hands. "Korman, I haven't had to haul you out of a ditch or come start up your generator for a while. You must finally be settling into the ranch," said Emory. The trio loaded up into Terry's Ford F-350 quad cab and drove over to the Buckhorn Restaurant and Bar. Flyers were posted on the front door announcing the annual late summer rodeo and an upcoming bake sale benefitting the local FFA chapter. In the entryway were recent pictures of local youth exhibiting their county fair blue ribbons alongside pictures of pigs, sheep, and steers that had won at the recent fair.

Terry selected a table in the back and he and Riggs proceeded to the table and then waited for Emory to finish exchanging greetings with several of the local cattlemen who were having lunch at the counter. Herb Rummell eyed Riggs and Terry suspiciously from his seat at the end of the counter. He had always considered the jojoba operation a front for French's real business activities, whatever those were. Farmers had tried to grow potatoes in the 1920s, until diseases from continuous cropping had made further farming impossible. Then alfalfa growers had moved in to access the cheap land for that crop, only to be put out of business from overpumping of the fragile groundwater aquifer that sat under the valley. Vineyards, fruit trees, and pistachios had come next, only to be proven as risky ventures at best due to the late frost hazards seen in the spring. Irrigation was now centered solely on carrots farmed by huge farming companies that had operations across the entire United States in order to provide fresh product 365 days a year.

As Emory walked by Herb's table, Herb reached out his hand and shook Emory's, joking about Emory coming out of retirement to help him gather some snaky cattle that the Rummell Ranch Company had left years ago on some leased pasture. He had never retrieved them from a long-ago forest service lease that he had abandoned due to environmental pressure from the local tree huggers. The two of them joked about how they would ride out there in the old way of working cattle, set up a camp, and start digging them out of the brush and tying them to trees to take some of the snort out of them before trailering them back to the ranch. In their minds they were still twenty-somethings, up for the challenge. They still had the heart, but no longer the legs to get it done. "Well, I'll let you gents get back to your business," Herb had proffered as the two old cowboys finished their conversation.

Riggs called the waitress over and she took their drink orders. "She looks as good walking away as she does comin' toward ya," remarked Emory as she left to get their iced teas.

"Damn hot today," remarked Terry.

"Yup, dryer than a popcorn fart, too," replied Emory. "So John, you drove all the way up here and dragged Terry along for the ride. What is so important that you need to get an old pensioner like me off the front porch and down to the Buckhorn to gnaw on a burger in the middle of the day?"

Riggs stared across the table for a moment as he considered how to approach the subject. Emory was just as cranky as Riggs remembered him to have been five years ago when they first met.

"I need to find out some information on a job you did for Rick before he died while you were still managing the ranch."

"What kind of job?" answered Emory. "I have told Terry all I know about the ranch and how things work and he seems to have figured out how the water and such works on the place. At least he hasn't called me in a while to bail him out."

"This is not that kind of work," answered Riggs. "As you know I was the attorney for Rick for some time and he entrusted certain information to me that is not generally known by the public. I don't know if you are aware of this, but the court determined that Rick is officially dead and I have almost concluded the matter of settling his estate. When I was going through my files the other day to store them away, I found some notes of a conversation I had with Rick about some packages that he had hidden on the Rummell ranch."

"Packages?" asked Emory.

"Well, small parcels of things that he had wrapped up and given to you from time to time that you were supposed to hide for him in certain locations. He told me before he disappeared that you did this for him over the course of several years and that you gave him a map of the valley showing where these items had been stored or hidden."

"Did he tell you anything about the packages or what were in them?" asked Emory. He was suspicious that Riggs was on a fishing expedition and that he might have no official capacity to be asking about those hidden items or their locations.

"They were long cylindrical packages wrapped in oilskin paper and burlap so that they could be preserved in a damp environment. The diameter of each cylinder would be no more than four or five inches across and they would be a foot or more in length."

"Naw, I don't know nothing about long cylinders," replied Emory. "He used to keep a metal box buried in the front yard by the old cottonwood tree. Said it had some traveling money in it but he never said anything about tubes of stuff for me to bury." Terry and Riggs looked across the table at one another for a moment and then they all stopped talking as the waitress interrupted them with their drinks and took their lunch orders.

"Strange," replied Riggs. "Rick specifically mentioned to me that he had asked someone on the ranch to hide these packages for him down inside old unused oil wells where the pumps had been pulled off and the holes were still open for access."

"Nope," replied Emory. "Does not sound like anything I ever did for him. I would have remembered something like that."

"Okay," replied Riggs. "I guess I will have to find out who else might have done some work for Rick while he owned the ranch."

"Well, I would have suggested you ask Pete Johnston, except he died last year. Pete did some day work for us from time to time and Rick might have asked him to do this for him."

"Did he have a wife or family we can ask?" asked Terry. Riggs put his hand on Terry's arm to silence him.

"No need. I have followed up on my duty to the estate and have reached the end of the trail. Who knows what was in those packages or if they were even real. It's a dead end as far as I am concerned." The trio finished up their lunch and they drove Emory back to his trailer to drop him off.

"Let me know if you come across anything more on those packages," Emory said to the pair as he gripped the handrail to his front porch and slowly climbed the steps. He disappeared into the shade of the porch and they could see his silhouette waving to them as they backed out of the gravel driveway and headed to town.

"Poor old guy," remarked Terry. "I bet he is dead by the end of the year. Kind of sad to see the old guy in that kind of shape, even with the load of shit he has given me over the years."

"The man's a liar," replied Riggs.

"Liar, what do you mean?"

"Rick told me in detail about those packages and how he instructed Emory to take care of them and hide them."

"Packages, what kind of packages and why were they hidden?" asked Terry.

"How much do you know about Rick and his former business activities?" asked Riggs. "I know you guys knew each other from when you sold him the ranch but did he tell you very much about what he did for a living or about his background?"

"Well, we used to party together from time to time and he had one of those surfing memberships on the Alistair ranch that he let me use. He knew about my surfing background and we shared that in common."

"Did you know how he made his money?" asked Riggs.

"You know, we never really talked about it. All I knew was he was trying to start up his jojoba farming business and that he seemed to have a lot of cash. From the conversations we had I got the idea that he had traveled a lot in South America and Spain and may have been involved in things which are not completely legal. Let's just say I did not ask, and he did not tell."

"My position as his former legal counsel and recent executor prevent me from giving you the details of his business activities. All I can tell you is that he did not trust banks and kept very large sums of cash on his person. The nature of his business dealings did not mesh well with the banking or tax reporting systems. He had developed a plan to have Emory periodically hide packages of money for him in certain locations in the Cuyama Valley. These stashes of cash were his personal liquid wealth and I know for sure that Emory did this for him and is playing dumb."

"If he knows you know, why would he lie about it?" asked Terry.

"I don't know. Maybe he is not one hundred percent sure I know that he was the guy who did all the hiding of cash for Rick and maybe he is just playing dumb until I come up with some better reason why I know about the cash. He could also be dipping into the cash and maybe he is afraid of getting caught."

"So how much cash are we talking about?" replied Terry.

"These tubes of cash were described to me to be about a foot or so long, about five inches in diameter. And contained various tightly rolled denominations of bills. Twenties, fifties, and hundreds. Each tube was to be worth about $250,000. There are other tubes though that are smaller and contain gold coins. These weigh about ten pounds each."

"So what is each of those tubes worth?" asked Terry.

"About five million dollars based on today's spot gold price. There are a total of twenty tubes. Emory may not have known about the value of each tube but he knew Rick was hiding cash."

"So how are you going to get him to fess up?" asked Terry.

"I don't know. He is a nice old guy, just suspicious and loyal to Rick. I will have to noodle on it awhile and see what I come up with."

The two of them bid each other goodbye and Riggs climbed back into his car for the drive back to the coast. He had the idea of his next move. Internet service was notoriously bad in the valley. He waited until he reached the top of the Figueroa Mountain Ranch before he turned on his phone and voice dialed the number for the Casebeer Detective Agency.

He was in luck. Craig Casebeer was still at work. "I need you to have your guys do some surveillance work in Cuyama."

CHAPTER EIGHTEEN

UPON HIS ARRIVAL IN HAVANA, JACK MORRISON HAD CHECKED into the Hotel El Presidente and spent three days posing as a tourist. He had mingled with crowds of visitors eager to view the former Russian island protectorate and spent the time lounging along the Malecon, drinking beer with the locals and interacting with street vendors and fellow travelers. He had engaged in all of the typical tourist activities, visiting the Habana Vieja and spending one evening at the always popular Tropicana Nightclub where pre-revolution-style shows were still being produced. He half-expected to see a 1950s mafia figure in the fringes of the crowd, overseeing the nightclub operations.

Three days had been sufficient to enable Jack to establish his character as a visitor from abroad on vacation to assume the role of a tourist. Now waves pounded on the bow of the container ship as it left the harbor in Havana and traveled to Houston with Jack safely aboard. Commerce between Cuba and the United States was limited. Regulations tightly restricted products between the two countries. Agricultural products were permitted for import as well as medical and humanitarian products. But consumer products and other raw goods were excluded.

Jack Morrison had been able to board the freighter with relative ease. Freighters usually had extra cabin space for passengers. Selling these quarters to passengers who were more interested in a cheap trip than a vacation cruise was a common practice in the industry. Local rules varied country by country and it was up to the captain to provide lists of these passengers each time he arrived at his destination port. Each captain had his own idea of what was proper and prudent and the captain of the *Misako Maru* had no compunction in looking the other way as Jack boarded the vessel and posed as a crewman in charge of checking the refrigeration units on the reefer containers. He had flashed the captain a fake union card and paid him five hundred dollars in cash for a quick ride up the gulf coast to Houston ostensibly to start a job on a container ship traveling from that port to Spain. The captain asked no questions even though the amount proffered was larger than he usually charged for steerage-quality accommodations. He expected to never see Jack again or have any knowledge of him leaving the ship once it tied up to the pier to unload its cargo.

Jack had dined with the other passengers and the crew for the evening meal and again for breakfast the next day as the ship started to enter the harbor. There had only been one couple making use of the empty cabins, a young couple who had taken advantage of the lifting of the Cuban travel embargo to see the country on the cheap. They had peppered Jack about where he had been and what he had seen while on his visit to the island. Jack was on the top of his game, a more gregarious self that his normal surly nature. In the event law enforcement found the need to follow up on his back trail, people he had met on his visit to Cuba would relate that he was just another fellow traveler, experienced in visiting countries abroad, and helpful in his suggestions in how to navigate in a foreign country.

As the freighter began to approach Galveston and the greater Houston area, Jack Morrison had chosen a refer container unit in which to stow away. He had dressed warmly to be able to survive the refrigerated container. He knew that the mechanics who checked and recorded that temperature of refrigerated units would not address the container unless there was a repair issue. After traveling for most of a day he had caught sight the Houston harbor.

Now Jack was ensconced in the container as the ship neared the dock where its cargo would be unloaded by large articulating cranes. He had pitched his backpack overboard early in the morning and would be blending in with the union workers who would be unloading the ship's cargo. The container sat on a perimeter row nearest the dock. It was one of the first to be unloaded and the container was quickly loaded onto a commercial flatbed trailer bound for Dallas. Jack stayed hidden just long enough for container to be taken off the deck and loaded onto the trailer. Jack quickly opened the container door and emerged onto the loading area next to the large crane. There he posed as one of the teamsters who were busy preparing their tractor trailer rigs to transport cargo to Dallas. Blending in with the other workmen, he had simply walked away from the loading area and away from the docks.

CHAPTER NINETEEN

THE LAST THING ELIAS ESPINOZA WAS COGNIZANT OF WAS the muffled sound of boots walking up behind him and the sudden blinding flash from the business end of a 1911 government model semiautomatic pistol, which had been pointed at his forehead from six inches away. The gun metal gray silencer muffled the sound of the explosion. A 45-caliber, 220 grain copper jacketed lead slug made a neat hole in the center of his forehead. The exit wound was five inches in diameter, a perfect circle. Beyond that on the inside of the front passenger seat window, a collage of brain matter and bone fragments had landed to form an impressionist painting of blood, gelatin, and skull fragments. Elias had been preparing for an evening snatch and run job in the home of Emory Calloway. He had been instructed to drive out to the remote town of Cuyama, wait until the occupant went to bed, and then sneak through the house to look for papers that would have notes about locations where items had been buried on the ranch. It could have been a hand-drawn map of the Cuyama Valley or a simple list with numbers on it. His job was to locate an item that looked similar to this, retrieve it undetected, and bring it back to Riggs. It was going to be a simple assignment. But the job was over before it got started.

A tall dark figure turned from the driver's side door of Elias's car and walked over to the front door of Emory Callaway's trailer. The muffled pistol shot had been no more than a puff in the night: the sound of a horse kicking a fence rail in the nearby pasture, a screen door knocking in the night wind. It had gone unnoticed by sleeping residents of the town. Jack Morrison put his black-gloved hand on the doorknob and slowly turned it. He entered the front room to the trailer and heard Emory snoring in the rear bedroom. Jack's eyes became adjusted to the dim light and he scanned the room. The room was neat and tidy. Emory kept a clean camp. A television complete with rabbit ear antenna sat opposite to an old green Naugahyde armchair. A well-worn saddle sat in the corner. A bridle and spurs hung around the horn along with a braided rawhide rope. A small table that served double duty as an eating table and repository of reading material and knickknacks sat to one side of the armchair. A recent issue of *Range Magazine* was on the table, opened to the section containing photos of rural ranch scenes submitted by readers of the magazine.

He could find no file cabinet or other likely places where papers or large maps might be located. Then he noticed it. A small gleaming object sitting on top of the ashtray on the table. He walked carefully over to the table and picked up the object. It was a gold-colored coin, the size of a quarter. On the front of the coin he found the familiar Indian head picture which had been used on Indian head nickels. The image of a buffalo was on the back of the coin. The coin was dated 1992. Jack knew what it was. Gold coins minted by the US Mint had become increasingly popular with the investing public after the 1989 financial meltdown. Their faith in the value of the dollar had been shaken. Speculators, survivalists, and the like had increased the demand for hard currency products in the form of gold and silver. People such as Jack who engaged in the underground economy had used them for years as a storage of wealth. They were easily exchanged as barter in a business transaction and in a pinch could be hidden and transported more easily than paper currency.

"Get your hands up where I can see them!"

Jack slowly put down the coin and raised his hands up high into the air. He turned to see an elderly man wearing boxer shorts and a white undershirt standing before him with a doubled barreled shotgun pointed at his chest.

"What the fuck are you up to, young fella?" shouted Emory, staring down the barrel of his shotgun.

"Take it easy," replied Jack. "I must be in the wrong house." "Wrong house! You can bet your ass you picked the wrong house," replied Emory.

"Take it easy, old man," said Jack. "I was down at the Buckhorn with a few old buddies and they told me to just come over to their trailer to crash. I just got in town from a long flight and could not make it to closing time. They told me to look for an old green trailer on this street and I figured this must be it. Sorry if I got the wrong one. They said it was not locked so I figured I had the right one and just came on in."

"Is that your car out front?" replied Emory. He lowered his shotgun and walked over to the front window.

In a flash, Jack was on him. He slammed the old cowboy up against the wall and threw him down to the floor in a limp heap. Placing his knee into Emory's chest, he began to choke him. Emory flailed at Jack's face with both hands, but his sinewy eighty-year-old muscles were no match against the younger man. His emphysema-ridden lungs quickly ran out of air and the last thing he saw were the dead cold eyes of a swarthy bearded man crushing the life out of him.

Jack rose from the dead form before him and bent over to retrieve the gold coin he had been looking at. Walking outside, he went over to the car, pulled the body of Elias Espinoza from the front seat, and dragged him partially out of the vehicle as if the driver had been trying to escape from the vehicle. He surveyed the side yard and retrieved a small gas can from a shed. He liberally poured the contents over the body and into Elias' car. He then poured a small trail of gasoline across the yard and up to the front porch of the house. He looked for an ignition source. All of the appliances for the home were propane powered, a common utility source for rural areas such as this. Inside the house he found a small wall heater in the bedroom that was manually operated without the modern convenience of a thermostat. He turned the wall heater on and then returned to the kitchen to remove the flex line to the propane-powered stove. The propane began to flow into the kitchen and Jack turned off the lights to the house and quickly exited the trailer and returned to his car, which he had left parked several blocks away. As he drove away, he saw the trailer erupt in a loud explosion. A second explosion followed as the trail of gas was ignited by the house fire and traveled back to the car. Lights began to come on in the neighborhood. As he drove down the highway he was passed by the volunteer fire department engine coming in the opposite direction from its station in New Cuyama. The usual compliment of a fire chief's car and the sheriff cruiser followed several minutes behind.

Isadore Rodriquez returned home from the trailer fire incident at seven in the morning. His wife, Angelica, was busy serving breakfast burritos to their two school-age sons and was stuffing sandwiches into lunch bags. "Long night?" she said. Isadore plopped down at the oblong pine kitchen table and took a bite out of the burrito she had placed before him.

"Yup, Emory Calloway's trailer burned up. It was a total loss," he replied.

"Too bad. Is he all right?"

"He did not make it out. We found him in the living room on the floor and another body in the yard next to a car. The body was too burned up to let us take fingerprints. The VIN number though ties the car to a low-level petty thief who operated a muffler shop in Santa Bonita. Not sure why this guy would be out late at night in Cuyama," replied Isadore.

"That's a lot of action for one night," Angelica replied. "Sounds kind if fishy to me. What's a guy from the coast doing out here late at night? Think he's connected to one of those stolen car chop shops you hear about?"

"Not likely, but you never know these days. Looked like Emory was trying to get out the front door and the smoke probably got to him," he replied. "Not sure what the relationship to the muffler shop guy is at this point. The investigator from county fire is coming out this morning to go over the scene. Probably got started by a cigarette. The old coot liked to smoke in bed before turning out the lights."

"How did the fire department do?" she asked.

"They got it out pretty quick after they got their hoses off the engine and untangled. Still using that old triple-fold method to stack their attack lines, you know."

The Cuyama Valley fire station was manned by a crew of volunteers from the community who trained weekly and responded to calls from their homes. It was a social club of sorts. Their calls were limited to the occasional highway wreck or inhalator call for one of the residents in the valley. They had few opportunities to use their firefighting skills. Training sessions many times ended as beer drinking sessions at the Buckhorn. Isadore had been part of the crew for several years upon first being assigned to the valley substation but had resigned from the department once he had been promoted to the station commander for the sheriff's office in the valley.

"The trailer was pretty much gone by the time they got there, being as old as it was, you know. I waited on scene until the coroner drove out from Santa Bonita to pick up the bodies. Guess they will do autopsies to confirm the causes of death."

Angelica stroked his shoulder as she poured him a second cup of coffee. "Well, they do the best they can under the circumstances," she acknowledged.

"I am turning in for a couple hours of shut eye," said Isadore.

"Okay," she responded, clearing his plate. "Don't forget we have that parent-teacher meeting tonight after dinner."

Isadore gave her a thumbs-up as he trudged up the stairs to their bedroom to catch up on sleep missed during the previous evening's late night fire.

CHAPTER TWENTY

ROB HIPNER HAD NOT SLEPT WELL THE PREVIOUS EVENING. He had risen from his bed in a mechanical manner as he had done every day since his retirement. He had been ready to leave his thirty-year position with a large life insurance company when he retired twelve months previous. His concern for becoming irrelevant and lazy had spurred him to continue with his habit of starting his day promptly at six thirty on weekday mornings. He of course was free to rise as late as he liked, start the day when the feeling moved him. But Rob was a plow horse of sorts in his work habits, unable to let go of a full day of activity.

The phone call he had received the previous evening had both excited and irritated him. A young female who had identified herself as Erika had asked to meet with him to discuss a long-ago case that he had worked on. It had dealt with a claim on a life insurance policy that his former employer, Western General Life, had written on a customer. He was happy to discuss matters of his former career so long as they did not violate the confidentiality agreement he had signed with the company upon retiring. When he learned that the case involved a policy in the name of Richard S. French, his interest had been heightened.

"Yes, I remember the French matter," he had relayed to Erika during their brief phone conversation. "It was one of my last big claims and I was unable to successfully defend the company against the claim. It cost them five million dollars and I think my career path at the company took a side track after that effort."

They had agreed to meet in a Red Robin restaurant in Westlake Village just down the road from his condominium. The previous night's conversation had dredged up all manner of memories and feelings he had been harboring for the past several years. The policy holder's lawyer had instituted court proceedings to have French declared legally deceased after having disappeared five years previous. Western General had petitioned the court to decline the request by way of the general rule that requires the lost to have been missing for at least seven years before being presumed dead. The two sides had quibbled in court about the length of time having been only five years. The petitioner had offered cases where fewer than seven years had passed with the person having gone missing and declared deceased by the court. Western General Life had stressed the dominant seven-year theme that had been upheld by courts in the majority of the missing persons cases. "Well, if he is alive, Western General should be ordered to present Mr. French to this court or at least provide some evidence that he is in fact still alive," the attorney, John Riggs, had argued before the court.

Hipner had been brought into the matter at the last moment once Western General had been successful in gaining a delay on the petition so that Riggs could provide more support for his petition to force the insurance company to issue payment on the life insurance policy. Five million dollars was a lot of money and Judge Slider, who was presiding over the case, was going to move with a certain amount of caution before making a ruling.

As he had laid in bed the previous evening, Rob had resurfaced all of the prior activity and stress he had undergone during his work on the claim. It had been exciting and potentially dangerous work surpassing anything portrayed on the popular television crime investigation shows. He had cleared his schedule to focus on only this claim but had failed to gather sufficient evidence to enable the court to deny the petition. Now that the matter had resurfaced again by way of the call from Erika, his juices flowed with the excitement of the old matter.

He walked out to the parking lot and unlocked his forest-green late model Toyota Camry. As a retired investigator, he was neither flashy nor portrayed any opulence. His had been a world of the nondescript and innocuous, someone who preferred to blend into a crowd as opposed to standing out or seeking attention. He quickly looked underneath his car as a habitual check against the possibility of a car bomb or other incendiary device having been planted. Former clients of his employer had been known to become angry upon receiving a denial of the claim on a policy written by the company and some of them were not averse to using violence against company employees who were responsible for rejecting claims.

Seeing nothing below his car, he drove to the restaurant. He immediately spotted Erika waiting in a booth in the rear of the eatery. She looked expectantly at him and raised her hand to signal him. "Rob?" she asked as he walked over to her. She extended her hand to greet him.

"Erika?" he answered.

"Yes, Erika McConika," she replied, shaking his hand. "I really appreciate you taking the time to meet with me on such short notice."

"Well, I am retired, you know, and the file you have been reviewing over at the courthouse was a high watermark for me in my career with Western General. When you mentioned the French disappearance case, it all came back to me just like it was yesterday. So tell me again why you are so interested in this old case and how you came about tracking me down?"

"It is a long story and all started with my boyfriend buying an old VW van that used to be owned by French. He purchased it from an auction sale at the Mendocino County impound lot and after he bought it we found some things in it that led us to French being the former owner. Also, there is an attorney, John Riggs, who keeps bugging my boyfriend about buying the van. He keeps offering more than the van is worth."

"Up until last night after we spoke, Riggs is a name I have not thought about for a few years," replied Rob.

"Oh, and before I forget," interrupted Erika, "someone tried to break into the van right after we brought it home and we found some sort of map hidden in the roof part of the camper that we think might be important to someone."

Rob was silent for a moment and took a sip from his coffee. "I think it might be best for me to start at the beginning of what I know about the missing persons matter I became involved in and lay out what I recall. I don't have any information on this map you found but I do have quite a bit of background work on Rick French and the activities leading up to his disappearance that might be helpful to you."

"Yes, that would be great. Anything you can tell me that helps us find out what this map is all about would be great," Erika responded.

Rob cleared his throat. "Before I start, I need to tell you that you and your friends are potentially in great danger if it turns out this map is of importance to the people who are trying to get it from you. During the course of my investigation, I found out quite a bit about French and his business dealings. His partners were not, should I say, members of the Rotary Club. Everything I tell you should not be repeated outside of your two friends and if you decide to look any further into what might have happened to French, you should prepare for the worst."

"Okay, I will keep what you tell me close to the vest and only share it on a need-to-know basis with Chester and Arnie," she replied.

"Let me start at the beginning then," said Rob. "About eighteen months ago I received a call from the legal department and was told to assign all the cases I was then working on to my staff. I was to only prepare to deal with one new large five-million-dollar claim on a life policy. This was going to be the largest case I had ever worked on, and I was excited for the opportunity. It was an unusual claim in that the covered party, French, had not actually died. To clarify, a body had never been located to confirm his actual death. At that point, he had been missing for about four or five years. Upon his disappearance, Riggs, as his personal attorney and conservator of his estate, was going to court to have French declared dead in order for the family to collect on the insurance policy written by Western General and receive the rest of his estate assets."

"I thought you had to be gone for at least seven years before it is assumed that you are actually dead," interrupted Erika.

"Yes, that is the general rule of law, but there are exceptions to everything. The court did not act on the petition, but they did not reject it either. Riggs was given some leeway to provide the basis for his petition to be granted."

"So the judge gave this guy Riggs time to prove he was really dead?" asked Erika.

"Yes. Judge Slider was one of those small town, I feel your pain type of judges and he kept the door open for Riggs to present additional support for his request to have French declared legally deceased."

"So what did he dig up that was so compelling to make Judge Slider willing to find that French was most likely dead?" asked Erika.

"It was a mishmash of personal testimony from French's former girlfriend, his parents, and Riggs himself that recounted how French had always kept in contact with his friends and family. His failure to contact anyone during the five years since his disappearance could only point to one thing, that French was likely dead."

"So just these people saying that he must be dead because they had not heard from him was all it took?"

"That and a sob story about French's parents being ill and about to be kicked off the Cuyama ranch they were living on and needing to be able to sell the ranch, which was in foreclosure," he replied.

"So this guy was a rancher in Cuyama?" asked Erika.

"French was an enigma," answered Rob. "I looked at all the court filings and did my own independent research and came up with many trails to nowhere. Each time I found a lead or someone to talk to about him I became more and more convinced that he was not dead and was living below the radar in a foreign country. I found some information after the case had been closed and French had been declared deceased. But I was never able to tie up all the loose ends in time to have the court reject Riggs's petition to distribute the estate. He was found to be deceased and Western General paid the claim plus five years of interest on the funds. It was well over five million dollars by the time they totaled it all up."

Erika pursed her lips and made a low whistle. "That's quite a payday for someone."

"Yup, I knew in my heart that the claim was bogus and that Western General should not have had to pay it but I was unable to provide the facts to the court in time. The judge ruled in favor of the petitioner based on testimony and the sob story from the parents and we wrote the big check."

"So you did more work after the end of the trial?" asked Erika.

"Yes, I was so convinced that French might still be alive that I continued to review the estate filings once Riggs had opened the probate for French's will. I found that much of the financial data for the estate was in conflict with how French presented himself to the world. In fact, this case led to a major shift in how Western General Insurance would underwrite large life insurance policies from that point on. It used to be pretty easy for a life insurance agent to bind a large policy like the one written on French. All you needed to do was have a physical to verify the customer did not have any major health problems, get the premium check from them, and you were done. Nowadays, you need to do quite a bit more in investigating the financial and business reasons for the policy and the requested amount of coverage."

"Do you mean that the insurance policy was bogus?" she asked.

"The policy was valid. Just the underwriting was sloppy. If someone had looked into French's finances a little more, like they are required to do now, the company would not have issued the policy and saved themselves the large claim. But a lot of that I found out after he was found to be deceased and Western General did not want to reopen the case. I guess they were embarrassed that they had not done a good job on the front end and wanted to move on."

"So what does all of this have to do with the map we found in the van that this guy Rick French used to own? And why are people so interested in getting the van from us?" she asked.

"I don't really know, but if my suspicions are correct, it all ties into my theory that French is still alive and that he still has access to funds that permitted him to drop out of society in this country and start a new life elsewhere. My theory has been that he went to Australia, somehow has access to money, and is living the life of Riley offshore somewhere."

"So why would a successful rancher type want to drop out from society and disappear? It doesn't make sense that someone would scheme up something like this with all the risks of getting caught. How did you come up with the conclusion of him living in Australia? Couldn't you have just gone down there, asked around, and located him and then told the court that he was still alive?"

"I guess I should give you a clearer picture of how things developed on this case," Rob replied. "When I was assigned to the case by Western General, I was given the petition Riggs filed with the court. The substance of his case was that French had been visiting in Tiburon and had gone missing. The first thing I did was to follow up on the missing persons report that had been filed by his then girlfriend, Mary Hurley. The sheriff's office in Mendocino County had a report of finding his van abandoned on the side of the road up in the forest and they found out that he had had a motel room in town and the motel reported that he had never checked out of his room. The report also had notes about a drug informant who had provided information to the DEA that French was in town to meet up with a known drug dealer named Jack Morrison. Jack operated out of a paint and body shop in Tiburon and both of them were under surveillance at the time."

"Surveillance," Erika repeated. "I guess French was a rancher of a different sort."

"I'll come to that later. You can see from my initial contact with law enforcement that my suspicions were aroused. The sheriff's office had also had calls from French's family members who were concerned about French's whereabouts. One of them was a sergeant with the Long Beach police department who was a brother-in-law of French's. No one ever found out what happened to him up there and his van was towed to the impound yard where, I guess, it was finally sold to you guys once the estate was closed."

"The drug thing must have made you think that not all was right with the world, right?" she asked.

"Western General is an A-rated company with the rating agencies and not accustomed to writing polices for people in the drug trade. Five years is a long time and usually a body surfaces in the mountains some-where that is eventually tied to the missing person by dental records or DNA. That never happened and some of the circumstances that happened about the same time as his disappearance led me quite a way down the road to what I suspect happened to French," he replied.

"Sounds like you spent a lot of time on your investigation," said Erika. "If you thought so strongly that the insurance policy was improper, what did you find out? Why were you not able to get the judge to toss out the case and let the insurance company off of the hook?"

"I was able to gather a certain amount of circumstantial information that I thought would lead me to French still being alive, but I was never able to connect the dots. The first thing I discovered was that on the night of the supposed disappearance of Rick French, a plane he owned crashed in the Everglades. No one was found at the scene, but the plane was loaded with hashish. The DEA had been tailing the plane based on a tip they received from an informant in Colombia."

"So the jojoba farmer French was really dealing in a different kind of crop," said Erika.

"Yes, I put two and two together based on the plane crash and the law enforcement missing persons report on French and his purported meeting with the guy they referred to as Jackson and came to the conclusion that French might have had different reasons for his need for a life insurance policy. My research indicated he had never been married and had no children so the need for such a large policy was always the big question."

"But you must have had some hard evidence to make you think that French was still alive. How would he be able to get the money if he was no longer in the country? Who actually got the insurance money? You must have found a pretty good trail on what happened to still believe that French is still alive today," pursued Erika.

"While the case was still open before the court, I did what I always did. I located people who knew Rick French and asked them about his lifestyle and what they suspected had happened to him. Most of the people were shocked that he disappeared but a couple of people also made me believe that he might still be alive and hiding somewhere."

Erika leaned back in her chair and took a drink from her water glass. The waiter approached and took their lunch orders.

"So what did these two people tell you that made you think he might still be alive?" she asked.

"The first matter dealt with the then soon to be ex-wife of John Riggs."

"You mean the John Riggs that has been trying to buy back our van!" exclaimed Erika.

"Yes. I learned that he and his wife were in the middle of an ugly divorce. I posed as a private detective and contacted her about her divorce and shared information I had on her husband that might help her in getting a better financial settlement in the divorce. We got chummy over the phone and I casually mentioned French's disappearance and how sad that had been. Angry wives many times will say things they would not ordinarily say if they were not under the stress of a divorce. She let it slip that the French situation was a dirty deal. As I recall, her exact words were 'all we got was $500,000 out of the deal.'

"I came to the thesis that French had taken out a large insurance policy, had faked his death, and had arranged for this guy Riggs to launder the money through his estate and somehow French would be able to get access to the funds later."

"So who was the other person and what did they say about French dropping off the face of the earth?" asked Erika.

"I talked to everyone who knew French and they all thought he had been killed in a dispute with one of his business partners. Some of them alluded to his drug connections but most just characterized him as someone who marched to his own beat and who made his living in nontraditional ways. There was one person who had dated him just shortly before his disappearance though, who stated emphatically that he was not dead but instead was living in Australia at a place known as Surfers Paradise."

"So, what made you think this person was not a crackpot?" asked Erika.

"Well, I had the statement from Riggs's wife, which I took to be significant. This other gal, Heather Houseman, had not known French very long and was not as emotionally tied to him as some of his longer-term friends. She stated to me that she had met him at a bar, Chanticlair, I believe, and had drinks with him and had taken him home after a walk on the beach. She had formed some kind of personal connection with him such that he had spoken to her in depth about his plans to leave the country and move to

Australia, leaving his life in the States behind him. They had spoken several times after that but had not spent any more significant time together. I was the first person to talk to her about Rick, and she had not heard that he had gone missing. She was firm in her belief that he had simply dropped out of the local scene and relocated to Australia. It was her assessment and the statement from Mrs. Riggs that made me dig deeper into his background and contact the informant in Mendocino County who had provided the intel to the sheriff's office regarding the pending drug deal between French and this guy Jack Morrison, the one they referred to as Jackson."

"So you called the informant up and asked him what he knew?" she asked.

"No, it is not as simple as that. This guy was actually located in Los Angeles. He was a convicted felon with connections to the drug trade and had worked out a deal for an early release in exchange for relaying information he came across on drug cases and pending shipments to this country from Colombia. You don't just call these kinds of guys up on the phone and ask them what they know. I was given his address by the local PD in Los Angeles, using some connections I have with a local investigator down there. I called in a couple of favors and showed up, armed, on his doorstep, and grilled the guy with a detective from the PD there along with me. The guy was scared silly and did not want to give me anything. The local detective started to press on him pretty hard and he finally told us that French was most likely living in Surfers Paradise in Australia, but we should not even consider going down there."

"Was he just trying to hold you off, scare you so you would not go down there and blow his cover by finding French?" she asked.

"Actually, he probably saved my life. He gave me some bullshit story about a group called the Cut Toe Gang and how they were real bad asses. He told us that a group of expat surfers and former drug dealers were all located down there, and they all looked out for each other. They had a business using the acronym CTG, which was a front for illegal activities and provided protection for its members. Anyone who showed up and started asking questions about people in the group was discouraged from further activity and urged to quickly leave the country."

"How were they able to protect themselves? They must have been pretty convincing to be able to pull this off," she replied.

"I naively had one of our contacts down there try to track him down. He disappeared shortly thereafter and I receive a small package in the mail with his big toe and a note telling me I would be next if I continued my search. I checked with law enforcement down there and found out the Cut Toe Gang was in fact the real deal. They advised me that the rumor was that any outsider who tried to investigate any of the group was later found dead and missing one of their big toes. I think they suspected that hoof trimmers, the ones used by horseshoers to trim horses' hooves, were used to lop off the toe. They would then kill the guy after he told them who he had been working for and consequently would send the toe as a message."

"Yikes!" exclaimed Erika. "That would stop me from trying to find French."

"Yes, it seemed to work pretty well. When you are dealing with an ex-wife or former business partner and the like, any dollar remuneration you think you might be able to get by finding one of these expats pales in comparison to being tortured by getting your toe cut off and then being killed."

Erika sat silently, letting the full weight of the information that Rob Hipner had relayed to her sink in. The excitement surrounding the mystery of the map had been dampened by the mental image of a severed toe and the terror associated with that circumstance. She flexed her toes instinctively, finding reassurance that all of her appendages were intact. Erika was not a quitter, but the recollections of Hipner were sobering and enough to make her rethink delving further into her search for the purpose and importance of the map.

"Well, Rob, if you found it wise to stop your investigation and recommend the company pay the claim, I guess I would be smart to cut my losses and just burn that old map so it does not cause us any further problems."

"I would say that that might be a smart move on your part right about now," he replied. "There are very few things that still keep me up at night. But the Rick French disappearance is one of them. I am always looking over my shoulder in case someone involved in the alleged scheme wants to take me out and close one of the few remaining trails to that scheme that still exists. I have often thought about working out a deal with Western General to take over their rights to any proceeds that might be forthcoming if Rick French was indeed found alive with all of his millions still intact, but I could never find a partner in Australia who was willing to take on the groundwork down there."

"So what would be my next step?" she asked as they finished their lunch and prepared to leave.

"You might go over the probate file again and review all of the financial filings and see if you agree with me that the insurance policy was purchased for a purpose not supported by the facts surrounding French. If you come to the same conclusion, you might then want to talk to the family and friends of the decedent. Perhaps after this passage of time one of them might be willing to talk. If they think that you have some official capacity and they might be subject to an investigation, who knows who might be willing to spill the beans," he replied.

CHAPTER TWENTY-ONE

THE CRUNCHING OF TIRES ON THE GRAVEL DRIVEWAY CAUSED
Terry Korman to look up from his noontime meal. Mego woke from her
slumber beneath the wooden steps leading up to the porch and ran to
the chain-link fence that surrounded the yard, barking furiously at the
intruder. As Terry opened the front door and peered through the rusty
web of the screen door, he saw Isadore Rodriquez exiting his patrol car and
reaching inside for his hat and a notebook.

"Morning, Izzy," Terry called out. "What brings you all the way out
here on such a fine day?"

Isadore was a periodic visitor to the Wasiola Canyon Ranch, especially once deer season opened in the early fall, or later, when the valley
was flooded with hunters partaking in the annual quail hunt. The pastures
and springs on the ranch provided plenty of feed and water for the local
wildlife, and Terry had enlisted a local farmer to plant an annual grain crop
to attract both deer and birds. In exchange for having a law enforcement
presence during the year, Terry was more than happy to let Isadore or one
of his deputies fill a deer tag or take a limit of quail. The police presence
kept out the riffraff from town and discouraged the townies who liked to

drive over from the coast in their four-wheel-drive trucks and take pot-shots at water tanks on the ranch.

"Well, I have some bad news to deliver about your old mentor Emory Callaway," replied Isadore. "He died in a trailer fire last night, and I thought you would like to know about it."

"Trailer fire?" exclaimed Terry. "What was he doing, smoking in bed after a bender at the Buckhorn?"

"We haven't received the coroner's report yet. But there was a car outside of his trailer and another body in the yard. We are trying to piece together what happened while we wait for the labs to come back."

"Yikes," said Terry. Dead guy in the yard, burned-up car, and Emory burned up in his home. "Sounds like something fishy went on over there."

"At this point we just don't know. The path of the fire went between the car and the house. Nothing else was burned. You knew Emory pretty well, didn't you? I just want to see what people know about his last few days. You know, was he depressed, acting unusual, stuff like that."

"I had lunch with him just yesterday," replied Terry. "That guy John Riggs, who has been handling the ranch for the French family, came out like he does every once in a while, and we all got together to talk about the ranch and how Emory was doing these days."

"Riggs, huh?" replied Isadore. He had an inherent distrust of lawyers, common to law enforcement, and had never had a good feeling about John Riggs. It had been suspicioned in the law enforcement community that Riggs's former client, the missing Rick French, had been involved in less than legal business activities. Car lights out on his ranch at all hours of the evening and an occasional nighttime landing of his small plane on the dirt runway on the adjacent Rummell ranch were activities not common to the Cuyama Valley. They drew suspicion from Isadore, and he had informed his commander of these activities. County budgets being what they were, however, no funds existed for further surveillance in that rural community.

"How was the old guy when you last saw him?" asked Isadore.

"Pretty much the same old Emory. You know, still full of horse shit and gun smoke. He seemed to have aged a lot recently though. I got the feeling he might not be around much longer, all stove-up and with emphysema, you know."

"Okay, just checking. Did he say anything unusual over lunch, like he was expecting a visitor, something like that?"

Terry maintained his poker face as best he could. "No, nothing out of the ordinary. He had a good lunch and a couple of drinks, and then we dropped him off at his trailer. He was in good spirits when we left him. Whose car got burned up? Was it that old sedan he had out front that had not run in years? Maybe the old guy tried to start it up, and something started to smolder in the wiring and set things off later that night."

"Maybe," replied Isadore. He sensed that he might not be getting the full story from Terry. Terry seemed more animated than usual. Too eager to proffer ideas on how the fire might have happened the previous evening. He could see beads of sweat beginning to emerge on Terry's forehead. "Well, that about does it, I guess. Just wanted to see if you might know something that would shed some light on the fire." He made a few notes in his notebook and returned to his vehicle. "There was that body in the yard. Burned up. It would be strange for a car to catch on fire, have the driver burn up in the fire, and then have the fire burn over to the house and get to Emory without anyone noticing what was going on."

"Yeah, that is pretty strange," replied Terry. He wanted Isadore to leave in the worst way. Surely it was no coincidence that Riggs had wanted to have lunch with him and Emory and that now his aged cowboy mentor and nemesis was dead. Something had been set in motion, and he had the fear that he was being dragged into something that he was not prepared to deal with. He needed to find out what it was so he could get ready to protect himself.

"Well, if you think of anything further, if you remember something, please give me a call," Isadore said. He handed Terry his business card and returned to his patrol car. Terry looked at the business card, which sported the official seal of the county of Santa Bonita and an image of a sheriff's badge. Dust wafted up behind the black-and-white patrol car as Isadore drove back toward the highway. The vehicle faded into the cloud of dust and disappeared from sight.

Mego trotted over to Terry, who sat down on the front porch in silence, gazing at the business card. She whined at him for attention and he absently stroked her neck, deep in thought. Reaching into his pants pocket, he retrieved his cell phone and dialed the number for John Riggs's personal cell phone. He spoke bluntly when the call picked up. "We need to talk. Emory died last night under suspicious circumstances. I just got a visit from the sheriff. I have your maps for you but you need to be square with me about what you are up to."

"Emory is dead?" exclaimed the voice on the other end of the line. "How?"

"Burned up in a fire in his trailer. They found another body outside his trailer near a burned-up car. The sheriff is waiting for more information from the coroner."

"Meet me here Monday at one o'clock. Bring your maps and we can go over all of this then."

Terry arrived just before one o'clock Monday and found the office locked. Riggs and Manita usually closed the office down for lunch every day. That practice was announced to the public in the out of office voice-mail message. Terry fidgeted anxiously outside the office door as he waited for Riggs to return. He had a single problem to deal with and was energized to get to the bottom of it as soon as possible.

At ten minutes after the hour, Riggs and Manita returned from their noon lunch break and sauntered up the stairs. Riggs was a man with many problems to deal with and numerous deadlines. He was practiced in prioritizing numerous client crises and had been unaffected by Terry's emotionally charged demand for a meeting. His favorite phrase, which he often shared with excited clients, was "Wait to worry."

The pair greeted Terry and opened the office door, directing him to the conference room next to the waiting area. "Have a seat, Terry," offered Riggs.

"Would you like a water?" asked Manita

"No, I'm fine," replied Terry.

"We'll need just a few more minutes. I have asked Craig Casebeer to attend the meeting as well and shed some light on some of the happenings of late concerning the French estate and some of the estate property." Terry knew of the Casebeer Detective Agency.

A few minutes later, Craig entered the office and Manita showed him to the conference room. He and Riggs exchanged greetings, and Riggs introduced Terry. "Terry is handling the management of a ranch in Cuyama for one of my deceased clients. I asked him here today so we could discuss what you have found out from your surveillance work in Cuyama and how it might tie in with a recent event there."

"Terry, how about going first and telling us what you know about the death Friday night of Emory Calloway?" Riggs asked. He turned to Craig and added, "Emory was the former manager of the Wasiola ranch that Terry handles for the French estate. We had lunch with him on Friday and he may have died under suspicious circumstances."

Terry turned to face Craig. "All I know is that John asked me to get maps of the ranch and the surrounding properties from the Department of Oil and Gas. We took these with us when we had lunch with Emory, and John asked him about the maps and old oil wells and wanted to know if Emory knew about some of the wells being used to hide things. The old guy said he was clueless but John did not believe him. We all went home. The next day, I learned Emory had died in a fire in his trailer that night."

Craig stroked his chin. "That may all be just coincidence. Was Emory a smoker? He might have just fallen asleep in bed and been overcome by the smoke before he could get out of there. Happens all the time. What about the dead guy they found in the yard outside though? He was burned up too. The fire trail led from the house to the car."

"Let's not go jumping to conclusions," interjected Riggs. "It is quite possible that the guy in the car was passed out from a night at the Buckhorn and was in the wrong place at the wrong time when Emory's trailer went up in smoke. Don't you think?" From the quick glance he gave Craig, Craig surmised there was more to the story than Riggs was letting on.

Craig took the lead from Riggs. "Yes, let's not go jumping to conclusions. Unlikely but still possible. Stranger things have happened. Now, tell me more about the maps of the ranch that showed old oil fields and wells. What might the maps have to do with these deaths and the French estate? French is the guy who used to own the van whose new owners I'm tailing, right?"

"What van?" asked Terry.

"What I am about to tell you is confidential and cannot be shared outside of this room," replied Riggs. "Remember the van that Rick French used to drive when we would all go surfing at the Alistair Ranch? When Rick came up missing, they found the van parked up in the forest near Tiburon and determined he had checked into a motel but never checked out. The van was taken to the local impound yard. I was unable to retrieve it since French was missing. I was able to get an order directing them to keep it until such time as Rick turned up again, or was declared legally deceased. They would not release it to me but agreed to hold it from the impound sale until the court finally determined that Rick was officially dead. I was aware that Rick had kept some important papers in the van but I was unable to buy it at the auction sale last month when it finally came up to be sold."

"The van was purchased by a couple of guys who are trying to restore it," Craig took up. "John has tried to buy it from them with no success. Unfortunately, the papers were found in the van that consist of maps similar to the ones you acquired from the DOG for John. They are of no value to anyone except French and now his estate, but one of the buyers' girlfriend has been looking into the maps and why they were hidden in the van. The ranch, the van, and the maps are all linked to something of financial importance for the French estate, but what we really needed to find out from Emory was what the maps' purpose was and how he and Rick used them in order to store items of financial importance to Rick."

"Craig, what has the girl been up to since you found her researching court records on Rick's disappearance?" Riggs asked.

"She has looked at the files on your petition to become conservator as well as all the files on your petition to have Rick declared deceased. She also made a trip over to Bakersfield to find out more about the oil field maps. More problematic than that is her recent meeting with the retired insurance adjuster who was battling you on your petition to force payment on the life insurance policy taken out on Rick. We observed her having a meeting with him recently, no doubt to discuss the case. I am sure he relayed all of his findings and suspicions to her. She strikes me as someone who will not let this drop. I am willing to bet her next trip to the records hall will be to review the estate file for more information."

Riggs wrinkled his brow with concern. "Traveling to the DOG office in Bakersfield wouldn't get her close to anything important, but I am a little concerned that she is looking at the court files relative to the petition to declare him deceased. If she looks at the probate files she might become even more suspicious, but it is unlikely that she will be able to connect any of the dots between the financial affairs of the estate and that map."

"But if she and her friends have the map, who knows what she has learned from it?" replied Craig.

"So what is so important about this map?" interrupted Terry. "Did Rick bury things on the ranch he did not want anyone else to know about?"

"The less you know about the map the better," answered Riggs. "That goes for you as well, Craig. Both of you are currently on a need-to-know basis. I have some attorney-client privileged information that should never see the light of day unless absolutely necessary. What I would like to know, though, Terry, is if you ever noticed Emory acting funny during the time you dealt with him on the ranch? Did he ever do anything you found strange? Ever observe him nosing around the place after hours or on week-ends? He was playing dumb about the map. I think he knows more than what he was letting on."

Terry was silent for a moment. "I remember one time about a year or so ago. I was out driving a gal around the valley in the evening and came upon Emory on horseback out in the abandoned area around the old gas plant on the Rummell ranch."

"Saw him at night on horseback? What was that all about?" asked Riggs.

"Yeah, I had had a few drinks with a gal at the Buckhorn and had taken her out onto some of the back roads in the valley to look for jackalopes."

"Jackalopes?" injected Craig. "That proverbial fabrication of the mythical animal resulting from the union of a jack rabbit and an antelope."

"Yeah, there is one hanging on the wall over the bar at the Buckhorn," continued Terry. "It is the front of a jack rabbit with horns attached from an antelope. Tourists are pretty gullible and I had this gal convinced we could spot one if we drove out of town into the rangeland."

"I don't care about your nighttime romance with some tourist out on the range. What was Emory up to? What did you observe?" grilled Craig.

"We came over a rise down into the area where the old gas plant buildings are located, and he had his horse tied to one of the oil wells out there and was huddled over the well with a long rope. Looked like he was fishing for something in the well."

"What did he do when you discovered him?"

"He was startled as hell. It was a moonless night and the sound of the truck must have been muffled by the hills as we drove up. I had the headlights off to make things kind of scary for this gal. When we came up over the rise, Emory looked like he was going to have a heart attack."

"What did he say he was doing out there?" asked Riggs.

"He told me he was schooling a new colt and was getting her used to being out at night. He said he was breaking her to be ground tied and was tying her up to the old well to get her used to standing still in one place when he got on and off her. At the time, I thought nothing of it. But now with him dead and you guys being interested in the old oil field, there might be more to this than I first thought."

"It's unusual but believable," answered Craig. "If a cowboy is training a new horse, they put them into all kinds of situations that they might come across, such as night riding or being ground tied."

"Is that all you recall out of the ordinary?" asked Riggs.

"You know, there is one other thing I thought was strange. One time when we were in the bar and Emory was pretty drunk, he got into a big argument with the bartender over how he was going to pay for his drinks. Seemed that he did not have enough cash, so he reached into his pocket and dragged out a small gold coin that he said was pure gold and worth a thousand bucks or more."

"Gold coin?" repeated Riggs.

"Yeah, you know, the kind you see advertised for sale in magazines. It looked just like one of those old Indian head nickels with the buffalo on the back except it was a little bigger and made out of gold."

Riggs's jaw tightened and he looked ever so much like someone trying to pass a kidney stone. He saw Craig's eyes flicker for an instant.

"Okay," Riggs continued. "Doesn't seem like much to be concerned about. Just an old cowboy breaking a horse and probably using one of the only things of value he had besides his truck and saddle to buy a drink."

"But Emory is dead and the house fire looks like a messy deal," replied Terry. "I know strange stuff happens out here but come on! We see him the day before, asking about the map, he dies in a trailer fire that night, and all at the time you're working on some secret project for the estate involving the map. Riggs, you need to come clean and come clean right now. I don't want to be involved in something underhanded or have to be looking under my car for a bomb."

"Settle down, cowboy," soothed Riggs. "We both know how Rick got his money and it was not all from his farm. There are a couple of loose ends I need to tie up for the estate, but you are not involved in any of them. You don't need to worry. Just keep overseeing the ranch for me for a little while longer. Once the estate is ready to close, we can sell the ranch and then you are off the hook."

Terry left the meeting feeling better about things and began the long drive back to the ranch. Riggs and Craig were left alone in the room. After a long pause, Craig opened his notebook and asked, "What would you like for us to do next, John?"

"I am curious how much farther this girl Erika will look into the French estate files. Keep surveillance on her and report to me what she is doing in this endeavor. If she starts to dive into the estate filings, I want to know."

"Fine," replied Craig. "I will provide weekly reports unless something surfaces that looks like it might be of importance. By the way, here is my bill for services to date."

"The estate is illiquid presently," replied Riggs. "You will of course wait until I can get the ranch sold and the estate closed?"

"I am not a bank, John" replied Craig. "Payment is due in thirty days. If you are cash constrained, I suggest you get a credit line from your bank."

Craig could see that there was more to the French estate and the missing map than met the eye. It was not his custom to pry or dig further into details surrounding an assignment. Sometimes less is more and he was not in the habit of digging into details that were not part of an investigation assignment. He also knew that sometimes things went south and the best way to protect his interest was to ask for prompt payment for his services.

John Riggs stared at the bill for a moment and placed his hands before him, fingertips touching, making a triangle. "Wait here a moment," he said, rising from his chair. He left the conference room and entered the file room at the rear of the office suite. Craig could hear Riggs turning the dial on what sounded like an office safe. He heard the lock click open and the opening and closing of a door. Riggs returned to the room with an oil-stained sack and plopped the container down on the conference room table. "I can pay you now in gold coin or in a week after I convert some of this inventory over to cash. Which do you prefer?"

"Gold coins, let me see what you have," replied Craig. Riggs reached into the leather pouch and pulled out three small gold coins. Stamped with the familiar images of the well-known buffalo nickel, they were bigger than a nickel but smaller than a quarter. They had the dull shine of gold that has been circulated and touched by human hands. "How do I know these are real?" asked Craig. He reached over and picked one of the coins up, feeling its weight. Pulling out a pocketknife from his pants pocket, he touched the point of his knife to the surface of the coin to test its hardness.

"Oh, they are the real thing," replied Riggs. "Give me a week to get some of these sold or you can take three of them now to settle the bill. Each coin is one ounce of 99 percent pure twenty-four-carat gold, worth about twelve hundred bucks each in today's market. You can wait for the cash but you might consider taking payment in kind. In never hurts to have some non-traceable gold for an emergency."

"Where do these coins come from?" asked Craig.

"Let's just say my client did not totally trust the banking system in this country and directed me to hold some of his wealth in precious metals," replied Riggs.

"Are these coins from the same source as the one Terry talked about seeing Emory with at the bar?" asked Craig.

"I suspect so," replied Riggs.

Craig grunted, looked at Riggs for a moment, and then stacked the three coins and placed them into his coat pocket. "Payment in kind will be fine," he said. "Expect my next report in a week." The meeting quickly ended, Riggs returning to the safe to deposit the bag, and Craig driving back to his office to give directions on further assignments for this case to his staff of investigators.

CHAPTER TWENTY-TWO

THE 1600-CC ENGINE ROARED TO LIFE, BELCHING FUEL-RICH blue smoke, as Chester worked the ignition key in the van and Arnie fed fuel from a small gas can into the carburetor. Given that the van had five years of sitting idle in the impound yard, the pair had been concerned that the pistons might have frozen in the engine bores and that the walls might have become scored. They had decided to pull the spark plugs and liberally spray each cylinder with WD-40 to help unlock the engine in the event that any of the pistons had become frozen in place. Each day while they were working on brakes and electrical systems, they had lubricated each cylinder. After the passage of a week's time, they had taken the van off of the jack stands and gently rocked the vehicle back and forth, leaving the transmission in gear. At last, the weight of the van had helped to free the stuck pistons and the pair were able to verify that the engine now turned freely when manually turned by a wrench on the end of the crankshaft.

All that had been left to do was fire the engine up and see if it still ran on all four cylinders. They had drained the remaining five-year-old fuel from the tank and had blown out the fuel lines to remove any lingering gunk that might impede the flow of new fuel into the engine. Instead of priming the fuel system, Chester had chosen to simply pour fuel down the throat of the carburetor to get the engine started. The fuel pump would start to do its thing once the engine was running and they would be able to find out quickly if they had an operating power plant.

At first the engine fired up, sputtered, and then died. Elation was followed by frustration. "Let's try it again," said Chester. Arnie poured another shot of fuel into the carburetor and held the choke closed as Chester tried to start the engine again.

Putt . . . putt . . . putt . . . putt noises again sounded as the engine caught, cleared the excess fuel, and then roared to life, free of smoke as the fresh fuel began to flow through the system. Arnie manually worked the throttle and revved the engine to a high idle and held it there for a few minutes, returning it to an idle as it came up to operating temperature.

"She purrs like a cat!" exclaimed Chester as he came to the rear of the van to listen to the engine.

"Yup, she sounds pretty tight," replied Arnie. "Whoever used to own this van must have done a recent rebuild. That valve chatter will even out once she gets hot. All eighty-five of those ponies are running now!"

"Well, the brakes work and she is now road worthy. I say we take her out tonight with Erika for her maiden voyage."

"That's a plan, Stan," replied Arnie. They had a week of work into the van and had now gone over all of the operating systems. It had been completely rewired, brakes had been replaced, and it sported a new set of whitewall tires on all four rims. All that was left was a redo of the interior and to give the van a new paint job. In her present condition, she was road safe and able to be used as a daily driver until the finishing touches to the restoration could be completed.

That evening when Erika returned home from work, she was greeted by the duo and quickly escorted over to the van for a ride downtown for an early evening dinner. The van was only slightly more sanitary than when they had first brought it home. All the trash and detritus of the years of being stored had been removed from the interior and the exterior had been washed to remove the years of grime, dust, and mold that had formed a patina on the van. Erika had a clean Mexican sarape to sit on, which had been thrown over the front passenger seat, and the van had aired out sufficiently so that only a lingering trace of the former mustiness could be detected. A mid-workweek dinner out was a welcome surprise for Erika and she did not complain about the condition of the van's interior as they sped off for the surprise celebration.

They arrived at their favorite Mexican restaurant, Tres Arroyos, and Chester let them off in front of the eatery so he could search for a parking place in the city lot across the street. There were three sets of eyes on the van as Chester paused for his parking lot stub from the automated parking machine. He located a parking spot close to the street. One observer of the van quickly walked up to Chester as he was locking the door and began to comment on the van and how rare it was. "What is it, a '70?" the guy asked as he looked the van over.

"Nope, she's a '71," replied Chester as he locked the door and proceeded to the restaurant. He was in a hurry and not interested in walking down memory lane with a stranger to hear all about how the guy used to own one just like his when he was in college. "She's a beauty," the guy called back to him as he walked across the street to Tres Arroyos. "Thanks," Chester replied. He ignored the question that followed about if the van was for sale and entered the restaurant as if he had not heard the guy.

Following close behind Chester into the parking lot was a nondescript dark-colored sedan driven by a second observer. The driver of the car circled the lot several times and chose a parking spot that provided a good view of both the van and the front door to the restaurant. The driver of the car remained in his vehicle, pulled out a notebook, and made a notation about the time of day and where the trio had gone for dinner.

The third set of eyes were those of a tall swarthy bearded man with silver rings on his fingers who just happened to be drinking a beer down the block at Mel's Bar. Jack Morrison had been killing time in Santa Bonita waiting for further information to develop from Rick French as to when he could expect to receive payment on the long overdue sum owed to him by French. He had been surprised to see the familiar van turning the corner and entering the parking lot. There were hundreds of the green two-tone vans still running in California, but he had recognized the telltale flower power decal on the bumper and the Yater Surfboards sticker in the rear window. He had seen the van many times at the Alistair ranch during his surfing days and several times when he had conducted business with Rick French in various purchases of hashish and marijuana. He noted the trio of people who were riding in the van. Snuffing out a cigarette, he paid his bar tab and walked over to Tres Arroyos and sat down at a table within hearing distance of the table where Chester, Arnie, and Erika were seated.

"She is one sweet ride, isn't she," chortled Chester as they waited for their dinner orders to arrive.

"Yes, I admit, the van runs well. But what is with all that pumping on the brake pedal when you try to stop?" Erika asked.

"We just need to bleed the rest of the air out of the brake lines," answered Arnie. "We did the best we could while she was up on blocks but once we hook up a power bleeder to the brake lines, she will tighten right up and be stopping on a dime."

"So now that you have it road safe and running, have you thought about calling up that guy who wants to buy it from you?" Erika asked.

"Nope," replied Chester. "I have ordered all new interior upholstery and after that all she needs is a paint job. We can get twenty grand for her once she is all restored. If I paint her myself, we will have a ten grand profit in her, easy. Besides, that guy Riggs who left us his card is kind of pushy. I got a bad vibe from him. When she is ready to sell, I will give him a shot though."

"Something tells me he might just be your best buyer, even with the van not fully restored," Erika answered. "I found some pretty confusing facts today when I looked over the probate files down at the county courthouse."

"Confusing, how so?" replied Chester.

"Remember the insurance guy, Rob Hipner, I had lunch with the other day?"

"The guy who handled the insurance claim?" asked Arnie.

"He thought the claim was bogus but could never put his finger on how to track down French and prove he was still alive. It was an insurance policy for five million dollars. He said this was an unusually large sum and he could find no evidence in the probate records to justify this guy French having that amount of coverage."

"So what did you find in the court file?" asked Chester.

"It seems that this guy French owned a house in Santa Bonita, a surfing parcel interest at the Alistair ranch and a ranch in Wasiola Canyon in Cuyama. He had bought the house from a convicted drug dealer who had been busted and needed to raise cash for bail. The surfing parcel and the ranch in Cuyama were heavily mortgaged and French had very little equity in them. The inventory for the estate lists a total of $294 in cash at three banks and a few cars, but no other listed assets. The only asset of any value is this five-million-dollar insurance policy with some accrued interest that Western General Life had been fighting payment over. They never found French so it became a valid claim and an asset of the estate."

"So why is that so confusing?" asked Arnie. "The guy goes missing, no one ever finds him or his body, so they look at the will, find out what he owned and just settle up his estate and fold their tent, right?"

"Yes," Erika replied, but why does a guy with only a couple of hundred dollars to his name and some real estate that is worth about what is owed on it go out and take out a five-million-dollar policy? The guy is not married and has no children. He only has a longtime girlfriend, his parents, who are retired, and five siblings. Who is he trying to provide for with this large insurance policy? If you only have a couple of hundred bucks to your name, how are you operating a jojoba farm paying monthly interest on all the land loans, and a paid in full for a life insurance policy that must have had a hefty premium"?

"It does not really add up unless this guy was off the grid and got his income from less than legal activities," answered Arnie.

"Did I forget to mention he took out his life insurance policy five years ago in January and went missing two months later?" asked Erika.

"So?" replied Chester. "What is the big deal? He was worried about dying and being able to have his debts paid off so he bought some insurance. People do that every day. Guilt for not providing for your loved ones is the tune salespeople use the most in selling insurance."

"Did I tell you about how he wrote his will only six months before he took out this life insurance? And that he named this guy Riggs as his executor and also gave him a durable power of attorney to act in all financial affairs for him? He had never had a will before that. I don't know. It all looks pretty fishy to me. According to the estate filings, he had not filed an income tax return for several years yet he had cash sources to make large payments on notes he gave when he bought some of his real estate. This guy used to own an airplane and had invested in a jojoba ranch. Money doesn't grow on trees. I looked up some old news reports on the Internet and it seems that the DEA had been looking at possible drug dealings in Cuyama in recent years and had suspected that product might be flown in from Mexico or Columbia. A plane loaded with drugs crashed in the jungle in the Everglades right about the time this guy French went missing."

Chester and Arnie sat quietly for a moment, letting the facts of Erika's recent file review sink in.

"So this guy French who used to own the van was a drug dealer and had to skip out of the county on short notice when a deal went bad?" proffered Arnie.

"And this guy had a lawyer on the payroll, maybe a judge too, to get himself declared dead so that he could collect on a big insurance policy," answered Erika. "Plus this guy Riggs starts using the power of attorney French signed just months after French goes missing to deal with some of his real estate and sells or trades some of them when the guy has only been missing a short while."

"That sounds like a guy who does not expect his client to turn up again any time soon," replied Arnie.

"Just to close the loop on all these sales and trades, Riggs also got the court to validate all those transactions while French was deemed missing during the period of estate administration. He specifically asked the court to find that all these transfers and trades were valid and proper under his POA."

"Why would he ask for that confirmation five years after the fact?" asked Chester.

"Remember when we bought our house with our reward money from the Terra Auri affair?" asked Erika. "We have a policy of title insurance that the bank required as part of our loan to ensure that the people selling us the house actually owned it and there were no other banks with loans against the property that would need to be paid off before our bank made the new loan to us so we could purchase the home. Maybe the title insurance company did Riggs a favor when he was selling and trading some of French's property under the power of attorney and had him clean up things once he was in a position to do so when they had French declared dead and opened up the estate."

"So tell me how a title insurance company guarantees that you own something if they have less than perfect documentation about a guy being missing and/or dead?" asked Arnie.

"Think back to the Terra Auri deal," replied Erika. "They had such an extensive relationship with several title companies who were all competing for their business that they were able to get them to write around some of the title issues on some of the problem transactions with the understanding that they would get them fixed when the opportunity arose down the road. That is what title insurance companies do, measure the risk, charge a title fee to take on the risk, and then wait for a claim against the policy later. It is no different than fire insurance or life insurance."

"This is all intriguing," replied Chester "but what does it have to do with that map we found hidden in the van?"

"This guy French must have had some financial resources to keep his lifestyle going with no apparent sources of income," replied Erika. "When you put the missing persons report together with the map and the markings we found, along with the strange things that went on in the estate, there is only one answer."

Chester and Arnie stared across the table at her, waiting.

"The oil wells that have those markings on them have something to do with what that map is all about. I don't want to jump to conclusions but hear me out on this. Suppose for a moment that this guy French is someone who used to make a living in the drug business. He lived off the financial system grid, had no traceable financial assets, owned a home in Santa Bonita, surfed at the ranch, and had his jojoba farm in a remote area of the county that served as a front for his drug dealing lifestyle. He was able to avoid the DEA for a while by ferrying his product to his ranch and things were going fine until the Feds caught on to his distribution system. French was no dummy. He saw how others in the drug trade were caught from time to time, and the drug trade is probably riddled with informants, snitches, and people willing to testify from prison in exchange for getting a lighter sentence. What if he had the forethought to hide his drug profits on his ranch and on some of the surrounding properties? Kind of an insurance policy against the day when he would need cash to flee the country on short notice or pay legal bills to fight charges if he was ever caught?"

"What good is a bunch of cash hidden in Cuyama to him if he drops off the face of the earth and hides somewhere offshore?" asked Arnie. "It's not like he can just take the time to drive out there with a shovel and go looking around for his stash."

"That is the beauty of his plan," replied Erika. "He does not simply bury his cash on his ranch. Instead, he chooses multiple locations that consist of old oil wells that are already in remote locations that no one is ever going to access for years, if ever again. He does not just use wells on his ranch. He uses other locations in the area on other property so that in the event anyone finds one of his locations, he still has plenty of other stashes that he can go to to get cash when he needs it."

"Okay, I follow you," replied Chester, "but if this French guy disappeared real fast and no one ever saw him again after the night of his disappearance, when that plane they tied to him crashed with all the drugs on board, when did he have the chance to drive seven hours back to his ranch to get to his hidden cash?"

"He probably had some arrangement with someone who he trusted to get his cash for him," she replied. "I don't know, maybe his attorney, or someone he knew in Cuyama. Maybe one of his siblings or his girlfriend. The part I think that is important is this insurance policy he had on his life that his attorney, John Riggs, worked so hard on to collect. French must have been a smart guy and covered all of his bases. He must have known that his number would be up sometime, and he might not be able to access all of his cash as soon as he needed it. He had to have partners in this arrangement. Money heals all problems, be it angry drug customers that got shorted on a drug transaction, corrupt judges who are willing to rule in his favor on petitions to get him declared dead before the customary seven-year period is up, or lawyers who are willing to participate in fraud and lie to the court about missing people they know are still alive and well. It's a bit of a stretch, I admit, but not out of the realm of reality," she said, tapping the tips of her fingers together while she let her wild theory settle on Chester and Arnie.

"Holy smokes," exclaimed Chester, "that is a lot of moving parts."

"You're right. The money is still there," Arnie said coldly. "That is why the guy tried to break into the van to get the map. That is why Riggs tried so hard to buy the van from us. Who goes to the trouble of tracking people down like he did to buy an old van like yours? The money is there, all right; all we have to do is go out there and dig it up."

"I bet we can find all of those marked wells without too much trouble," added Chester.

"I don't know," replied Erika. "This lost treasure map thing looks pretty dangerous to me. Drug dealers kill people all of the time, don't they? You guys watch those crime shows on TV like *Forty-Eight Hours* and *NCIS*. I don't think any amount of money is worth getting killed over."

"Let's step back a moment," replied Arnie. "Maybe the money is there and maybe it isn't. What is our fallback position if it is already gone?"

"It's still there, I just know it is," replied Chester, eager for an exciting treasure hunt expedition.

"Maybe it is but hear me out on this. Who else might have an ax to grind in this situation besides French and his attorney?"

"How about the guy the police referred to as Jackson in the missing person's report? You know, the DEA report said an informant told the local sheriff Jackson was supposed to meet up with French for a drug purchase," said Erika.

"Yes, that might be one player who would bump us off in a heartbeat if he was still involved and looking for the map," replied Chester.

"What about Western General Life Insurance?" said Arnie. "They must have been pissed off that they were defrauded on the policy and had to pay the five million bucks when the judge ruled French was dead. Would they not be someone we could align with to get some reward money if we could prove that French is still alive, you know, show how the deal was all set up with the lawyer, French, maybe the judge, and who knows who else in funneling the insurance money to French?"

"That could be a viable alternative, some reward money from the insurance company if we could pull this off," replied Erika. "Let me see if this guy Hipner knows someone at the insurance company I can talk to. Maybe we can pull off another Terra Auri–type deal and get a bigger reward."

"I'm pulling out the cape again," chortled Arnie. "I know I promised you guys to never use my transportive powers again when we pulled off the Terra Auri deal, but I bet no one is going to object if we can solve this case and expose some of these people for who they really are."

"Slow down, Arnie," replied Erika. "Let me feel out the insurance company first and see if they are willing to help us out financially if we are successful, maybe let us look at their old files for anything that might be useful. Let's pay the bill and get out of here."

At a table behind the trio, the sole occupant paid his bill in cash and left the restaurant. He walked behind the restaurant to the parking lot, entered a car, closed the door, and dialed a number on his cell phone. In Surfers Paradise, Rick French picked up the call on his cell phone.

"It's time to meet," the caller announced. French knew immediately who it was at the sound of the gravelly voice.

"The deal was we would never meet again. I said I would get you your money and things are in motion to get you paid. There is no reason for us to meet."

"Think again," came the reply. "There are three people who have found out about your hidden money and they have your maps of the locations. They have also looked at court files on your disappearance and your estate and may have partially closed the loop on what went down. As we speak they are planning to contact your old insurance company and negotiate getting a reward if they can prove you are still alive and conspired with others to defraud them."

"I know all about the people with the map and that one of them has been digging around. Perhaps they have been able to connect some of the dots but no one is ever going to believe their story without solid proof. They are not going to be able to prove anything about me still being alive. No one is going to talk. Everyone who is involved in my disappearance received cash for their part in my scheme and no one will risk going to jail by spilling the beans to these people. I have surveillance in place. If they start to get close to anything I will know about it and take the appropriate action then. Just sit tight."

"I have been sitting tight for five years while I waited for Riggs to get you declared dead, and more time for your estate to go through probate," came the reply. "Every pot has a lid and I am tired of waiting. This deal gets done in a week, or I am going to track you down and end it once and for all."

"Cool your jets, Jackson," replied Rich French. "You are getting paid regularly to wait. Another few weeks is not going to matter one way or the other."

"Okay," replied Jack, "but I am here on the ground now and watching everything that is going on. I will know just as much as your surveillance people. If you try to screw me you will end up floating face down in your favorite lineup for the sharks to chew on."

The call ended abruptly. French knew the stakes had risen but the end game result would still be the same. He would retrieve his cash hoard, pay off Jackson, and be able to finally close the loop on his financial scheme. No longer would he have to look over his shoulder for Jackson, insurance investigators, or law enforcement trying to tie him to old drug transactions or the like. He was not a run-of-the-mill participant in the drug trade. He did not personally indulge in the use of his products. He had carefully saved his money over the years and crafted an exit strategy he had already employed. He would close the loop on the only outstanding issue between him and his new identity, namely resolving the Jackson issue, and then resume his life of surfing and leisure.

CHAPTER TWENTY-THREE

KATE REILLY WAS PREPARING TO LEAVE HER OFFICE IN Carlsbad early in the afternoon when she received a call from the front desk. "There is someone here that would like to discuss one of our old insurance policies with you. She says she was referred to you by Rob Hipner." Kate was about to travel up the coast to Ojai to participate in a tennis tournament over the weekend. She had a level-four rating with the amateur tennis association and held the prospects of reaching the tournament finals. Trim and athletic, she exuded an air of physical fitness and conditioning required for her level of play in the tennis ranks. Ordinarily she would have refused the request for an unscheduled meeting, but Rob was one of her favorite investigators whom she had worked with on a variety of insurance claims during her tenure with Western General Life. Though he had retired the previous year, the two still kept in contact and had an occasional coffee.

"Send her in," she replied. In a moment, she was greeted by Erika, whom she invited into her office, offering her the chair in front of her desk. "So, you're a friend of Rob's?" she asked.

"Sort of. We just met the other day to discuss an old case he had investigated for you, and he recommended that I speak to you if I wanted to dig any further into the case."

"Rob's a great guy," replied Kate. "He would go the extra mile and put in the legwork necessary to be sure we only paid out on life policies that were appropriate under the terms of the policy."

"So is that your job, processing claims for people who had a policy and then died?" asked Erika.

"No, not exactly. I am part of the fraud unit. Most of the claims we get are pretty simple. People die of old age, disease, or an accident. The paper trail from the doctor, the coroner, and law enforcement is usually pretty clear cut. We close most of those claims in thirty days or less if the beneficiaries can find the policy. Many times, they cannot locate that document so those cases take a little longer to close. We want to be sure someone else does not surface later with the original policy and try to make another claim."

"So what do you remember about the policy the company wrote about five years ago for a Richard French who lived in Santa Bonita County?" asked Erika.

Kate's eyes narrowed as the memory of that case flashed before her. The details of the case quickly returned to her.

"Rob and I worked on that one for almost a year. We had good reason to suspect that the decedent was not at all dead. We suspected that he had concocted a scheme to disappear and collect the policy face amount with the help of a few well-positioned players. We had reason to believe he had gone underground and eventually surfaced in Australia. It appeared that he was being protected by a group connected with organized crime down there. We were never able to put the resources together that we needed to track him down."

"Let me cut to the chase," replied Erika. "My boyfriend and his buddy purchased a van at an impound auction sale in Mendocino County that French used to own. After they bought the van all sorts of strange happenings have taken place and we think that we found something in the van someone is trying to get from us. Something that is important to this guy French. Something that shows where French may have hidden most of his drug smuggling money over the years. His estate is about to be closed by an attorney named John Riggs. Riggs has been trying to buy our van and we had a break-in just last week. That is how we found a map hidden in the ceiling of the van with some notations that we believe identify locations of money that was possibly hidden years ago by French."

"This is all interesting, Erika, and personally, I would love nothing more than to nab Rick French and bring him up on insurance fraud charges along with Riggs and whoever else was involved in this mess. But we were never able to locate French, and believe me, we spent a lot of time investigating this before we were finally stopped in our tracks by the judge who was presiding over the petition to have French declared legally deceased. I think we were home towned by the local judge, Judge Slider, I believe was his name. At any rate, the case is closed. We could not find French. Without a live body, there is no proof of insurance fraud, and besides, unless there is some way to recover our financial damages, Western General Life would have no interest in reopening this case."

"Would you object to us looking at your old case files?" asked Erika. "My friends and I strongly suspect that French is still alive and that he possibly is about to access a large amount of cash now that his probate is almost concluded. We were instrumental in bringing down a large investment fraud scheme last year and have the resources and capabilities to dig into this case for you and see if there is any potential recovery. We have some unique resources that we employ that no one else can duplicate."

"How does your group propose to be compensated in the event you are successful?" asked Kate, her interest piqued, but still suspicious.

"We would be willing to work on it on a fifty-fifty split. We pay all of our own expenses."

Kate glanced at her watch. She needed to leave soon for her travel to Ojai. "I tell you what," she replied. "Let me look at the case summary again and go through the files to be sure that there is nothing in there that is confidential to Western General. I will ask my supervisor if they are interested in your proposal. Let me find out and I will get back to you in a few days."

"Agreed," replied Erika. "We can start just as soon as you give us the okay."

When Erika returned home later that evening, she found Chester and Arnie in the office sitting in front of a white board. The pair had spent all afternoon laying out the issues and locations that would need to be visited in order for them to solve the mystery of the Cuyama oil field map and retrieve the riches which might be hidden there.

"So what did the insurance company say?" asked Chester "Are they willing to play ball and let us take a shot at finding Rick French and sharing in the insurance recovery?"

"They will let us know next week," answered Erica. "What is all this on the white board?"

"These are the action steps for us solving the case and getting part of the fortune," replied Arnie.

He first pointed to a picture of a two-story office building with an arrow pointing to a window on the second floor of the building. "We first need to get inside of Riggs's office and look at his files. He probably has a file about this guy French and we may find out more about where this guy might be hiding or how much money is hidden out there in Cuyama."

From the picture of the building, a dashed line was drawn down to an image of Australia with the line ending on the east coast. A stick figure of a man riding a surfboard marked the areas of interest.

"You said this guy Hipner thought French was living in the Surfers Paradise area on the coast. We also need to go down to this Surfers Paradise place in Australia and nose around. If he is still alive, we will have to send someone down there and find out where he lives and get a picture of him or something like that to prove he is not dead," continued Arnie.

Another dotted line ran from the picture of the office building in Santa Bonita over to a drawing of an oil well and a treasure chest on which the image of a dollar sign was drawn. "We will need to get out to Cuyama and start to find the wells and see what French buried out there," continued Arnie. "This is a lot to do, and we may have to divide up the duties among ourselves. I of course will take on the office break-in since I am the only one of us who can get in there unnoticed by using my fax transportive capabilities."

"But you have not fax machine traveled since we solved the Terra Auri scheme. It's been almost a year now," pointed out Erika. "How do you know it will still work?"

"I have little confession to make," replied Arnie. "I know I told both of you I would not become some fax travel junky and start sending myself around the world after we solved the Terra Auri case. But I could not resist using my abilities to scope out the van before we drove all the way up there to bid on it."

"You mean you faxed yourself up to Mendocino County to check out the van before we drove up there?" asked Chester.

"Exactly. I did not want to spend two whole days going on a wild goose chase to look at a van that might be rusting into the ground, so I got the fax number for the office and sent myself up there a few days before the auction just to look around. The van looked solid so we ended up making the drive up. I have been faxing myself to various locations every few weeks just to be sure I do not lose my capabilities."

"So, you say you still have the same ability to send yourself anywhere in the world as long as you have a fax machine number. Are your powers still the same or are they starting to fade away?" asked Erika.

"It's a funny thing," replied Arnie. "Each time I fax myself I find that I have a better ability to actually interact with things I find that are being sent at the same time I am traveling. I have also been able to determine that things that have been sent, like letters, maps, and pictures all leave a trail of sorts. Just because I sent myself through the communication channels at a particular time, does not mean I cannot find out what was sent before me."

"You mean like following tracks? Like tracking a person or animal?" asked Chester.

"Kind of. Each time something is faxed, it leaves an energy trail of sorts that slowly fades over time, kind of like ripples on a lake. They follow behind the fax and eventually fade out. I have been able to discern these image trails but have a lot of work left to do to try and perfect my ability to actually see what the old faxes consisted of. I can look at recent data, but as they become older, it is harder for me to pick out the details of those kinds of faxes."

"Wow," exclaimed Erika. "I had no idea you were still doing all of this. I guess I can't criticize you too much about that. If I had those abilities I suppose I would still be keeping them sharp."

"That's not the only thing," continued Arnie. "I can now scan myself to any printer or computer that has internet capability."

"What the hell!" exclaimed Chester. "What do you mean, scan yourself?"

"It's pretty simple, Chess," he replied. "It was not a big leap for me to deduce that if I could break down my molecular structure into electronic signals and travel over the communication lines in the form of a fax, I should be able to also send myself in the form a scanned image along the same transportive process. Really, all a fax machine does is take your image, break it down into a file of electronic data, and then send it to another fax machine where the data is translated back into an image that is printed onto paper. An image that is scanned undergoes much the same process. One day when I was just screwing around, I used one of the large commercial copiers at one of my customers' offices to scan something back to my home office. It was pretty easy. I just opened up the scan function on the copier, dialed in the number for my home fax and printer, and stuck my watch into the machine with my hand. It was kind of like what happened the first time I found out about these powers when I found my watch lying on the floor of my home office after I sent the fax from the Onyx Financial office last year."

"You mean when you got home your watch was lying on your fax machine paper tray again?" asked Erika.

"Not exactly. I sent the scan of the watch to my home computer via e-mail. When I got home I simply opened my e-mail and downloaded the scan and printed it off. Voilà, my watch arrived just as it would have if I had sent a fax instead. I have not yet sent myself via a scan, but think I can simply scan myself to anyone's office computer and once I am inside all I have to do is manipulate the printer command to print myself off. It is going to take a little more investigation, but I am pretty sure I can get this all ironed out. I may also be able to look around at what is stored on the computers' hard drive before I send my image to be printed in order to get out of the machine."

"So now what do we call you instead of Faxman? Scanman?" replied Chester.

The trio laughed for a moment and made jokes about the new pseudo superhero operating under the guise of this widely used document transfer method.

"Having the ability to scan myself will be important," Arnie continued. "After all, the fax machine is old technology nowadays. Many offices are doing away with those machines and just scanning documents instead. When I get ready to try a test scan, I will call one of you so that you are ready to access my scan and print me off. I am pretty sure that I can work the innards of the PC where I send the e-mail and send the print command to a printer, but just to be sure, I will have one of you ready to print me off."

"That's right," exclaimed Erika. "You don't want to get trapped inside someone's desktop if you can't print your scanned image off on the printer."

"You could end up in someone's computer forever," added Chester. "Don't guess you would starve though. There are plenty of bytes for you to chew on," he joked.

"Enough of the levity. I can still fax myself anywhere I need to. Let's concentrate on the plan of attack to turn this old map into a cash reward or to lead us to the pot of gold at the end of the rainbow," replied Arnie.

"Agreed," said Erika. "Arnie, you will of course dig around in Riggs's office for anything that can help us out on this guy French and what he might have hidden out on his ranch. I will see if I can make some contacts in Australia and find a private investigator who can see about French living down there and verify that he is the guy and that he is still alive. Chess, you will be in charge of planning the trip out to the ranch to locate where these well sites are and to plan the logistics of getting out there unseen so we can see if French actually hid his fortune out there."

Things were heating up for the trio. As Erika watched Chester walk out with Arnie to his car, she was both excited and concerned. She was sure Arnie would be able to come up with more information about the missing Rick French from nosing around in Riggs's law office files. Finding out that he might still be alive and part of a scheme to defraud an insurance company might be troublesome. If French had indeed been a drug dealer and connected to an expat community of former dealers in Australia, finding him and extraditing him back to this country would be potentially dangerous. She remembered the matter of the Cut Toe Gang and shivered at the image of a big toe being severed by razor-sharp hoof trimmers. "One step at a time," she murmured as she watched Chester wave to Arnie as he sped off in his car. Arnie was impulsive. He might even make his first fax journey to the Riggs law office this evening. She could not worry about Arnie now. Her part of the plan was to track down Rick French and determine if he was still alive. If he was, they might share in splitting the insurance recovery with Western General Life. If not, then Chester's part of the game plan to visit the Cuyama Valley and nose around in some of the old oil well sites marked on their map would be the fallback position, perhaps the most lucrative of all the alternatives available to them.

Chester returned from seeing his friend off and retrieved a beer from the refrigerator before joining Erika at the kitchen table. "The little guy is all charged up over this deal," he said. "He said if we can pull this off and make another big strike like we did in the Terra Auri deal, he thinks you and him should quit your jobs and we should all start an investigation company. We can join forces using your analytical skills and his faxman powers to dig into corporate or political scandals. We could become the crime solvers of the century. No one would be able to figure out how we do it. We would be the go-to company to solve the unsolvable, break open cases that no one has been able to crack. He thinks we could make a fortune."

"The thought has crossed my mind," replied Erika. "We just fell into this map thing when you bought the van. But I bet there are hundreds, maybe thousands of things just like this out there that people have not been able to solve that are just waiting for someone like Arnie to dig into. Let's not put the cart before the horse though. Arnie will dig up what he can from the Riggs files and then we will see what the next step is."

She reached over and took a swig from Chester's bottle of beer. Chester let out a satisfying burp and smiled at her. Their next faxman adventure was about to begin in earnest.

CHAPTER TWENTY-FOUR

THE CELL PHONE IN HIS PANTS POCKET VIBRATED. RICK French reached for it to view the screen for the number of the caller. He had been thinking hard about all the possible courses of action since speaking with Jack Morrison two days previous, and he had made the careful decision to remain in Australia surrounded by friends to wait out his current predicament. Jack was now impatient and wanted to see results. He was no longer willing to continue with the installment plan that French had provided to him. A double cross in the drug trade normally meant immediate payback in the form of getting whacked. Jack wanted his long-overdue cash.

"Your old foreman is dead along with the private dick you sent out to spy on him," French heard the gravelly voice state on the other end of the call. "Now how are you going to play this with no one to dig up your stash and send your monthly payments to you?"

"Dead, how?" asked French.

"I am on the ground just a few miles from your ranch. I'm keeping close tabs on your people's comings and goings. I thought I would be able to find the map you talked about in your old foreman's house, but I ran into a problem with some investigator who was casing the house, and then the old guy inside got the jump on me when I was looking through his stuff. They left me little choice."

"You killed Emory Calloway and another guy casing the place?" exclaimed French. "I told you I had things in motion and you would have your funds within the week. All you have done is to bring attention to the valley. Now people will be nosing around for months trying to solve a double murder."

"It should not be much of an issue. I torched the place and the car out front with the guy near it. Made it look like an accidental car fire that caught the trailer on fire. No prints, everything burned up. Just some guy who was drinking at the bar and passed out in front of the house. The old guy got caught up in the inferno and did not make it out. The only thing you have to know is that I want my money and you need to produce it now if you want to continue your lifestyle in the southern hemisphere."

"Killing Emory only limits my ability to get the money for you. He knew the locations of some of the stash but he did not know about most of the locations. Those are on a map which is in the possession of some people we are keeping a close eye on. I have them under twenty-four-hour surveillance and will know the second they have found out what the map's importance is. If they try to recover the money I can have people out there to protect my interests."

"Does a gold coin that your old foreman had in his possession have anything to do with your hidden stash?" asked Jack.

"Gold coin, where did you see one of those?" asked French.

"It was lying in an ashtray on a desk in front of the old guy's TV," answered Jack. "I picked it up just before he walked in on me with his shotgun."

"Let's just say I diversified some of my financial investments into precious metals that would be better able to withstand the environmental forces of storage for several years until such time as I could access them again," replied French.

"How much is hidden? Why should I trust that you still have the resources to finally pay me off?" came the reply.

"Emory was my trusted accomplice in the entire plan to leave the US and assume a new identity. We had an agreement such that once a year, he would visit various locations to dig up packages of gold coins I had secreted away. He of course did not have access to the map that showed all of the locations, just a simpler drawing of locations where he could provide me with financial resources to make payments to you and help me keep body and soul together down here until I could retrieve the rest of my stash. I let him keep one coin each time I sent him to a location and there were never enough coins in any location to tempt him to just take them all and cut out on me. He would deliver the coins to Riggs, who would then send them to different people in my family, and over time they would sell them and give the cash back to Riggs. Riggs would then wire the cash to a company down here for me to collect. I have five sisters, an old girlfriend, and both of my parents are still living. One of my brothers-in-law is in law enforcement in Santa Monica. I had enough people so that no one ever tried to trace where the money was coming from."

"Nice plan," replied Jack, "but it's time to put the rubber to the road. Your old foreman is gone, your estate is about to close, and the ranch will be sold, so you better get over here and get me my cash before it is too late. We can drive around together and pick it up."

"That would not be good for me," replied French. "I cannot ever show my face again in the States. I cannot risk anyone discovering that I am still alive and well. I have spent a lot of the money that was retrieved from the ranch. The life insurance money will be available when the estate closes and I don't plan on letting anyone getting their hands on the rest of my assets much less going to jail for insurance fraud."

"Seventy-two hours," replied Jack. "Three days. That's all I am giving you. If I don't have my money by then, all bets are off. We all know the same guys in Surfers Paradise. They will simply find you in the lineup one evening with tragic life-ending shark bites. I hear it can be pretty messy when you go out on one of those shark-watching gigs from inside the shark cage and the door is not shut properly."

The conversation ended as abruptly as it had begun. The threat to his life was ominous. Jackson had the ability to pull off no little amount of mayhem and murder. Emory's death was just a sample of his capabilities. Emory was not integral to the recovery of his fortune. But he needed some current intel on the ground, and he needed it now.

He called the law office of John Riggs promptly at eight the following morning. "What has your source found out about those kids and how much they know now about my map?" he asked.

"Let me look at the file they should have sent last night and get back to you," replied Riggs.

"Not enough time for that now," replied French. "I had a call from Jackson last night. Apparently, he has snuck back into the country and is on the ground in Cuyama as we speak. He has already killed Emory and another guy, probably one of the guys you hired to try and get the map back for me. I only have three days left to get the cash and pay him off. He is at the end of his rope and I believe him when he says to get him paid off or else."

"I heard about the unfortunate situation with Emory," replied Riggs.

"All I know is Jackson smells blood in the water and is not going to stand by and let us take our time figuring this thing out. Read your report to me," replied French.

"Okay, okay, it's loading," replied Riggs. "Let's see, girl met with a retired insurance investigator, girl met with someone at Western General Insurance, she also has looked at all the estate files and accountings as well as the old accountings for the conservatorship when you went missing.

They did a background check on this Erika woman. Let me see what it says. CPA, undergrad from UCSB, a principal in some securities fraud investigation dealing with something called Terra Auri. Bunch of guys went to jail or disappeared before they could be prosecuted. She sounds like a smart cookie. I think we need to expect the worst."

"How so?" replied French.

"If she looked at all the accountings, she will be able to deduce that the need for an insurance policy was bogus. No one with so little equity and no children or a wife would have needed a life insurance policy, especially one so large. If she meets with the old investigator, Hipner, she will find out that he was on the trail of solving the fraud issue but did not have the time or resources to find you down there." "Not to mention the physical disincentive of getting your toes cut off," added French.

"If she has any smarts at all, she will find some of the things I did with your ranch and properties unusual and she will only dig deeper into the reason for the map," said Riggs. "She will add two and two and find out the map is valuable."

"She might even determine that the markings on the map show where I have hidden my assets over the years and go out there to retrieve my cash. If she does this, I am a dead man," replied French.

"I am watching her every move and also those two other guys," answered Riggs. "If they make a move to go out there and start to dig around, I will be apprised and take proper measures. Besides, you can't come over here and access the locations, even if you could remember some of them after all these years. Let's see if they actually plan on going out there. They can do the dirty work for us by finding the locations and retrieving your stash. We can then swoop in and get the map from them or even let them dig up all the cash for us first and then arrange for them to have a terrible accident on the way home."

"Okay," replied French. "It's a dangerous highway out to Cuyama. I suppose we can make it look like an accident if we have to. Keep on it."

"There will of course need to be another fee for this extra service," answered Riggs. "This is no longer just a simple matter of me closing out your estate and distributing your assets to your heirs. They have all been complicit in this subterfuge, but any one of them could turn on us and cooperate with law enforcement if any whiff of impropriety surfaces before I can get the insurance money and ranch sale proceeds distributed, and I don't know how they all intend to get the hard assets like your gold and printed currency over to you."

"That is my concern. We have it all worked out," replied French. "Another five percent of the estate value?" he asked.

"Ten," replied Riggs.

"Split the difference"?

"Ten percent," Riggs replied firmly. "If you pull this off you will go about your life down there. If the plan fails, they still have to track you down and extradite you back into this country. As for me, my career will be ruined and I will be wearing stripes in some Federal prison."

"Agreed," replied French. "Do what you need to keep tabs on those people and be prepared to head them off if they are lucky enough to put all the pieces together."

CHAPTER TWENTY-FIVE

IT HAD BEEN EASIER THAN ARNIE HAD EXPECTED TO FIND the information on the estate of Richard S. French. That evening, he had faxed himself over to the law office of John Riggs around ten, late enough to ensure that no one would be in the office working late and early enough for him to return home at a decent hour. His first task was to take the easiest approach, look at recent documents on Riggs's computer. He had guessed that the sole practitioner attorney would not be following the usual office protocols such as requiring a log in and password to access the machine. He had located Riggs's computer shortly after emerging from his faxman journey that had commenced from his home office fax machine. He had fine-tuned his ability to travel within the communication lines and discern all nature of information that traveled alongside him in the fiber-optic transmission lines and found that he had become impatient with the process. He was no longer curious about data that others were sending or the faint trails of old fax communiqués that had been sent previously. He needed to find out more about the nature of the map that Chester had discovered, and about which Erika had strong suspicions.

He quickly moved the mouse across the mouse pad and immediately heard the familiar sounds of the machine booting up. On a hunch, he opened the word processing program and under the history tab located a file entitled CTG. Upon opening the file, he now sat in the shoes of the deceased Richard S. French. He read the notes of the recent activity that John Riggs had so carefully recorded. A chill settled over Arnie as he viewed the detailed notes and realized that all three of them had been under surveillance since the night that the van had been first broken into. "Christ, they know all about us having the map and Erika digging into things," he muttered to himself. The most recent notes included the conversation that day with French.

He saw that Bert at the impound lot was dead and two other men in Cuyama had died in a suspicious fire. One of them was a former employee of Rick French. French was still alive! A new guy, Korman, was still working for French. Riggs had been the key player in putting an insurance fraud plan together.

"Let's see," he muttered to himself. "Jackson is on the ground in Cuyama, the map showing the hiding places for gold and currency, people being killed, and they know about us looking into the missing persons case and the estate." He saw Riggs's note about five million dollars of insurance money plus more being hidden on the ranch. A computation showing ten percent of seven and a half million dollars had been made in the notes. He noted that Riggs intended to petition the court for extraordinary probate fees of $750,000 to compensate for the complicated level of work he had put into the protracted matters of the missing person and now deceased French. "This guy's dirty hands are all over this deal," he muttered to himself.

At that moment Arnie heard the key turn in the lock and the opening of the front door. Muffled sounds of people speaking Spanish came from the front reception area. Arnie quickly crouched down behind the computer screen. He peered out and saw a couple of people armed with cleaning implements beginning to empty the trash. Timing his keystrokes with the activity of the workers, he shut down the machine and waited. He thought for a moment to pass himself off as a computer repairman. But the lights had been off in the office and the front door had been locked. How could he reasonably explain this to the cleaning staff who probably spoke only broken English. He looked around the dimly lit office and located a fax machine in the front reception area behind Manita's desk. The custodians were dusting off surfaces with feather dusters and straightening magazines on the coffee table in the reception area. It would be difficult for Arnie to access the fax machine without being discovered. He crept over to the window and looked down from the second-story window. Below him was a trash bin. The lid was closed. It provided no means for a soft landing if he was to jump from the window. He looked out from behind the computer screen again and noticed that the janitorial staff had entered the file room. The front of the office was empty. Seeing his chance, he ran over to the fax machine and dialed the number to his home fax machine. As he entered the last number, the janitors reentered the office. The woman screamed, "Dios mio!"

"Quien es?" replied the man, pushing the woman aside as he entered the room behind her. "Es un robo?" asked the woman.

Arnie slipped one of his hands into the fax machine receptacle and punched the send button. Waving to the couple with his free hand, he offered them a weak smile as he disappeared into the machine. The janitors could only stand speechless at what had just transpired in front of them.

As Arnie entered the bowels of the fax machine, he was prepared to slow down his journey back to his office and look for remnants of old faxes and letters that had been sent through Riggs's triple function Konica machine. All images of copied correspondence, scanned material as well as fax communiqués, still resided within the circuitry and hardware of the apparatus. All Arnie had to do was move among the assorted images that were compiled in the sequence from which they were sent and look for anything that might shed some light on the missing persons case of Richard French or his probate.

The electronic images appeared as if each was a page of paper. They were stacked together like a bundle of newspapers that had just rolled off of a printing press. They resided in the area of the copier that was devoted to taking an electronic image of the document being faxed or copied. From this component the electronic signals could be applied to the copier or the receiving fax machine or computer e-mail on the other end of the transmission and enable ink to be applied to paper to reproduce the letter or image. The machine had been placed in service six years prior. Arnie began sifting through all the old images, looking for anything that would help them ascertain the purpose or importance of their map.

The bulk of the records dealt with divorce cases. Riggs seemed to specialize in representing the wives in dissolution of marriage matters. Arnie rifled through the assorted filings. Each had similar themes; requests for interim spousal support payments, requests for sole custody of the children, requests for all manner of documents and proposed orders for property divisions. He noted that many of the pleadings seemed similar and only the names of the parties and the case numbers were different from case to case. Here and there he noted a real estate transaction. Finally, he started to find records pertaining to the disappearance and later declaration of death for Rick French. All the court filings and related communication to the French family and creditors of the estate had already been reviewed by Erika when she had made her inspections of the court files, and Arnie remembered the highlights of those pleadings from Erika's recent summary of her findings in the court files.

His journey into the bowels of the copier appeared to be hitting a dead end when at last he found it. It was a fax from Commonwealth Bank of Australia that contained information to enable transfers of funds into a checking account at the bank. It was from Cecilia Rappaport, a customer services representative in their Sydney office, and contained a checking account number, an ABA number, and routing information the sender of funds would need in order to have cash delivered into an account at that bank from an account located in the US. In the fax, Cecilia had relayed information on how the funds being sent from the US would be converted to Aussie currency based on the currency exchange rate at the time.

The account had been set up for regular quarterly transfers from an account in California under the auspices of authority that Riggs had presented showing Commonwealth Bank of Australia that he was authorized to conduct business on behalf of the Estate of Richard S. French. Payments would go into an account owned by Certified Transfer Global, a company that purported to act as a factor for receivables for various Australian companies that exported commodities to Europe and South America. He noted that Cecilia had indicated that she would confirm with representatives of CTG when wires had arrived and verify receipt of those funds so that Riggs could track his wires to that offshore bank.

Arnie's interest was piqued. Certified Transfer Global? CTG? Cut Toe Gang. Didn't Erika mention this gang as being the reason the insurance investigator had terminated his search for the missing Rick French? It was too much of a coincidence. He could find no other records that pertained specifically to the map, but he did find an image of the fax from Cecilia that had been sent to Certified Transfer Global. Riggs's note indicated that the wires had been set up and would be sent quarterly.

Thinking that this document might be useful, Arnie manipulated the electronics inside the machine to capture a copy of the scanned document and then sent the copy to his home fax machine. He exited the machine, following closely behind the copied image and emerged from his home fax machine, landing on the floor on top of the paper. He wondered about the importance of wires from the French estate to Australia. Erika had not mentioned anything about this when she had looked at the court files. Perhaps she had deemed this aspect unimportant. Maybe the court file had no record of these transfers. All in all it had been a productive evening. He had found two items of interest and had scared the pants off the cleaning staff after being discovered in the fax room. The Australian connection opened up a whole new avenue to be investigated but also raised the level of danger that lay ahead for them.

When Arnie arrived at Chester and Erika's house the next morning, he found them working on the van. Erika was sitting in the driver's seat and Arnie was lying under the left front wheel of the van. He could hear the two of them talking as Chester directed Erika to pump on the brake pedal and then hold the pedal down as Chester attempted to remove any air left in the brake lines after he and Arnie and had replaced all the old brake cylinders. He waited until Chester had bled the air from the wheel cylinder and then exited his car and walked over to the pair. "How's she going?" he asked. "Got a firm pedal now?"

"Yup," replied Erika as she tested the brakes. "One inch of free play and she is firm as a rock."

"Good going," replied Arnie. "I have some rock solid stuff myself that I found over at Riggs's office."

The trio headed inside and sat around the kitchen table as Arnie relayed the results of his fax/copier investigation and the review of Riggs's CTG files.

"Certified Transfer Global. CTG. Cut Toe Gang. That is all too coincidental," said Erika.

"That is what I thought too," replied Arnie.

"I bet they are one and the same or have some kind of relationship," continued Erika.

"Did you see anything in the court files about Riggs getting orders to wire funds from the estate to this company in Australia?" asked Chester.

"No, there was nothing in the files about any of this. Just an order for ongoing preliminary distributions from the estate insurance money to his heirs that seem to have happened every few months or so once the insurance company paid the money to the estate."

"If you have cash or other financial assets that you keep out of the banking system, you are not going to report those to the court as part of the probate, are you?" said Arnie. "You will find some other way to get money out of your estate and make it look legit, like distributing money to the family instead, who can then figure out a way to get it over to you."

"Bingo," replied Erika. "If you make your money in the drug trade and keep it all in hidden liquid form, say for example hidden down abandoned oil wells on ranches in Cuyama, then only you are going to know about it. The world knows about the insurance money though since the court file is open to the public. There is always someone, an attorney, a low-level bank officer, some person who is willing to bend the rules in exchange for a payoff, to help you transact business and access those insurance funds. Remember, regular wires were sent from his private account to a bank in Australia. I did not connect the two until now."

"It took five years to get the guy declared dead," said Chester. "How did he survive in the meantime?"

"Those wires to the bank in Australia started about five years ago," replied Arnie. "Who knows, maybe Riggs was holding some of his cash for him or maybe he knew where some of the cash was hidden on French's ranch."

Erika frowned for a moment. "Maybe, but whatever the source of these wired funds, the important point for us is that the money was funneled out of the country under the nose of the court for some purpose. If the drug money is never reported to the court, but Riggs gets the authority to act on behalf of French while he is missing and later declared dead, all he would have to do is show his durable power of attorney or his appointment as conservator for the estate or his letters testamentary to enable him to open accounts or wire funds out of the country. All the bank in Australia needs to see is some form of authority to conduct business on French's behalf or at least verify the funds are coming from a legitimate bank in the US. They would have no reason to see accountings filed with the court or follow up any further on wires that came into a valid account at that bank. The court does not know Riggs has unreported assets in a bank offshore and the bank does not know Riggs is running the money through French's family and hiding this from the court."

"But what about all the money laundering regulations and terrorism laws that make banks report suspicious things like this?" replied Chester.

"I thought banks have to keep track of these kind of things, especially when large amounts of cash are being wired?" Arnie asked.

"SARS," replied Erika. "Suspicious Activity Reports. We used to have to deal with those at Capital Triangle when Morris would do one of his cash transactions that were over ten thousand dollars. The banks have to report large cash transactions to the Fed. How large were those wires you found over at Riggs's office to CTG?"

"I don't know," answered Arnie. "Five thousand, eight thousand, something like that."

"Well, that's how Riggs got around anti–money laundering laws," she replied. "He got money over to his heirs from cash he was holding for French or had the court approve preliminary distributions from the estate and then made his wires large enough to send sizeable amounts of cash but small enough to avoid being reported to the authorities. If his drug money was never inventoried in the estate, he would not have recorded his transactions in the court filings . . . pretty slick way of being able to move this money offshore."

The trio sat in silence for a moment, digesting what Arnie had discovered and their conjecture about what it all might mean

"Let's circle in on what we know for sure and what is likely to have occurred," said Erika. "First of all, we know that Riggs put us all under surveillance and they know what we have been doing to look into the purpose of the map. They know we think French might still be alive and that cash or gold might be stored in old oil wells in the Cuyama valley and that we have talked to Western General about the life insurance policy. There may be a third party that French owes money to from an old drug deal, this guy called Jackson they say is on the ground in Cuyama. Riggs, French, if he is really still alive, and this Jackson guy all have reason to bump us off or at least discourage us from trying to look any further into the location of what is buried out there. The guy with the most to lose is French. If we prove he is still alive and put this scheme together to fake his death and collect the life insurance money, he is going to jail for a long time, Riggs too."

"Yeah, but I am more worried about this other drug dealer, Jackson," said Arnie. "What did the police report say about him . . . a known dealer who used to live in Morocco? People have already died under suspicious circumstances in Cuyama this week. People in the drug trade kill each other all the time. I am more worried about this guy trying to get us out of the way than I am about some ex–jojoba farmer who is living the good life in Australia."

"The risks have gone up for us but if we move quickly, we can still try to put the pieces together and attempt to collect part of the proceeds from the recovery of assets that the insurance company will be entitled to if French is found to be alive," replied Erika. "I will get started on seeing what resources we can bring to bear in Australia in order to locate this guy French. Chester, you and Arnie start to plan the logistics of a trip to Cuyama to scout out the oil well locations and check if we can dig around at those locations for what French hid out there. We are going to need aerial photos of the land to see what the terrain and access is like, and we are going to need to plan for an extended stay in the valley while we look around to find these locations."

"That's my assignment," said Chester. Reading the clues to their fortune hunting map or trying to decipher how French had moved money offshore under the noses of the banking system and the probate court were topics that he was ill prepared to deal with. Putting together a plan of attack to head out to Cuyama and locate the oil wells in question was right up his alley, however. "We can use the van to camp out and set up a base camp. There are a couple of remote campgrounds in the valley. They are probably seldom used and we can use one of them as a base camp to stage our searches."

"Good," replied Erika. "If we are going to collect part of the cash French hid out there, we are going to also have to prove that this guy French is still alive and living down under."

"That is your part of the project," replied Arnie. "What do you have in mind?"

"Time is important now that we know that we are being watched. I will dig up an investigator who can take the project on down there and start looking around for this guy. I have an old picture of him I came across when I was doing my research in the court files. With what we know from the guy from the insurance company, it should not be too hard to find this French guy if he is in fact still alive."

"Then what?" replied Arnie. "Are you going to sweet talk him into coming back to stand trial for insurance fraud? I am sure he will just get on the plane with you and come on back over here once you locate him." He smirked.

"One thing at a time. The two of you find some air photos of the Cuyama area and put together a battle plan for how we supply ourselves, how long we need to be out there, and put together any stories we might need just in case people start to nose around in our business."

Chester and Arnie looked at each other and grinned. Their minds swam with the endless possibilities of things that would be necessary for the expedition. Jeeps, guns, food, metal detectors, these and more would be brought to bear to solve the mystery of the map. The excursion might lead them to riches far greater than what they had gained during the Terra Auri affair.

CHAPTER TWENTY-SIX

CEDRICK TORMEY PRINTED OFF A DEPOSIT SLIP FOR A BUSI-ness account from his office printer and examined the quality of his work. He was one of only three private investigators in the City of Gold Coast, Queensland, Australia, and his schedule of assignments was sporadic if not sometimes infrequent. The call he had received the day previous had come at just the right time since he had not had an assignment for several weeks. Ordinarily he did not deal with issues related to American expats who resided in the area. They had a reputation for being secretive, well-funded, and kept their dealings private. Rumors abounded about former drug activities of the group and why they had over the years congregated in the area. They were like a club. They watched each other's backs and were known to aggressively defend their privacy. The local police took a live and let live attitude toward them. So long as they were not breaking any laws or causing trouble, local law enforcement looked the other way. They put no effort into attempts to arrest and extradite the group back to their country of origin.

Cedrick was sorely in need of some work. He had agreed to take on the assignment Erika had approached him with concerning an American who had disappeared from the US some five years previous. He had been given a bank account number and the routing number for an account at one of the large banks in town. The missing person was alleged to be receiving periodic payments from the owners of that account. Erika had wanted to know if the account was still open and who owned or controlled the activities of an export company called Certified Transfer Global. It would be a simple matter to make a small deposit of a money order via the drive up window at the bank. If the account was still open and valid, they would accept his check. He had thought about making a fake check and depositing it into his own bank account but had decided that this would be too risky and would look like he was engaging in check fraud. It might draw attention that he was looking for someone related to that account. If the account was still open, he could then meet with the bank officer whose name he had been given, Cecelia Rappaport, and see what she was willing to share with him about the account principals.

Cedrick could trace his ancestry back to the early 1800s, when his long-ago ancestors were dumped onto the shores of the continent in Great Britain's effort to rid itself of undesirables and overcrowded prisons. His family had steadily climbed the economic ladder over five generations, rising from sheep shearers to landowners and businessmen. Family fortunes had waxed and waned for the Tormey family and Cedrick, having no interest in business or farming, had used his talents and position to open up a one-man private investigation business.

The City of Gold Coast was primarily a tourist area. The suburb of Surfers Paradise, called Surfers by the locals, would be the subject of his investigations. He gazed at the black-and-white photograph of Richard Sutherland French. He looked to be about six foot three, 190 pounds with dirty blond hair. The photo, which had been used on a passport some years previous, showed a confident middle-aged man, perhaps thirty-five years old. His face had a serene, almost godlike quality.

Cedrick looked over the missing persons report from the Mendocino County Sheriff's office. Mustache, small scar by the belly button, nothing else to help identify him more fully. The notes from his conversation with Erika indicated that an insurance company had investigated the case and had dropped further inquiry after a year's time once the court had ruled French to be dead. A five-million-dollar life insurance policy had been paid but the insurance investigator had leads that indicated French had avoided arrest in a drug transaction by fleeing to Surfers Paradise

Erika had not been fully forthcoming with information concerning the subject's secret life in Surfers. She had not relayed the CTG suspicion to Cedrick. The existence of the American expats was generally known to the local population and they had been given the Cut Toe Gang moniker due to their aggressive tactics in discouraging those who would seek to locate them. It was rumored that some of the group were ex bank robbers. Others had dealt in the drug trade. The one common theme among them was their desire to be located close to the beach so that they could continue a surfing lifestyle and play a few rounds of golf every week or so. Many of them were charming and popular with the female tourists who visited the area. A few were untrusting and distant and were suspected of being the muscle for the group when people showed up from time to time asking too many questions.

Cedrick surfed as well and was familiar with the local Americans. Richard French would of course have assumed a new name and identity but his facial features were distinctive enough to help identify him. A number of years had passed since the passport photo had been taken. The face might be a little fuller, the hair a little thinner, but all in all the man was distinctive enough.

His plan was simple and straightforward. A new southern hemisphere swell was being generated off the coast of New Zealand. In a day's time, large swells would start arriving on the local beaches. Serious surfers, including those in the gang, would be taking advantage of those waves.

There was only one point break in the area. Experienced surfers, especially those who lived a life of leisure, would time their surf session to catch the new swell as the tide went from low to high. He had checked the charts that morning and determined that this would occur in the mid to late afternoon. He would be there early so that he could screen the surfers as they arrived and suited up. He would observe them from a position that provided a good view of the parking lot.

He arrived at three thirty in the afternoon just as the tide had retreated fully and had just begun to retrace itself. Positioning his truck in the center of the parking lot with a full view of the beach, he climbed up to a viewing stand he had rigged on the top of his truck and posed as if he were a freelance photographer taking shots for a magazine. Hidden from the public was a second small camera on a movable camera stand that he could manipulate from inside his rooftop stand. The images from that camera were viewed on a small screen he had located inside the lens of his sunglasses. To the public, he appeared to be taking shots of surfers in the lineup. From his perch, he was viewing images to his left, right, and rear as cars pulled into the lot and surfers exited to don their wetsuits and enter the water. He operated a small joystick each time a new vehicle pulled into the lot. Beaters and small economy cars were quickly scanned and discarded as possibilities. He looked for BMWs, Audis, and Range Rovers, cars that wealthy expats drove.

All manner of vehicles were beginning to arrive at the beach parking lot. The usual crowd of tow-headed groms were already in the lineup. They had been surfing the low tide waves that consisted of fast long barrels that broke quickly over the shallow sand bottom. With the changing tide, older surfers consisting of the retired, tourists, and those with flexible work schedules were now showing up. Cedrick scanned each car as it entered the lot, looking for the person who would match the photo and the physical description he had been given. After an hour's time, he finally saw a tall gangly surfer emerge from a Range Rover SUV. This guy had similar features to those in the passport photo, and the hair style was very much like that in the photo. Cedrick thought he recognized him as one of the regulars at the surf break. The subject did not immediately suit up for a surf session. Instead, after giving a furtive glance around the parking lot, he walked quickly over to a late model Acura and stepped into the passenger's side of the vehicle. From his viewpoint, Cedrick could see the driver facing the subject. They appeared to be having a serious conversation. Neither of them were looking at the surfers in the lineup. After ten minutes, the subject left the Audi and returned to his car. He did not put on a wetsuit or pull his surfboard off of the rack on top of his car. Instead, he took a beach chair and an ice chest out of the back of his SUV and walked down to the sand. He set up his chair in good view of the surf break and took off his shoes and shirt. As he removed his shirt and bent over the ice chest to remove a beer, Cedrick could clearly see the small scar located next to the man's belly button. "An old knife wound?" thought Cedrick. "Or an appendectomy?" This had to be the guy.

Cedrick continued to pose as a photographer. It was easy now to keep track of his subject. He took pictures of the surfers as they rode waves on the incoming tide. He also took pictures of his subject as the opportunity arose. He observed him make several phone calls on his cell phone over the course of an hour's time. The swell continued to build and his subject folded up his beach chair, returned to his car, and donned a wetsuit. Cedrick's van was parked next to the stairway that led down to the beach. As he pretended to observe surfers in the lineup, he followed the subject with his hidden camera and snapped a photo of him as he walked past his van down to the shoreline. Cedrick pulled the old passport photo from his pocket and compared it to the image on his camera. There was no doubt. This was the missing and legally dead Richard Sutherland French. All Cedrick needed to do to complete his assignment was determine the status of the checking account at Consolidated Transfer Global and report his findings to Erika. She would want to know his new name and details about where he lived and where he spent his time, but the hard work had been done.

On the way home Cedrick deposited the small money order into the Consolidated Transfer Global account at Commonwealth Bank of Australia. The cheery teller at the drive up window had quickly looked up the account, verified the account details, and that there was no hold on the account, and handed Cedrick a receipt for the transaction. "Thank you, young lady. Is Cecelia Rappaport in today?" he asked before he drove away.

"Sorry, today is her day off, but she is back in tomorrow. Shall I leave a note for her?" she asked.

"No worries," he replied." I will circle back later with her."

He spent the rest of the day buttoning up loose ends on the assignment. He was able to get the name and address associated with the vehicle French had been driving. He was using the name Mitchell Davenport. Davenport's address was located in an upscale enclave of Surfers Paradise where the occupants kept modest estates behind security gates. These were people who did not want uninvited guests showing up on their doorsteps. Cedrick cruised past the home later in the evening and noticed French's auto parked in the garage and a wetsuit hanging up to dry in a tree nearby. This had been too easy. For someone who had taken great pains to drop off the face of the earth and take on a new identity, French had been easy to find. Cedrick thought there must be more to the story.

The next morning Cedrick returned to the bank and met Cecelia Rappaport for a ten o'clock meeting. She was not at all what he had envisioned a bank officer to look like. She was a deeply tanned woman, possibly with some Aborigine heritage. Her athletic body suggested that she was a health fitness aficionado and possibly a surfer as well. The blond ends of her wiry hair bespoke of hours in the sun, possibly from surfing in the local waters of Surfers Paradise. She had the square, well-muscled shoulders of a swimmer.

"Good morning, Mr. Tormey," she had greeted him, extending her hand to give him a firm businesslike handshake. "What can I help you with this morning?"

"I want to open a business checking account for my export business and some of my surfing buddies recommended your bank. I need to be able to deposit proceeds from my customers in the US, and account for the exchange rates and such, and track my receivables."

"Yes, good to be recommended. CBA is the largest bank in Australia and many of our business customers have multinational sales. We can convert dollars into the Loonie and report the exchange rate on the day you make deposits or send out funds to the US or any other country, for that matter, where a rate of exchange is maintained."

"That will be fine," replied Cedrick. "Let me have the documents that you need to open the account and I will have my secretary complete them for you and then bring them over so you can open the account."

"Thank you for the business," she replied. "Tell me who was kind enough to give us this referral. I always like to send a thank-you card when clients send us business."

"Mitch Davenport at Certified Transfer Global," replied Cedrick. "Have you been banking them very long?" he continued. "They were very high on your services and your ability to deal with the unique aspects of their business." He noticed a slight pause, but in the next second she smiled and rose to bid him goodbye. "Privacy laws restrict me from discussing other people's accounts, you understand, but we are grateful for referrals from our customers."

"Of course," he replied.

She continued, "Just have your staff drop off your articles of incorporation and local business license and I will have the paperwork ready for you to sign the next day." Her eyes followed Cedrick as he walked away from her desk and left the building. Watching him get into his car and drive away, she scribbled his license plate number on a notepad. She then picked up the phone and made a call. She spoke in a low tone. "Did you refer a guy named Cedrick Tormey to me?" There was a pause. "He came in just now to open an account and said he knew you." After a moment she picked up her notes and relayed the name, address, and the car license number Cedrick had given her.

"If he shows up again let me know right away," the voice on the other end of the line said.

"You know I will," came her reply.

CHAPTER TWENTY-SEVEN

CEDRICK PUT ON HIS WETSUIT FOR A LATE AFTERNOON SES-
sion. He pulled into the same parking spot he had used earlier. The lot was
almost empty. Young school-aged groms had already returned home for
the approaching dinner hour and a slight chill in the air had convinced
many of the tourist sunbathers and beachcombers to retreat to the more
temperate climes of the local eateries or their hotel rooms. Cedrick pulled
his longboard out of the back of his van and headed toward the surf break.
He had been a lifelong surfer and entered the water with an economy of
ease, finding the faint rip current that ran alongside a jetty to help him
make an effortless paddle out into the surf zone. Now in his early fifties,
in good physical condition but with a slight belly bulge, he had given up
riding short boards and beefy thrusters in favor of a nine foot six Soft Top.
Some of his fellow surfers had given him grief when he had first showed up
in the break with his new longboard, but many of them had since migrated
to this model. "I never worry about ding repairs, just throw it into the back
of my truck," he had retorted to the criticism. "I can knee paddle all day
too."

An onshore breeze had come up. Not enough to make for crummy surfing conditions, but just enough to put diamonds on the surface of the water. Cedrick entered the pack and took a respectful place at the end of the line of surfers waiting to catch waves as the sets rolled in. He was not a wave hog and even though he was considered a local and entitled to priority over the tourists and young groms, he rarely exercised that privilege. He had caught fifteen head-high waves by the time the sun began to approach the horizon. The wind had picked up and he began to feel a chill. He paddled in and walked up to his truck, noticing that a car was now parked next to him. It felt odd to him but he rationalized it being some tourists wanting to park close to the walkway that led from the parking lot down to the sand. A couple dressed in street clothes were standing by the wall looking down at the beach and taking pictures of the ocean.

He put his board into the bed of his truck and began to pull off his wetsuit. The donning and removal of his wetsuit was a systematic procedure. He removed it in the exact opposite sequence that he had used to put it on. First off was the head bootie. Next, he unzipped the zipper that ran behind him along the middle of his back and removed his arms from the wetsuit sleeves and peeled the upper part of the wetsuit down to the waist. As he leaned over to remove the booties, he saw the couple approach him.

"G'day mate," the man called out as they walked up to him. He was a large middle-aged man in good physical condition with the body of a weightlifter. His short blond buzz cut gave him a military appearance. He spoke with an American accent. The woman was a trim opposite of him. Small and petite, she wore a close-fitting jogging outfit and sunglasses. Cedrick guessed they were government workers from the military base at Alice Springs on vacation from that lonely central Australian burg. The United States and other Western nations maintained facilities in that part of the continent to operate tracking devices for military defense purposes. Rocket launches, satellite orbits and communications from their home countries as well as those from hostile nations were monitored from this remote location. Military veterans from the US typically signed up for three-year commitments. Periodic vacations to the coast were a common diversion from the extreme hot and cold weather, boredom, and having to deal with the strange customs and rule of law that pertained to the Aboriginal population living in the area.

"Do you know of a good place to eat nearby with views of the water?" the man asked.

"Nothing fancy, just one of the places the locals like to go to?" the woman elaborated.

"Well, you can try Jocko's," Cedrick replied. "It usually is crowded this time of day, but they get them in and out pretty fast. Just walk down the boardwalk about five hundred meters and you will come to the place."

The couple thanked him and got into their car, a black Mercedes, and started to drive out of the parking lot. Cedrick resumed taking off his wetsuit. Booties now off, he applied himself to the most awkward part of the disrobing process. He worked the rest of his wetsuit down to his ankles and began the strenuous process of working the legs down around his ankles so that he could take each leg and foot out of the wetsuit. He had each leg of the suit down to the calf and was beginning to work on the left leg when two vans pulled up, one on each side of his car. And they didn't just pull up—they came to a screeching stop. At the next moment, the black Mercedes pulled up in front of his truck, in a blocking maneuver. In an instant, a sack was thrust over his head and a drawstring was pulled tightly around his neck. He was wrestled to the ground. His feet were tied and he was picked up and thrown into one of the vans. He fought against his restraints but quickly determined that his efforts would be futile. The van exited the parking lot quickly. He could feel the vehicle lurch toward the highway leading away from the downtown area. He struggled for breath. The noose was tight. Did they intend to kill him? He felt a needle in his neck. He lost consciousness.

When he revived, he had been removed from the van and was now sitting on a chair in the middle of an industrial building. Around the perimeter of the room were assorted barrels, boxes, and pieces of steel. The room smelled of old oil and solvents. Light came into the room from chicken wired glass windows running along the top of the walls of the room. The shadows of a rooftop ventilator, turning slowly in the breeze, played lazily in front of him on the stained concrete floor.

Three people stood around him, shielded from clear sight by the shadows of the room.

"Who are you working for?" he heard one of the three say to him.

Cedrick thought better of trying to take a macho attitude. He was tied tightly to the chair, and though the hood and noose had been removed from his neck, he feared the worst but hoped to extract himself from his dilemma without revealing the entirety of his assignment.

"I am a private investigator researching a missing person assignment."

"Who are you looking for?" came the reply.

"Richard Sutherland French. I am working for someone from the States who has a failure to pay alimony claim from an ex-wife," he lied. Fearing the worst, he reasoned that if his assignment appeared innocuous, perhaps they would consider him a small player.

"Who hired you?"

"Some private dick in California that has been hired by the ex-wife's lawyer to find this guy," he lied again.

"What is he paying you?"

"I get one hundred and fifty dollars an hour with a five thousand cap on this assignment," Cedrick replied.

"If we pay you ten thousand dollars, are you willing to tell them that no such person exists?"

He thought for a moment. What did he have to lose? His captors were organized and serious about protecting French. They had not physically harmed him yet, but he had no reason to believe they would not resort to such tactics if needed.

"I guess so," he replied. He heard one of the group walking up behind him.

"We have gone to your office and removed all of the images you took today on your camera at the beach. You will send a report to your client that you exhausted all channels to locate the subject, including law enforcement, and that the subject is nowhere to be found."

"All right. When do I get out of here and when do I get my money?" replied Cedrick.

"The money will be in your truck at the beach," came the reply." We are going to put a disincentive in place in the event you try to change your mind." He felt a hand on his neck and the prick of a needle again. As he lost consciousness, he heard a voice say "Prop his foot up."

It was dark when he awoke. He was sitting behind the steering wheel of his truck. The dashboard clock showed that it was now nine o'clock. He recognized the interior of his townhouse garage. "They must have driven me back to my place and parked me inside," he thought. As he regained his full senses, he saw a paper bag next to him on the seat. He opened it and observed a stack of tightly bound bills, several photographs, and a note.

He became aware of an intense throbbing in his left foot. He looked down. His foot was tightly bandaged. There was bloody gauze at the end where his toes were. A wave of nausea passed over him and he nearly passed out from the pain. He reached into the bag and retrieved the photos and note. The first photo was an image of a foot, his foot, being held by two hands with a pair of horse hoof clippers positioned around his big toe. The next photo showed his foot, now missing the big toe, with the toe laying on the floor below. He vomited at the realization of what had happened to him. The final image was of a sutured stump where his toe had been formerly located and a roll of gauze and bandaging being applied to his wound. The note was concise and to the point. Make the report that French is nowhere to be found in Surfers Paradise and he could resume his life. If anyone else showed up to continue searching, he would lose more than just a toe. He had been properly stitched and bandaged. A bottle of pain pills had been placed in the paper bag beside him on the seat of his truck. He was not to go to the police or a hospital.

The pain was intense. It throbbed as he hobbled up to his townhouse. He gripped the paper bag tightly. Sitting down on a living room chair, he surveyed his options. He could go to the police and file a report. He could go to the hospital and be sure that his foot had been properly cared for. He could do nothing and just write his report to Erika as agreed and take solace in the bag of money sitting beside him and be grateful that he was still alive. He chose the latter. Downing some pain pills from his bathroom, he went over to his computer and sent off a quick e-mail to Erika. "In the matter of Richard Sutherland French, no such person exists in Queensland. This concludes the assignment. He attached a bill for $5,000 for his services. He had made a total of $15,000 on the assignment but was now minus one big toe. But he was alive. Things could have turned out far worse.

When Erika read the e-mail that evening, she walked outside to where Chester and Arnie were mounting five-gallon gas cans on the rear of the van. "No luck in Australia, boys," she said.

"That was fast. Is your guy sure?"

"He was referred to me by corporate counsel at one of the firms we did business with when I was working for Capital Triangle," she replied. "Maybe this thing is just a wild goose chase after all and this guy French really did come to some unfortunate end back when his drug deal when bad."

"Maybe so," replied Arnie, "but that doesn't explain us being put on surveillance by Riggs and the other stuff that has happened to us."

"Yeah, and besides, all of the other pieces to the map puzzle point to something valuable being hidden out there by French or someone connected to him," added Arnie.

"Well, my investigator could have run into the same people down there that the insurance investigator Hipner sent down there did. Maybe

Hipner's guy crossed paths with these guys and ended up dead. Remember, that's when Western General decided to throw in the towel on their case and decided to stop trying to find the guy," Erika replied. "If we don't have French, we can't collect the insurance reward money."

"We can still go after the stuff that is hidden in those wells," replied Chester.

"Allegedly hidden," corrected Erika. "Who knows how much is still left after all of this time has passed?"

"Okay, where do we sit on this now?" Arnie asked. "What if French is still alive but has protection down there. We think the gold and cash is still in some of those wells, and we need French if we want a cut of the insurance recovery."

"And we are being followed by Riggs, probably to report to French if we get too close to finding his hoard," said Erika.

The three sat quietly for a moment, musing to themselves on the next course of action, if any.

"I am going to fax myself down there and see what I can find out," said Arnie. "You two get ready to get out to Cuyama and use the map and air photos to locate each of the marked wells. You guys find the wells, I will find this guy French, and maybe if we are lucky we can bring all of this to a head, deposit him with the insurance company, and claim our share of the recovery from the insurance money or those Cuyama oil wells."

"How are you going to get started in Australia?" asked Erika. "You don't know anyone down there. I assume you will fax yourself to some office in Surfers Paradise but what next?"

"Let me start with this guy Tormey. I will talk to him and look around his office first and circle out from there. You guys get out to Cuyama asap and start the search on the ground. I can be back here in an instant if you run into trouble."

The plan was set. The stakes had risen, and time was of the essence now that they knew they were being watched.

The next morning Chester and Erika began obtaining the provisions they would need for their excursion to Cuyama. Fuel cans had to be filled. Ample food for a week in the field was procured. The camper van already had a functioning stove and refrigerator, both of which ran on propane. They had borrowed two five-gallon plastic water bottles from a neighbor, telling him they were going on a camping trip to a remote area of the county. They loaded up provisions and a box of sundry items they always took on their camping trips. Fire starters, lamps, toilet paper, and mosquito repellent together with rope, duct tape, and a small camping ax and a shovel rounded out their supplies for the trip.

"We leave late this afternoon," said Chester. "We will camp in the Cottonwood Canyon campground. No one ever goes there. Our story will be that we are on a camping trip and are hiking some of the back-country trails and doing some star gazing. That should explain any after-dark exploring."

Erika was resigned to her fate. She too had felt the thrill of the fortune hunting expedition. But she had the sense to know the potential danger involved. Any number of things might happen to them on this trip, but if they could pull it off and find the fortune that French had hidden in the area before his disappearance and prove he was still alive, they could become rich beyond their wildest dreams. They could earn a lifetime of salary in the matter of a week. It seemed worth the risk.

They left their house at three p.m. and traveled north from Santa Bonita, passing by vineyards and wineries. As they went farther north, they came into the Santa Maria Valley, the salad bowl of the county. Both sides of the highway were bright green with lettuce, broccoli, and other truck crops. A gray haze from the nearby ocean still hung over the valley. They eventually turned east onto the Cuyama Highway. In the short distance of only several miles, the climate turned warm. Chaparral-covered hills ran along both sides of the highway as they climbed out of the Santa Maria Valley on up to the plateau of Cuyama. There were long stretches of highway where no homes or buildings of any kind could be seen. Here and there the foundations and walls of adobe structures dating back to the time of the Spanish and Mexican settlers could be seen. They were slowly melting back into the landscape, the mud and straw walls returning to the source from whence they had originated over the previous two hundred years. The harsh climate, poor soils, and lack of a steady water supply had dashed the hopes and dreams of the original settlers. As they had given up and abandoned their homesteads, larger surrounding landowners had acquired those properties, leaving the buildings to decay with the passage of time.

As they drove out of the canyon onto the valley floor of Cuyama, it became hot. The sun was at their back as they headed east. Trucks hauling double trailers loaded with carrots passed them going in the opposite direction. The trailers swayed back and forth behind the semitrucks that were pulling them. Cars on this two-lane highway darted in and out from between the trucks in a hurry to get through the heat and reach the cool of the coast.

After ninety minutes, they came to the turnoff for Cottonwood Canyon that ended in a forest service campground at the end of the road. The terrain had changed dramatically from the coast. To the north sat the Caliente Range, a dry set of mountains that reached from the valley floor elevation up to thirty-five hundred feet. Sparsely vegetated, they spoke of scanty intermittent rainfall for the region. To the south lay the San Raphael Range. They were covered with a dense growth of chaparral. Chamise, coyote brush, and toyon evidenced a higher level of rainfall that could make the journey over the coastal mountain range and fall on that set of mountains. Small dust devils whirled across the empty landscape of the valley floor. Ground squirrels hid in their burrows from the heat of the midday sun. They spotted a coyote panting beneath the shade of a juniper tree. It melted into the brush at the sight of their van.

As they drove up from the valley floor, they passed an occasional ranch. These were not the luxurious homes and buildings they had seen in the wine country near the coast. These ranch houses were simple, sparsely maintained structures designed for the utilitarian ranching purposes of the area. None of them were new. They were wood-sided structures, many whitewashed with green trim. Some appeared to have been abandoned years ago. Several still had large overhead water tanks used to store water pumped from the ground by ancient metal windmills. Time had not been good to this remote hardscrabble area of the county.

They came at last to the campground. A signboard, filled with bullet holes, greeted them at the entrance. Following the instructions, they selected a camping spot, filled out the envelope they had picked up, and dropped the envelope with their fee into the steel pipe receptacle constructed for that purpose. The campground was almost empty. Across from them, several spots away, they saw one other occupied campground. A Ford van was located in the spot. The occupants were nowhere to be seen.

"I wonder who our camping neighbors will be," mused Erika. "It is a little spooky out here," she added.

"It is the perfect spot for what we have to do," answered Chester. "The fewer people we come across while we are looking around for those wells, the better for us. If we are still being observed by Riggs and his guys, this is the last place they will go looking for us."

They began to set up their camp and settle in for the week. Chester positioned a ground cloth where their tent was to be located and then dragged the large bag of camping gear over. They had been in the car for some time. It would be up to them to create some measure of peace and tranquility. That would start with creating the space to sleep and get out of the weather.

Erika had assisted in putting up their tent in the past. It had resulted in various amounts of arguments, yelling, pinched fingers, and looking at the diagram of how to set up the tent. The eventual success of raising the tent had always been bittersweet. Several beers and glasses of wine later, each of them off by themselves to handle other tasks of setting up their camp, they would finally be able to speak to each other again when they realized there would be no TV, no beds, and no restaurant. It would be up to them to work together to make the experience positive.

"Let's look at the directions before we try to set up this new tent," Erika suggested.

"No need. Stand aside," Chester replied. "It's one of those new dome tents with flexible poles." He pointed to the picture on the cover of the bag that held the tent. Dumping the tent unceremoniously onto the ground cloth, he located four corners and pulled each one out to form a square. "Help me put all of the poles together," he asked as he dumped four sets of collapsed black fiberglass poles. They each began putting poles together and placed them into the nylon straps on top of the dome of the tent. Chester instructed Erika on how to form the poles into half circles and lock the base at each end into the straps at floor level. In a moment, their abode for the next week stood erected before them, a two-tone, cool-green refuge. They retreated to the picnic table where they had laid out the rest of the camping gear and dug out a couple of beers from the ice chest.

"That was easy," said Chester.

Erika giggled. "You sound like that Staples commercial where they press that stupid button."

"It's a lot easier than that old tent we used to use. We can spread out all of our gear in here and still sleep in the van if we want to."

They went over their dinner supplies for the week and began to settle in for the evening's dinner preparation. Hot dogs and chili were the logical choice. They were both tired and dirty and neither of them wanted to spend a lot of time cooking a complicated meal. They paid the fee to purchase a bundle of firewood from the campground hosts' kiosk. In no time, the meal was done, dishes had been washed, and the two sat in front of their campfire in the coolness of the early evening breeze.

The campers across from them returned shortly after dark and introduced themselves to Erika and Chester. Mark and Mary McAllister were baby boomers who were clinging to the back-to-nature life of the post–Vietnam War era. Their four-wheel-drive Ford Econoline van was equipped for extended stays in the backcountry. It sported a large roof rack for carrying supplies and was equipped with a gas generator and solar panels to provide power in remote locations. Distrustful of the political process, they were equipped to survive the chaos that would certainly occur after a meltdown of the new global economy.

"We were just getting ready to pack up," Mark informed them after the couples exchanged greetings. "We've been out here for a week and have pretty much explored the entire area. If you are looking for some isolation, you have picked the perfect spot."

"We haven't seen a soul since we pulled in here," added Mary.

"Except for one guy who cruised through here a couple times at night but did not stay to camp," added Mark. "What are you guys planning to do while you are here?"

Chester and Erika shot quick glances at each other. "We plan to just spend a few days alone, do some hiking and exploring and check out the town, maybe grab one of those famous buffalo burgers we have heard about at the Buckhorn Café in Cuyama."

"Ah yes, the famous Buckhorn," replied Mary. "We went there for dinner one night. Of course we are vegetarians and everything on the menu has meat in it. But we managed to get by with the spaghetti and meatballs by asking them to hold the meat! You have to go there for breakfast or dinner. It's like stepping back in time, a real kick. Everyone is dressed like cowboys or oil field workers. It's a very fifties type of a motif in there. You will love it," she added.

"Come on," Mark said. "I want to get out of here before creepo drives by here again tonight."

"Creepo?" repeated Chester.

"Yeah, this guy we told you about drives through the campground every night just after the sun goes down. He doesn't stay. Maybe he is looking for some friends. Maybe he does not want to camp here with other people. He gave us a good looking over the first time he was here, but after that, he just drives through and then leaves."

"Sounds harmless enough," said Chester.

"Probably," replied Mark, "but we have had enough. We are off to the Saline Valley for some star watching. I know we can find some seclusion out there."

The couple retreated to gather the rest of their camping gear and tooted their horn as they drove away from the campground.

"Do you think that guy they talked about will be back tonight?" Erika asked.

"Not sure but it should not be a problem. I brought my 45 semi-auto. We should be fine if this guy shows up and gets nosey. Did you bring your Target Master pistol?"

"Yup," she replied.

They had not started up as a gun enthusiast couple. Chester had owned guns all his life. Erika had not. When they had first begun dating, Erika had refused to have anything to do with shooting sports or firearms in general. She had refused to even hold one of Chester's guns. With the passage of time, increased crime and the effort of the government to clamp down on gun ownership, Erika had finally been persuaded to go target shooting and eventually gained a proficiency and pleasure in shooting sports. Her twenty-two caliber pistol was a popgun compared to the large caliber semi-auto pistol Chester had brought along for the trip. Hers had been a birthday present from Chester, complete with pink pistol grips. His had been a hand-me-down gift from his father, a World War ll relic he had been able to hide in his duffel bag upon returning stateside from the war. What it gave up in accuracy in any target over twenty-five feet was more than made up by the sound it made when fired and the impressive muzzle flash.

Secure in the knowledge that they were well armed against any harm from man or local beast, they turned off their propane camp light and retreated to the safety of their tent.

CHAPTER TWENTY-EIGHT

THE HEADLIGHTS OF JACK MORRISON'S RENTAL CAR BOUNCED
and gyrated up and down on the road in front of him as he drove slowly
along Cottonwood Canyon Road toward the campground at the end of
the road. Beyond his headlights it was pitch black. The poorly maintained
road had originally been used by the first settlers in the region to access
their remote ranches. The road had later been upgraded by the oil companies that had flocked to the area during the oil boom of the 1950s. But
with their withdrawal from the region, it had become a poor remnant of
its former self. It was only intermittently maintained by the county. Jack
zigged and zagged around the foot-deep potholes in an effort to keep his
tires on what remained of the old blacktop and oiled base road. As he jolted
and swerved along, he caught brief glimpses of the surrounding landscape
and local wildlife. A flock of buzzards were highlighted for a second in the
branches of an oak tree. They huddled in clutches, appearing ever so much
like black-robed court justices, poised to cast down their rulings upon the
rangeland below. A coyote bolted from the brush and shot an accusing look
back at Jack as it slinked off into the safety of the dark.

As he had for the past several evenings, Jack continued up the road, his eyes peeled for campers who might fit the description of the people who had come into possession of the map. There were only two local campgrounds in the region to observe and the Buckhorn Café sat next door to the only motel in the valley. He had received information via John Riggs that the trio who had come into possession of the map were going to be staying in the valley to work on identifying the locations of Rick French's hidden stashes. Jack Morrison had not had any contact with John Riggs since the disappearance of French five years previous. Riggs had been instrumental in setting up the periodic wire transfers to an Australian entity that provided payments to Jack, but Riggs had left it up to French to deal with Jack on communications thereafter and the final outcome of money French had promised to pay to Jack once the court proceedings on his disappearance and later probate had been concluded.

"Two is company, three's a crowd," he had stated at the conclusion of his phone call from Riggs. French owed him money and had concocted his plan to settle the debt once and for all. All of this was about to happen, but the introduction of Chester, Erika, and Arnie into the mix had inserted an unwanted third leg to the arrangement, a leg that could potentially disrupt his payout. And so he had methodically cruised through each of the campgrounds in the Cuyama Valley looking for any sign of the trio who would be looking for the French fortune. Being ensconced at the Buckhorn Motel, he had observed all of the comings and goings of those staying at the establishment and had been able to determine that the clientele consisted of oil field workers and deer hunters preparing for the opening of the hunting season that weekend.

Campers were known to camp alongside several of the other remote roads in the valley and Jack had also driven along Wasiola and Bell Roads looking for signs of his party. But law enforcement was also on the watch for illegal campers and Jack concentrated his efforts on the three target locations that the trio might use as their base camp. The Cottonwood Canyon campground was a little maintained, semi-abandoned venue that was a shadow of its former self. He drove up the hill past the bullet-ridden sign at the entrance to the campground and looked at the abandoned Forest Service buildings that had been used in the past by rangers and maintenance personnel. Windows to the low-set building had been broken out and the front doors were ajar, hanging lazily on sagging hinges. His headlights scanned quickly into the open buildings, casting a fleeting image of derelict furniture, trash, and broken glass. A mattress lay partially in the doorway of one building, evidencing someone's willingness to use the old mouse infested structure in days past.

Jack drove around the campground circle and spotted a Volkswagen Campermobile in a secluded spot parked among some large juniper trees. A small tent was located in the campsite. He immediately recognized the van as belonging to Rick French. He had conducted drug transactions with French many times in years past and recognized the vehicle as one of several that French had used to deliver product to him.

Someone turned on a flashlight inside the tent. Jack continued to drive slowly past the tent as if looking at the other spots in the campground. The couple who had been staying there earlier in the week were gone. A smile curled on Jacks lips as he exited the campground and returned to his motel room. It was game time. The people who had the information to locate the oil wells that held the money that was due to him were now on the scene. The situation was now in play. Jack knew that the time for action had come. He was willing to kill again. It would probably come to that, but he reasoned that keeping surveillance of the campers and letting them work the map was a more efficient way to retrieve his fortune. If he killed them now, law enforcement would become involved, possibly before he could retrieve the money and gold coins and make his exit from the county to a safer location.

He returned to his room at the Buckhorn Motel and prepared his plan of attack for the next morning. The campers in the campground would likely rise early and perhaps begin their survey of the area the next day. He would be prepared for that. The plateau that rose to meet the mountains to the west of the valley floor was dotted with dense groves of junipers and digger pines. It would afford him the advantage of hiding his car in the trees while at the same time giving him a view of the campground and the highway below. All he had to do was lie in wait and observe the couple with his high-powered binoculars. If they indeed had the map and were successful in retrieving anything from the old wells, he would have no trouble determining this fact. He could then make his move and bring an end to the wait for his long overdue payment.

Chester and Erika rose just before dawn the next morning. The early fall day was going to be another hot one and Erika wanted to get an early start to beat the heat. They had decided on the area of their search and had honed in on the western portion of the Rummell Ranch Oil Field where the majority of the marked wells had been noted on the map as being inactive, shut in from production.

"If we concentrate on areas where no wells are operating, we should have less chance of running into oil field workers or anyone else who might be working in the area" Erika had reasoned. They were less concerned about running into a rancher or landowner. The entire valley was devoid of grass at this time of the year. Cattle had been shipped out of the valley in the early summer at the conclusion of the short, high desert grazing season.

They approached a dirt road that lay across the highway from an old gas plant in the oil field. They were surprised to find no gate or locks of any kind. "Must be easier for the truckers and roustabouts to just keep things open instead of having to get out and open and close gates all day long," Chester reasoned as they left the highway. They began to bump along the dirt road that headed out into the rangeland. The van bounced and jerked, sending a trail of dust behind it as they followed their progress on the map. "Slow down!" Erika yelled as she became concerned with the cloud of dust that they were raising. "Someone is going to see all of this dust and come to see what we are up to."

"Don't worry," Chester replied. "If someone stops us we will just act like we are lost and will ask for directions back to town. We can tell them we are looking for the trail to Santa Bonita Canyon.

They continued on and began to drive by abandoned oil wells and tank batteries. Some of the wells were still complete with jack pumps in place as if someone had just walked off the job that day. The rust on the pumping rod bespoke of the inactivity of those wells. Some wells were devoid of pumping apparatus. Old rusty tanks were still on site, with holes in their sides evidencing the long ago cessation of use. But the well bore locations were clearly evident. Some of the wells had been welded shut while others had been closed off with threaded steel caps. The old abandoned oil wells stood as silent headstones of a past vibrant oil field, its participants now long gone from the area. "I bet the wells we are looking for will have those caps on them," Chester had reasoned. "No one is going to weld a casing shut if they want to come back later and get something out of it."

Just as they approached the tree line, they came upon the object of their search. "This should be well 355," Erika said as they rolled up on a well site. The well bore was located several feet from a partially dismantled pump jack that had a sign proclaiming this to be well 355. As they had hoped, they noted a threaded steel cap on the well. They drove past the well and looked around for any signs of cars or oil field workers in the area. Several miles off on a ridgeline they saw what appeared to be an oil well service rig, which was positioned over a well. They could hear an engine running as the crew pulled lengths of pipe from the well. The crew was several miles off and did not appear to notice Erika and Chester as they circled back and stopped alongside well 355.

"Do we get out and pop off the cap?" asked Erika.

"We have come this far, let's see what we find," replied Chester.

They got out of the van and walked over to the well. Chester placed his hands around the cap and tried to remove it. It did not budge. He returned to the van and retrieved a large pipe wrench. Straining mightily, he tried to remove the cap. Still no success.

"Who put this thing on," Erika exclaimed, "Mighty Mouse?"

Chester kneeled alongside the well, looking at the threads on the well pipe. "Hey, this thing is spot welded!" he exclaimed. "Just a couple of small spots, but we are not going to be able to unscrew this thing until we get a chisel or something else we can use to cut through those small welds."

He looked through the tools they had brought from home and brought back a small sledgehammer and a chisel. Pounding at the welds, he made short work of the task and was able to unscrew the cap on top of the well. They peered down the well bore, holding a flashlight to illuminate down inside the shaft. Near the top, a chain was welded to the inside of the well. They could see something hanging at the end of the chain about ten feet down. Far below Chester could see the shimmering surface of a liquid, water with an oily sheen. A strong odor of petroleum wafted out of the bore hole. Chester reached down into the well and began pulling on the chain. In a moment, a burlap-wrapped cylindrical package emerged. Chester cut the wired package from the chain and threw the chain back down the well.

"Put the cap back on this thing and let's get out of here!" he yelled as he picked up his tools and the burlap package. Erika screwed the cap back on the well and jumped into the van. As they made a speedy retreat back to the highway, they looked across the hills to the crew that was working on the nearby ridge. They still did not appear to have noticed the couple.

"I think we can make a clean break out of here!" exclaimed Chester. "No one will even know we were here." Smiles began to appear on the couple's faces and they reached the highway and returned to their campground.

On the plateau above the valley, Jack put his binoculars away and sat smoking a cigarette. Hidden from view among the scrub oaks and cedars, he had observed the couple find something in the well but had not seen them open their find to expose its contents. Their hasty retreat meant that something was up. He would need to monitor their activity and follow up.

He quickly returned to his motel, paid his bill, and checked out. Making a quick stop at the store for provisions, he continued on to the Cottonwood Canyon campground and pulled off to spend the night at a turnout before getting to the campground. He did not want to alarm them needlessly by making his presence known to them. If the couple decided to make a run for it with what they had found in the well, he would be the first to know.

Back at their camp, Erika and Chester quickly parked the van and opened the side door to access the rear seat and eating area. Chester placed the burlap sack squarely in front of them on the folding table. It was heavy and clanked as he set it down in front of them. The sides bulged with the weight of the contents. It was tied with a plastic zip tie. It smelled musty with notes of petroleum.

"Get out your knife," exclaimed Erika, "and cut that thing off."

Chester sawed on the zip tie with no success. Reaching down into a small toolbox under the table, he retrieved some wire cutters and made quick work of the zip tie.

"Wait a minute!" cried Erika. She got a towel and placed it under the burlap bag.

"Who knows what is in this thing. Now, go ahead and pour it out."

Chester grabbed the sack with both hands and heaved it upside down holding the neck closed with one hand so that the contents did not spill out all over the table.

"This thing weighs a ton. Are you ready?" he asked.

"Dump it," Erika replied.

Chester loosened his grip on the neck and slowly released the bag's contents. Gold coins began to emerge from the bag, making a clinking sound as though a slot machine was paying off at a casino. The slow clinking sound turned into a roar as the contents of the bag poured out in a rush before them. They sat silent, dumbfounded as they surveyed the large pile of gold coins. Erika reached into the pile and retrieved one of the coins.

"One ounce of .9999 fine gold," she stated as she looked at the back of the coin. They were the size of a quarter but contained the familiar image of an Indian's head on the front and a buffalo on the back.

"Minted in 1910," she continued. "Looks like we have some of those coins that were minted for collectors to buy or people who don't trust our own currency anymore."

Chester reached over and dug his hand into the pile with both hands. "We're rich!" he cried out as he let the coins dribble out of his hands back into the pile. The tinkling of the coins brought a smile to both of their lips.

"What are they worth?" he asked.

"The spot gold price right now is about sixteen hundred dollars an ounce," she replied.

"You mean each one of these is worth sixteen hundred bucks?" he asked.

They began counting the coins in the pile, making neat stacks of ten coins each in front of them.

"Four hundred and eighty," said Erika as they finished stacking the rows of coins. "That's thirty pounds of gold."

Chester took out his phone and accessed the calculator function. "Seven hundred and sixty thousand dollars," he exclaimed. "This beats the Terra Auri reward all to hell," he continued.

"Don't count your chickens just yet," replied Erika. "There are twenty more well locations we still need to find. What are we going to do with this stuff while we are out looking for the other wells? We can't just carry it with us and we certainly can't leave it in the tent. What if one of those oil crews comes over and finds out what we are doing?

"Let's give Arnie a call and let him know what we found and see what he thinks."

"Okay," she replied. "We will have to drive into town to get cell phone reception so let's eat at the Buckhorn and make the call." The couple cleaned up and quickly changed clothes.

As they bumped along the Cottonwood Canyon Road, Chester could not help reaching down and touching the bag of gold coins they had placed on the floorboard between them behind the floor shifter, verifying that their newly found fortune was still in their possession. As they rounded a bend and began the descent into the valley, they noticed a late model SUV parked alongside the road in a turnout area. A swarthy bearded man was leaning up against the side of the car smoking a cigarette and gazing down on the valley below. His dark eyes stared at the couple as they drove by.

Erika shivered. "I hope that guy is not hanging around tonight when we get back," she said.

"We are well armed," Chester replied, patting the bulge under his shirt that concealed his forty-five semi-auto. "You brought your Target Master along, right?" he asked.

"No, I left it in the tent when we changed," she replied.

"Everything will be fine," he continued. "He's probably just some guy out hiking around and taking a smoke break."

They remained concerned as they pulled up to the Buckhorn and parked the car. Nearly a million dollars lying between them in the van was enough to heighten their senses and raise their suspicions of people and places they would not ordinarily have given a second thought to.

"What do we do with the stash?" asked Chester.

"Just stick it in the refrigerator," Erika replied. "We can get a seat by the window so we can keep track of the van while we are eating."

They entered the café and chose a booth in the back of the restaurant with a window overlooking the parking lot. The restaurant was empty except for a trucker at the counter who was eating an early dinner and an older gentleman with a cowboy hat who was looking at a menu. Chester pulled out his phone and gave Arnie a call. "How's it going out there?" he heard Arnie say on the other end of the call. "Did you have any luck finding the wells?"

"We found the first one," replied Chester, "and it was a doozy!"

Erika grabbed the phone from Chester, looking around the diner to see who might have heard his remark. "Shh!" she exclaimed under her breath. "Arnie, we have confirmation on one location and will be heading out tomorrow to locate more of the product. We have a logistical problem though and want your thoughts on how we handle this recovery project."

"What is the problem?" replied Arnie.

"The first package weighed nearly thirty pounds and has a value of seven eight zero."

"What is that, seven eight zero?" replied Arnie.

"Just add three zeros to that number," she replied quietly.

The phone was silent for a moment as Arnie digested that information. He did the math in his head to estimate the total financial fortune that might be hidden in the rest of the marked well locations.

"I understand the problem," he replied. "If you are looking at additional locations with similar amounts of product you might have twenty times this value by the time you are done. You can't risk hiding it in your van under a blanket or something. My snooping around Riggs's office indicated that some of this might be in paper bills. I am just about ready to fax myself down to Surfers Paradise to see what I can dig up on the CTG entity. Let's do this. I will make that trip and get back in a day or so. You and Chester go out tomorrow and try to locate another well or two and find out what is in there. Get the number of the fax machine in the motel and check in there tomorrow so you have a safer location to work from. I will fax myself to the motel when I get back and start transporting what you find back home. I'll take it to a safe deposit box at the bank for safe keeping. I can do this in a day and can start helping you with the hunt. You need to hide the map just in case someone busts you. Put it back in the headliner. It should be safe there."

"Okay, we will check in to the motel tomorrow night," agreed Erika. "Let us know when to expect you."

With a solution to their problem, they ordered dinner and discussed their plan for the next day. As they left the restaurant, the older gentleman turned his head to watch the couple leave and get into their van. Herb Rummell smiled slightly from his table. He had been close enough to their table to determine that something important was being discussed on their phone conversation. Hushed tones and code words were enough to pique his interest.

As Chester and Erika bumped along Cottonwood Canyon Road back to their campsite, they were filled with apprehension. The stakes now were higher than when they had first started their treasure hunt. Three quarters of a million dollars in gold coins, most probably gained and hidden under questionable circumstances. Their best and worst hopes and fears had all come true. Their remote camping location in unfamiliar territory of eastern Santa Bonita County, seeing edgy people, and trespassing out on the local ranches to make the quick grab of the hidden fortune did not make them feel at ease or satisfied. They sensed grave danger; a feeling that was amplified as their headlights panned over the campground when they pulled up to their campsite. In the flash of the light, they observed the SUV they had seen that morning in the turnout to the campground as they had left that morning to begin their search. It was now parked in a campsite across from them.

Erika shuddered as they noticed the vehicle. Quickly getting out of their van, they entered their tent, bag of gold coins in hand, and zipped up the tent opening. "Put out the light," Chester said quietly. They sat silently in their tent. "That guy makes me nervous" whispered Erika. "Should we get back in the van and leave?"

"Just let me think," he replied. Erika could feel her heart pounding in her chest as the two sat in silence.

"Maybe he is just camping," Chester said finally. He had a sinking feeling that he was wrong about that statement.

"What if the guy is on to us and is connected with the money and the guy that French owes money to? We should get out of here and make a run for it."

"Quiet," he whispered. "If we make a dash for it, he could run us down in a few miles and push us off the road or get in front of us and stop our getaway. The van is not a speed machine, you know."

"Well, let's get back into the van and spend the night. At least he can't break into it as easy as the tent," she suggested.

"No good," he answered. "If he is armed he could just knock us off from his campsite and take the money and run. I think we act as if nothing is wrong and then look at our options in the morning."

"I wish we had taken a satellite phone with us," moaned Erika. "At least we wouldn't have to deal with cell phones that don't work out here and would be able to call for help if we needed to."

"What would we tell the police? We have been out here taking property that does not belong to us and the guy that might own it is trying to kill us and get it back?" he replied.

Erika sat a moment in silence. "You're right," she whispered. "We are in this too deep. Let's just act like nothing is wrong and we can get up early and decide what to do then, maybe make a run for it."

The couple turned in for the night for a fitful rest.

CHAPTER TWENTY-NINE

CEDRICK TORMEY APPLIED OINTMENT TO HIS FOOT, WORK-
ing the antiseptic cream in and around the sutures on his recently altered
appendage. Deep purple lines were burnished into his skin where his
assailants had sheared off his big toe and crudely sutured up the wound.
Their message to him had been clear. Richard S. French was no longer
alive. Anyone asking about him was to be told that Cedrick had performed
a thorough search of all available sources and had determined that no such
person existed within the borders of Australia, in particular the Surfers
Paradise area. Erika, his client in the States, had been disappointed when
he reported the results to her, but she had seemed to have accepted the nil
report, asking only a few follow-up questions as to the sources he had used
to complete his task.

Now that he was missing his big toe, he questioned her story about
having located some Australian real estate assets in an estate and the need
to clear title on the assets to enable them to be sold. He had no idea what
the larger picture of her investigation looked like, and frankly, he no longer cared. His foot would heal, he might walk with a slight change of gait,
but life would go on. The five-thousand-dollar investigation fee and the

ten-thousand-dollar cash payment from his abductors were of little solace, but at least he was alive. His cell phone rang on the kitchen counter where he kept it attached to its charger. He hobbled over to it and saw a number he did not recognize, a number from an area code in the United States. Hesitating for a moment, he decided to pick up the phone. He was greeted on the other end by a male voice.

"Hello. My name is Arnie Jensen. I am working with Erika McConika and want to follow up on your assignment to locate Mr. French."

"My assignment has been completed," replied Cedrick glumly. "As I informed Ms. McConika, I could find no trace of the subject anywhere in the region or on the continent, for that matter, or even that he had entered the country."

"Yes, Erika told me about your search results but I want to discuss where you looked and what records were researched to reach your conclusion," replied Arnie.

"Look," Cedrick replied angrily, "I spent quite a lot of time on this project at some peril to my life and came up with nothing, not even a hint that such a person ever came to our fair shores. If you have some hard-on to locate this guy, you will need to look elsewhere. Save yourself the time and expense of flying down here and just drop it. I am done with this assignment!"

"Look, we spent five thousand dollars for you to do this work for us. Cash paid in advance. I am already down here staying at a hotel. I just want to meet with you for a few minutes to go over the resources you used to look for French so I can make sure that there are no other places we should be looking down here. I can pay you for your time."

"No. I am not willing to meet. I have performed my duties and given a report of the results. This assignment is now closed," Cedrick answered abruptly. He hung up the phone and hobbled over to his living room arm-chair. "Pesky people, just won't take no for an answer," he mumbled under his breath. He raised his foot and placed it on the footrest and waited for the throbbing to lessen. He stared at his bandaged foot and weighed the value of the fifteen thousand dollar addition to his finances from the recent debacle. Five from Erika and ten from the masked foot surgeons who had waylaid him in the beach parking lot. He looked at his remaining big toe. Was it worth another fifteen grand to him? What was the whole set of toes worth? Would he be able to walk normally again? Was there any amount of money that would make him take this kind of risk again?

Arnie clicked off his cell phone, angry that he was unable to convince Cedrick to meet. He was not in Australia at all but could be there in the time it took to locate Cedrick's office fax machine number, walk over to his home office multi-function copy machine, and fax himself to that location. He picked up the copy of the e-mail from Cedrick that Erika had shared with him and Chester. At the bottom of the communiqué he found Cedrick's full contact information. Quickly accessing time zone information on his laptop, he determined the appropriate evening hour when he should fax himself to Cedrick's office in Surfers Paradise and then made the conversion for his time of departure from California. He would travel light. No suitcase or change of clothes. Cash and credit cards in his wallet would be sufficient for this trip. He could exchange dollars into the local currency at any bank and he had sufficient space on his credit cards to enable him to stay in that country for an extended period of time. Not that he would need to. An early morning search of that office and perhaps another day or two of fax snooping would be sufficient to tell if any further clues as to the location of the missing French existed. He could buy what he needed to when he arrived and could arrange for accommodations later.

He looked at time zone information again and determined that there was a nineteen-hour time difference from his home office and the east coast of Australia. Quickly doing the math, he made plans to fax himself to Cedrick's office. He would leave at 9:00 a.m. to get to that office at 2:00 a.m. He would be leaping ahead a full day with the time zone differences. Finding out if Richard S. French still existed was key to collecting the insurance company reward for the suspected fraud he and his friends had fleshed out from the events to date. If such a man really ever existed and had spent time in Surfers Paradise, Arnie was determined to find out.

He awoke from a fitful sleep at the appointed hour in his La-Z-Boy recliner. The television was still on, playing a delayed taping of one of his late night TV shows. Jay Leno was going through his monologue routine to an enthusiastic audience. Fully clothed, Arnie was ready for his fax journey. Approaching his fax machine, he glanced down at his note, dialed the fax machine in Cedrick Tormey's office, and pushed the send button. With hands placed into the feeder, he began his journey.

It was dark in Cedrick's office as Arnie emerged from the fax machine. Partially opened venetian blinds let the dull amber glow of a streetlight show through. Arnie picked himself up from the floor and walked over to the window. He peered out onto the scene of a mixed-use industrial neighborhood. He could see large concrete and brick buildings across the street with shipping docks to the side and behind the buildings. From the second-floor vantage point, he could see various businesses were located up and down the street. Cedrick's office was located above a carpet and flooring warehouse boasting the company name of Wallaby Industrial Flooring. From the window, he could see a large plastic kangaroo with a roll of carpet sticking out of its pouch, advertising the business.

Arnie took note of the security alarm components that adorned the buildings. Taking no chances, he slowly closed the blinds and closed the curtains. When he turned on the office lights, he found a small one-room office filled with cheap office furniture. Spartan but neat in its appearance, it served the business purposes of its occupant. The office provided a business address for the few meetings necessary in the detective trade, while at the same time keeping down costs. There was no need for paneled walls or plushy office furniture in a private investigator's line of business. An air of seediness and an office location off the beaten path was essential to creating the cloak and dagger atmosphere Cedrick's clients were interested in.

Arnie looked around the office and located a large, four-drawer metal filing cabinet. The bronze-colored filing cabinet was old and the drawers groaned on dry rollers as he looked through each of them for files that pertained to French, Certified Global Transfer, or Erika's search assignment. He could find nothing in the cabinet. Looking around the office, he saw an older couch, a couple of chairs in front of Cedrick's desk, and an antique coatrack. "Damn," he muttered under his breath. He pulled open the drawers to the desk and found files pertaining to the detective business in general but no case files. Old tax returns, billings for past cases, and a file containing vacation plans for an upcoming surfing vacation to Hawaii did nothing to help Arnie in his search. He strode back to the filing cabinet and began pulling random files, taking note of the general contents of each. "This stuff is all old junk," he exclaimed as he scanned the latest pages of each file. "What the hell has this guy been doing for the past few years?" he muttered.

Then it hit him. People did not keep physical files anymore. Even the most rudimentary of businesses made use of computer hard drives or flash drives for storing documents these days. It took only a moment for Arnie to decide his next course of action. He did not have the password to access Cedrick's computer. He had only just begun to explore his newfound ability to scan himself into his multifunction home office machine but he had successfully been able to store himself in a scanned file stored onto his office computer and manipulate the machine to create an e-mail. From there it was a simple process to attach the scanned image of himself to that e-mail and send it to someone. Once there he could manipulate that machine to open the document and print it off. He picked up a business card from Cedrick's desk and then faxed himself back to his home office fax machine. In a matter of minutes, he scanned himself into his office machine, manipulated his computer from within the bowels of the apparatus, and then sent an e-mail back to Cedrick and attached himself to that e-mail.

In the next instant, he was aware of being transported across communication lines back to Cedrick's office. He was no longer inside the dimly lit office. Instead, he became aware of multiple electronic files in the directory of Cedrick's office computer. The directory to Cedrick's computer was well laid out and organized. He had created numerous files, some personal and some business. Arnie saw a directory for case files, organized by year and month. Quickly finding a file for the preceding month's work, he located the file pertaining to Erika's inquiry and began reviewing the documents and notes in that file. He passed by the retainer agreement and saw that the file had only a few pages of documents to review. First were the notes of his conversation with Erika followed by a written contract outlining the scope of his work to locate Richard S. French. The last document contained notes relating to a bank account number with the account title in the name of Certified Transfer Global. A copy of an endorsed check into that account was stored in the file. At the bottom of the last page was a report to Erika indicating Cedrick had exhausted all avenues and had come up empty handed as to the existence of the subject person. At the bottom of the page was a final note, "Case Closed."

Arnie made another check of the files and directories in the computer and could find no other associations to the French assignment. He needed to get out of Cedrick's computer. He manipulated the machine and located the scanned image of himself that he had sent from his home office machine. Printing off that scanned image of himself on Cedrick's copier, he re-emerged from the office printer.

The sun had begun to cast a dull glow into the window. Arnie walked over to the window and checked for activity below. A large truck was now parked in front of the carpet store. Its flashers were blinking on and off while the truck idled near the loading dock. There was no other activity on the street. Arnie determined that he would be needing to spend some time in the city to uncover references to Certified Transfer Global. That was the only lead he had discovered from the scanty case file he had reviewed. He exited the office and walked down a steep set of stairs that provided access to the ground floor offices. The exit door was a glass-paned affair with a crash bar that permitted occupants to quickly leave the building while providing security against intruders by way of a keypad located on the exterior of the building next to the door.

Arnie arranged for a taxi via his cell phone. After being quickly picked up, he made arrangements to be taken to a hotel on the beach in Surfers Paradise so that he could continue his investigation of Tormey and the French missing person's assignment. He had found it odd that Cedrick had been unwilling to meet with him. His offer to pay him for his time had been rejected outright. His office did not reflect a person who was in a position to pass up the opportunity to make a few extra bucks. There was more to this than met the eye and Certified Transfer Global was the only clue he had discovered that might lead to the whereabouts of French. It was a long shot but Arnie sensed that he would need to be on the ground in Surfers Paradise if he had any hope of closing the loop on the disappearance of French and laying claim to part of the life insurance.

"Tell me, my good man, what hotel do you recommend that is located along the shore?" he had asked after getting into the taxi.

"There are plenty of fine establishments along the shore," the driver had replied. "Are you here for business or pleasure?"

"A little of both," replied Arnie.

"I would recommend the Crown Plaza. It is close to the water and has all the amenities you need for office support during your stay. And it is close to all the good restaurants and nightlife."

"That would be great," replied Arnie.

He was driven to the entrance of the hotel and was shown the check-in desk by the bellman as he entered the lobby.

"Do you have availability for a few nights' stay?" he asked the receptionist.

"Let me check," she replied, consulting her reservation system. "Yes, we have an ocean view room available at three hundred and forty a night for two nights only."

"That will be fine," Arnie replied. "I should be done with my meetings by then."

"Can we help you with your bags?" she offered, looking over at the bellman's desk.

"They misplaced them at the airport" he replied. "Guess I will just pick up a few things until they arrive."

"We will bring them up to your room as soon as they get here," she replied, handing him the room key card. "Enjoy your stay."

CHAPTER THIRTY

THE CIGARETTE GLOWED IN THE PREDAWN MORNING LIGHT from an outcropping of boulders overlooking well number 495. With each inhalation, the face of Jack Morrison was illuminated for a moment. Silver rings on his right hand shone brightly for an instant and then disappeared back into the dark as he exhaled and lowered the cigarette from view. He had left the campground during the early morning, packing up his camp completely to signal his departure to Chester and Erika. He had chosen the current well sight not for any reason other than it sat high up in the foothills and provided a good view of the Cuyama Valley and in particular the highway and its intersection with Cottonwood Canyon Road. If Chester and Erika chose to make a run for it in the dark, he would be able to see their headlights.

As the sun began to light the sky over the top of the Caliente Range to the east, he set up a spotting scope and trained it on the Cottonwood Canyon Campground. He could see the glow of a small light inside their tent. The silhouettes of the occupants moved in and out of view as they moved inside the tent. The couple emerged from the tent and looked surprised, relieved, as they saw they were the only occupants of the campground. The man went inside of the van and returned shortly with a large rolled-up piece of paper which he spread out on the camping table. The couple bent over the paper, pointed, and talked to each other for a while and then rolled up the paper and returned it back to the van.

The couple loaded the van with their tent and camping equipment and drove down the canyon toward the highway. Turning north onto a dirt oil field road, he watched as they drove past oil well locations. They slowed down each time they came to the circular patches of ground where pump jacks were located. Jack observed that they seemed to have no interest in wells where the pumps were operating. Instead, they seemed to be interested in the abandoned well site locations where the pumps had been removed or had been dismantled and set off to the side. Several times he saw the couple exit the van and walk around the well sites. They walked up to the rotting storage tanks and picked up fallen markers that held the well naming information, discarding the markers each time they proceeded to a new well location.

Finally, the couple stopped at a well about a mile east of where Jack had positioned himself and began to withdraw tools and gloves from a chest located in the rear of their van. The man began pounding on a well cap with a hammer and chisel while the woman watched and appeared to offer encouragement each time he stopped to rest. After a while, Jack saw the man return to the tool chest and retrieve a large pipe wrench and a long bar which he placed on the handle of the pipe wrench and positioned around the well cap. The cap was removed and the couple bent over the exposed well and looked down into the bore hole. They began pulling on a chain and pulled up a circular burlap sack. Jack had seen enough. Quickly dismantling his spotting scope, he jumped into his car and began to drive back to the highway. He located the dirt oil field road that would intersect with the well Erika and Chester had opened and he turned his wheel sharply to enter onto the ranch. Clouds of dust kicked up behind his car and he sped to cut off Chester and Erika's retreat. He could see the dust from their van kicking up from the canyon they were traveling down as they drove toward the highway below them. Jack's SUV fishtailed wildly as he swerved along the dirt road, avoiding pot holes and dodging oil wells and tank batteries. He reached the mouth of the canyon before Chester and Erika and stopped short, out of sight. At the moment their van came into view from around the corner of the canyon, he pulled his car out to block the road.

As Chester and Erika came around the corner, Jack was standing behind the hood of his car holding a pistol. "Chess, stop!" screamed Erika. "Hold on!" cried Chester as he slammed on his brakes. The van started to slide sideways, slowing to a stop parallel to Jack's car.

"Show me your hands!" yelled Jack, leveling his pistol at the couple. Erika and Chester froze in their seats. Jack raised his pistol and fired off a shot into the sky. The empty cartridge made a tinking sound as it hit the rocky ground alongside Jack. "Get them up!" he yelled again. The couple raised their hands, the color drained from their faces. Reaching into his back pants pocket, Jack retrieved two large black zip ties and threw them through the van window onto Erika's lap. "Tie his hands together" he rasped at Erika.

"Don't shoot! We will give you anything you want," she replied.

Chester grabbed for his door handle to exit the van. Jack fired off another shot through the side window behind the couple, sprinkling broken glass over them.

"Okay, okay," Chester said. He placed his hands behind his back and leaned forward. "Just put the band around my wrists and pull it tight," he said to Erika.

Erika did as he instructed and then turned to face Jack again. "You're the guy from the campground. Don't shoot us. What do you want from us?"

"Just trade seats with your boyfriend and drive back to the campground. I will follow behind. I won't hurt you as long as you follow my directions. Don't get any ideas of being the big hero," he said to Chester. "If you don't cooperate fully, I will put a bullet into each of your heads."

Chester exited the van and Erika traded seats with him after helping him back into the passenger's side of the van. As she got behind the wheel and started the drive back to the campground, she glanced behind her and verified that their accoster was following closely behind in his SUV.

"Who is that guy? What does he want with us?" asked Erika.

"I don't know. He must have some connection to the French money. Why else would someone be out here on this ranch or have been staying in the same campground as us?"

"He is going to kill us, isn't he?" she asked.

"Probably. Let me think a minute. Don't drive so fast, give me some time to sort this out," he replied. Chester tried to recall the events of the weeks leading up to the past few days' search in the oil field. The guy who wanted to buy their van at the auction, the break-in of the van, and seeing their captor staying in the same campground and skulking around the countryside.

"I think someone has been following us all along and has some connection to this van," he stated. "Whoever hid the map in the ceiling of the van probably hid all this money and gold we are finding and had planned to retrieve his van when it was finally sold from the auction yard. We got in the middle of this thing without knowing what it was all about."

"Do you think this guy is Rick French?" asked Erika.

Her question remained unanswered as they drove off the road into the campground and pulled up in front of their former campsite. The bearded stranger in the SUV pulled up beside them and motioned Erika to roll down her window.

"Not here," he said in a gravelly voice. He motioned with his pistol toward the derelict abandoned forest service buildings near the entrance to the campground. "Over there behind those buildings," he barked.

Erika started up the van and slowly drove it over to the parking spaces behind the buildings. Jack Morrison motioned for them to get out of the van and walked over to a door at the rear of the abandoned office. He grabbed the doorknob and pulled the door open. It sat crookedly on its hinges and rubbed along the ground as he forced it open.

"Should we run for it?" whispered Erika. Each of them was filled with dread as they looked into the dark recesses of the office. Jack stood before them, pistol in hand, motioning them into the building.

"He would shoot both of us before we could get ten feet," muttered Chester. "I don't think he is going to kill us, at least not immediately. We have something he wants and he is going to try to get it out of us. If he is this French guy, maybe all he wants is his map back so he can get his money and disappear again before anyone finds out."

They walked toward the faded green building. He stopped them at the door. "Turn around and put your hands behind you," he said to Erika. A black zip tie was quickly tightened around her wrists.

"Go on, get inside," he directed.

It took a few moments for their eyes to adjust to the dark interior of the building as they left the bright sunlight outside. They found two straight-backed wooden chairs and sat down uncomfortably, arms still tied behind their backs. As they became accustomed to the dark interior, they could see an old metal desk, some filing cabinets, and assorted papers and trash strewn about the office. Naked wires hung from the ceiling where light fixtures had been removed. The smell of dust and mouse excrement permeated the air. In the corner were two soiled mattresses.

"Let's make this short and sweet," their accoster said. "What are you doing out here and who are you working for?"

Erika spoke first. "We are camping and looking for old bottles and antiques from back in the days when the oil fields were booming."

"Yeah, we are collectors and were told we could find some good stuff if we looked around the old drilling sites," said Chester. "Drillers used to camp out for weeks at a time and would leave their stuff in pits or drop them down wells that were dry holes."

Their assailant rose from his chair and went outside. They heard him open the door to their van and he returned holding the burlap bag they had retrieved that morning. He dragged an old card table over in front of the pair and pulled a large folding buck knife from a sheath he had on his belt. Cutting the cord that held the tightly wrapped bundle together, he dumped the contents in front of them. Several handfuls of gold buffalo nickel coins fell out of the bag and spread out in front of them.

"Doesn't look like bottles to me," Jack said in an accusing voice. He shook the bag some more and several rolled bundles of paper currency fell from the bag on top of the gold coins. The bills were musty and smelled of crude oil. "Doesn't look like trash to me, either," Jack stated. "Is this what you found yesterday in the other place you were digging?"

Chester and Erika looked at each other. He knew what they had been up to. There was no point in lying. "Uh-huh," they both answered.

"You have a map or a list of where to look, right? Give it to me."

Chester spoke first. "We don't have a map. We just looked at an old oil field map to see where all the wells on this ranch are located and we just started driving around to find spots where the wells were no longer being used so we could dig around and find stuff. We were not expecting to find cash and gold and looked some more today to see if we had been lucky to find the first stash or if there was more hidden out there."

"We were going to turn all of this stuff over to the sheriff and make a claim for abandoned property if no one showed up to claim it," Erika added.

Jack sat for a moment and considered their stories. These people lacked the fidgety edginess of people involved in the drug trade. They appeared to him to be a couple of yuppies with no ties to his line of business. They were in over their heads. If they indeed were as innocent as they stated, killing them would complicate things unnecessarily. If there was more to the story, then he was at risk as well as anyone else connected to the French fortune. He could care less about what happened to French, but he did not want to alert local law enforcement of his presence or raise the ire of the Cut Toe Gang down under and risk retribution from them if harm came to French.

"I am going to give you some time to think about things and then I will ask you again what you know and who you are working with," Jack said. He rose from the table and reached into a backpack he had brought with him. Taking a coil of rope, he began wrapping it around Chester so that his legs and torso were tied securely to the chair and then did the same to Erika. He then walked out of the building and closed the door behind him.

They heard him start the engine to his car and drive away. "What do we do now?" cried out Erika. "I never should have let Arnie get us involved in this."

"This is seriously bad," answered Chester. "He is coming back and is going to want answers. He doesn't believe our bottle hunting story and even if he does, he might just kill us for the cash we have found and disappear."

"No one will find us for days out here. Arnie is the only one who knows we are out here," said Erika. "We could be dried-out jerky by the time someone finds us. I say we give him the map and hope he lets us go."

"That map is the only thing keeping us alive right now," replied Chester. "Look at us. We are not hardened criminals or professional treasure hunters. You're a CPA and I am a former stockbroker looking for my next career. He might believe us and just leave us here to finally escape. If he is just a thief who stumbled upon us, he will be more than happy to take the $750,000 and what we found today and run for it."

"Maybe," answered Erika. "How much do you think was in the bag today?"

"Looked like another 100 coins or so," replied Chester. "That is $150,000 or so, and the stacks of bills, one hundreds, they looked like, probably another $200,000. With what we found yesterday, that is about a million bucks. I bet we never see him again."

"I don't know" she replied. "People get greedy when money is involved. That is the whole premise on TV shows where people compete for prizes and money. People risk everything and end up losing just for the chance of getting more money."

"This is a little different, babe," replied Chester. "He has a gun. I bet this is not his first rodeo. He holds all the cards right now."

"I don't want to die here in this urine-soaked rats' nest for any amount of money. Let's just give him the map and get out of here," she replied.

"Do you think this guy is French?" he asked.

Erika stared back at Chester and thought for a moment. "Let's be logical about this," she answered. "If he is this guy French, he is the guy that hid the map in the ceiling and knows all about it and where it was hidden. I bet he tears the ceiling apart again when he gets back and finds it. If he is French, he might just take the map, leave us here to die, and get his money out of all those wells. Someone will eventually find our carcasses after he is long gone."

"And if he is not French?" asked Chester.

"That scenario has an equally poor outcome. If he is not French, he is either a friend of his or someone French is connected to, maybe someone who has a beef with French, maybe the Jack Morrison guy, 'Jackson', who was mentioned in the DEA report. If he is this Jackson guy, we are of more value to him alive because he does not really know about the map and its marked wells. If this is the case, he cannot afford to bump us off immediately. He will break us down until we tell him why we are really here and then he shoots us or leaves us to die here in this building."

The couple became silent, staring at the floor, considering their alternatives.

"We buy the most time by playing the part of a couple of city folk who are out looking for stuff around the old well drilling camps," said Chester. "If we spill our guts now, he tortures us to be sure we have told him everything and then shoots us. If we play our roles as naive bottle hunters, it buys us some time. Maybe someone will drive by and find us here or Arnie will get back from Australia and come out looking for us when he doesn't hear from us."

"Let's hope Arnie found out where French is hiding out down there and gets what he needs to have him extradited back to the US. Once we do not check in with him, I bet he gets back over here in a hurry and comes out looking for us," she replied.

Several hours passed. The pair struggled against their ropes from time to time in desperation as the building heated up in the midday sun and their thirst began to increase. Then they heard the sound of a car approaching the building.

Jack Morrison opened the door and strode inside holding a plastic water bottle and a bag of tools. He threw the bag down on the floor and walked over to Erika and Chester, water bottle in hand. After opening it, he offered them each a drink. Water spilled down their chests as the each eagerly drank from the bottle.

"That's enough for now," Jack growled. Walking over to the bag, he dumped the contents onto the floor. Chester's sledgehammer and chisel fell out in front of them. "You left these at the well where you found the sack of coins and bills," he said. "You are not bottle hunters. If you were, you would have been digging around with picks and shovels, not chiseling into the tops of abandoned oil wells. It is time to tell me what you know. No more stories. No more stalling."

"Okay, okay," said Erika. "Are you Rick French? Is this money all yours?"

"I am not French and who I am is of no concern of yours," replied Jack. "Let's just say I have an interest in the financial assets Rick owns and I am out here to collect a debt."

"Owns?" said Chester. "You mean the guy is not dead?"

"Dead, missing, disappeared. None of that matters. All you need to do is tell me what you know and how I find the rest of his hidden cash to save your skins."

"If we tell you what we know, will you let us go?" asked Erika.

"I will leave you both tied up here in this shack with enough food and water to give me a head start," he answered. "All I want is the money he owes me. Once I find that I couldn't care less about you two."

"We bought this van at an auction sale in Mendocino County," blurted Chester. "When we got the bid, a lawyer tried to buy it from us at the sales yard and then tracked me down at my house and tried again to get me to sell it to him."

"Lawyer? What was his name?"

"John Riggs," answered Chester.

"Continue," replied Jack.

"Well, we did not think much about it until someone broke into the van. We thought they were trying to steal it but later found out they had started to pull apart the interior and it looked like they did not want the van, just something hidden in it."

"So we found the ceiling fabric and trim all pulled apart," continued Erika. "And we found a map of the oil field. I thought things looked strange so while the boys continued with their van restoration, I did some digging around and found out the van had been owned by Rick French and that he had disappeared during a drug transaction in Tiburon and had finally been declared dead. He had been up there to conduct a deal with a man called Jackson and I looked at the DEA report in the probate file that suggested French had disappeared sometime while this deal was to have occurred."

"That is when she found out an estate had been opened in the local court and she started to track down what was going on," added Chester.

Jack's eyes narrowed as he listened to the pair lay out for him the substance of the sequence of events which had happened five years previous. Before him sat a couple who had stumbled into the facts of the transaction between himself and Rick French and which an insurance investigator and the local police had been unable to solve. "Go on, what made you think that French might have hidden stuff out here in Cuyama?"

"Well, I looked at the probate files and found out he owned a lot of real estate out here. He was posing as a jojoba farmer. He also owned a place in Santa Bonita and an expensive parcel on the Alistair ranch that he used just for surfing. He died with only a few hundred dollars to his name plus all this real estate and a lot of debts against his ranch. He also had this five-million-dollar insurance policy that had been taken out just a few months before he died. I thought it was strange that someone with no cash and no wife or kids would have an insurance policy on his life."

"Tell him about the insurance guy and what he thought about all of this," added Chester.

"Yes, tell me about that," urged Jack.

"I tracked down the guy who investigated the disappearance for Western General Life. He told us he had found out everything we had about French and his finances and had concluded from interviews with friends of French that he had skipped out to Surfers Paradise in Australia and was living off of his drug money cash under the protection of the Cut Toe Gang down there."

Jack's eyes narrowed at this reference.

"Cut Toe Gang"?

"Yes," blurted Chester. "These guys must be some bad hombres because the insurance guy said he was warned by an informant that French was still alive and was part of a cartel down there made up of former drug dealers that looked out for each other and protected the members from anyone who was looking for any of them. They were known to have cut the toes off of private investigators or law enforcement who they found out were looking for any of the group. They were sending a message to lay off of them and their members. He told us he was sure French was still alive down there but he had been prohibited from looking further by Western General due to the danger involved."

"So you decided to find this money before French did?" asked Jack.

"It is more than that," replied Erika. "When I looked at the court file I found a petition filed by Riggs to close and distribute the remaining assets of the estate. They are sitting on five million dollars of insurance proceeds that will go out to his parents and sisters. We think French will get the money somehow from his family, get the rest of his stuff hidden on the ranch, and then conclude forever his disappearance, pay off Jackson and the Cut Toe Gang for their help, and live out his life surfing and leisure, never having to look over his shoulder again."

"So you two are good Samaritans trying to expose his scheme and collect some reward money for your trouble?" asked Jack.

"Kind of," replied Chester. "We worked out a deal with Western General where we will split any insurance money recovery and what we find from our search on the ranches in the valley. They will have the satisfaction of exposing the insurance fraud and recovering the money they had to pay out to his estate."

"Can you let us go now?" asked Erika. "We have told you everything we know."

"Maybe," he replied. "Where is the map?

"We hid it in the ceiling of the van," replied Chester.

Jack rose from where he was sitting and walked outside. They could hear him slide open the side door to the van and prying sounds as he disassembled the ceiling trim and fabric that hid the contents in the ceiling of the vehicle. He returned with the rolled-up map and spread it out over the piles of gold coins and cash on the desk.

"So which locations are the ones where French stored his cash?" asked Jack.

"They are the ones where the symbol by the wells are marked with a cross, not an X as listed in the map legend. They are not on the legend of the map and were drawn on by someone to look like they are official. These are the wells where we found the first two bags of cash and coins," said Erika, looking down at the map.

Jack looked at the map for a moment longer. "Looks like there are ten or fifteen more of these out there." He glanced at his watch and looked outside. "It will be dark soon. Let's see if you are right tomorrow morning. If I get my money, I will let you go. If you are screwing with me or hiding something, I will leave you out here for the coyotes."

CHAPTER THIRTY-ONE

ARNIE SAT IN HIS CAR, FRUSTRATED WITH NOT BEING ABLE TO get any information from the local branch of Commonwealth Bank about Certified Transfer Global. He had been referred to a commercial banking officer by the receptionist and had sat for some time in the waiting area while she had concluded a discussion with a client. "How can I help you?" Cecelia Rappaport had finally greeted him. The thirty-something, attractive brunette was deeply tanned with blond highlights in her hair, suggesting a beach-going lifestyle. Her handshake was firm and her gaze steady as she directed him to a chair at her desk.

"I am from the States and am in the process of arranging marine shipping services for some components I am importing from Melbourne. Certified Transfer Global has provided your company as a bank reference and I am doing my due diligence before I execute an agreement for services with them. Can you tell me what you know about the company?"

"Certainly," she replied. Her gaze did not waver. "First, who are you dealing with at CTG who gave us as a reference?"

Arnie was prepared. "I had a local investigator screen companies for me and he came up with a short list. His name is Cedrick Tormey. Certified Transfer Global is one of the names on his list of candidates."

"Very good. Next, we will need someone from CTG to authorize us to provide you with information they would like us to release to you. You understand, with all the privacy rules and such today. We cannot divulge information without our client's approval."

"Of course," replied Arnie. He could see he wasn't going to get any information from Cecelia. He decided to roll the dice. "I can contact them directly and discuss what services I need and ask them to authorize a banking reference from you. I looked at their Dun and Bradstreet report online. I see a Rick French as one of the principles. Is he the contact person I should deal with on this?"

Cecelia's eyes darted for just a moment. She quickly regained her composure. "No, that name does not ring a bell with me."

"No worries," answered Arnie. "I will meet with them and then circle back with you once I have decided on using them as my carrier."

Arnie concluded the meeting and returned to his car. "That ought to heat things up," he muttered. He looked up the address for Certified Transfer Global and found their location in the industrial section of the Surfers Paradise harbor. He mulled over what the likely future events might be as he drove across town to the harbor. Cecelia Rappaport's subtle yet detectible pause when he'd mentioned French had turned her hand. She knew French. CTG was going to lead him to French but Cecelia Rappaport had probably already alerted someone at CTG that he was snooping around. They probably had his description. Other than that, he was still flying under the radar.

He drove into the entrance of the parking lot that serviced the fishing fleet and cargo ships and located a low-slung metal industrial building where the offices of Certified Transfer Global were located. He observed a small building compared to the companion businesses around it. It had two roll-up doors and a small front office. Several roll-off containers were positioned alongside the building. The adjacent businesses dwarfed CTG with multi-story-high banks of shipping containers, cranes, and other transfer equipment.

"Some small fry outfit," mused Arnie to himself. "Just the front we are looking for to launder drug money in and out of the country for a group of expats on the lam." Positioning his car with a full view of the entrance to the building, he slouched down in his seat and began surveillance on the building.

He had been there less than an hour when he observed a tall middle-aged man exit a dark SUV with surf racks enter through the front door. "Rick French?" he wondered. Arnie had seen a copy of the police photo Erika had copied from the missing person's report that had been part of the probate file for the French estate. He could not be sure without a closer look. Trucks carrying loaded containers drove up and down the street in front of the warehouses. A forklift was parked alongside the road across from the CTG building. On a whim, Arnie left his car, pulling his jacket collar up around his face, and walked over to the forklift. He crawled into the driver's seat and pulled out his phone and sat there, posing as the operator of the apparatus. In twenty minutes, the tall man he had observed entering the building came out through the front door and drove away from the parking lot. Arnie was satisfied. The face was a little older than the one he had seen in the probate file picture, but the sun-bleached blond hair and dark tan were still the same. Rick French was still alive! All he had to do now was figure out a way to get him back to California and collect their part of the insurance recovery proceeds.

Quickly jumping into his car, he began to follow French at a distance. French drove out of the harbor and continued along toward the tourist section of the oceanfront. Arnie parked in the parking lot across from French and watched him as he walked up to one of the restaurants and sat down at a table. In a moment, two men drove up in a van, entered, and sat down at the table with French. The trio were serious, businesslike, not at all like the rest of the guests at the eatery, who were ordering lunch and observing the surfers in the lineup in front of them. In the next moment a black Chevrolet Suburban drove up in front of Arnie, blocking his view, its brakes screeching as it slid to a stop. The driver had a beanie on his head and dark sunglasses. As Arnie sat transfixed, the driver pointed a pistol equipped with a large silencer at him through the side window. His door was opened quickly and he was grabbed from behind, a sack was wrapped around his head, and he was dragged out of his car onto the ground. The sack gave off a chemical smell and the last words Arnie heard were "Get him back to the warehouse" as he lost consciousness.

When he awoke, he was lying on the cold concrete floor of a dimly lit warehouse building. Alongside the loading dock area were stacked pallets that held sealed cardboard boxes. As he regained his senses, Arnie could read the labeling on the boxes. "Didgerydoo Jojoba Oil, a product of Australia." At the front of the building were two workmen. One of them was loading bottles of clear honey-colored jojoba oil into Styrofoam boxes. The other was putting plastic bags filled with a white powdered substance inside of the bottoms and lids of the Styrofoam packaging. Arnie could see that the containers, once assembled, contained these hidden compartments in which the white bags of powder were being placed. The first workman then took the containers and loaded them onto the pallets. Next, they wrapped the palletized loads with clear plastic wrapping. The two workmen, dressed in worn clothing, appeared to be Aborigines. They labored silently, without direction, constructing boxes with the compartments for the bags of white powder, and then filling them with the bottles of oil.

The door to the office in front of the building opened and light streamed in onto the concrete floor where Arnie was lying. He could see the forms of two men walking into the room, blocking for a moment the bright sun that was streaming into the room through the blinds on the windows of the office. The shadows of the two men approached him and they presented themselves in front of him. The workmen continued in their labor, not even glancing for a moment in Arnie's direction.

As his eyes adjusted to the sunlight, Arnie saw two middle-aged men looking down on him. They were tan, physically fit, both wearing casual shirts and slacks. One of the men spoke. "We received a call from our banker that you were inquiring about our company and one of our associates. What is your business and what is your relationship to Rick French?"

Arnie's mind whirled with a range of responses. These guys were not trying to sell him shipping services. Rick French was part of their organization, whatever that was, and the white powdered substance they were hiding in the Styrofoam containers was most likely cocaine. He instantly regretted dropping French's name to Cecelia. The next words out of his mouth would determine if he would meet the fate of others who had tried to break into the secret of the business dealings of the Cut Toe Gang, or perhaps suffer an even worse fate. He decided that he was already a dead man. He took the risk.

"I don't know what you're talking about. I am just trying to get some components shipped to my company in California and I was given French's name by my attorney John Riggs. I am dealing with some electronics that have been restricted by the Department of Homeland Security for resale to certain governments and Riggs told me he had connections down here that could accommodate my need for confidentiality."

The two men glanced at each other. Arnie could see that the taller of the two was Rick French.

"How do you know Riggs?" asked French.

"My CPA turned me on to him," lied Arnie. "I had a tax problem a few years ago and Riggs did some things for me with offshore companies and accounts that helped me get some funds out of the country before the IRS came in and froze my accounts. He said he would clear things with you when I was ready to look at using your shipping company. I guess I jumped the gun and should have told him I was coming down here first before I started to look into your company."

French and the other man looked at each other again, appearing to relax as they digested Arnie's story.

"We can verify your story pretty easily," answered the other man. "While we are waiting, we are going to ship you off to a location where you will not get into any further trouble. If your story checks out, we can discuss business. If not . . ." the sentence trailed off into nothing.

The pair returned to the office and closed the door. In a few minutes French returned. "With the time zone difference, it will be a while before John Riggs gets into his office. We left a message with his answering service." He walked over to the two workmen and spoke with them for a moment. He returned to address Arnie again. "Neville and Emile will take you with them to their tribal clan's village and wait for us to check you out. If you are who you say you are, they will bring you back and then we can discuss your transportation needs." There was no need to discuss what might happen when they found out that Arnie's story was a complete fabrication.

Arnie was left lying on the floor for several more hours. When the workmen had completed their work, they walked over to him and picked him up. Releasing his legs so that he could walk, they motioned him to follow them out a side door, leading him over to an older model four-wheel-drive Toyota Land Cruiser. They pushed him into the back seat and began driving west out of the Surfers Paradise locale.

As they drove toward the interior of the outback, the country became hotter and drier. The lush coastal vegetation changed to sparse groves of tall eucalyptus trees congregated around small watering holes. For miles he looked out on desert sand, sparse plants and areas where seasonal water puddled during the wet season to cause occasional patches of yellowed grass to grow. He observed gangs of kangaroos and wallabies. In the tall trees sat black-necked storks overlooking small ponds of water where their next meal of frogs and small fish were hiding.

After an hour, the Toyota drove off of the paved highway and onto a dirt road. The four-wheel-drive vehicle bounced wildly as it crossed over railroad tracks that paralleled the highway, lurching back onto a red dirt road. At the railroad crossing were several eucalyptus trees on which tattered clothing hung. The two Aborigines stopped and removed their clothing and hung it up in the tree. They returned to the vehicle clad only in loincloths and sandals. Clouds of dust billowed up behind the vehicle as it sped along the road. The driver swerved as they came across potholes and washouts. Arnie's head bounced off of the metal roof of the Toyota each time the driver bottomed out on a dry river crossing.

They eventually entered a small Aboriginal village and came to a stop in front of a decrepit single-wide trailer that was home to Neville and Emile. A crowd of villagers ran up to the vehicle, shouting in their Aboriginal tongue, greeting the pair and welcoming them home. The ties around Arnie's hands were cut before he exited the car and the crowd escorted the trio over to the trailer, shouting and singing as they entered the residence.

Arnie did not know what to expect. There was no one inside the trailer except for Neville and Emile. It appeared to be a poor man's bachelor pad. The kitchen was dirty. The counter was piled with dirty plates and glasses. A small propane-powered refrigerator served double duty, acting as both a cold storage unit and a counter strewn with papers, magazines, and clothing. Arnie guessed that the pair were brothers, both being of the same slender body type and having similar facial features. He guessed they were considered in high regard in the village, having income from their jobs on the coast. He hesitated to think what their other duties for CTG might entail in addition to packaging up illegal drugs for shipment out of the country.

They motioned for him to sit down on a well-worn sofa in the living room and brought him a bottle of orange soda. "Aren't you worried I am going to try to escape?" he asked the pair.

Neville looked at him soulfully and said, "What, are you going to run across the desert to escape? Where are you going to go? If the dingos don't get you first, the heat will burn you up, man. Go ahead. Make a run for it. You won't last a day. We will just follow the buzzards and bury you in the outback. They will call tomorrow and tell us what to do with you."

"Where am I?" Arnie asked.

"We are part of the Jindalee community, the Bare Hills Tribe. We inhabit much of the interior of the continent and you are in one of our tribal villages while we wait to hear what to do with you. You are free to walk around the village but stay out of people's homes and do not go where you are not wanted." The two men made a quick meal of meat sandwiches and offered one to Arnie, which he gobbled down.

"Thanks," he said after finishing his sandwich. He saw the hide of a kangaroo, its head still attached, hanging up on the porch on the house across the street from the trailer and felt his stomach turn as he realized what he had just eaten. He guzzled the rest of his soda, hoping to keep his meal in his stomach as he contemplated his predicament.

Neville and Emile left the trailer and walked down the village street to meet with the villagers of the tribe. Arnie contemplated his fate. In a few more hours, Riggs would get the message from Rick French and let French know that Arnie was not a client. If he put things together, he might even guess that Arnie was at the impound auction and connected to the French's van. "Was the guy in the campground that Chester and Erika had talked about connected to CTG?" He wracked his brain to remember what Erika had shown them about the missing person's report for Rick French and the DEA report on his contact in Tiburon. "What was the name? Morrison, Jackson? Jack Morrison," he recalled. He reasoned that French would soon find out what Arnie's involvement was. Jack Morrison, or Jackson, as the DEA referred to him, was probably on the ground in Cuyama at this moment. There were three people who did not want the facts of French's disappearance five years ago to be resurfaced to the light of day. Chester and Erika were in grave danger. He had to do something, to warn them, to get them out of there!

His options were poor. He knew he could not make it across the desert. An Aborigine would be fine but not a California boy from the city. Could he steal a car and make a getaway back to the coast? He reasoned that his captors would run him down even if he was able to hot wire the car and drive away. The road into the village had been windy and tortuous. He might very well find himself trussed up again with no options of escape. It would all be over in just a few more hours. The men would get the phone call and then they would drive him out to some lonely canyon and shoot him or leave him tied up for the dingoes to feed on. They would make it look like another unprepared tourist had died in the outback. Then he remembered the train track. It traveled in a straight east and west line. He could catch it back to the coast and go to the police and save his skin as well as Chester's and Erika's before Riggs or Jack could cause them harm.

After Neville and Emile had returned to the trailer and finally gone to bed, Arnie made his move. The slow rhythmic breathing of the brothers signaled to him it was time to make his escape. He walked out of the front door and slowly made his way down the middle of the dirt road back toward the highway. A dog huffed at him as he walked down the street. Glancing fervently over his shoulder, he did not see anyone coming after him. As soon as he was out of sight of the village, he began trotting along the road. In the distance the elevated railroad bed and tracks appeared before him and he ran down into gulches and back up on the desert floor. Then he heard something moving in the brush to his side. In the moonlight, he could see the tail of a dingo moving through the brush, waving its tail as it signaled the wild dog's pursuit of his scent. "One dingo should not be a problem," he thought. Then he heard the yipping sound of a pack of the dogs far off in the distance. A single dog would not be a problem for him. But a pack of the wild dogs could easily surround him and tear him to shreds. He envisioned the pack circling him, the leaders darting in and out snapping at him, wearing him down, drawing blood as they attempted to make him their next meal. He shuddered at the thought. Then he heard it, a different sound. The whistle of an approaching train as it sped toward the crossing of the highway. It was headed in the wrong direction though, traveling west across the interior of the continent. The pack was approaching, he was a quarter of a mile away from the tracks and the small platform that served as a station for the itinerant Aborigine travelers seeking to travel to the coast. The train began to slow. Arnie took off running, cutting across the desert in a straight line to the platform. He could hear the train slowing even more. He tripped on a large root and face planted across the sand in front of him. He was still four hundred yards away. The pack of dingoes yipped as they closed on him. Jumping to his feet he resumed his sprint. He could see the large male off to his right in the bushes as he sprinted toward the train. Would it try to bring him down? The train began to speed up. It had not stopped at the platform. No riders could be seen waiting for the train. "Shit." Arnie yelled as he ran at top speed. "Stop!" he yelled. He approached the tracks and made his way up the steep embankment, crawling and slipping in the soft red sand. He felt the teeth of the large male dingo tear into his ankle. He could see the glowing eyes of the rest of the pack below him charging up the embankment. Only a few cars were left to pass by him. He was sprawled on the ground next to a rail, dingo attached to his ankle tugging vigorously, trying to drag him back down, back among the pack. He reached up to grab at the stairway on the boxcar. He latched on to it and the train tugged him forward. The dingo lost its grip and slid away, falling under the train. It was instantly cut nearly in half by the steel train wheels. Arnie could not hold on. He lost his grip and fell hard, back onto the gravel rail bed. The pack of dingoes had reached the top of the embankment and were running fully extended down the track toward him. Four cars were left to pass by him. Then three, then two. With superhuman effort, Arnie stood up and leaped for the steps at the rear of the last car, putting his arm through the railing and catching his wrist with his other hand. He lurched forward with the train and saw the dingo nearest to him snap at his leg, barely missing as the train dragged him to safety. Arnie drug himself fully onto the stairway and looked back down the tracks. He could see the large male that had nearly dragged him off the train laying on the tracks, struggling in its death throes. The pack circled around it. One of them dashed in to finish him off. The pack began tearing the dying alpha male apart, glowing eyes and bloodstained jaws glancing back at the train as Arnie lay gasping on the railcar stairs.

He awoke the next morning as the train slowed on its approach to a small town sprawled on both sides of the track. He had dragged himself inside of the last car on the end of the train, an empty boxcar, and had collapsed into deep sleep after a full day of playing private eye, getting kidnapped, and finally escaping his captors. It had been a close call with the pack of dingoes. As the train came to a full stop, he saw the sign on the station building announcing his arrival in Alice Springs. Quickly looking up the town on his cell phone, he discovered he had traveled nearly half of the width of the continent of Australia during the night's journey.

His mind returned to his fears for the safety of Chester and Erika. French and his companion no doubt had learned of his escape by now and were taking measures to counter Arnie's next move. French would be calling Riggs to alert him of Arnie's discovery of him. Measures would be taken to track down and terminate Chester and Erika, to tie up those loose ends so that French could retrieve his hidden fortune and finally close the last door on his disappearance plan.

Arnie exited the boxcar and walked into the station bathroom to freshen up. The bite wound on his ankle was only skin deep, the bite marks not having gone into the muscle. He washed it, carefully blotting off the caked blood, and saw that it had not continued to ooze. Walking out of the bathroom, he observed that the train tracks bisected the town of Alice Springs. He turned toward what appeared to be the commercial district and walked down the main thoroughfare and found a café. He was famished. It had been nearly a full day since he had last eaten. The café was filled with a collage of the Alice Springs population. Ranchers from a sheep ranch, shopkeepers, and workers from local businesses filed in for their noontime meal. In a booth at the back of the eatery he saw a group of men who appeared to be engineers or having some connection with a professional trade. An American Air Force officer in uniform sat with them. They were a serious group, talking in low tones with the uniformed officer.

"G'day, mate," the waitress greeted Arnie, pouring a glass of water in front of him. "What will it be today?" she continued. He ordered the lunch special. "I just got into town. What is up with the airman at that table over there?" he asked. "Is there a military base around here?"

"Pine Gap. It's a few kilometers north of town," she answered.

"Seems like an out of the way place to have an air force base," said Arnie.

"Radomes," she answered. "Those are cloak and dagger boys out there. It is a satellite tracking station for all of the Western world. They monitor missile launches that take off from anywhere in the world and keep track of who is doing what in outer space."

She returned to the counter in front of the kitchen area. She rang the bell sharply to alert the cook of Arnie's order and spun the metal ring into which she had inserted his ticket. He had to get back to California and alert his friends that they were about to be discovered. Any of the businesses in the downtown area might have a fax machine. Copiers with scanning capability might be few and far between in the tiny town. The military base would have all of those and more. He decided to access the base and locate the nearest apparatus that would permit him to transport himself back to his home fax machine. He quickly finished his meal and hailed a cab to take him to the Pine Gap radar base.

The cab driver stopped in front of a concrete block guardhouse at the entrance to the base. "This is as far as I go, mate," announced the cabbie. Paying him with the remaining cash he had on him, Arnie walked up to the entrance to the facility and waited for the guard on duty to come out of the guardhouse. The entire site was surrounded by chain-link fencing.

The top was festooned with concertina wire. Several hundred yards within the facility he observed a number of nondescript, military-style buildings. Behind those sat a number of large circular metal balls, elevated off of the ground by tall, circular pedestals. No one was in sight around the buildings.

The uniformed guard approached him. His white helmet and light-colored khakis were accented by white gloves, a belt, and a holster, which carried a semiautomatic pistol. "Good morning, what is your business today?" the guard greeted him.

Arnie thought for a moment. "Do I come right out and tell them who I am and what happened to me?" No one would believe his story about the map, French, getting kidnapped, and then escaping on the train. He needed to get to a fax machine or a multifunction copier in a hurry before his friends came to harm in the Cuyama Valley.

"I am a US citizen vacationing on the coast and was interested in a tour of this facility," he stated confidently.

The guard looked at the thirty-something man standing before him in rumpled clothes. To him he looked like a homeless person. He noticed the shredded pants leg and dried blood. "I am sorry," he replied. "This is a restricted area. No one is permitted entry unless they have a signed pass by the base commander. The only tours are conducted by base staff for visitors approved by the State Department or the Pentagon."

Arnie could see that trying to get in the front gate would be impossible. There was no story he could concoct that would let him get on base and into one of the buildings. "Could I use your phone to call a cab then?" Arnie asked.

"Sorry, we are a military base. Phones are for official business only," replied the guard. "Town is back that way about a mile," he furthered, pointing toward the city of Alice Springs.

Arnie started to trudge back towards the town, thinking of his alternatives. He could look for a fax machine in one of the local businesses, but that might take some time. "Who knows if anyone even has a fax machine in that tiny burg?" he reasoned as he walked alongside of the road back into town. Then he saw a culvert pipe that ran under the road in a wash coming from the Pine Gap base. Quickly running over to the pipe, he slid onto his belly and began crawling under the roadway through the pipe. When he came to the end of the pipe, he jumped up and began running toward the compound. Someone would find him soon, he thought. Surveillance cameras were mounted along the chain-link fencing surrounding the base. He heard the sound of a jeep come into view over a rise behind the radoms. Two uniformed soldiers were speeding toward him as he approached the building nearest to him. One of them was holding an M16 rifle and was pointing it at Arnie as the jeep turned and headed toward him.

Arnie beat the jeep to the building and jerked open the door and ran inside. The building was empty. It had what appeared to be long rows of tables and highbacked swivel chairs, which were all facing in the direction of large television screens that were hung alongside one wall of the building. The rows of tables and chairs were arranged in a semicircle around the screens, each row of tables descending lower into an open central pit area. The screens had images of the continents and countries around the world and were otherwise blank except for lines that marked the various time zones across the globe.

The lights in the room were off; only background light from the large screens back lit the room. He searched desperately for an administrative area, somewhere where phones, copiers, and other office equipment might be located. Then he spied it, a long glass-lined area at the rear of the room where desks, computers, and other office equipment were located on an upper level. A blinding rush of light entered through the door to the room as the two guards entered. Guns were drawn as they searched for Arnie in the room down the barrels of their M16s. Arnie crouched down in the shadows and made his way to the room, quietly opening the door and worming his way toward a large copier. The apparatus was in a sleep mode. Arnie crouched over the copier and found the machine had both scanning and faxing functions in addition to being a copier. Below him he could see the two guards working their way down along each row of desks, guns and flashlights searching for him in the dimly lit room.

Arnie located the fax button and pressed it.

"Enter the fax number" came the instruction on the front panel. Arnie entered the number for his home fax machine and pressed enter as he placed his hands in front of the paper feeder. The lights to the copier panel came on.

"Machine warming up," read the information panel.

"Damn," Arnie hissed under his breath. He raised his head and peeked over to where the guards were searching for him. They were almost down to the central pit area of the room and were now pointing their guns and flashlights up along the ceilings and back toward the top of the room where Arnie was hidden.

A beam of light flashed across his face, blinding him for a moment. "There he is!" he heard a guard yell. The other guard trained his light on Arnie. "Freeze. Get your hands where we can see them," ordered one of the guards.

Arnie turned around and looked back at the copier and saw it had completed its boot-up process and was ready for use. "Enter the fax number," he saw on the screen of the machine. Arnie bent over the machine and frantically entered his fax number. Bullets from the guards' M16s began to splat on the bulletproof glass that separated the command office from the rest of the room. Each bullet made cracked, spiderweb circles on the glass.

The guards stopped firing and looked up along the barrels of their weapons to see the effect of their shots. To their amazement they saw Arnie grinning back at them and waving as he inserted his hands into the paper receptacle of the copier and began to enter the machine and disappear from sight. The guards opened fire again and rushed the room. Their intruder was nowhere to be found. Walking over to the copier where they had last seen Arnie, they looked down at the input panel. The screen read "fax transmission complete, pages sent, 1."

CHAPTER THIRTY-TWO

TERRY KORMAN WHISTLED FOR MEGO AND OPENED UP THE door to his pickup truck. He had been at the ranch for a week and was tired of bumping along the ranch roads while he looked for strangers who might be casing the ranch. Riggs had been insistent that he keep up the surveillance. His ranch foreman position had gone from a part-time getaway from the life of a city real estate broker to something that was now keeping him from his main line of work and his social life. Riggs's threat had been clear enough though. If something was about to come to a head, he would give the alert and then get as far away from Cuyama as he could. He made his usual circle of the ranch using the dirt oil field roads that crisscrossed along all of the ranches in the valley. Everything seemed normal to him. A tanker truck passed by as it left the tank farm on the adjoining ranch to deliver crude oil to a refinery in Bakersfield. He stopped and let Mego out of the cab to chase a jack rabbit he had busted out of the salt brush. The dog yipped in excitement as it chased after the bounding rabbit, steadily falling farther and farther behind as the rabbit ran in circles and took advantage of the brush and rocks to evade its pursuer.

Retrieving Mego, Terry resumed his circle of the ranch. He bumped along in low gear, the melodic humming of the engine lulling him into a place of serenity and calm. Then he saw it. From a ridge on the west edge of the ranch, he could see a vehicle parked in the campground below. It was rare for anyone to be using the old unmaintained site, but there was something familiar about the vehicle. Terry stopped his truck, left it idling, and took his 30/30 Winchester rifle out of the gun rack behind him. Placing the rifle across the hood of the truck, he trained the scope down onto the vehicle to get a closer inspection. He centered the cross hairs and saw a green, two-toned van with its sliding side door open, parked in front of the abandoned campground office building. He inspected the van. There was no one around. The doors to the building were closed. Something was hanging down from inside the van. At that moment he observed the door to the building open and a bearded man, holding a large rolled-up set of papers, walking around behind the building out of site. A second vehicle, a non-descript SUV, drove out of the campground and down toward the Cuyama highway and out of sight.

There was something about the van. Terry could not quite get his mind around it. Something familiar. He trained his scope back onto the van. Then he froze. The faded decal on the rear window of the van was barely legible. "AR, Allister Ranch," Terry muttered. "It can't be." The memories returned, flooding back to his recollection of his surfing adventures on the ranch with Rick French and John Riggs. He recalled summer surf sessions when he had been able to access the private surfing spots on the ranch through his contact with Riggs and his friend Rick French, an owner of one of the coveted surfing parcels that comprised the reconstituted Allister Ranch.

Terry recalled sunny summer days, surfing spots known in the surfing world for their unmatched quality waves and lack of crowds. Lefts and Rights, Auggies and Razors, the offshore winds that kicked up in the afternoon and howled through the lonely steel railroad trestles that crossed above the arroyos that cut across the ranch out into the ocean.

Through John Riggs, he had been introduced to Rick French. They were all part of the working professionals party scene in Santa Bonita. Their mutual surfing interests had led to the offer by French to get Terry access to the private surfing beaches on the ranch. He recalled how he had parked his car in the lot at the local state park next to the ranch and waited with Riggs to be picked up by French. The van below him was unmistakably the van French had been driving. How could it be after all these years that the van was still in existence, out in Cuyama and in a campground next to the ranch French owned? Who was the guy who'd driven away from the campground and what was his connection to French's old van?

Riggs would want to know about this. Terry looked at his cell phone and saw that he had no signal. It was nearly noon. He climbed back into the truck and drove back to the ranch headquarters and onto the highway, speeding toward the Buckhorn. He pulled up in front of the eatery and raced past the waitress to the phone booth. He dialed Riggs's office and received the message machine announcing the office was closed for the noon hour. Terry left a short, excited message. "You are not going to believe this. I found French's old surf van. It is parked in the Cottonwood Canyon Campground. Some guy was there too in another car. Call me as soon as you can!" He hung up the phone and walked back through the restaurant into the bar. He ordered a drink to steady his nerves and chose a seat near the swinging doors into the bar so that he could observe the phone booth. A noon crowd began to file in for lunch. Herb Rummell walked in, glanced into the bar and walked over to Terry, sitting down on a stool next to his.

"Well, Korman, having chow today after a hard morning on the ranch?" His sarcasm did not go unnoticed. Terry did not have time to be offended. He glanced over Herb's shoulder, keeping his eye on the phone booth.

"Just the usual rounds, checking water and fences, you know," he replied.

Herb was unusually talkative. "It's going to be another dry summer. We are starting to ship steers out already. How are your jojoba trees doing?"

"Err, they are doing okay, I guess," answered Terry.

"Great, that's just great," replied Herb. "Maybe I might get around to planting some of them on my ranch. Not much money in cattle these days, you know. Where did you get your root stock from?"

Terry heard the phone ring in the phone booth and jumped up quickly from his barstool. "I gotta go," he replied, downing the rest of his drink and running out of the bar.

He closed the doors to the phone booth behind him and picked up the receiver. "John?"

"Yes, are you where you can talk?" asked Riggs.

"Yeah, I am in the phone booth and no one else is sitting back here. You are not going to believe this. Well—what do you think of my news?"

"Did you see anything else? Was anyone else out there with the van?" asked Riggs.

"No one in the van but I did see some guy in another car driving out of the campground. Maybe another camper," answered Terry.

"What did he look like?"

"I didn't get a good look at him. He walked over to a car that was behind the building and drove away. Dark complexion with a beard. Kind of dressed like a biker type."

"Did you see where he went?" asked Riggs.

"No. He just drove out of the campground and down to the highway. I lost him after that. He was carrying something though. Some rolled-up papers. Like a map or poster or something like that."

"Okay, that is what I needed to know. You can come back to town in a few days. He is probably some guy who is checking out the area in advance of the estate sale for the ranch next week. I will let you know if I need you for anything else," said John.

"But what about French's van being out there? How weird is that? Someone has his old van and is camping right next to his ranch?"

"Might not be the same van or if it is, just a coincidence. Stay close to the ranch and wait for a call from me tomorrow," replied Riggs.

Terry hung up the phone and walked past the bar and out to his truck. "Don't forget to get me the name of the place you got your jojoba plants from!" yelled Herb from the bar.

As he drove away from the Buckhorn he tried to think about the purpose of his last five years keeping watch over the ranch and how this chapter of his life was apparently coming to an end. The ranch would be sold next week, the sale confirmed in court by Judge Slider. His services would no longer be needed. But for some reason, he had the uneasy feeling that there was more to the story than what Riggs was telling him.

In his office, Riggs glanced at his watch. It was eight o'clock in the morning in French's time zone. It was also the following day, technically, but this had no importance to the matters at hand. He dialed French's number and recognized his voice on the other end of the line.

"I think you need to get back over here," said Riggs. "Your van has been spotted in Cuyama near your ranch and I think Jackson may be over there snooping around. With Emory getting killed, all signs point to Jackson being on the ground here. And if the van is here, then those kids are also out here looking around, probably using your map. I think you need to expect the worst and get out here so you can head them off and retrieve your stuff before the ranch gets sold."

"Jackson!" exclaimed French. "I told him to hold tight and let me get the insurance payout from the estate to pay him off. My family is all set to get the funds to him after the estate is settled."

"Jack is tired of waiting and doesn't trust you," replied Riggs. "You can't blame him. Five years is a long time to wait, even if you have been sending him money from time to time. His handprints are all over the murders out there last week. He is playing for keeps. It's time to end this thing so we can all get on with our lives."

Riggs waited for a response.

"All right. I will make arrangements through CTG to get over there. I'll let you know when I am expected to arrive," French said.

Riggs hung up the phone and sat back in his chair. "Manita, pull the CTG file for me if you would, please."

She brought the file to him, placing the dark brown, sealed legal-size Smead portfolio on the desk in front of him. "Anything else before I go to lunch?" she asked.

"No, that's fine for now. I am going to take a few days off, and I may not be able to call while I'm out. Send me a text if anything comes up and I will get back to you when I can."

He stared at the sealed file in front of him. He had thought about the matter from time to time when he made wire transfers to CTG. Hush money to keep Jack quiet until he could get French declared legally dead, collect the insurance funds, and get them funneled to Jack. But he had not really played out in his mind how the matter would be concluded or what his involvement might be. He had always thought the best case scenario would be to have French declared deceased, collect on the insurance policy, settle his estate, and then assist French's heirs in funneling the insurance funds to Jack. Once the long overdue debt to Jack was paid, Riggs could get on with his life, and French could remain deceased in the eyes of the court and continue living under the protection of the Cut Toe Gang in Australia. Any danger of Riggs losing his license would vanish into thin air. Life would go on for all of them, but first, Jack had to be confronted and controlled. Riggs could ill afford any connection to the van and its new owner and friends, especially if they turned up dead in some dry Cuyama Valley wash.

Rick French arrived the following evening at LAX and boarded the Airport Express bus that provided daily trips to and from the central coast for travelers catching flights out of Los Angeles. In two hours, he was dropped off in Santa Bonita and thirty minutes later he was sitting in Riggs's living room. The pair had not said much as Riggs drove French to his home. He was not surprised that French had arrived scarcely twenty-four hours after their last phone discussion. He surmised that the CTG transportation connections and network of workers at airports, ports of entry, and the like had been extensive enough to allow French to get back into the country under an assumed name, complete with a passport, visa, and identification.

"I have supplies already packed in my car so wash up and let's get out to the airstrip," said Riggs. "As soon as we can get on the ground out there, I will feel better about how we track down Jackson and get him under control. The key to this recovery is keeping him from killing anyone else and getting your cash out of there as fast as we can before the authorities gather too many facts about Emory or that other private investigator getting whacked out there."

"I agree, but let's first see what Jackson has been up to. If your foreman spotted the van out there and your private investigator is correct, then the kids that have the van have the map. We should assume they have found out about the wells and are already getting into them and taking my stuff. If the guy Terry spotted with the van is Jackson, we can assume he had already accosted the kids, has the map, and has probably killed the kids. If he knows which wells I hid my stuff in, it will take him three or four days to retrieve all the sacks."

"We don't have much time," agreed Riggs. "Let's get going."

CHAPTER THIRTY-THREE

THE NEXT MORNING FOUND THE PAIR ON A RIDGE ON THE edge of French's ranch overlooking the Cottonwood Canyon campground. John Riggs had flown them there at three a.m. As instructed, Terry had left the ranch pickup truck parked on the Rummell ranch alongside the dirt road that had served as a runway for French when he had been posing as a jojoba farmer. Being careful to avoid detection, Riggs had not filed a flight plan. They had simply taken off and headed toward Bakersfield, but had circled back around and over the Caliente Range to the east, ending in a long slow glide path back into the Cuyama Valley and onto the remote landing site. They had landed undetected; the DEA had ceased cooperative drug ops with Santa Bonita County several years previous.

The predawn air was cool but without moisture. The day would begin to heat up as soon as the sun began to rise over the Caliente Range. Riggs had brought a large spotting scope, which they had trained on the abandoned forest service building. A second vehicle was parked beside French's green van. French had recognized his van instantly. He recalled the last time he had seen it, parked in Tiburon five years previous. He had barely escaped arrest. A local contact had warned him of the DEA surveillance and pending arrest. He recalled how he had walked away from the motel during the evening rainstorm and made his way to a remote cabin where one of the local marijuana growers presided over illegal cannabis cultivation in secluded forest locations. A quick explanation of his predicament had resulted in an escape out of the area. He had eventually made his way to Australia.

French had not been naive about his line of work or what might result if he was arrested. His participation with fellow people in the drug industry had led him to his contact with the Cut Toe Gang, a group of expat drug dealers who had formed a consortium of sorts. His participation and payments had been a form of insurance for him against the day when he ultimately would have to cease operations and flee the country. Participation in the CTG was a retirement vehicle, a place where he could ultimately hide funds from his illicit drug career and create a stream of cash flow to use in his retirement years. It was like a 401(k) plan for its members, who had made their fortunes dealing in illegal drugs. The membership came with an aspect of protection from investigators and law enforcement seeking to locate and extradite members of the group and was a feature French had been especially interested in.

The sun came up over the mountains and the country began to warm. French returned to the truck and sprawled out in the seat of the cab to sleep. In a couple of hours, he felt Riggs tugging on his boots. "They're up. Let's go," hissed John. The two crawled on their bellies over to the rim of the bluff and observed the campground. They observed Jack Morrison sitting on top of a wooden campground table while a man and a woman were cooking something over a portable Coleman stove. The couple were not talking. Jack was presiding with a semiautomatic pistol.

When the group had finished their meal, Jack ordered something of the couple and they walked over to the sedan and retrieved tools and shovels, which they placed in the van. Jack retrieved a rolled-up map and then got into the back seat of the van. The trio drove out of the campground down to the highway.

"Let's go," said French. They headed west toward the foothills and stayed among the trees on a forest service road that was screened from the valley below. On reaching a promontory, they again set up an observation point and waited for the van to come into view in the oil field below.

It was slow going in the van. Jack had directed Chester to travel high up into the oil field to an area where abandoned wells were located. The road had not been maintained in years. Any semblance of asphalt was long gone. They came to a well site and Jack directed them out of the van. "This is it, well 454. Let's get started," he ordered as they came to a stop. Chester picked up the sledgehammer and chisel and walked over to the well head. To the side of the well sat an abandoned pump jack. As he walked by the equipment, he heard a sudden buzzing in the brush.

"Look out!" cried Erika as a rattlesnake raised itself in a coil and aimed itself in Chester's direction. Chester froze. The snake continued to buzz, its black tongue flicking in and out as it attempted to assess the danger it sensed coming from Chester.

"Hold still," ordered Jack. The buzzing of the snake's rattles began to trail off. It slunk off into the brush, shaking its rattles occasionally as it disappeared.

"All right, the show's over. Get that cap chiseled off so we can see what's down there," said Jack. Chester began chiseling away at the spot welds on top of the casing and then removed the cap with the large pipe wrench. Jack motioned Chester aside and peered down inside the well. "Okay, let's pull this stuff out and see what we have here," he ordered. Chester reached down into the well and started pulling on the rusty chain that held the cylindrical burlap sack below. "Now open it up," rasped Jack as Chester retrieved the sack from the well. The contents were similar to the other sacks. Gold coins, a few bars, and currency wrapped and bundled as if they had come right out of a bank vault or armored car.

"Okay, let's get to the next well," ordered Jack.

"Come on, let us go!" cried Erika. "You don't need us anymore. You have the map and know where to look. Let us go."

"You're going to help me get all of this money out from the rest of the wells first," replied Jack. "Then you can go."

The couple returned to the van, resigned to their fate, and began driving to the next well site that Jack had identified.

From their vantage point overlooking the valley, Riggs and French saw the pattern of the movements of the trio. "He is making them dig up the stash at each of the wells!" exclaimed John.

"Smart guy," answered French. "Let them do all the work and then leave them at the last well buried in a shallow grave. At the rate he is going, he will be done with them by tomorrow."

"Okay, what do you want to do? Wait another day and let them collect all of your stuff, or hit them tonight and settle for what they have collected so far?" Riggs asked. "It's your stuff, your call."

"Jack might take off tonight if he thinks he has recovered enough of the value out there. If he covers another five or ten wells today, that leaves maybe two or three more for tomorrow. If I were him, I would take what I have and run. It probably covers what I owe him. The longer he waits, the better the chances are that someone discovers him out here or that the couple tries to escape."

"He's not going to leave any of the cash," replied Riggs. "He has been waiting a very long time. One more day in exchange for maybe a few million more is a good payoff for him."

They waited until the van had driven out of view and then retraced their route back in the tree line and returned to the ranch headquarters to prepare for their next move.

Upon driving up to the ranch house, Riggs and French could see that the house was empty. Terry would waiting for Riggs to give him further instructions. "Having Terry keep track of things worked out pretty well," Riggs commented.

"If all my stuff is still down those old wells like it seems, it was well worth it," agreed French. "But Jackson has messed things up by getting involved and killing Emory and the other guy. We did not need law enforcement looking around to solve those murders. After a while, someone is going to go look for those kids too."

The pair prepared a quick meal from the canned goods stored in the kitchen pantry and began to make plans to accost Jack Morrison and his captives the following day. "What kind of guns do you still have out here?" asked John.

"Not much, a few handguns and rifles as insurance. Just enough to defend myself in case an old customer or supplier came calling. Come see."

French motioned for Riggs to follow him and they walked outside over to a round concrete grain bin that sat alongside the derelict barn across from the house. "Up here," French motioned as he began climbing up the rusted steel steps that wound up and around the forty-foot-tall cylinder.

Riggs hesitated. "All the way up there?" he asked, pointing to a landing at the top of the structure.

"No, not that high," replied French. He stopped by the first of a series of rectangular inspection doors that signaled four levels inside of the grain storage silo. "Hurry up, come see," he said as he pried open the rusted latch that held the door closed and swung it open. Riggs timidly climbed up the stairway, grasping the rail and testing each rusting, flaking step before putting his full weight on it. He reached the landing and joined French to peer inside of the silo. It took a moment for his eyes to fully adjust to the darkness.

"Come on," French urged as he placed both hands on the ledge of the window and swung himself inside of the bin. He landed softly on top of the grain, sinking in up to the top of his ankles. Riggs followed slowly and eased himself down onto the top of the grain pile. "What are we going to do with this stuff, throw wheat at them?" he asked.

"Over here," French directed. The grain was hard to walk in, like walking in quicksand. They sank up to their calves in it as Riggs followed French over to the opposite side of the silo. French began digging down into the grain, sinking his hands and arms up to the elbows as he pushed downward through the wheat. "Give me a hand here," he asked. "Help me pull this stuff up." Riggs shoved his hands down into the grain and felt the top of plastic cases. There were four of them, buried deep down in the grain. Working them back and forth, they pulled them up and carried them down the stairs and back across the yard and into the house.

They were soft-sided plastic gun cases. French placed them on the kitchen table and opened the clasps on each case and removed the firearms. "Nice!" exclaimed Riggs as he picked up each weapon. An AR-15, .223 caliber with a large capacity magazine would be capable of providing a show of power from its spray of bullets. A Winchester model 70 fitted with an 8 x 43 Uberti scope was capable of providing long-distance kill shot capability from its 30.06-caliber cartridge. The third case held a single shot Remington Target Master .22 caliber rifle. Riggs looked at French, amused.

"Rabbit gun," French commented.

The last case held boxes of ammunition and three pistols. Riggs inspected each handgun, a .45 ACP semiautomatic government-issue relic from World War II, a .357 magnum Smith and Wesson wheel gun, and a .32 caliber Colt snub-nosed revolver. The guns were lightly covered in gun oil and grease.

"Pick your poison." said French. Riggs selected the AR-15 and removed the clip and worked the action to verify it was unloaded. "I am not much of a shot these days," he said. "But this should do the job if we get into trouble."

French smiled and grabbed the Winchester. "Okay, I can handle any long-term surgical shots with this. I sighted them all in before I left the country. You are zeroed in at a hundred yards. I am set up for a thousand yards just in case we need to make a long shot. Let's get them cleaned up and ready to go." They spent the rest of the evening getting their weapons ready and discussing the plan of attack for the next day.

"If we try a nighttime raid on the camp, someone might get shot," reasoned French. "Jackson is ex-navy, used to be a SEAL. He will set up a perimeter with sensors so we have zero chance of surprising him. Our best shot is surprising him tomorrow when he is thinking about digging at the next well and having to worry about his captives and the chance they might make a run for it. He has no idea I am out here and probably thinks I am just waiting for the estate to close and for the insurance money to get funneled to him. He might even kill the couple tonight and make a run for it with what he has collected so far."

"Well, there is only one road out of the campground," replied John. "We can try to surprise him when he leaves or just let him get away. After all, if he has already found most of our hidden stash, then you can let him keep it and just have your family send the insurance funds back to you."

"When I hid my financial savings from the business, gold was worth nine hundred dollars an ounce. The cash is still worth what is was, about a million dollars, but with the price of gold now running around sixteen hundred bucks, there is probably closer to ten million dollars of value out there in those old wells. I told Jack I would get him his five million. I did not say anything about any more than that. Besides, five million does not go as far today as it used to."

Riggs smiled ruefully back at French. His obligation to his old surfing buddy would be coming to an end soon. All he had received for his participation was a hundred-thousand-dollar legal fee hidden in the form of probate fees and conservatorship fees to deal with the missing persons matter through the court. Part of that had been paid to the campaign fund for Judge Slider, who had been up for reelection to help grease his petition to the court to have French declared dead.

"Rick, our original deal did not include me providing paramilitary services to deal with Jackson. Five million does not go as far as it used to, but you have to admit you got great value out of the fee you paid to me to set all of this up for you."

French sat in silence, staring back at his old friend. Friends were expendable in his line of work. He had no illusion that his fellow CTG members would not fail to cut him off in an instant if he violated any of the provisions of his participation in that venture. But Riggs had been loyal, if perhaps a little reluctant in his duties, thought it was understandable given what he risked to his career and reputation. "Okay, how about another hundred thousand to follow through the rest of the way on this?" French proposed.

"I don't know. The ante is a lot higher now. Five hundred sounds better to me. That is only one of those bags they have been digging up."

"Two," countered French.

Riggs saw that his eyes had a steely, cold sheen to them. Friendship only went so far.

"Done," he replied. "I am going to give Terry a call. I think we can use the manpower."

CHAPTER THIRTY-FOUR

"THERE'S SOMEONE HERE TO SEE YOU," SAID SHARON Callaway. The plump middle-aged receptionist held court over the sheriff substation in Cuyama and provided the initial contact with the local population who came in seeking assistance. Isadore Rodriguez had just returned from an FFA Booster Club breakfast where the parents of the children participating in the club had discussed the logistics of traveling to Santa Maria to participate in the annual county fair and livestock auction.

"Anyone I know?" asked Isadore. He was used to the occasional drop in from any of the locals. Complaints of loud late-night parties, suspected camps of illegal farmworkers, and reports of suspicious neighborhood activity comprised the bulk of his daily calls.

"It's a guy from Santa Bonita. An Arnie Jensen, who has a wild tale of being kidnapped and nearly killed. He scared the shit out of me. I was out here going over the incident reports for the month and when I went back into the copy room, there he was lying on the floor by the fax machine. He springs up and says his friends are in grave danger somewhere out here and he needs you to find them before something bad happens to them."

"Is he a nutcase?" asked Isadore. He was used to dealing with people who had imbibed a little too much at the Buckhorn or had perhaps consumed to excess one of the several popular new drugs that were easily obtained.

"I don't know," she replied. "He looks homeless, or like he just crawled out of a ditch, but I don't think he's a junky or anything like that. I put him in the conference room."

"Okay, let me see what it's all about," Isadore said, taking a thin file from Sharon and walking into the conference room.

He closed the door behind him. Seated at the table facing the two-way mirror was the very disheveled Arnie Jensen, the man of the tales of kidnapping and impending danger. Isadore kept an open mind. "Mr. Jensen, I'm Officer Rodriguez. Your report indicates that you have two friends camping in one of our local campgrounds and that they are in imminent danger."

"That is it!" replied Arnie "They came out here a few days ago to look for old bottles and such and the last time I talked to them they were worried about some strange guy who seemed to be following them around."

"Let's start at the beginning" answered Isadore. "What are the names of the missing persons?"

"Chester Sullivan and Erika McConika."

"Can you give me a physical description of each person?"

"Chester is six feet tall, twenty-five years old, about two hundred pounds. He has blond hair and blue eyes."

"And Erika McConika?" asked Isadore.

"Five eight, also twenty-five, red hair, green eyes, I don't know, maybe around one fifteen."

"When did you last see them?"

"Three days ago."

"And where was the place of last contact?"

"At their house in Santa Bonita."

"Is this the location they left from on their camping trip?"

"Yes, they left the next morning. I gave them a call to see how they were doing and that is when I found out about this strange guy who was lurking around their campground. I have not been able to contact them since then. Something bad has happened or is about to happen to them, I just know it," Arnie answered.

"We get a lot of strange people camping out here. That is not in of itself enough to justify me putting resources into the field. You are going to have to have more concrete evidence on why they may be in danger before I send someone out to patrol the area campgrounds."

Arnie knew it was time to lay out all of his cards and save his friends. "Okay, there is more to the story than just a bottle hunting trip." Arnie began relaying the story of the van auction, the discovery of the map, and the sequence of events and findings that had put Chester and Erika into their predicament.

Isadore felt as if an old movie was being played again in front of him. Five years ago, he had been a recent graduate of the sheriff's academy with less than a year of patrol experience when the position for an officer in the tiny burg of Cuyama had opened up. His fellow officers had discouraged him from applying for the position. But a friend in the DEA had turned him on to a pending task force that would be conducting surveillance on suspected drug trafficking. Cuyama was to be the focus of the task force operations, and if he was in the right place at the right time, there was a strong possibility of Isadore being assigned to the task force as one of the local law enforcement personnel.

Rick French was a name well known to Isadore. He knew of his role as a new jojoba farmer in the valley and that he had not quite fit in with the other local farmers and ranchers. His clothes were too fancy, his van did not blend in with the pickups common to the area, and he never seemed to spend much time on the ranch or participate in any of the local community activities. French had been a target of interest for the task force.

They had been on the verge of connecting the dots to a drug transportation scheme that used small private planes flying out of South America, the remote Cuyama Valley, and panga boats that would ply the coast of California during the early morning hours. The task force had received a tip about some late night landings of small planes on a remote ranch in the valley. The investigation had come to an abrupt halt with the disappearance of Rich French.

"Wait here for a moment," he said as he left the room. Returning with a weathered manila file, he opened the file and removed the photo of two tall thin men standing on a beach, each holding a surfboard. "Is French this guy?" he asked Arnie, pointing to one of the men in the photo.

"I don't know, I've never met the guy" replied Arnie. "But the other guy . . . If you cleaned him up and put a suit on him, he looks like a lawyer who followed us home from the auction sale and tried to buy the van from us."

Isadore flipped through the file. "John Riggs, was that the lawyers name?"

"Yeah, that's the guy" replied Arnie. "His mitts were all over the court stuff we looked at about Rick French disappearing and later being declared dead by the court. Erika tracked all of this stuff down. We figured out what the old map was for and now they're telling me they found gold coins and bundles of cash inside the first well they opened up. French must have had guys tailing us all along to see if we were going to be able to break the code on the map and go out there to find all the stuff. You gotta get going on this and find out what has happened to them!"

"Okay, Mr. Jensen, let me check with my superior and we will get started on this. This will take a little time. You can wait in the reception area or you might just check into the Buckhorn Motel and get cleaned up and wait for us to follow this down."

It was a wild story. But it was plausible. Isadore was trained to consider every action he took as having the potential of being viewed with twenty-twenty vision by a review panel after the fact if things did not turn out as planned. His first impression of Arnie had been questionable. His story, though a little on the wild side, had some basis in fact from the information contained in the closed DEA file. Rick French was known to Isadore. Arnie had recognized John Riggs. The insurance adjuster who had been nosing around five years ago when French had gone missing had alluded to Isadore that French had probably made a clean get away to Australia and the drug cartel down there would provide the protection he needed to live out his life as an expat on that continent. Isadore picked up the phone and made a call to the district attorney's office in Santa Bonita. By noon, he had received the fax containing a signed search warrant for the French ranch.

The sheriff substation in Cuyama had limited resources. Normally only one officer at a time was on patrol. The three uniformed officers assigned to the valley rotated shifts, and off-duty officers would be sleeping or perhaps out of the area until they were required to man their shift. Isadore grabbed his hat and headed out the door to his cruiser. "I am going out to the French Ranch to follow up on Mr. Jensen's missing person's complaint," he said to Sharon. "See if you can track down anyone for an early shift change just in case I need some backup."

"Copy that," she replied.

The valley spread out before him on both sides of the highway as he left Cuyama and made the twenty-minute drive out to Wasiola Road and the ranch. Finding the couple, if they were indeed missing and in danger, would be difficult. The valley ran for thirty miles and was easily ten miles wide from the base of the Caliente Range on the east to the coastal range to the west. They could be hidden in any number of dry washes, along the steep banks of the Cuyama River, or inside an old barn or abandoned ranch house anywhere in the region. Isadore started methodically at the

French Ranch. Picking up his microphone for his car radio he signaled his arrival at the ranch. "I am 1097 at the French Ranch. What is the status of my backup?"

"Copy that," Sharon replied. "Unable to contact sheriff backup but CHP is 1023 if you need them."

Isadore walked up to the door of the ranch house and knocked loudly. There were no cars in the yard and he knocked again, verifying the house was empty. "This is the sheriff. Open the door. I have a warrant to search the property." He heard no answer. He tried the front door and found it to be locked. He made short work of the door with a swift kick of his boot. Drawing his gun, he eased into the room, pointing his weapon left and right as he verified that no one was hiding inside.

"I am coming in, come out with your hands raised so I can see them!" he yelled. He circled through the house and verified that no one was inside. In the living room he found four open gun cases, one small-caliber rifle, and two handguns. Boxes of rifle ammunition had been opened. He picked up his handheld radio from his waist belt. "Base, this is unit 4800. Proceeding to the Cottonwood Canyon Campground to follow up on the missing person's report. Stand by for a status."

He drove up the canyon road toward the campground. He was no stranger to the site. Looking for missing people in possible danger from long-ago drug deals gone wrong was a far cry from his usual practice of breaking up high school beer parties at the campground, however. He considered parking down the road and walking in quietly or driving into the camp. He chose the latter, deciding that anyone on the lookout would have already spotted his patrol car coming up the road.

There was no one in site. No people, no cars, no camping paraphernalia in any of the campsites. The door to the abandoned forest service building was ajar. He walked inside, gun drawn, and surveyed the room. A couple of water bottles and granola bar wrappers indicated that someone had been in the room recently. He saw several white plastic zip ties that had been connected and then cut off. Arnie's wild story of his friend's abduction was gaining traction.

He walked out of the building and surveyed the campground. Someone had been under duress here and had been kept in the abandoned building. No one would voluntarily stay inside that filthy place. But where had they gone and under what circumstances? Then he saw it, black smoke boiling up out of a canyon to the north of him. It was a hot day with little moisture in the air. No one would be issuing a burn permit during this time of the year—this had to be a wildfire. Isadore keyed the mic to his radio and called the fire in. "Dispatch, this is 4800. Fire located north of Cottonwood Canyon Campground. Request a type three from County fire in Cuyama and additional resources from BLM and Cal Fire."

"Copy," replied the dispatch officer in Santa Bonita after a few minutes. "County fire requests a better location of the fire."

"Proceed to the Rummell ranch and stand by. 4800 proceeding west up the road to get a better visual," he replied.

The street farther up into the mountains degraded to a dirt road filled with potholes and boulders. Isadore navigated his way around each obstacle until he could go no farther. He started walking to gain a view of the fire below him. Rounding a bend in the road, he froze. A young man and woman were crawling away from a Volkswagen van and were being surrounded by ten-foot-high flames from their crashed van. To their right he saw another car, an SUV that was positioned on the side of the hill, by an outcropping of rocks. He heard shots being fired.

CHAPTER THIRTY-FIVE

JACK MORRISON HAD RISEN EARLY THAT MORNING TO PRE-
pare for the last day of digging into the remaining wells on the ranch. He
did not plan on spending any more time out there than necessary. He had
calculated the value of all of the hidden gold and cash and determined that
he had more than enough to consider the debt from French settled. He had
to get rid of the couple first though. All he needed was a head start. He did
not have to kill them, just tie them up for a day or two to give him time
to make a clean getaway. He had untied their bindings and thrown some
power bars and water at their feet. "Eat up," he had barked. "It's time to get
out of here."

"You said you would let us go if we showed you where all the wells
are located," Erika said.

"I will cut you loose. I just want to make sure you don't have a change
of heart and decide to turn me in before I can get far away from here,"
he replied.

The couple got into the van and began driving toward the oil field
with Jack following in his SUV. The two vehicles began to climb up onto the
ranch from the valley floor. The old oilfield road ran mid-slope along the

side of an increasingly steeper canyon wall as they drove higher. Ahead of them, a ridgeline began to loom, forming a box canyon that cut off further access to the distant coastal range. To their left was the edge of another ridgeline, not as steep, and with cow trails that led over to the next canyon to the north. Below, the slope dropped off steeply. Erika glanced nervously down the slope as they bumped along to the location of the next well site. "Do you think he's going to kill us?" she asked quietly.

"I don't know. Since he took his car this time he's probably planning to leave us out there after we dig up the rest of the wells. Maybe he will just tie us up. He has no reason to kill us. He has his money and who knows what happened to this French guy. He could already be dead. Who else would even know about the money? He can fade into the woodwork and let us go. What are we going to say? We found all the money that some dead drug dealer put out here and this guy took it away from us? Who is going to believe a story like that?"

At that moment a bullet splintered the front window of the van, passing between the two of them. "Chess, look out!" cried Erika. The van lurched wildly as Chester swerved off the road and tried to regain control of it. Tires spinning wildly in the soft red dirt, he regained the road and brought the van to a stop. Following, Jack Morrison had felt his right front tire go flat from a well-placed shot from Rick French's scoped 30.06. He spun the car sharply to his left and slipped it back and forth, uphill, to reach an outcropping of sandstone boulders that would provide him with protection from his attackers.

Seeing that the road was now clear behind them, Chester and Erika turned the van around and made a run for it back down the road and away from their hidden attackers. A second bullet passed through the rear window of the van, smashing between them and into the dashboard. "Chess! Erika cried out again. "They are going to kill us!"

"We have to get off this road," Chester said between clenched teeth. He saw another outcropping of rocks and turned the van uphill, trying to reach the boulders that ringed the top of the canyon above them. They were not as lucky as Jack had been. Halfway up the hill, the van skidded and rolled onto its side and then started sliding down the slope. It came to a stop in a dry wash. Spilled gasoline from its ruptured gas tank exploded into a yellow ball of flame.

Erika and Chester were dazed but unharmed from the crash. Camping gear, tools, and clothing had hit them during the rollover but their seat belts had kept them from being thrown from the van. Smoke began to fill the interior as the fire from the rear engine began to spread.

"Erika, are you all right? We gotta get out of here!" Chester yelled at Erika through the dust and smoke.

Erika pushed a pile of camping gear off of her and stared through red rimmed eyes in a dust-covered face.

"Erika!" Chester yelled again. "Come on, let's go!"

They both began to cough as the black smoke from the fire surrounded them and hid them from view. Chester tried his door and found it to be jammed shut. He grabbed an ax from the floorboard and broke through the front window, running the ax head around the window frame to clear away the glass shards. Shimmying through the opening, he reached back in and grabbed Erika with both hands and dragged her out onto the ground and over to the dry ravine where they would be hidden from their assailants.

The fire from the van began to extend out into the rangeland around them and found the ravine below them. They looked uphill at Jack and saw that he was wearing the large backpack he had been keeping the coins and paper money in. Glancing uphill, they could see the flash of sunlight coming from the scope on Rick French's rifle as it panned back and forth between them and Jack.

The fire began to move up the gulch toward the couple. "It's starting to come up the draw. It's being driven toward us by the upsloping winds!" yelled Chester as the flames and smoke moved in their direction.

"What do we do now?" cried Erika.

"We can't go down and we can't make it up out of this ravine without them spotting us," Chester replied. "All we can do is stay in this gulch and move up ahead of the fire and try to make a run for it if we make it till dark. The wind is not too bad right now so we may just luck out."

"I'm scared, Chess!" Erika wailed.

"Just stay on my tail. We will be okay," he assured her. But he was not so sure himself. The odds were certainly against them. If the shooter did not pick them off as they traveled uphill in their direction, they had a good chance of being overcome from the flames and smoke below. Visions of Erika and him lying in a ravine, burned to a crisp, flashed across his mind.

Uphill from them, they saw Jack Morrison had positioned himself behind an outcropping of rocks. He was calmly removing a rifle from a scabbard and attaching a curved, high-capacity magazine. "What is he up to now?" Chester muttered. With his backpack with cash and gold coins he looked like he was getting ready to make a run for it up to the top of the ridge and over into the next canyon. There he would be out of sight from the shooters above.

"He looks like he knows what he is doing," observed Chester. Jack alternatively raised his semiautomatic weapon and sprayed bullets toward the position the shooters had taken up, quickly moving each time to a new position higher up on the ridge to another grouping of boulders. For their part, one shooter did not have time to sight in a shot with his scope, and the other was frozen with fear each time Jack sprayed a hail of bullets at their position.

With the assailants now under attack from Jacks weapon, Chester and Erika had time to fully survey their situation. They were hiding among an outcropping of red sandstone boulders. The fire from their van was working its way uphill toward them. The air was still. Black smoke boiled up from the fire. The van had been fully consumed. It was now just a charred metal shell lying on its side with the front and back windows shattered by rifle fire.

"We are all right for now," said Chester. "But we have to make our move out of this ravine before the fire gets to us."

They could not go up over the ridge without being spotted by the two shooters above them. Down the slope to the side of them Erika spotted a small green patch of grass surrounded by ancient cottonwood trees. A small muddy pond sat in the middle of the grove of trees.

"What about that pond over there?" she exclaimed. "If we can get down to that water maybe we can wait out the fire."

"I don't know," replied Chester. "Those guys could pick us off before we made it halfway." He peeked up over the boulders that shielded their position and saw their former captor shooting bursts of shots uphill at the shooters' position above and then moving up toward the ridge top to a new position of shelter. Each time he moved, the shooters hidden in the tree line would return fire. Their bullets ricocheted harmlessly off the rocks hiding Jack's new position. The shooters were now fully concentrating on Jack's position.

The fire was getting close. The smoke from burning brush and grass began to overtake their position. Radiant heat from the flames became unbearable. Chester surveyed the muddy spring below them. They had no choice. They could stay where they were and become overcome by the smoke and burned to death, or risk getting shot on their dash to reach the water source at the bottom of the canyon. If they did not act soon, the fire would cut them off from reaching the spring.

"Okay, let's go!" he yelled. He grabbed Erika's hand and they took off running downhill toward the grove of cottonwood trees. A bullet kicked dust up in front of them. The shooters had spotted them. They fell flat on their bellies behind a small mound. Another bullet kicked dust up just inches from where they were taking cover. Then they heard a burst of fire from Jack's rifle. "Let's go!" yelled Chester again. The fire was almost on them and would reach the grove of trees in a matter of minutes. The two took off running again. The fire reached them just as they jumped into the muddy spring. Jack grabbed a handful of bulrush reeds and waded out into the center of the spring. It was no more than three feet deep at the center. The flames burned around them and ignited the leaves on the trees surrounding the spring.

"Here, take this and get under the water. You can breathe through this until the fire passes by us." He thrust a hollow reed into Erika's hand. She watched Chester put a reed into his mouth and then he ducked down into the spring. He sat up out of the water, yelling at her again. "Come on, it's our only choice!" The roar of the fire was deafening. The heat was intense. Erika felt her ears begin to burn. She took the reed and began to breathe out of it and slipped down below the water and settled into the mud-filled bottom. The ooze closed in around her face. Her instinct was to hold her breath. She felt Chester's hand grab hers. He gave it a reassuring squeeze. She relaxed and began to breathe through the hollow reed.

Things were not going as planned for Rick French. Jack Morrison had used his shoot and move strategy successfully so that French had not been able to use his sniper rifle to neutralize Jack or the couple pinned down behind the wrecked van. The fire from the smoke had allowed them to move away from the van down to the circle of trees surrounding the pond below them. Now the fire was moving past the pond and rapidly approaching them. They saw Jack disappear over the ridgeline with his backpack loaded with French's gold. The fire was beginning to make its own weather. The wind swirled up around them in a vortex, sending ash and smoke into the trees and brush behind them. Spot fires erupted uphill behind them.

"We are going to burn up here where we are if we don't make a run for it!" yelled John, his eyes wide with panic. French looked around behind them and saw the wall of flames beginning to encircle them. He was frozen in fear. He took off running across the slope back to his truck. "You will never make it!" yelled John. French continued to run toward the pickup truck. The wall of flames from below met the fire from above. The red wall closed around French, he collapsed ten feet from the truck, and the heat and smoke sucked the last breath of air out of his lungs. Within a minute, he had drowned from the fluids of the burned and collapsed alveoli in his lungs. Riggs looked at the spring below and saw that it was now encircled by flames. But the grass had been fully grazed around the water source. The flame lengths were only a foot or two in height. He began running downhill toward the water hole. He held his breath as he approached the circle of cottonwood trees. The flames were dancing around the spring but he could see water behind them. Limbs began to fall from the trees as the heat from the flames weakened them. His clothes were on fire now, the pain excruciating. He plunged through the circle of flames and jumped squarely into the middle of the pond, feeling the respite from the fire as the cool water and mud encased his body.

Isadore had watched the scene develop. He had driven as far as the road permitted and then walked over to a turnout and had seen Chester and Erika making their dash to the water hole in the bottom of the canyon. He had thought he had heard gunfire, slow methodical shots as well as bursts of semiautomatic fire from a second location farther away. Uphill from the water hole he observed two men hidden in the brush. They were arguing. The fire was about to reach their position. One of them started to run toward a truck parked in the trees. The second man tried to hold the runner back, unsuccessfully, and then made his own dash downhill to the water hole. Isadore watched incredulously as one man was consumed by the flames, the other, on fire, apparently making it to the safety of the grove of trees and the water hole. There was no sign of the occupants of the burned-out van. He could see a line of brush trucks from the county fire department and Cal Fire turning off the highway and making their way up toward the fire. He keyed his handheld radio.

"Dispatch, this is unit 4800. Request info on who will be the incident commander and the command frequency. Advise the IC that there are four civilians in the path of the fire near the location of the pond and grove of trees to their west and by a pickup truck above that location. Probable 1144 near the truck. Fire is heading upslope to the west in heavy fuels with spot fires. Advise the IC that gunfire heard in the area."

"Copy that," replied the dispatcher.

Isadore remained in his position. Below him the brush trucks came to a halt in a line. A four-wheel-drive Ford one-ton truck pulled up in front of the group and he observed the battalion chief for the local Cal Fire base begin to talk on his radio and develop an attack plan with the responding engines. Isadore switched his handheld radio to scan and determined the command frequency. He could hear the Cal Fire chief giving instructions to the dispatcher.

"Dispatch, this is Cal Fire 3100. Request a D-8 from the Pine Creek Forest Service yard. Request air support from Santa Maria helitack. Advise that we will want them to paint the fire along the western slope before it gets any farther into the backcountry."

"Copy that."

Isadore watched as the various fire units began to accomplish their tasks. The teams of Cal Fire and Santa Bonita County brush trucks began to cut fire lines from the burned-out van uphill around each side of the fire, slowly trying to get control in an effort to pinch it off and contain it. The low rumbling of an air attack unit including a spotter airplane came onto the scene. Isadore could hear the radio traffic between the command center and the air attack units. The small spotter plane circled around the fire several times and then flew away from the fire. Then the DC 10 lumbered in low over the top of the mountains and dropped its cargo of liquid Phos-Chex directly in front of the wall of flames. Within minutes, the roiling white smoke turned to black as the oxygen-starved fire began to lie down. A second airdrop stalled the fire further. Isadore could see the hand crews working up both flanks around the fire while a dozer created a firebreak along the ridgeline to the north of the fire. It worked its way along the top of the fire to grub out a line ahead of the now smoldering line of fire still punking around in the forest above Isadore's location.

Isadore called into the incident commander. "Request you send a unit over to the area of the pond, near the burned-out van, and search for the disposition of three civilians at that location. Also check the pickup truck for an additional victim."

As the wind cleared the smoke from the still smoldering cottonwood trees, he saw two people stand up and walk out of the pond. A third person crawled to the edge of the pond and collapsed. A brush truck drove up to the group and began to administer first aid. Isadore wondered if he had just located the two people who had been listed on his missing persons' report. Who was this third person and the other man who had been running toward the truck? He glanced over at the disabled SUV parked by the out-cropping of rocks. Was there a fifth person? There was no one to be seen.

He walked back to his vehicle and drove back down the road and over to the command center that had been set up for the initial attack on the fire. "Looks like you are making good progress," he said as he walked up to Wally Freeman, the Cal Fire battalion Chief. The white helmeted chief was looking up in the direction of the pickup truck, which was now a fully burned out shell. A crew had driven over to the site to look for victims.

"Better call the coroner, victim is deceased," he heard the captain of the brush truck crew relay back to Wally.

"Okay, is everyone else accounted for in the area?" Wally looked over at Isadore. "We have three by the trees and one by that truck. Anyone else out here we have not found yet? Who was driving that SUV over on the side hill?"

"I will run the plates and check it out" replied Isadore. He accessed the unpaved ranch road and drove over in the direction of the vehicle. He came to the place where the van had skidded off the road and had rolled after its driver had attempted to drive away from the road. Twenty feet behind he found the tracks from the SUV, which had proceeded uphill to its present location. He exited his car and began to walk the scene after calling in the license plate to the dispatcher. "Run a plate on Alpha Gary Zebra One One Niner," he requested. He approached the SUV. Both the driver's door and front passenger's door were open. The car had several bullet holes through the side windows and doors. A scattering of spent rifle casings was strewn around the driver's side of the vehicle. Isadore crouched down instinctively by the side of the car and surveyed the scene around him. The angle of the shots through the car came from the uphill position of the pickup truck. He wondered who the shooter was and who had returned fire from the SUV. He reached over and picked up several of the spent casings. They were .223 caliber Remington. It was a common rifle cartridge still used by the military and also by hordes of semiautomatic-rifle-toting weekend warriors who owned AR-15-style weapons and frequented their local shooting ranges or laid waste to beer bottles and cans in backcountry areas.

"Where could this guy have gone?" wondered Isadore. He had not seen anyone running from this car. He looked uphill and spotted more cartridges next to an outcropping of rocks. He continued uphill and noticed footprints leading up to the rocks. He glanced over to the location of the pickup truck, seeing the rocks provided cover from that location. Farther up was another group of rocks and another small pile of spent cartridges. Isadore surmised that this shooter had been trying to get away from gunfire that had been coming down from the truck shooters' location. He obviously had some military training, methodically providing his own covering fire and then moving uphill, away from the location of the shooter positioned by the truck. Isadore reached the top of the ridge and got down on his belly to survey the next canyon. He could not tell if the shooter had gone down the canyon or on up into the forest. He returned to his car. He had three potential witnesses to interview and possibly had found his two missing persons. He had no idea who the third person might be who had emerged from the pond or any of the group's connection to the deceased found beside the truck. And there was the fifth guy who had been driving the SUV. He was nowhere to be found. How was he connected to all of this? He saw two ambulances driving away from the fire base camp, which had been set up near where the chief's vehicle was parked. The fire crews would be days getting the fire totally out and ensuring that no hot spots still existed in the burn area. "Dispatch, this is 4800. Is CHP still available for back up?"

"CHP is on scene and providing traffic control on the highway."

"Request they follow medic one and two to the hospital and detain all subjects until I can get there to interview them."

"Affirmative," replied the dispatcher.

Erika and Chester had emerged from the pond covered from head to toe with mud. They staggered out, coughing and wheezing from the inhalation of smoke from the surrounding fire, and were quickly approached by members of a fire department brush truck. The four-man crew pulled medical bags from their rig and began to question the pair on injuries and their condition. "Let's get them both on ten units of oxygen," instructed the captain of the crew as they continued to monitor the vital signs of the couple. "Check the pond for any more survivors," he directed to one of the crew. On reaching the edge of the pond, the firefighter saw a male collapsed on the edge of the pond. "Bring a litter over here. I've got one more!" he yelled. A second crew member came running over and they dragged John Riggs out of the water and placed him alongside the red plastic backboard. Riggs was barely breathing. He had severe burns to the back of his legs and back. His clothes were destroyed and he had suffered third-degree burns.

"Let's place him on his front and get him up to where they can package him for transport," said one of the firefighters. They gingerly placed Riggs onto their litter, strapped him down, and carried him up the slope to an area where the ambulances were waiting.

"Put the two males into one ambulance and the female can ride solo in the second unit," directed the battalion chief.

"No!" Erika cried out. "He tried to kill us. He was up there in that truck shooting at our van."

"You need to arrest that guy," added Chester, removing the oxygen mask the medics had placed over his face. "There were two of them up there and a third guy who was holding us hostage and took off the other way after the fire started."

The chief held up his hand to stop his crew from loading the victims into the two ambulances. He was used to civilians being upset and agitated at the scene of a fire or accident. This was a wild story though. He had heard the radio traffic when Isadore had requested the CHP to follow the victims back to the hospital and detain them.

"All right. The two of you go together in one ambulance and this third victim can go in the second unit."

Erika and Chester climbed into the ambulance and sat down on the bench reserved for the ambulance crew for monitoring patients. As they left the scene, they observed a crew of firefighters spreading a blanket over the still body of Rick French. Riggs was loaded into the second ambulance. He was breathing but nonresponsive.

"You two doing okay back there?" asked one of the ambulance crew. Erika and Chester still wore their oxygen masks and were breathing better. Each had been hooked up to a pulse ox monitor, which showed their heart rate and oxygen levels on a screen the crew was monitoring.

"I guess there were two of them shooting at us," said Chester. "Doesn't look like that second guy is going to be a problem anymore."

"Who were those guys?" asked Erika. "I am sure the creep that had us tied up was the Jackson guy I read about in the French disappearance file, so those other two must have some connection to French. Why else would they try to kill us and be shooting it out with Jackson?"

"I don't know. Maybe they were hired by French to track us down and make sure we did not get away with any of the money. Maybe French is the guy in the other ambulance or the guy that got burned up in the fire."

"I think we are going to find out pretty quick who those two people are," replied Erika. She pointed out the rear window of the ambulance. A highway patrol cruiser was following closely behind the second ambulance. Its red and blue light bar was fully lit as it escorted the procession to the hospital emergency room in Santa Maria.

John Riggs was in severe pain from second- and third-degree burns to his back and legs. He continued to lie on the gurney and tried to appear unconscious. The fifty-minute ambulance ride gave him time to evaluate his predicament and devise a plan to deal with the questions he knew would be posed to him by law enforcement upon his arrival at the hospital. He assumed French was dead. It might be some time before they fully identified him from fingerprints or dental work. But they would eventually discover his identity and start to connect the dots to Riggs. He had to assume the worst and formulate a plan, a story, which though fantastic, might explain why he was in the presence of a supposedly deceased former client. A client with guns that had been used against a pair of weekend treasure hunters and Jack Morrison. His mind whirled. Had they found Jack? Had he been able to make a clean getaway with his backpack of gold coins and cash? If he did not come up with a good story his neat and tidy life of a family law lawyer would all come to an end. He did not relish the possibility of being disbarred and spending the rest of his life in a federal penitentiary.

CHAPTER THIRTY-SIX

THE PHONE RANG ON HARRY CRUISER'S DESK, NAGGING HIM to stop looking at his retirement projection and get back to work as the assistant DA for Santa Bonita County. He looked at the readout on the phone and saw it was coming from the detective's office at the Santa Maria Sheriff's substation. "Cruiser," he answered.

"This is detective Lyons in Santa Maria. We have a kidnapping and attempted murder case for you to take a look at," he heard on the other end of the line.

"Okay, what do you have?" Harry replied.

"I have a couple, a young man and woman, who say they were kidnapped while on a camping trip and held for a few days in some old, abandoned forest service buildings in the Wasiola Campground. They escaped during a forest fire. They tell me a couple of guys were shooting at them, trying to kill them and their kidnapper. They crashed their van trying to get away and started the fire. One of the assailants died in the fire. They have a wild story about the shooter that survived the fire. Their kidnapper appears to have left the scene before he could be taken into custody. Their other assailant is still in the hospital being prepared for transfer to a burn center for skin grafts. I spoke with him briefly. He has his own story of being held hostage by a former client named Rick French who he originally thought was dead and being forced to go to a ranch in Cuyama to help this man retrieve some hidden property. He says he barely escaped with his life after the fire started and he was able to run away from him during the fire. Says he is an attorney, a John Riggs, and that you know him and can vouch for him."

Harry digested what he had heard for a moment. "Yes, I know who John is. A small-time divorce guy who does some trip-and-fall work. I heard about this incident on the news. Sounds like a made-for-TV movie. What do you know about the other two?"

"Just a man and woman who live in Santa Bonita. They were in the news a few months ago for exposing some investment fraud scheme and getting a reward. I checked them out. They have a story about Riggs and some guy named French and how Riggs helped him disappear and got him declared legally dead so that his family could collect on a five-million-dollar life insurance policy. They say they found out about all of this by chance after buying a van this guy French used to own and finding a map that had locations marked on it showing where French had buried gold and cash. They had been out in Cuyama driving around in the old oil field looking for the stuff when they were kidnapped by another guy named Jack Morrison, alias Jackson. He had taken all the money the two had found and hightailed it out of there during the fire."

"What happened to the French person?" Harry asked. "Do you have him in custody?"

"Dead. He's the guy that burned up in the fire," replied Lyons.

Harry was no longer thinking about his pending retirement plan from the county. He had some interesting cases over the years but this one was not the usual murder or drug bust. He recalled the name French from his work with Federal and local drug task forces but did not remember what had happened in those efforts. "Do any of your suspects pose a flight risk?" he asked.

"The couple seem pretty benign," replied the detective. "You tell me on Riggs."

Harry considered the situation for a moment. "Riggs is an attorney. You have this couple claiming he tried to kill them, but according to his story he was a hostage of French's and was able to escape just like they did. Without more questioning, it is their word against his. On their story of being out there looking for buried treasure, unless they have permission from the landowner, all you have is a trespassing charge against them and possession of stolen property if they indeed dug up money on someone's ranch. The kidnapping allegation against this guy they call Jackson might be valid, but you need more evidence for us to file charges. You need to produce Jackson if he even exists. Do you have that guy in custody too?"

"No, this is what they relayed to me during questioning. At this point there is nothing to corroborate their story. The deputy in Cuyama indicates a rental car was found at the fire scene with bullet holes in it, and he was able to trace a trail from the car away from the fire. Looks like the driver made it out undetected. He appears to have been armed. They found rifle casings along his trail."

"All right, I don't think you have enough evidence to hold any of them. This guy Jackson, if he is real, is the key to putting any of this together. No one has made a complaint of trespassing and we can question Riggs and this couple later if we connect any of the facts they are alleging. If this guy Jackson turns up, that will be a different story."

"We have a helicopter in the air and are looking for Jackson as we speak," replied Lyons.

"Okay, let me know if you find him. I will look at some old files and see if I can connect any of these dots to what you have out there currently."

Harry Cruiser hung up the phone and brought up a list of probate records from the local court on his computer. As he read over the missing persons reports from Mendocino County that were exhibits in the probate file for Richard S. French, it all began to come back to him. The drug task force had been working on surveillance for possible drug trafficking in the Cuyama Valley. French had been a suspect. He had known ties to dealers in Mendocino County and an informant had alerted them of a pending transaction with a suspect Jack Morrison, known as Jackson, who operated under the guise of running a paint and body shop in Tiburon. French had been under surveillance but had dropped out of sight at the same time a plane suspected of carrying a delivery of drugs from Florida had crashed in the everglades. The file was replete with testimony from Western General, who wanted more time to locate the missing French who was suspected of having left the country to live under a new identity in Australia. Judge Slider had quickly shut this effort down. French had been gone for five years, and Western General had spent several years looking for him. The judge had proclaimed French legally dead and set in motion the events that would require the insurance company to pay off on the life policy and allow Riggs to open and settle the estate and distribute the assets.

Harry Cruiser exited out of the court records program and leaned back in his chair. He had brought many criminal cases before Judge Slider during his career and knew Slider to be a liberal judge who gave light sentences and great leeway to the defense teams. If Judge Slider had erred in finding French deceased and if Harry could show impropriety in how this case was handled, it would be a nice conclusion to the end of his career with the district attorney's office.

The next day, Detective Lyon was in attendance while the coroner began his autopsy of the burned body found next to the pickup truck at the Cuyama fire. The coroner began to narrate into his recording device as he made his initial survey of the deceased.

"Victim was found in a prone position with extensive burns all along the posterior torso. The clothing is completely destroyed. Moving the body into a supine position. No tattoos or other markings except for a small scar near the navel. The balance of the torso is unremarkable."

He began to open the body cavity and removed the lungs for inspection. "Victim died from smoke inhalation. Burns to the torso occurred after the victim became deceased, after the fire burned over the body. No other apparent wounds or causes of death," he concluded. He made a cursory view of the rest of the organs and then concluded his report and had the transcript sent over to Cruiser's office.

Before he left the autopsy, Lyon lifted prints from the deceased and had them sent to the FBI for identification.

The results were waiting for him in an e-mail the next morning. Richard Sutherland French. Date of birth April 1, 1948. "Here's a first for you," he said to the district attorney, Kathrine Shuelman. "Lazarus has returned from the dead. Remember that DEA task force we worked on a few years ago in Cuyama where the subject just disappeared? Well, the courts declared him officially dead and have a probate about ready to close in Judge Slider's court. Seems like the guy was not dead after all. They just found him out in Cuyama. Got himself caught in a range fire and it burned right over the top of him."

"Interesting," Shulman replied. "What kind of charges are you going to file?"

"Not sure yet," he replied. "We have three other people that were caught in the fire who survived. Two of them say this guy French and his attorney, John Riggs, had them pinned down and were trying to kill them. They also said they were kidnapped by a former drug accomplice of French's and were able to get away from him during the fire. That guy's name is Jack Morrison."

"So you have three people trying to bump off a couple of kids camping in Cuyama?"

"Not exactly. Riggs is saying he was also taken hostage by French and he had made his escape during the fire also. All three of them ended up in the same pond when they escaped from the flames. We have not found this Morrison guy."

"What does Lyon say about motive?" Kathrine asked.

"It is pretty early in the investigation here but it looks like three things are going on. The couple say they were following up on a treasure map they found in a vehicle that French used to own and had found several stashes of gold coins and cash. They thought this guy French was not dead and had signed an agreement with the life insurance company to split the insurance payout that had been deposited into the French estate if they were able to prove that he was still alive."

"Splitting an insurance recovery by proving insurance fraud. That's a long shot," Kathrine commented. "But let's assume that they are correct and were able to locate French, which certainly seems true from the fingerprint identification you just received. What is the second leg of this fiasco?"

"French must have found out that his soon-to-be-distributed estate, including the five million dollars of insurance, was now in jeopardy with the kids nosing around in Cuyama having found some of the assets he had hidden out there. So, French gets back over here from Australia where he had been living in order to protect his assets and get rid of these kids."

"Fine. Dead guy comes back to life and comes back to protect his hidden assets. That explains them all being out there. Riggs could have been under duress just like the kids. But what is the third leg of this stool?"

"Jack Morrison, aka Jackson. The missing person's report has him as the contact in Mendocino County the DEA had under surveillance at the time a deal was supposed to have gone down. Things went bad and French disappeared. So did Jackson. Now they both show up in Cuyama after five years just as all this is coming to a head. A retired foreman who worked on a ranch French owned turned up dead along with a private investigator someone hired to stake out the foreman's house. I think Jackson and French had been in contact during the years of disappearance. Maybe some payoff or a deal tied to French's estate and his assets was going to take place. Now

Jackson has disappeared without a trace. Looks like Jackson was operating independent of French. Maybe he had some interest to protect out there. He is ex-navy, a seal, special ops stuff that did some things for the CIA after he left the navy. I don't think we will ever find him."

"Okay, a drug dealer who never got the shipment he paid for has been waiting all of these years for a payback. Doesn't trust French so he appears on the scene to protect his interest. This is all speculation at this point, with no hard evidence. Do we have a dog in this fight?" she asked.

"The couple say they were kidnapped by Jackson and he is long gone. Unless the detective can find him, we have no case. They say Riggs and French were firing down on them and Jackson. That is how they crashed their van and started the fire."

"Did they see Riggs fire a gun at them?"

"No, it was too far away. They said that Riggs and French were uphill from them about half a mile in the trees. They crashed just after the bullets hit their van and after they rolled downhill, the fire started, and they made a run for the pond."

"What does Riggs have to say about the shooting?"

"He says French showed up at his house and forced him at gunpoint to go out to the ranch and help him with this couple. He said he was shocked to see him still alive after having gone missing and with all the work Riggs did to get his estate resolved and the insurance money collected. He claims he knows nothing about where French has been all of these years or the connection to Jack Morrison. He said all he ever did for him was his estate planning work and handling his probate."

"What do you think?" she asked.

"You couldn't make up this kind of a story if you tried. Who knows what really went on out there? French is dead so you have no charges against him. It is their word against Riggs as to who was shooting at who, and Jackson is long gone. You have an uphill battle bringing a case of participating in insurance fraud against Riggs without better proof. You don't want to go down the road and try a high-profile case like this unless you are sure you can win it. The taxpayers are not going to be happy with an O. J. Simpson result. Next year is an election year."

"All right then, I think we tell the couple that the case is under investigation. It can reach a timely demise. If something surfaces later from the investigator, we can always reopen the matter and deal with it then."

"Okay," he replied, "I will let them know what we think."

CHAPTER THIRTY-SEVEN

"YOU UNDERSTAND THAT THIS IS GOING TO BE A FREE-FOR-all today," said Andie McDougal as she sat at her desk and surveyed her new clients. She had been contacted two days previous by her friend Erika McConika about a case before Judge Slider that was on the morning's docket of probate matters. The attractive five-foot-four Hispanic woman had inherited dark black hair and a solid plump stature from her stay-at-home mother, and her Scottish surname from her surgeon father. She had met Erika while working for Capital Triangle Properties and had done accounting work for her while she attended night classes at UCLA School of Law. She had completed her classes and was one of the fortunate few who passed the bar exam on the first try. After working for a local law firm for a few years, she had opened her own practice, taking on a variety of family law cases and the occasional business transactional work.

Before her sat her friend Erika, boyfriend Chester Sullivan, and Arnie Jensen. Erika had filled her in on their tale of adventure and near death and the predicament that they had found themselves in. After all of their detective work to sort out the secret behind the hidden map, working out a reward plan with the insurance company and suffering danger and almost death, they had found themselves in the remarkable position of being left out in the cold. No reward money, no sharing of insurance proceeds recovery, nada. Indeed, the district attorney had alluded to potential trespassing charges that could be directed at them by the landowners on whose property they had been looking for the lost treasure. Whether the recovered gold and cash belonged to the person who owned the land on which the stashes had been found, or if ownership resided with the person who deposited the contraband down the old abandoned wells was a separate matter to be brought before the court at a later date. The matter at hand was the disposition of five million dollars of insurance funds the estate was holding. Interest had accrued on the funds so that the amount that the court was considering for distribution totaled nearly five and a quarter million dollars.

"But what about all the stuff we dug up on them about French skipping out to Australia and the Cut Toe Gang helping him send money to Jack Morrison all those years until his estate could be closed? We saw enough in Riggs's files to connect him to the scheme," said Arnie angrily.

"First, you say you found out all of this by getting into various offices for Riggs and CTG without permission. You don't have any copies of documents or other solid evidence to prove any of these facts. These are just things you state you saw in their files or on their computers. Even if you saw these documents, you did so illegally. The court will not let it be admitted as evidence."

"What about French coming back over here to collect his hidden wealth? We found the map and all of that cash in the wells that were marked on the map. French and Riggs just happened to be there at the same time after five years had gone by?" asked Chester.

"And they were trying to kill us and that guy Jack Morrison," added Erika.

"What about the agreement we made with the insurance company to split the insurance recovery?" said Arnie. "That is five million dollars."

"The court is going to consider the facts and apply the law," replied Andie. "We can raise all of these issues, but frankly, your position is weak on all points."

"How so?" asked Chester.

"If you did not have permission to be on the land where you found the sacks of coins and cash, that then is a matter between the landowner and the estate as to who owns such property. French, and possibly Riggs, shooting at you is a criminal matter, which the DA has, at this juncture, not agreed to take up. I am informed that their investigation is still ongoing. That will be a separate matter for the court to consider if, and when, any charges are brought against John Riggs. The alleged kidnapping by Jack Morrison is also a pending matter. The sheriff's investigation unit is looking for the suspect, but they believe he has already left the area and possibly the country. It might take years tracking him down through Interpol before he is ever extradited and brought back over here for trial. Again, this is a criminal matter and none of the estate assets are subject to any of your claims against Morrison unless you can tie the rightful ownership of what you found to him."

"So we went to all of this work and endangered life and limb for nothing?" concluded Chester.

"At this point, it seems so. Court commences at ten o'clock. I think we need to go on over and lay out our case," she replied.

The walk over to the court took only a matter of minutes. An assemblage of briefcase-toting lawyers, clients in tow, were congregating around the steps leading up to the entrance of the Mediterranean-style building. The red-tiled roof of the complex and courtrooms, decorated with murals of the Spanish colonial history of Santa Bonita, were in sharp contrast to the other pedestrian governmental buildings in the city. The courthouse spoke of a former era of wealth when the icons of the pre-Depression period flocked to the city to build their winter mansions and begin the long process of converting the city from its former Spanish cow town period to a modern cutting-edge repository for high-tech business incubators, the arts, and social liberalism. As they walked inside the building and climbed the circular stairs to the second-floor courtroom where their case would be heard, they passed by small groups of attorneys with their clients huddled around them listening to what might happen today in court.

"Sit here," Andie instructed them, pointing to the first row of long wooden bench seating. They sat down. Before them was a wall mural depicting the arrival of Juan Rodríguez Cabrillo on the shores of Santa Bonita. To his side, a priest was giving a blessing. Chumash neophytes knelt in front of the pair, unsuspecting of the travails that would befall them over the next several hundred years.

"The court will come to order!" barked the bailiff. "Everyone please rise, the honorable Judge Slider presiding."

Judge Slider entered through a door behind the judicial bench from where he would hear the arguments and testimony associated with the day's cases. He swirled his black, floor-length judicial robes around and sat down.

"I have the following matters to be heard this morning," he called out. He began reading out cases one at a time and asking if the parties were ready to go to trial. "Gates versus Foss?" he asked. "Are you ready for me to assign this case out yet?" Two attorneys rose from the gallery and approached the judge. After stating their names, law firm, and which client they represented, each informed the judge they were ready for trial.

"Fine, I am assigning this case out to Judge Flavershine in department four." He went down his list of pending matters and assigned or delayed them according to the wishes of the parties.

"I have the following probate matters preapproved," he then stated. "If anyone objects, please let me know now." He read of the names of the estates on the list, looking up periodically to see if there were any objections.

"Objection," he heard as he read out the last case on the list. A thin, balding attorney rose and approached the bench, followed closely by a young woman. Each held files filled with case material.

"I represent the guardian ad litem for the estate and we have just determined that the decedent fathered a child out of wedlock, the child just having been born. We ask for a delay to determine the child's interest in the estate and propose an amended division of the estate."

"Your Honor, this is preposterous," interjected the other attorney. "There has been no mention of any minor children belonging to the estate or unborn children of his. At this late date the court should not permit any further delay of these proceedings." She glanced back at her clients, middle-aged children of the deceased, children in tow. They looked expectantly back and forth at their attorney and the judge.

"Your Honor, the decedent had become engaged to a Ukrainian woman with whom he was having a child. She returned to that country but has just informed us through her own attorney that she has just given birth to his child."

"I will allow a two-week postponement so that you can get me the appropriate affidavits from Ukraine to support this request. Hearing no further objections, the approved list is confirmed and I will sign the orders as they are submitted to me."

"When is he going to get to our case?" hissed Arnie under his breath to Andie. She put her hand on his shoulder and motioned for him to be quiet.

"And now for the current probate items. Petition in the Estate of Richard S. French for approval of a final accounting and final distribution. I see there has been an objection filed and a claim made against the estate."

Andie rose together with John Riggs and a tall female attorney wearing a conservative dark blue pantsuit. "Andie McDougal representing Arnie Jensen, Chester Sullivan, and Erika McConika."

"John Riggs for the petitioner."

"Kate Reilly for Western General Life Insurance, which has filed an objection to proposed distribution."

The judge leaned back in his chair and peered at the trio over the top of his reading glasses. "I must say, this is a case that just will not go away. I am inclined to grant the petition to distribute the estate as proposed. The family has suffered the tragic loss of a son and brother through his untimely disappearance. I will hear arguments of course on the positions of the objector and the parties who are making a creditors' claim against the proceeds of the estate, but you should all know my initial take on these matters."

Kate Reilly stepped forward first. "Your Honor, my client objects to the distribution of funds resulting from their payment of funds from the life insurance policy purchased by the decedent. We have determined that Mr. French had been alive since the time of his disappearance and has only recently become deceased. We allege that the policy holder was engaged in an act of insurance fraud against our company and we intend to seek recovery of the insurance proceeds the company has paid into the estate. We request a two-month continuance so that we can provide the court with points and authorities to support our claim."

"Ms. Reilly. Was your insurance policy issued on the life of the decedent Richard S. French?"

"Currently, yes. But at the time this court made its finding, Mr. French was apparently still alive and we assert that one or more people, possibly his personal attorney, Mr. Riggs, may have known this and participated in a scheme to defraud Western General and this court in the payment of insurance proceeds to his estate!"

"That is outrageous!" shouted a still heavily bandaged Riggs. The courtroom began to murmur at these outbursts.

"Order, order in the court," demanded Judge Slider, banging his gavel several times as order was restored to the court. "There has been no case filed by the district attorney for such a matter against Mr. Riggs and until such time as any charges are proffered, this court will hear no arguments along this vein."

He turned his gaze back toward Kate and resumed his line of questioning.

"This life insurance policy, was it a term policy or a universal whole life policy?"

"The latter, Your Honor," she replied.

"Had the premiums been fully paid during the policy period?"

"Yes, Your Honor."

"Is Mr. French deceased?"

"Yes," she replied. She did not want to elicit another outburst from the judge. "But we have recently learned that at the time we paid on the policy, Mr. French was still alive and possibly living out of the country. We have reason to believe that this was known to one or more persons and we want time to bring evidence to this court concerning possible fraud perpetrated against our company."

"Well, if he was not dead when this court established his death per my decree, he is certainly dead now," replied the judge. "The policy premiums were paid in full. The insured has been positively identified as deceased. Your objection to the petition to distribute is denied."

He looked over at Andie. "You represent the creditor who is making a claim against the estate assets?"

"Yes, Your Honor," Andie replied. "My clients entered into an agreement with Western General Life Insurance to share in the recovery of proceeds that company paid to the estate as a result of the insurance policy they issued to the decedent. They have fully fulfilled their part of the contract by finding lost assets hidden by the decedent on property in the county. As a result of their actions, Mr. French was determined to still be alive at the time this court was handling his probate and preparing to hear this matter of a final distribution. The fact that Mr. French is now truly deceased should have no bearing on the sharing of the assets held in the estate, which were forthcoming from Western General, which Western General agreed to pay to my clients."

"Ms. McDougal, you have already heard my ruling on Western General's objection to the petition. They receive nothing from this estate. It appears to me any claim you have against them should be handled separate and apart from these proceedings."

"Yes, Your Honor, but it seems unfair that my clients have uncovered substantial additional assets and unwittingly caused the missing French to again show himself, proving for Western General their allegations of fraud with respect to his alleged disappearance and presumed death. If he had survived the tragic fire in Cuyama, you would be handling their objection in quite a different manner. The estate should not be rewarded simply because Mr. French was unlucky and died in the recent fire. That constitutes unjust enrichment. My clients have fulfilled their part of the agreement with Western General and should be treated fairly."

"Ms. McDougal, what is the period during which creditors' claims must be made against the estate?"

"Nine months after the opening of the estate," she replied.

"This estate has now been open for almost a year and a half. The time for filing creditors' claims against the estate has passed. I am inclined to deny your clients' claim."

"The estate has not properly been open for a year and a half," she replied. "Mr. French has only recently become deceased. The fact that this court made a finding of a presumption of death after only five years from the date of the disappearance by French is an error that can be corrected by this court. I request a thirty-day postponement to prepare a petition to support my clients' position and to give the court time to reassess this matter in light of the recent findings concerning the true date of the decedent's death."

"Okay," replied the judge, looking over at Riggs. "How about we postpone this matter for four weeks. That will let Ms. McDougal get her ducks in a row and let each of you get your points and authorities on this for me to consider. I can have my clerk look for any prior precedent for this situation. Okay, councilors?"

John Riggs gripped his folder of court papers tightly. "No objection, Your Honor."

"I would like to revisit your ruling with respect to the disposition of the insurance funds," interjected Kate. "It appears that you have several things in play with respect to the decedent and I would also like the opportunity to revisit the fraud aspect of this case and determine what options might be open for my client."

Judge Slider glared back at her. He was clearly irritated. But he did not want to risk a reversal of his ruling on appeal. "Fine, you get four weeks as well to come back and tell me why I should rule otherwise with respect to these funds. Is there anything else for the court today in this matter? Very well then, see all of you back here in four weeks." He looked over at his clerk. "Schedule this for me then please."

"What just happened?" asked Erika as they were quickly ushered out of the courtroom by Andie.

"We just bought some time," she replied. "I bet no judge in this jurisdiction has ever had to deal with somebody being declared legally deceased after going missing and then having to deal with them reappearing and dying all over again just as they are ready to button up the estate. I am going to research case law to see if this has ever happened before in California and if not, then in another state. If I can find a similar situation and a ruling that supports our claim, we stand a good chance of getting something from the estate. Jackson may have gotten away with all the stuff you retrieved out there, but the cash in the estate and whatever else exists is our potential recovery. If I can get even the threat of a case to attack some of these assets, I bet Riggs will agree to settle with us. If General Western comes up with some case law about insurance fraud and how other courts have ruled, that gives us more of an edge. I will keep you all apprised of what I find out in the next week or so."

The trio returned to Erika and Chester's house and sat around the kitchen table. In a matter of less than a month, they had gone from auction sale van owners, to treasure hunters, to being nearly killed by a missing drug dealer and his attorney as well as a cartel in Australia that had a reputation for mayhem and murder. "If we had known how all of this would turn out, would we have just sold the van to Riggs and cut our losses?" wondered Erika.

"I don't know," replied Arnie. "How could anyone have suspected such an elaborate scheme or all the players that were involved, or that we might have been at such risk of getting killed? I say we would have gone for it anyway."

"Twenty-twenty hindsight?" replied Chester. "I think I would have sold the van and taken my profit then. We could still end up with nothing. You weren't there, Arnie, when they had us tied up and later when they were trying to kill us and we barely made it out of the fire."

"How about me?" Arnie replied. "I was held hostage by some Aborigines, nearly had my leg chewed off by a pack of dingoes and had to sneak onto a secret military base to fax myself to safety!"

"Well," replied Erika. "Andie said to give her a couple of weeks. Let's hope she comes up with something that helps us."

CHAPTER THIRTY-EIGHT

BLUE SMOKE BILLOWED OUT OF THE TAILPIPE OF THE RED and white former fire department truck that was parked alongside Chester and Erika's house. Erika looked out the kitchen window and saw Chester leaning over the engine spraying carburetor cleaner into the open carburetor. The truck sat where the van had formerly been located before it met its untimely demise in the Cuyama Valley.

Andie McDougal had exhausted her research to support the trio's claim to part of the estate and had come up short. She had determined that the insurance company would have to prevail first in its recovery of the insurance proceeds from the estate before she had any hope of a division of those funds with them. Their agreement for a finder's fee stood on solid ground but that ground had to be plowed first by Kate Reilly to convince the court that French had indeed planned to perpetrate fraud by pretending to disappear and be declared dead so his heirs could collect the funds for him.

General Western had been embarrassed by being sucked into the case again. The company had rewritten its underwriting requirements for large insurance policies so that this type of situation would not occur in the future. They were willing to share the recovery if the judge found in their favor on the matter of fraud and put the matter behind them.

Riggs had denied any knowledge of French's scheme and was taking the high road. His clients, the family and sole heirs of the now deceased French, were open to settlement discussions though. They had no interest in being questioned about their possible role in French's plan and Riggs was sticking to his story about being in the dark about French and his sudden reappearance.

Judge Slider was equally as willing to grant the wishes of the parties. He had ruled on French's death after he had been missing only five years when the standard for this situation was normally seven years, possibly longer in large estates with substantial financial assets. He did not want anyone nosing around in his reelection campaign funds and discovering that Riggs had been a sizeable contributor just eighteen months ago. He had taken the unusual step of sitting in on the settlement conference between the three parties of interest in the estate funds while they all argued their respective legal positions back and forth. "This is speculative at best," he had admonished Kate when she had discussed case law regarding disappearances and life insurance policies. "If you intend to bring all of this before me you still have to convince me that French had planned this in advance and he was not the victim of amnesia or some other unfortunate circumstance. Without concrete proof that he was complicit in a fraud, the funds remain in the estate."

Riggs had been eager to conclude the negotiations. He made it known that his clients were not greedy and would give up a portion of the estate if everyone was willing to settle and waive away forever future claims against each other. Riggs had opened the door and Kate had walked through it with Andie. Kate had reaffirmed the agreement to split its recovery of funds from the estate with Andie's clients. All of the parties had been willing to approve a large extraordinary fee request from Riggs as the executor of the estate for dealing with these complicated matters and selling off the remaining assets of French's estate.

Twenty percent of two and a half million dollars paid to Western General had resulted in a nice pot of money to be split up between the trio. The retired fire truck had been a replacement purchase for Chester now that the van had been destroyed. The county of Santa Bonita had sold it during a disposition sale of surplus equipment and Chester had eagerly purchased the old one-ton four-wheel-drive truck as his next project. He intended to turn it into a desert camping vehicle.

He gunned the engine by working the throttle linkage and alternately sprayed the cleaner. The engine backfired with a loud bang. Chester jerked back from the truck and glanced back at Erika to see what had just happened. He smiled sheepishly and began to spray the cleaner into the engine again. In a few minutes, the motor was idling smoothly. The cloud of smoke had drifted away.

She saw Arnie drive up and wave his hands, pretending to be coughing as the cloud of blue smoke drifted away from the truck. The two of them were laughing and joking as they walked inside and sat down at the kitchen table.

"So, you got big red running," said Arnie.

"More like Blue Thunder" said Erika, pointing to the cloud of smoke disappearing down the street. "Guess we won't have a mosquito problem this year in the neighborhood."

"I had a funny message on my cell phone today," said Arnie. "Some guy out in Cuyama said he heard about what happened to us out there. Said he wants to talk to us about something he thinks we might be interested in."

"Cuyama. No way!" yelled Erika, turning her back on them and walking away.

"Who is he?" asked Chester.

Arnie reached into his pocket, retrieved his cell phone, and played the recorded message back. They heard the gruff voice of an elderly man.

"My name is Herb Rummell. I own one of the ranches you were nosing around on a few months ago when you started that fire and nearly burned up half the country out here. I understand you have a map with some markings on it and you found some stuff my dead neighbor Rick French had buried out here. Story is that you found some valuable stuff but could not hang on to it because you had been digging around without the landowner's permission. I would like to join forces with you and use your map to look around my ranch and see if anything else is left." He had left a phone number for Arnie to call.

"Tough luck," said Chester. "Little does he know the map is a goner with the fire."

"Even if we had it, there is no way I would ever go out there again," said Erika from down the hall.

"By my count we left five of those wells still unexplored. That might mean there is still a couple of million dollars still hidden out there," replied Chester.

Arnie sat in silence looking back at Chester. Chester recognized the look.

"What are you thinking?" he asked.

Arnie was recalling what he had seen in the computer files during his fax machine journey and his review of scanned files on Riggs computer. "Nothing is ever really lost," he said. "Sometimes you just have to look in different places. If memory serves me right, I think I remember a file I saw that had a string of handwritten numbers written on it with a note indicating to save this list until he heard from French later. I think it is time for another fax trip over to Riggs law office."

The trio sat in silence for a moment. Grins began to spread over each of their faces. The safety and security of their day jobs paled in comparison to the excitement and monetary rewards of this next leg of the Cuyama Valley treasure hunt. With an enthusiastic high five, they signaled that they were all in.